as dust dances

As Dust Dances

Edited by:
Jennifer Sommersby Young

Cover Design by:
By Hang Le

Interior Design & Formatting by:
Christine Borgoford, Type A Formatting

OTHER ADULT CONTEMPORARY NOVELS

Play On
Into the Deep
Out of the Shallows
Hero
One Day: A Valentine Novella
Fight or Flight

On Dublin Street Series:
On Dublin Street
Down London Road
Before Jamaica Lane
Fall From India Place
Echoes of Scotland Street
Moonlight on Nightingale Way
Until Fountain Bridge (a novella)
Castle Hill (a novella)
Valentine (a novella)
One King's Way (a novella)

Hart's Boardwalk Series:
The One Real Thing
Every Little Thing

YOUNG ADULT CONTEMPORARY TITLES

The Impossible Vastness of Us
The Fragile Ordinary

YOUNG ADULT URBAN FANTASY TITLES

The Tale of Lunarmorte Trilogy:
Moon Spell
River Cast
Blood Solstice

Warriors of Ankh Trilogy:

Blood Will Tell

Blood Past

Shades of Blood

Fire Spirits Series:

Smokeless Fire

Scorched Skies

Borrowed Ember

Darkness, Kindled

OTHER TITLES

Slumber (The Fade #1)

Drip Drop Teardrop, a novella

about the author

SAMANTHA YOUNG IS A *NEW York Times*, *USA Today* and *Wall Street Journal* bestselling author from Stirlingshire, Scotland. She's been nominated for the Goodreads Choice Award for Best Author and Best Romance for her international bestseller *On Dublin Street*. *On Dublin Street* is Samantha's first adult contemporary romance series and has sold in thirty countries.

Visit Samantha Young online at:

www.authorsamanthayoung.com
Twitter:
@AuthorSamYoung
Instagram:
@AuthorSamanthaYoung
Facebook:
www.facebook.com/authorsamanthayoung

Want to keep up-to-date with all of Samantha Young's latest sales, preorders and new releases? Never miss out on these sexy, emotional stories with their hot Scots and sassy heroines by simply following Sam on BookBub.

acknowledgments

FOR THE MOST PART WRITING is a solitary endeavor but publishing most certainly is not. I have to thank my wonderful editor Jennifer Sommersby Young, a talented, witty lady who always keeps me right. You've made me a better writer, friend. Thank you.

Moreover, thank you to Viviana Varona for giving Killian and Skylar's story that final look-through, ensuring I'm sending their love story out into the world as polished as can be.

This is a story I became truly immersed in while writing. The world around me ceased to exist until all of Skylar's tale spilled out of my fingertips. In order to have that kind of extraordinary alone time with this book, I have to thank my mum and dad for taking care of my wee babies while their momma was off living in another universe. I love you all. Thank you for understanding!

And thank you to my bestie and PA extraordinaire, Ashleen Walker, for handling all the little things and supporting me through everything. You're *my* Rockstar.

The life of a writer doesn't stop with the book. Our job expands beyond the written word to marketing, advertising, graphic design, social media management and more. Help from those in the know goes a long way. Thank you to my awesome publicist KP Simmon of Inkslinger PR. KP, you make my life easier! Thank you for all you and your team do!

And thank you to every single blogger, instagrammer and book lover who has helped spread the word about my books. You all are appreciated so much! On that note, a massive thank you to all the fantastic readers in my private Facebook group *Sam's Clan McBookish*. You make me smile every day!

Moreover, thank you to Hang Le. You create the most beautiful art and the cover for AS DUST DANCES is no exemption. It's one of my favorite covers EVER. I can't stop staring at it. It fits Skylar's story so perfectly.

And thank you to Christine at Type A Formatting for making this book look stylish for my readers.

As always, thank you to my agent Lauren Abramo for making it possible for readers all over the world to find my words. I'm so grateful for you.

Finally, to you my reader, the biggest thank you of all.

as dust dances

A Play On Novel

New York Times Bestselling Author
SAMANTHA YOUNG

one

Glasgow, Scotland

My music filled the air, creating a surrounding bubble of melody and familiarity in a city still strange to me in so many ways.

It was an overcast day on Buchanan Street. The gray clouds silvered the blond buildings and dulled the boldness of the red sandstone architecture that made up a part of Glasgow's identity. Busking on the main shopping thoroughfare in the city center, I stood far enough from the shop entrance behind me to not bother the staff, but not far enough out that I'd feel in the way of shoppers passing by. I played my beloved Taylor acoustic guitar and sang. Unlike some of the buskers I competed with on a regular basis, I didn't have their fancy portable PA systems with amps and mics. I had to rely on the quality of my voice and my playing to draw people in.

I never felt like a nuisance busking in Glasgow. It was the only time in fact the city didn't feel like a stranger to me and I to it. I felt like a part of a city that loved its music. If red sandstone was Glasgow's skin, music was its heartbeat. While I'd made peace with the idea that life had broken me down to dust, the joy of being a beat in the rhythm of Glasgow's soul smoldered within me.

Sometimes, especially if I was feeling upbeat and decided to do a twist on a well-known pop or dance song, I'd draw in a crowd. That was usually on a Saturday, like today, when people were shopping and feeling relaxed, where they weren't rushing past on their lunch break to get back to work.

Mostly, however, people either kept walking on by, or they dropped some change in my guitar case as they briskly marched on. I even had some regular workers who dropped the change in like it had become a habit. Not that I minded. Unlike those buskers with their fancy PA systems, I actually needed the money. I wasn't trying to "get found" on the streets of Glasgow by having my bestie film me on his camera phone and upload it to my YouTube channel.

I was busking so I could buy a meal for the night. And if it was a particularly good day, money to get into the swimming center so I could use one of their showers and a hair dryer. On the days I didn't make enough money, I had what the local homeless called a "tramp's wash." I had to strip off in my tent and use baby wipes to clean my body as best I could.

Glancing down at my guitar case as I sang, I thanked God that today it looked like I'd have enough for that shower.

Nodding my thanks at a couple of teenage girls as they dropped some change in my case, I kept singing the melancholy song I'd chosen to fit the weather. "Someone Like You" by Adele. A firm crowd pleaser, it was drawing one like it always did. I pulled it out of the bag when I really needed the cash. I have a good enough vocal range to sing Adele but anyone can have a good vocal range and still not be able to sell a song. You have to be able to fall into the lyrics and sing a song like *you* wrote it. Which is much easier to do if you did write the damn song. For the longest time, I only ever sang my own songs so that wasn't a problem for me.

Busking was different. People didn't really want to listen to unfamiliar tunes. That might have been an issue for me a few years ago. I wasn't very good at putting myself in someone else's place. Or empathizing.

But now . . . well, now I could sing sad songs like my heart was truly breaking. I'd look into the small crowds gathered around me and see more than a few tears in strangers' eyes. I loved that part of performing. Making people *feel* like that. I just hated all the other shit that came with it.

As I sang about time flying and yesterday being the time of our lives, I felt those words deep in my soul. I controlled a voice crack on the word "lives" and found a familiar face in the crowd.

Ignoring the frizzle of awareness that zinged down my spine, I kept staring at him, singing to him, telling him with that stare I could give a damn that he was there. He didn't scare me. He didn't creep me out. Didn't he know that I was unshakeable these days?

I didn't know the man's name. I didn't know anything about him except that he had the kind of presence that made everyone else around him fade. At around six foot he wasn't overly tall; he had an athletic build so it wasn't really his size that made you look. It was a quality. I couldn't tell what color his eyes were because he'd never gotten close enough, just that they appeared dark, and they were intense. There was a hardness to his expression, a remoteness that seemed at odds with his apparent interest in my performance. Today he stood apart from the small crowd, his hands in the pockets of his jeans, his head tilted slightly as he listened with that aloof countenance.

When I got to the part about finding "someone like you," I drew my gaze to the darkening sky from beneath the brim of my fedora, my tone as mournful as those heavy clouds above. After the final strum of an F-sharp minor lingered in the air, I lowered my head and let the gentle applause settle over me.

I didn't take much of a break before I immediately began singing an original song. Like I said, most people wanted to hear songs that were familiar to them, but I was a singer/songwriter and it was difficult for me to not sing what I truly felt at least once during a set. Plus, I'd noticed over the last few weeks that the stranger only walked away after I sang one of my own songs.

Weird but true.

Almost everyone who had been standing to listen to the Adele song stayed to listen to my perky, upbeat song with its sad lyrics. When I finished, a few came over to drop change in my case, some offering me praise, even thanks. It was hard to watch the people who walked away without offering me a token of appreciation, so I let them fade out in my peripheral and smiled at those who were kind enough to give me money.

There was enough there for a meal, a shower, and use of the laundromat.

If someone asked me for advice about sleeping rough, I'd tell them how important it is to keep your feet clean and dry. Change your socks every day. There was a laundromat a twenty-minute walk from where I'd pitched my tent and a ten-minute walk from the swimming pool. I could wash and dry the few clothes I had and keep my socks fresh.

Feeling grateful, I was filled with smiles as I thanked people in my fake English accent. I would've faked a Scottish accent if I could but it always came out sounding Irish with a hint of Australian. I was good at a generic southern English accent so I went with that. Why fake an accent at all? Well, I didn't want anyone recognizing me, and if they put my face to my voice and then to an American accent, things might get complicated.

As people dwindled away, I decided to pack up for the day. It was only three in the afternoon but I wanted my shower badly. Plus, those clouds looked ready to break any minute. It was nearly an hour's walk to the swimming center from here and as I pocketed my cash, I wondered if it would be foolish to use some of it on bus fare. If I got soaked I might get sick and then what the hell would I do?

I glanced back up at the clouds and saw one looking ready to give birth to a whole shower of raindrops.

Yeah, I was going to get the bus.

Feeling a familiar prickle on my skin, I looked up and saw the guy was still standing there, his arms crossed as he studied me. I scowled at his assessing attitude.

He'd started showing up to watch me play about four weeks ago. Since then he'd appeared every Saturday, watching from a distance. I knew it wasn't about physical attraction because I wasn't really looking my best these days. It had to be about my voice and it freaked me out. Busking was a risk because all it would take was that one person to guess who I was from my voice.

Hence the fake accent.

Had this guy figured it out?

Fuck off, I tried to send him the telepathic order.

He began walking toward me. I tensed as I put my guitar in the case. This was new.

He stopped a couple feet from my case and I straightened to full height. I wasn't diminutive at five foot six but I wasn't tall either. Still, it was better than being crouched down while this stranger towered over me.

My expression was challenging.

His was blank.

Which was why I was surprised when he offered without

preamble, "You can sing. You can write."

I frowned, tilting my head slightly as I studied his face. Finally, I replied, "I know."

His lips flattened and I wondered if that was his version of a smile. "Let me buy you a coffee."

Suspicion flooded me.

Despite my best efforts to stay as clean as possible, I couldn't rid myself of the aura of someone who slept rough. I had a large rucksack I carried everywhere and inside was my one-man tent. Once a week I had a shower and on the days that I couldn't, I sprayed my hair with a can of cheap dry shampoo that I used sparingly. I was careful with the few shirts and two pairs of jeans I had, attempting to keep them as clean as possible. But there was dirt under my fingernails I couldn't seem to get rid of and most importantly hard flecks of cold reality that I couldn't wash out of my eyes.

I was homeless and most people seemed to sense it intuitively. That meant I was familiar with strange men approaching me to proposition me as if I were a common prostitute.

"Why?" I bit out, hating him as I hated all the men who thought they could take advantage of me.

He responded with a look of derision. "I'm not looking for sex. I just want to talk. About your music."

"Why?"

"Let me take you for a coffee and I'll explain."

"I don't drink coffee."

He scowled, dragging his eyes down my body again. It was reassuringly nonsexual and insultingly disdainful. When we locked gazes, he said, "Then save your cash and let me buy you a hot meal."

"Right now?"

"Right now."

I pondered this, severely tempted. It was broad daylight, we were on Buchanan Street. If his plans for me were nefarious, there wasn't a lot he could do to me. I glanced to my left, up the street. The red-and-white, candy-striped sign of TGI Fridays beckoned like a seasoned seductress.

However, the concern over what his interest in me was, and whether he'd discovered my secret gave me more than pause. I bowed my head, hiding my face behind my hat. "Find another form of amusement. No thanks." I strode past without looking at him.

He didn't call out after me, and the more distance I put between us, the more I felt the tension in my neck muscles loosen, my hunched shoulders lowering to their normal position.

The north end of Buchanan Street started on a hill at the Glasgow Royal Concert Hall. It sloped downward at a gradient, leveling out at around the halfway point. I'd been busking on the level, so it took me less than five minutes to get to the bus stop to the left on busy Argyle Street. Less than five minutes to put the guy to the back of my mind. There was no time for worrying about trivial things in my new life. That was the whole point of it. I only had time to worry about the basics. It was liberating in a way I couldn't have ever imagined.

"Busker Girl!" I heard as I approached the bus stop.

My attention was drawn to the two homeless people sitting in sleeping bags outside the Argyle Street Arcade entrance. Old shopping arcade, not an amusement arcade.

Since my bus hadn't arrived yet, I walked over to Ham and Mandy. I met them not long after I'd arrived in Glasgow and found myself without enough cash to stay in a hostel. I think I'd been sleeping in the cheap tent I'd bought for about a week when they approached me one day while I was busking.

"Hi," I said as I walked over, staring down at them with

sympathy twinging in my chest. It was odd, but I didn't feel like I had anything in common with them other than that we were all homeless. I just couldn't picture myself looking as uncared for as these two.

"How ye doin', Busker Girl?" Mandy grinned up at me. Her teeth were thick with grime and decay that I no longer flinched at the sight of. I bought a new toothbrush every six weeks. It wasn't electric but it was better than nothing and I used little disposable dental floss harps too. I was vigilant about keeping my teeth and gums healthy.

"She has a name, ye know." Ham rolled his eyes at his woman.

I'd given them the false name of Sarah.

"Busker Girl is closer to the truth," Mandy said, giving me a knowing smile.

She saw through me. I didn't think she recognized me, but she knew I wasn't called Sarah and she made me squirm with the way she seemed to be able to peer into me. Still, I liked her because she never pushed me for real information.

"Ach, leave the lass alone," Ham said. Ham, short for his surname of Hamilton, wasn't the first heroin addict I'd ever met. He *was* the most tragic. Tall, all lean muscle and tattoos, he had beautiful green eyes and a face that would've been incredibly handsome if it weren't for the physical effects of the heroin. It was thin, drawn, his skin a grayish color, and his teeth were even worse than Mandy's. Not only yellow and diseased, but his left canine tooth was broken and his right incisor was missing entirely. They had told me their stories the first time we met.

Mandy ran away from an abusive home life. Her mom's boyfriend sexually assaulted her on a regular basis and her jealous mother liked to slap her around in punishment, as if it were her fault. I'd felt sick to my stomach listening to the casual way Mandy told her story. As if she'd grown numb to it. I understood the numb part.

Living on the streets led Mandy to prostituting herself to survive. She developed severe anxiety and depression and was one more awful sexual experience away from committing suicide when she met Ham. Where Mandy wasn't originally from the city, Ham was from a place called Ibrox that was less than fifteen minutes outside the city center. He got hooked on heroin at fifteen and his addiction cost him his family, most of his friends, and the ability to hold down a job.

Ham's addiction didn't bother Mandy. At least that's what she told me. I felt sad for them both, not only because of what they'd been through or because they were sleeping on the streets. I felt sad because I could tell Ham loved Mandy. But when Ham had wandered off that day to speak to another homeless guy they knew, Mandy told me she was only with him because he protected her from other men and he didn't mind the bad days she had with her untreated anxiety. *Don't you love him?* I'd asked. *As a friend*, she replied. But it was clear she was offering him more than mere friendship for his protection, and I wanted to cry for her, because she was still prostituting herself . . . just in a different way.

"What's up?" I asked, not really wanting to spend much time around them because they were too much of a dose of harsh, cold reality for my liking.

Before either could answer, the first fat raindrop fell from the sky.

"Fuck," Ham glared upwards. "Knew it."

"Are you guys going to find shelter?"

"It's just a bit of rain. First wash I'll have had in days," Mandy laughed.

"Where ye off tae?" Ham asked.

I shrugged. I didn't tell anyone where I camped out. "Going

to get a wash, a meal."

Mandy suddenly scowled at me. "Ye still on yer own? What did we tell ye about that, Busker Girl? Ye need a man. Or ye need tae find yerself some other women."

Ham gave me a look of concern. "Or stay with us. We'll protect ye."

I knew he didn't mean anything sexual by it, but I still shuddered at the thought. They both insisted that I was leaving myself vulnerable to assault by being on my own. Having wandered the city for a good few months now, I did see quite a few homeless people in pairs or as they'd suggested, women who camped out in small packs.

But I was being smarter than all of them. I slept where no one ventured, far away from the city center. I didn't need anyone else to keep myself safe.

"I look like a slight breeze could knock me over but it's only a façade. I can kick arse, you know." I grinned, trying to reassure them as I took a step back. "I can look after myself. Promise."

"Ye're going tae find yerself in trouble one of these days, Busker Girl!" Mandy called after me, and her words sounded prophetic in a way that sent a blast of cold shivers down my spine.

You're being silly, I told myself, shaking off the feeling. I was fine.

I didn't have their problems. I was being smart because despite my age, I had a lifetime of experience to fall back on.

This was my life right now. I liked it like this. I worried about important, basic-necessity stuff and all the other shit went away. I'd keep being smart as long as it meant not having to think about who I used to be.

two

The bus was only a fifteen-minute journey north. I got off at a stop that was a mere five-minute walk from the swim center. It was always this particular center because it was a ten-minute walk from the laundromat I used and a twenty-minute walk from where I slept.

Every Saturday it was the same receptionist behind the desk. She was a nice girl who graciously held onto my guitar for me after I paid for my swim ticket. There was a sadness in her smile when she handed me the ticket, so I knew she knew I wasn't there to swim. Still, she let me in.

Her kindness pricked my pride a little, but I didn't have time for pride, I reminded myself as I wandered into the ladies' changing room. The tiled floors had puddles of water here and there, the tiled walls glistened with condensation, and the large space was thick with the now-comforting smell of chlorine. I found one of the larger lockers free, hauled out my cheap shampoo and conditioner, my shaving cream and razor, a towel, and my body wash. After putting the rucksack into the locker with care not to damage my tent, I stripped down to my underwear.

Growing up, I'd never really been body conscious. As a teenager I developed slim curves, I fit into a size four, and no one ever mentioned my weight to me so it was never a factor. I didn't fit in with the popular kids but I had a band, a fun group of friends, and we were too busy concentrating on finding success in the music industry to care about stuff our peers cared about. So truthfully, I'd only ever grown insecure about my looks when the band took off.

Anytime we posted to our Instagram, there were always comments about how I looked in the photo. If the angle was weird, had I put on weight? Was I pregnant? Who knocked me up? Maybe I should get a boob job? And I'd be so cute if I got a nose job.

Not all the comments were negative. Most were positive. Some were sexually creepy and invasive. It was amazing how easy it became to concentrate on those negative assholes though. To let them get to me when I'd never worried about my looks before. It was also disheartening that the negative comments racked up when some tabloid magazine announced I was dating a beloved famous guy because we'd been pictured together. They'd done that a few times over my career. Women could be vicious when they thought you didn't deserve a guy they were fangirls over. Sad, but so fucking true.

Now I didn't care about any of it. I didn't have to.

I knew I was too thin now, but if anyone stared at me as I walked across the locker room in my worn underwear with my inexpensive products in my arms, I didn't see it. I didn't care.

Thankfully, finding a shower free, I stepped inside, ignoring the strands of strangers' hair clogging the drain, and pulled the wet shower curtain over for privacy. After carefully stripping off my underwear, I rolled it up in my towel and set it outside the shower, hoping, as I always did, that no rat bastard would come along and steal it.

When the hot water hit, I closed my eyes and salivated over the sensation. There was nothing like a shower after days and days of going without one. I'd always taken a shower for granted. Now that it wasn't a regular thing—being lucky if I could make enough money for one once a week—it was a pure joy. Not that I could really take the time to enjoy it because there was always someone waiting outside to use it next.

So I got to scrubbing. My body. My hair. Then I shaved. Mandy told me not to bother shaving. That leg hair kept you warmer in the winter. I'd been sleeping rough since late April and it had been pretty goddamned cold at night. Scottish summers weren't exactly hot during the night but it had been manageable. It was September now. In a few short weeks, the nightly temperature would drop to not so manageable and I was trying not to worry about it.

Or the fact that my visitor's visa was about to expire.

Feeling my stomach churn, I threw the thought out. I'd worry about it when the time came. My life was about working everything out on a day-to-day basis. It was simple. Easy.

After my shower, I felt more human again. I reached out, glad to find my towel and underwear still there. I wrapped the towel around me and walked out, ignoring the huffy look of the woman who was waiting to use the shower next. I locked myself in a nearby cubicle so I could dry off in private.

Back in my underwear, I left the cubicle to retrieve my stuff out of the locker. Once I was dressed and organized, I got out my hairbrush.

I was blow drying my hair, trying not to look too closely at myself in the mirror when it happened.

The feel of a penetrating stare began to niggle until I couldn't ignore it, and my eyes slid across my reflection to that of the young teen standing next to me. She was staring at me openmouthed with an excitement glittering in her eyes that I recognized. Fear slammed through me and I quickly looked away, blasting that hair dryer all over my head as if it would speed up the process somehow.

When I eventually switched off the dryer, I knew she was still staring.

Crap.

I grabbed my stuff and turned to leave. Quickly.

"Hey!"

Oh God.

I glanced over my shoulder, scowling at her.

Her smile faltered. "Ye look like Skylar Finch. Anyone ever told ye that?"

My English accent in place, I lied, "I don't know who that is."

The teen's face fell at my response or the accent, I wasn't sure. "Yeah . . ." Her voice lowered to a mutter, "As if Skylar Finch would come swimming here."

I left without replying, forcing myself not to feel anything about the encounter. Well . . . forcing myself to *pretend* to not feel anything about the encounter.

My next stop was my focus. The laundromat, or launderette as they called it here. What little clothes I had I put into the washing machine and instead of waiting, I took a walk to the local fish-and-chip shop and bought my dinner along with two bottles of water. It was still raining, so I ate my fish and chips in the sheltered doorway of the laundromat. To be honest, I struggled to finish it, throwing half of it away. Fish and chips were cheap and filling, but after weeks and weeks of eating cheap junk food, I thought maybe my body was starting to reject it.

It was a monotonous wait for my clothes to come out of the dryer, but I didn't mind. I was warm and dry in the laundromat.

Apparently there was a God, however, because the rain cleared up as I headed toward my sleeping quarters. It had taken me a while to get used to the lighter nights here. During the summertime in this part of the country, it didn't get dark until close to eleven o' clock at night. But the nights had started to grow dark earlier and earlier over the last few weeks and as it approached seven thirty, the sky darkened.

By the time I reached my destination—the large, padlocked gates of the cemetery—night had fallen. The gates of the cemetery sat on a busy main road. Streetlamps lit the way, as did the glare of headlights as cars frequently passed.

I waited until there were no cars, then I stepped up onto the ledge of the brick pillar the gates were bolted into, grabbed hold of the iron bars, and hauled myself up and over, taking care to not let the spear-pointed tips of the bars bite into me.

Landing on the other side, the impact vibrated up my legs but they were strong from walking everywhere. Taking out my mini flashlight, I lit up the path in front of me and began to make my way through the cemetery.

Weirdly, the place didn't freak me out at night. It had become my sanctuary where I was safe from the outside world. It was a quiet place to rest my head and I fancied my silent neighbors were somehow protecting me.

It was a large cemetery and I walked for quite a bit toward my spot. The council had been out to mow today—I could smell the freshly cut grass along with the usual familiar smell of damp earth and mingled floral scents from the flowers left by people visiting their relatives. The smell grew fainter as I moved toward the small copse of trees way up in the back that I liked to set my tent by. The stones close to the trees were so old, the engravings had faded until some were near impossible to read.

Once I had my tent up, my sleeping bag out, a pillow, the throw blanket I'd got on sale and used for extra warmth, I got in, got comfy, and pulled out one of the two books I carried with me.

Poison Study by Maria V. Snyder. I'd read it a million times, but it had become a comfort read. It and *Graceling* by Kristin Cashore. I was a fantasy fan. And I loved reading about wicked-strong heroines who kicked ass despite the odds.

As I read, I forgot about where I was, or that it was cold. I forgot about the outside world entirely for a while. I knew Ham, Mandy, and a lot of the other homeless folks in the city kept in touch with the outside world with their phones. I didn't know how they got phones. If they stole them or stole money to buy them. Or if they saved up all the money strangers gave them to buy a cheap phone so they could connect with each other and the world. But they did it. They charged them at charging points in coffee shops and used free Wi-Fi there to go on the internet. Some of them even had Facebook pages. No home. But they had a Facebook page.

I, however, didn't want anything to do with the outside world. The outside world was a distant memory.

Instead I read about Yelena learning about poisons as she studied to be a food taster. I read about her survival and her strength. And that night I closed my eyes and fell asleep in the cemetery that had become my home, knowing I had what it took to survive this life I'd chosen.

three

The air held the coppery scent of rain. Diesel fumes, coffee, and rain. However, I wouldn't let the thought of impending rain worry me as I stood on Buchanan Street the following Saturday. I was too busy trying not to let the little shit who had set up close beside me with his PA system bother me.

He was *trying* to bother me, making that clear when he'd thrown a smug, arrogant smirk my way as he halted closer to my spot than was polite to set up. There was a code among buskers, and he was breaking its most important rule; he was deliberately attempting to drown me out. And doing a great job of it. Anyone who took the time to stop was stopping to listen to him mimic Shawn Mendes.

Yet, I continued. I'd become a master at pretending young male musicians weren't getting under my skin. I mean, I'd been in a band with three of them and we traveled on a tour bus together, for God's sake. This kid had no idea how good I'd gotten at pretending assholes like him didn't exist.

And when to take my opportunity for payback.

It happened as soon he lowered his voice to sing a Coldplay ballad.

I belted out "Chandelier" by Sia. A notoriously difficult song to sing and one that tended to impress people when you could. People drew to a stop, crowding around me as my voice rose above the kid's PA system.

Then the camera phones came out, making me lower my head, shielding my face with my fedora. One of these days, those goddamned camera phones were going to get me in trouble. How long before someone on the internet went, "Hey, she sounds exactly like Skylar Finch. Wait . . . that *is* Skylar Finch!"

I dreaded it, realizing I wouldn't even know if it happened because I refused to go online. It was my worst fear to be playing on the streets of Glasgow one day only to look up and find one of my guys there, glaring at me accusingly.

I shook off the worries and kept singing.

As the applause died down, someone in the crowd called out, "Gonnae sing 'Titanium'?"

Between the constant rainfall during the week and the dropping temperatures in the tent at night, I'd had to spend most of my money on a raincoat and a couple of fleece-lined hoodies to wear in bed. What little it left me with I'd spent on a shower and the laundromat. I needed the money, so I sang "Titanium," particularly enjoying the moment when the kid with the PA system started to belt out a rock track and was told to shut up by one of the guys standing in my crowd.

My amusement died a sudden death, however, when the sky abruptly opened up—fast, hard, fat raindrops drenching people in seconds and causing them to yelp and duck for cover. They left me, dripping cold and wet, with a guitar case full of small change that wasn't even enough to buy a coffee. There was only enough there to buy fries from McDonalds.

I took a deep breath, bracing myself to go to bed hungry, trying not to let the panic set in that my life here was taking a turn for the worse because of the weather. Deep down, I knew it was only going to get more difficult, but I'd have to find a way to survive it.

Part of me wanted to go over to the kid who was hurriedly packing up his PA system with the help of some friends and kick him in the nuts for ruining most of my day. He was dressed in good clothes, wearing expensive sneakers, and he looked well fed and taken care of. He didn't need the money. He just wanted the attention. I felt like screaming over to him, "We've already got one Shawn Mendes. We don't need another, sweetheart!" But that was petty and I didn't have the energy.

Forlorn and truly worried for the first time since I'd gotten to Scotland, my fingers trembled as I packed my guitar away. Not only would I go to sleep hungry tonight, I would go to sleep soaked to the skin. The rain had stopped almost as abruptly as it had started, but the damage was done to my clothes and cash flow.

I sucked in a shaky breath, my stomach twisting with nervous butterflies.

Standing up from my haunches, about to turn for my backpack, I almost bumped into a guy no more than an inch taller than me. He stepped into me, holding an umbrella over both our heads, and I shuddered in revulsion as his gaze dragged down my body in a way that couldn't be misconstrued. Close to his mid-fifties, I'd seen the man before. He was dressed in a nice shirt that was dragged down over his jeans by his large, drooping gut. His broad shoulders were stuffed into a leather jacket that strained with his movements. But it was his face that was hard to forget. He had a distinct bulbous nose and pockmarked cheeks.

I remembered him because he had bothered Mandy one day

when I'd stopped to talk to her. Ham had shown up and scared him off.

Obviously, word had gotten around that I was homeless.

I straightened, taking a step out from under his umbrella, my already jangled nerves blasted to hell by my sudden fury.

His leering eyes moved up to my face and at the sight of my glare, he gave me a placating smile. "Let me buy ye a hot meal, love."

"No thanks."

"I think we both know ye need it." He gestured to the now-closed guitar case in my hand.

"Not that badly. Piss off."

Eyes hardening, he took a step toward me. "Now that's not nice, when I'm trying to be friendly. Ye need a friend if ye're going to survive on the streets of Glasgow, love."

"Sweetheart, even if you weren't some slimy little prick with a beer gut, I still wouldn't let you touch me, so if I were you, I'd do as I say and *piss off*. Oh, and a heads-up," I sneered at him as I lied, "if I ever see you around, bothering me or any of the girls, I know some very scary guys that will be happy to 'deal' with you. Got me?"

Anger mottled his cratered face and he made to take another step toward me when a large, masculine hand wrapped around his bicep and shoved him none-too-gently back.

My gaze flew up to the taller man, my fury now mixed with suspicion and confusion. It was my original song stalker from last week. Except this time, he was close enough for me to see the genuine anger blazing from his dark eyes as he stared down the shorter, older man.

"I think she told you to piss off."

To my increasing annoyance the older man, who had not been intimidated by me in the least, seemed to shrink under my rescuer's gaze. "My mistake," he muttered and hurried away with his bloody umbrella up like a shield.

Little cowardly shit.

"What do you want?" I snapped at my unwanted rescuer.

He was staring after the sexual predator and slowly turned to look at me. Although his jaw was still hard, those dark eyes softened and for a moment, I was held suspended under them. Everything about him seemed carved in stone. Implacable. Cold. But his eyes were a warm, dark brown rimmed with thick, long black lashes. They were smoldering, bedroom eyes, and completely at odds with the rest of him.

Then he spoke, breaking whatever spell his eyes momentarily had me under. "You're an idiot."

The words were harsh with irritation.

"Gee, thanks," I said, the words suspiciously American. I turned away from him to collect my large backpack.

"You keep this up, you're going to get hurt."

"Is that a threat?"

"No."

"Look, I've got to go." I turned and tried to brush by him.

This time it was *my* arm he took hold of.

Renewed anger and fear lashed through me and I glowered up at him, ignoring the heat of his closeness, the smell of cologne and shower gel. He smelled clean, he felt warm. All the things I wasn't. I envied him and hated him in equal measure, forgetting for a moment that I'd put myself in this position.

Without me having to say a word, he let go, holding his hands up, palms out. "I've already said I don't want sex from you. I just want to talk. Let me buy you dinner."

As if on cue, my stomach grumbled and I could feel my defenses crumbling. It was go to bed drenched through and hungry or merely drenched through. Tempting . . .

"They have hand dryers in the bathrooms of restaurants. You could dry off some of your things." He gestured to my drowned rat–like state.

Dammit.

I knew this guy wanted something from me, I just didn't know what.

However, the priority right now was getting fed and dry.

It was five o' clock in the evening, it was Saturday, and the busy streets of the city center would not only soon fill up with club-goers but also the accompanying police. There was nothing this guy could do to me here.

"Fine. TGI Fridays." They served salads and actual meat, not the processed shit I'd been eating lately.

Thankfully, he didn't offer me a smug, triumphant smile. He gestured toward the restaurant up the street as if to say, "After you."

I walked, far too aware of him as he fell into step beside me. I shot him a look out of the corner of my eye. He must not have gotten caught in the rain because his clothes were dry, so where had he been? I hadn't seen him in the crowd as I sang.

This was weird.

"Can I carry anything for you?" he offered.

"No thanks." Nobody touched my stuff but me.

He didn't reply but rather strode ahead to open the restaurant door for me. The gesture almost caused me to stumble up the steps. It had been a while since anyone had held a door for me.

I refused to acknowledge the little tingle of warmth it gave me, just as I refused to acknowledge that I missed anything about the time in my life when I wasn't one of the invisible.

The hostess at the podium raised an eyebrow but was immediately distracted from whatever she was going to say as the stranger pulled up beside me.

I realized I didn't even know his name.

"Table for two," he said.

She smiled. "Do you have a reservation?"

"No."

I snorted at his abrupt manner. What a charmer.

The hostesses smile dimmed a little. "Well, you're in luck. We have a table. Right this way." She grabbed a couple of menus and led us through the busy restaurant. I was assaulted by smells: burgers, barbecue sauce, ketchup, beer, all of it clenching my stomach with need. And noise: loud chatter, laughter, clinking of cutlery, and clash of dinnerware that made me flinch, the sounds making me feel slightly claustrophobic. I was used to crowds but out in the open air. It felt like forever since I'd sat in an enclosed space with so many other people.

She took us toward a tiny table where there would be no room to put my stuff. The stranger touched her shoulder to halt her.

"The booth." He gestured to an empty booth behind us that would take all my stuff and the two of us.

"That's reserved."

He reached toward her and I caught the glimmer of money in his hands as he discreetly tucked it between her fingers on top of the menus she held. She glanced down at it and then gave him a wide grin. "Right this way."

I slid into the booth first, putting my guitar on the floor at my feet and pushing the backpack toward the end of the booth. In hindsight, I should've slid in after my backpack, using it as a barrier between me and the stranger, a thought that occurred to me too late as he moved in beside me.

As it did among the small crowds that stopped to listen to me sing, his presence seemed to swell over the table, and I felt more than a niggle of annoyance as he sat close enough for me to feel his body heat.

I tried to shift inconspicuously away from him as he looked at the menu but was caught when he shot me a quizzical look out of his periphery.

Not wanting him to think he unnerved me, I turned to my own menu and immediately felt almost faint with hunger. I wanted to order everything. EVERYTHING.

Silence descended over us as I was lost in the heaven of choice.

"Don't order too much," the stranger suddenly said. "You're too thin and I imagine not used to eating large portions. You might make yourself ill."

Disappointment filled me because he was annoyingly right, so when the waiter came to take our order, I only asked for sautéed sea bass and not the wings, loaded skins, nachos, and ribs I wanted as well. Saliva was building up in my mouth.

"Why don't you go dry off while we wait?" the stranger said once the waiter left.

I immediately glanced down at my expensive guitar.

He grunted. "I'm not a thief."

"Then what are you? What do you want?"

"Get dry first."

I nodded, but when I got out of the booth, I swung on my backpack and grabbed hold of my guitar case. I trusted no one. He got the point, seeming almost amused by it. Now hungrier than ever, more irritated than ever, I almost snarled at him as I passed by the booth to make my way to the restrooms.

Now that the panic of going hungry wasn't messing with my mind, I remembered I had dry clothes in my backpack from the laundromat this morning. It was amazing what fear could do to you because in that moment, I'd completely forgotten about them.

Relief flooded me, and I grabbed a bunch of paper towels before I ducked into a stall to change. Once I'd stripped down, I dried off with the paper towels. I luxuriated in the feel of dry underwear and clothes as I pulled on fresh pants, jeans, socks, T-shirt, and hoodie. I folded up my wet clothes and raincoat, refusing to put them back in the backpack because they'd only get the rest of my socks, underwear, and books wet. Feeling naked without it, I tucked my fedora into my backpack.

When I returned to the main restaurant, I put the folded-up wet clothes beside me on the bench, my underwear tucked out of sight.

I couldn't meet the stranger's eyes as I reached for the Diet Coke I'd asked for, savoring the taste. On tour, I'd needed lots of energy so I'd eaten well and drank plenty of water. Soda was a treat at the best of times. But I hadn't had a Diet Coke in months, and it tasted great.

"Excuse me," my companion's voice jolted my gaze upward and I saw him wave down a passing waitress. "Do you have a bag?"

"A bag?"

"Carrier bag, paper bag. A bag."

"Um . . . let me check."

It was my turn to stare at him quizzically, but he didn't acknowledge the look. He sipped his water and stared around the restaurant as if this weren't awkward and weird. His nose had a slight bump in it, his cheekbones high, and his jaw chiseled and angular. Overall, he had a very hawklike profile, masculine, rugged, and intimidating. And at that moment I felt like prey, stupidly allowing myself to be caught.

Still, I couldn't shake the feeling that he genuinely didn't want anything sexual from me.

I stared at him unabashedly, wanting answers.

He remained steadfast, ignoring me, until the waitress he'd called out to returned with a plastic carrier bag. "Will this do?"

"Aye." He took it from her. "Thanks."

He held it out, staring at me with those eyes that would've been much more suited to a Lothario, to someone who knew how to be charming. "For your clothes."

Oh.

It was a kind gesture, also at odds with his demeanor, and my suspicion increased. I took the bag, however, sliding my wet clothes into it and out of sight. Exasperated, I said, "What the hell do you want?"

"Food first."

"So I'll be well fed, satisfied, and more amenable to whatever the hell it is you want from me?"

He looked at me now, really looked at me, and the corner of his mouth curled up ever so slightly. "Exactly."

"A good villain doesn't admit to his plan, you know."

"I'm not a villain."

"What are you?"

"Fo—"

"Food first. Yeah, yeah."

And so we sat in silence until the food arrived, and the smell of my sea bass made my stomach grumble loudly. Years ago, it would've embarrassed me. Now I couldn't give a shit. All I cared about was that fish.

I dug in, closing my eyes in joy as I ate.

When I opened them to scoop up buttery mashed potatoes, I felt his gaze on me.

The furrowed brow, the glimmer of concern in his eyes, made me stiffen. But just like that, his expression cleared, blank, and he went back to eating his burger as if I didn't exist.

I savored every morsel of that meal, including the Chocolate Fudge Fixation I ordered for dessert.

My belly felt full and satisfied, and exhaustion began to force my eyelids to droop.

And I knew it was time to pay the piper. "So . . ." I pushed away my empty dessert plate and slumped back against the booth, my expression baleful. "What the hell do you want from me?"

His answer was to reach into his wallet, pull out a business card, and hand it over.

I stared down at it, disbelief flooding me.

four

Killian O'Dea
A&R Executive
Skyscraper Records
100 Stobcross Road
Glasgow
07878568562

My fingers bit into the fancy embossed business card in my hand and I looked up at Mr. Killian O'Dea frowning. He was an artist and repertoire executive. Someone who found new artists and built the repertoire of a record label. "A record company?"

He stared blandly back at me. "If you don't believe me, I can give you my phone so you can google us." Before I could respond, he rhymed off who they'd signed; I recognized a few of them as successful British artists. "We're the only record company in Scotland worth discussion and on our way to eclipsing the top labels in England. Between our eye for recognizing relevant talent and a marketing team that knows better than any how to sell talent to a digital generation, we've had a succession of number one albums in the last five years and a handful of our artists have gone global."

There was a spark in his eyes as he spoke that hadn't been there before. A light. Of passion or cold ambition, I wasn't quite sure. Moreover, I wasn't one hundred percent sure why I was getting his pitch.

"Why are you telling me all of this?"

O'Dea turned slightly toward me, his intense focus unnerving. "We don't merely grow commercially successful singers, we nurture real artists. You have a gift. Do you think I stop by every bloody busker out there listening to them do Adele covers? No. You made me stop the first time I heard you singing an original song. You have my interest. I'd like a chance to hear more of your stuff, and if it's as good as I think it is, then I'll want you to write an album for me."

"I don't have a manager." It was a lie.

"I can help you with that."

There was a small part of me that would always be pleased to hear someone appreciate what I could do, but there was an even bigger part scared shitless that this guy had approached me. My heart pounded in my chest at the thought of what he was proposing. Putting me out there again. It would only take seconds and all my secrets would be uncovered. Sweat slickened my palms and I felt cold and shivery. I reached for my stuff. "Thanks, but no thanks."

"That's it?" he bit out, and I glanced up to see him glaring at me.

"I don't have anything else but the songs you've heard me sing."

"I don't believe you."

Anger mingled with the fear, making my cheeks flush. "I don't care what you believe." I made to slide out of the booth but he grabbed my elbow.

My eyes blazed with warning but O'Dea didn't let go. "Why would a person choose to stay stuck on the streets rather than take up an offer to change her life? That doesn't make sense to me."

I laughed unhappily at his naiveté. "Do you think fame and fortune are all they're cracked up to be? It's an emptier existence than mine."

"And how would you know?"

"Let go of my arm."

"How would you know?"

"You only have to look at the lives of famous people. How many of them seem truly happy to you?"

"I happen to know a few who are genuinely happy."

"Then they're probably self-medicating."

"You're awfully cynical for a young girl."

I lifted an eyebrow. "How young do you think I am? If you're looking for a new teenybopper to burst onto the scene in short skirts and fake pointy nails, you're barking up the wrong tree."

"If you think that, then you haven't been listening. How old *are* you?"

"Why the twenty questions?"

"That was one question. I haven't even asked for your name. Why the evasion?"

"Because you're a strange man who is buying me dinner because he wants something from me. It might not be what most men want, but it's still something I'm not willing to give. You can dress it up anyway you want, but we both know you couldn't give a shit about me. You want to make money and I don't want to make you that money. Still going to pay for dinner?"

O'Dea reluctantly let go of my arm. "Aye."

Relief flooded me but I didn't let it show. I pretended I wasn't shaking all over and got out of the booth, hauling up my backpack onto my shoulders.

"You're right," he said.

I paused reaching for my guitar case and waited for him to go on.

"I couldn't give a shit what age you are, what your name is. I couldn't give a shit that you're homeless. All I care about is your voice, the songs you write, and your ability to sell records." He stood up, pulling a wad of cash out of his wallet and dumping it on the table. It covered way, *way* more than the meal. His dark eyes were steely with disappointment and annoyance. "When you're ready to pull your unwashed head out of your arse, give me a call."

Outraged pride suffused me. "You condescending, pain in—I washed my hair this morning."

He strolled around the table and stopped to stare down at my head, making me squirm. When he finally met my eyes, the hardness in his didn't soften as it clashed with the fierceness of mine. "In a public shower somewhere. Let me guess . . . a swim center?"

Shame prickled my cheeks, and in that moment, I hated him for mocking me. "What kind of man shames a homeless person?"

"I'm trying to shame someone who doesn't need to be a homeless person, unlike the thousands of other poor souls in this country who don't have a choice but to sleep rough. You think *I'm* mocking *you*. *You* mock *them* every day."

I flinched. "Bullshit."

"No? They don't have a choice. You do."

"I don't."

"I just offered you one." He grabbed my hand and slapped his business card into it. "Do with it what you will."

And then he was gone, leaving me sweating hot and cold in TGI Fridays. My legs felt like jelly and my head swam with lightness. I refused to put it down to his harsh words and instead stumbled for the booth, slumping into it. It was just the food and excitement of the day—that was all.

Still, my fingers trembled as I reached for the money he'd thrown on the table.

"Would you like the bill?"

The new voice made me clench my hands around the money in a panic that took me by surprise. I nodded at the waiter as I drew my hands under the table so the cash was out of sight. When the bill came, I counted out what we owed along with a nice tip, and I felt the burn of tears when I realized what was left.

The bastard had given me two hundred pounds. Small change to some, but it meant I wouldn't have to worry for a few weeks about making money busking.

I hated him even more for his charity. Why give me money if he thought so little of me?

Try as I might, I couldn't get his voice out of my head as I took the bus out of the city center. And that night as I layered up in my tent, I tucked the money into a hidden compartment in my guitar case and then pulled out a notepad I hadn't touched since arriving in Scotland.

When everything went to shit, I'd taken off. I left everything behind and I backpacked through Europe for over a year. The whole time I'd written new music. Music that was unlike anything our band had produced. It wasn't about looking for a new sound or a new hit. I didn't want that life anymore. But music would always be the way I expressed myself and I'd hoped that the songs I was writing would bring me peace somehow.

They hadn't.

I knew then if music couldn't help me, nothing would.

So I stopped when I got to Scotland. I used the last of my money on a cheap flight from Paris to Glasgow. And for five months

I'd kept singing, but I didn't write.

My visitor's visa was about to run out. Although I had the money from O'Dea, soon there would be nothing. No money to get home. Frankly, I didn't want to go home.

Staring down at the notepad, at the lyrics I'd written, at a song that was too honest for me to sing while I busked, I felt an urge I hadn't felt in months. I'd spent all my time here trying to forget, forcing all the bad stuff out so I could pretend I was someone else. Yet . . . I wanted to finish what I'd started.

After fumbling for a pen, I began frantically making changes to the lyrics. I stopped when the song was half finished, needing to hear how it sounded.

Then I opened my guitar case and pulled out my Taylor.

And I sang.

"No, I didn't understand then
That your soul was part of mine and
When yours faded out
Mine broke down to du—"

My voice broke before I could even get the last lyric of the first verse out. I lay back in the tent, curled around my guitar, my song discarded beside me and for the first time in months, I fell asleep with tears on my cheeks.

five

During the summer the city had a distinct smell, a homogenized scent that was difficult to describe until you broke it down into all its separate parts. One of those parts was hot asphalt. The summers here were nothing compared to back home but on those elusive warm days, the many buildings, people, and traffic built up the heat until the sidewalk was so warm to the touch, it gave off that distinct smell of hot concrete.

Now as the temperatures dropped, I found myself surprised at the underlying smell of wet concrete everywhere, even when it hadn't rained for days. Scotland was damp in the fall no matter if those gray clouds overhead deigned to stay full.

It was the kind of damp cold that seeped into your bones.

The following Saturday, Killian O'Dea didn't show up to hear me sing. I'd like to say it didn't bother me, but I knew there had to be a string attached to the money he'd given me. I was so desperate, I'd taken it, but that didn't make me naive. It wasn't really kindness that had caused him to leave it. So I was on edge. Waiting. I wanted to return to being invisible. Yet my eyes searched for him beneath the brim of my fedora and I had an unpleasant restless feeling itching in my fingers and toes as I packed up for the day.

But it wasn't Killian O'Dea himself that was the cause for the feeling. He'd merely helped unveil them. Popping open my emotions like one of those joke snakes in a can. They'd jumped out in an unraveling mess and now I couldn't figure out how to neatly fold them back in. Instead I swept them under an imaginary rug. A lumpy, untidy rug that reminded me every day those feelings were there.

Along with a now dawning fear of approaching winter.

It really hit me the next evening.

After a fitful sleep of hugging myself and attempting and failing to keep my teeth from chattering, I got up on Monday morning feeling like hell. Even with the money O'Dea had given me, I was hungry. The goal was to make that money last as long as possible, so I ate cheaply and sometimes sporadically. That meant I was used to the gnawing hunger pangs and the constant ache in my stomach when I woke up. But that morning it was the queasiness of a lack of sleep mixed with the damp chill in my bones that really killed.

Despite the low temperatures during the night, the sun was shining as I wearily packed up my tent. Birds twittered in the trees, a sound I usually loved waking up to but today made me irritated with envy. Those damn birds seemed so happy while I couldn't be any more miserable if I tried.

Knowing I needed to get some heat in me, I headed for the swim center and grabbed a hot shower. Feeling marginally better, it wasn't until I was getting dressed and I saw the tampons in my backpack that I faltered.

My pulse picked up a little as I tried to work out the date.

What the . . .

Hurrying to dress, I got myself together and stopped at

reception on my way out to collect my guitar. "Thanks. Can I ask what date it is today?"

"It's the 24th."

Shit.

My period was over a month late. How had I not noticed this?

Feeling my skin prickle with worry, I tried not to let it show. "Do you have a scale that I could use?"

"If you go back into the dressing room, you'll see scales in the corner right at the far end of the room, at the last row of lockers."

Nodding my thanks, I hurried back into the dressing room, my pulse racing. Glad it was quiet this early in the morning, I shucked out of all my stuff, kicked off my shoes, and got up on the scale.

Despite an average height of five foot six, I've always looked petite because I have such small shoulders, a slender waist, and average boobs. If it weren't for my fuller hips and ass, I would've felt like a little girl.

I was losing my hips and ass. They weren't completely gone but it was getting to that point.

The weight on the scales was not as bad as I'd been anticipating. I wasn't a doctor but I didn't reckon I was dangerously underweight. But I'd stopped getting my period.

If it wasn't my weight—and I wasn't sure it wasn't—then was it malnutrition? Was it anemia? Was it all the walking? Hell, I didn't know.

All I knew was that if I didn't have my period, there was something wrong.

Out of what felt like nowhere, a sob burst up from my chest before I could stop it and I grabbed my stuff, fleeing to the sanctuary of a changing cubicle where I slapped my hand across my mouth to muffle the sound.

Suddenly I could see Mandy and Ham, both waif-like, unkempt, and so obviously not taking care of themselves. I thought I was above them. That sleeping rough wasn't affecting my ability to care for myself.

But it was, wasn't it.

What the hell was I doing to myself?

I had to stop this.

But how?

I couldn't go back. I couldn't, I couldn't, I couldn't . . .

There had to be a way to survive this life better than this. And wasn't this what I wanted? To only have to worry about basic survival?

I laughed bitterly at the thought. O'Dea was right. My head was shoved so far up my ass, I hadn't even realized it wasn't on my shoulders anymore. It turned out this life was pretty fucking scary in reality when your health started to suffer.

Shit.

It took a while, but I finally managed to get myself together, trying not to look at how frail my wrist looked, the bone protruding more than I remembered, as I fumbled to get my gear together. As I slid my hands into the pocket of my raincoat to make sure the change I had in there hadn't fallen out, my fingers rasped against a piece of card. Frowning, I pulled it out.

Killian O'Dea

A&R Executive

Skyscraper Records

100 Stobcross Road

Glasgow

07878568562

The business card seemed to glare at me like O'Dea had a habit of doing.

"They don't have a choice. You do."

"I don't."

"I just offered you one."

I blew out a shaky breath and for some reason, instead of crumpling the business card, I opened my jacket, unzipped the inside pocket, and slid the card in where it would be safe.

I didn't allow myself to analyze why.

JUST AS I'D BEEN WARNED, the weather surprised me that day. How it could've been so bitter during the night only to grow into a beautiful, warm, late-September day, I didn't know. I could only hope the heat would seep into the ground, keeping it warm for me tonight.

I refused to let my concern about my physical health affect today's performance on Buchanan Street. Since it was a weekday, I was the only one busking. The unseasonable weather meant those who didn't work were milling around and those who were working wanted to be out in the sunshine during their lunch hour. Wanting to feed their need for sunshine and summer, I did a quirky, upbeat rendition of The Ramones "Rockaway Beach." It proved to be a crowd pleaser and the coins in my guitar case began to multiply. I followed it up with "Summertime" by Ella Fitzgerald, and subsequently every summer-themed song I could think of.

I made more cash than I would have on a normal Saturday.

However, as I played song after song, I became aware of two young men who didn't move on. They stood in the ever-changing small crowd gathered around me, and something about them made my spider senses tingle. There was something *off* about them, as if they weren't really there to listen to me sing. I couldn't put my finger on it, but I'd been warned by Ham to watch my back after I busked if I'd had a good day. Anybody could see how much money I was pocketing by looking in my guitar case.

Taking a break after singing "Cruel Summer," the first thing I did was remove all the notes and pound coins from my case. The bottom of the guitar case popped off, so I put the money underneath it and clipped the base back into place so the money was hidden from sight. Then I hovered near it, guitar hanging over my shoulder on its strap, while I took a much-needed swig of water.

I felt them approach before I saw their feet appear on the ground at the edge of the brim of my fedora. Tensing, I lifted my head and glanced between the two young guys. They both wore tracksuit bottoms and T-shirts, baseball caps pulled low over their faces.

The hair on my neck rose in warning.

"That a Taylor?" The tallest of the two lifted his chin toward my guitar.

The question threw me. "You know your guitars?"

"My dad is intae his guitars. Yours is nice."

My tension grew tenfold. My guitar was *expensive*. "Thanks." I turned away, inviting them to leave.

"That a Dreadnought?"

It was a Presentation. But I didn't want him to know that so I lied. "You *really* know your guitars."

"My dad's always wanted a Cocobolo. He can only afford a Harley Benton. But he says one day he'll get a Cocobolo. He cannae play as well as you, though."

"Dinnae say that tae him," his friend snorted.

They chuckled between them and I considered the idea that I was being overly suspicious. "A Cocobolo." I looked up at them. "That's a nice guitar."

"Aye." He nodded, his stare intense on my Taylor. His friend suddenly nudged him again and he shrugged. "Anyway, we better go. Just wanted tae say how good we think ye are."

"Well, I appreciate it, thanks."

They gave me a small wave and strolled away. As they disappeared into the crowds, I waited for the tension to melt away with their departure, but something about the encounter unsettled me. The assessing manner of the young man who'd done most of the talking was disquieting.

My instincts told me to pack up and leave. I'd made enough money. Adding it to what O'Dea had given me, I decided it was time to trade in the raincoat for a cheap winter jacket.

After packing up, I wandered in and out of some of the less expensive high street stores. Most of them only had sales on their summer lines, which made sense, but I finally found a half-price coat that was a season out of style. I wavered handing the money over since it was a good chunk of what I had left, and then I remembered how awful the night before had been.

I needed that winter coat, and I might as well buy it while I had the money. I threw in a cheap winter hat, scarf, and gloves too.

Afterward, I splurged on a fresh chicken salad, sick of junk food, and made sure I had enough water in my backpack. Not wanting to waste the nice weather, I strolled to Glasgow Green, a park a twenty-minute walk from Buchanan Street. Laying out my raincoat on a spot of grass, I sat, ate my salad, and read a book I bought for fifty pence in a bargain bookstore.

It made me forget this morning.

It made me feel normal.

And I realized that as much as I wanted to disappear, maybe every now and then, it was okay—in fact, *important*—to feel normal.

IT WAS A NICE EVENING so I decided to walk back to the cemetery. The tall buildings of the city center disappeared as I headed north, and everything became much grayer as I strolled down a sidewalk of a busy road above the motorway. It was pretty much a straight walk along a busy main road all the way to the cemetery.

By the time I jumped the gates, it was dark. My hardened feet were sore and swollen in my boots from the heat that had cooled considerably. I eyed the shopping bag in my hand with my new coat in it, glad I'd bought it so I could sleep in it tonight.

As I began the long walk uphill toward my cluster of trees, I thought I heard a whisper in the air and put it down to the rustle of fallen leaves along the pathway.

But when I heard it again, I froze like a deer caught in a hunter's sights. The blood whooshed in my ears as I strained to hear, strained to see as my eyes swept the darkened cemetery. The moon lit up everything within near distance, but beyond the near glow of its beams, there was thick, discomforting darkness. I lifted my torch toward it but saw nothing out of the ordinary.

Yet, for the first time since I'd made this place my home, fear seeped into me.

Heart racing, I continued toward the trees, hoping the whisper had merely been my imagination.

I shrugged off my backpack and pulled out the tent. As I started to set up, however, I heard the unmistakable sound of thudding steps on the ground. I shot up, whirling around, alarm freezing me to the spot at the sight of the two young men from earlier standing in front of me.

They'd followed me.

I could feel my chest constrict, my breaths coming short and shallow, as the worst possible scenarios raced through my mind. Why had they followed me? Scared out of my mind but determined not to show it, I tilted my chin up and demanded, "What the hell do you want?"

"The guitar," the tallest of the two immediately replied. "We know it's worth a couple of grand."

Wrong. My Taylor was not only a Presentation Series acoustic, it was specially made for me. Technically, it was worth just under ten thousand dollars, but it could go for a lot more than that at a fan auction.

My guitar case lay behind me on the grass, not only protecting my Taylor but all the money I kept in there for safekeeping. Fear of losing the guitar, of losing that money, turned the shakiness in my limbs to steel. I stepped in front of it, blocking it from their view. "Go home, boys. This isn't worth the trouble."

The tall boy grinned and it was so full of malice, it made my pulse race. "Ye think anyone is going tae care that a homeless bitch got her guitar stolen?" He gestured to the cemetery around us. "There's nobody here tae care. Now give us the guitar and we'll leave ye in peace."

"Look," I turned to the shorter boy who was fidgeting restlessly, wearing an extremely nervous expression, "this guitar has a lot of sentimental value to me. Please."

"For fuck's sake," the taller of the two growled and strode toward me. I braced myself for attack but he merely attempted to brush past me for the guitar.

Instinct made me reach out and grab his arm.

I'd look back on that moment later and wonder how I could've been so foolish.

The boy, taller, broader, and better fed than I was, halted momentarily. He then shook off my hold only to pull back his arm and let it fly. His fist connected with my cheek in an explosion of fire that caused lights to spark across my eyes, blinding me.

The ground slammed into my back and I blinked, disoriented, as my cheek throbbed with an aching heat. As the cemetery stopped wavering, I realized he'd knocked me off my feet. I was lying in the grass as he crouched over my guitar case. He unlatched it, opening it I assumed to make sure the Taylor was in it.

Adrenaline ignited my fury and suddenly I was not only on my feet but I was charging him. I slammed into him, knocking him away from the guitar. I grabbed chunks of his hair, pulling with all my might and feeling satisfaction roar through me as he yelled out in pain. As he managed to shake off my hand, I drew my fingernails across his face, drawing blood.

"Fuck!" he cried out, his face contorted with rage, and he grabbed my hand and twisted it hard.

Sickening pain made my head swim as I dropped to my knees. The world wavered around me, nausea and dizziness making me sway. Tears dampened my face as my breaths stuttered out at the agony blazing up from my wrist.

"Johnny, what ye done?" the other boy cried.

"Grab the fucking guitar and shut up," Johnny said before I found myself pushed onto my back.

"Johnny, let's go."

"No before I teach this bitch a lesson." His hard hands squeezed both my wrists, pinning them to the ground beside my head. I whimpered as nausea rose from my stomach.

I was so discombobulated, it took me a minute to realize Johnny had let go of my injured wrist to unzip his jeans.

What?

No.

No!

"No," I tried to scream but it was like my vocal cords had snapped, the words coming out scratchy and pathetic. "No!"

"Johnny, no," his friend begged. "Come on, let's go."

"Get off me!" I tried to push against the hands holding me down.

His cold fingers fumbled under my raincoat for the zipper on my jeans and panic set me off. I began to kick up my legs, trying to unpin them from his. He punched me.

Again.

And again.

Until I was dazed enough that he managed to shuck down my jeans.

"Johnny, no!"

"Stop fucking saying my name. Go hide behind a fucking tree if ye cannae stand there like a man," he spat, his saliva speckling my throbbing, wet face.

Cognizance was returning and with it my determination.

He'd loosened his hold on my injured wrist while he'd been shouting at his friend so I used that moment of distraction to force every ounce of strength I had into twisting out of his hold and clawing his face. Ignoring the pain that screamed down my arm, I scratched at his eyeballs, his nose, his lips, and he fell off me, trying to protect himself. I rolled, digging my fists into the hard soil beneath the grass and using it as an anchor to pull myself out from under him, my legs scrambling like I was in deep water and trying to propel myself to the surface.

His cursing, foul insults rent the air as my fear-soaked body somehow did what I needed it to do. I had just gotten up on one foot when I felt his hand curl around the other, yanking me back down, face first, the impact on my chin causing a horrible burning in my nose, spots in my vision momentarily blinding me. But I didn't stop.

I whipped around, preparing to batter him with my feet, when through blurred, darkening vision, I saw the other boy bring a rock down across Johnny's temple.

My attacker slumped to the ground, out cold.

The boy stood, my guitar case in his hand, and stared at his friend in shock. His pale face suddenly turned to me. "Run," he said, and then he did just that.

With my guitar.

With my money.

My gaze dropped back to the boy who had tried to rape me, blood trickling from the hair at his temple, and the whole surreal mess swirled in my stomach. I promptly threw up on the grass, hoping the blood I saw in it was from the cut I could feel throbbing on my lower lip. Shaking uncontrollably, I got to my feet, feeling hard and cold as I pulled up my jeans with my uninjured right hand and zipped them.

After struggling to get my backpack on my back, I protectively curled my sprained wrist into my chest and I ran, leaving behind my tent and, later I'd realize, my new coat.

My left eye started swelling shut, and what was left of my vision was hazy. I stumbled a few times and even fell at the sight of the cemetery gates. And by some miracle I got myself over those gates.

Having walked the streets many times, I was on autopilot. It was like my brain had made up its mind what to do before I could really process it. Keeping my head ducked down, I marched until I found the payphone I'd passed daily but had never used.

The change in my pocket was all that I had.

I had nothing.

No money.

And no guitar to make any more.

I had only one option.

After a few rings his masculine voice answering my call felt strangely reassuring. I couldn't explain why.

"O'Dea?"

"Who is this?"

"Busker Girl," I said, taking Mandy's nickname for me. Then I swallowed my pride. In fact, the pain in my wrist swallowed my pride for me. "I need help."

six

The heartless bastard agreed to come get me if I promised to audition for him.

I had little choice in the matter.

He was just one more person I could add to my list of people I resented.

I was standing facing the phone booth when I heard the car pull up behind me. I tensed, not wanting to turn around in case it wasn't him. Then I heard the car door slam and his voice asking, "Busker Girl?"

Turning to him, I finally understood how much of a mess I must have been in because O'Dea's face slackened under the yellow glow of the streetlamp. Then it hardened and darkened with rage as he strode over to me. "What the fuck happened?"

"Can we get in the car?" I said, not wanting anyone else to see me.

He gently took hold of my right arm and guided me over to a black Range Rover. He pulled the door open and then helped me remove my backpack. I got in while he put my backpack in the trunk. Exhaustion hit me as I slumped against the car seat, the smell of leather and his cologne weirdly comforting. O'Dea jumped into the driver's side.

"You left a few things out on the phone. What happened?" he demanded.

So I told him everything about that day and the boys.

"His friend hit him pretty hard," I murmured, wondering if he'd hit him too hard.

There was utter silence from my right. I glanced at him out of my eye that wasn't swollen shut. His fists were curled around the steering wheel, his knuckles white.

"I'm okay," I said, realizing this was the first time I'd seen any real emotion from him.

"You're pretty far from okay," he snapped, starting the engine. "First we go to the hospital and we'll let them contact the police."

A new fear sprang up inside of me. "No. We can't go to the hospital. We can't contact the police."

"Don't talk shite," he huffed, his SUV racing down the street. "Your wrist is sprained, possibly broken. If you don't get that seen to, you'll never play the guitar again."

The thought made my chest ache worse than the blazing pain in my wrist or the throbbing in my face.

"He took my Taylor. It was . . . special. My mum had it specially made for me. I should have fought harder." I sighed, shaking my head, decided. "No hospital. No police."

"Drop the martyr act, Skylar. We're going to the hospital and that's final."

My breath caught.

"You can drop the fake British accent too. As good as it is."

Disbelief made my head swim even more. "You know who I am?" I asked in my own accent.

"Almost from the first moment I heard you play."

"H-how?"

"Music is my business. I know music. At one point Skyscraper were actively on the lookout for a band like Tellurian." He referred to my band by name. "A social media phenomenon, a commercially successful teen pop-rock band with more substance than most and millions of teenage followers that would make us lots of money."

"More substance than most?" Despite my current situation, I still had pride. It could still be pricked. Something he had a knack for, it seemed.

"You. You were the substance. You have a four-octave range. *Rolling Stone* magazine once named you in the top ten greatest singers of the twenty-first century. They never once named your band in the top ten greatest bands of the twenty-first century, mind you. Too many angsty, angry teen love songs to be truly respected. But *you* were, *are*, respected. Your talent is respected." He shot me an assessing look. "And the industry has no idea about your songwriting abilities."

"I wrote nearly all the songs for Tellurian," I argued.

"Aye, but those songs are nothing like what I've heard you singing lately. The songs you're writing now can make grown-ups feel, not just preteens who are sick of feeling invisible at school."

"Wow, you're really into that 'hitting them when they're down' thing," I said, disbelieving that he was talking to me about this while I was struggling to stay conscious. "Let me out of your fancy car, Nurse Ratched."

He ignored me. "Why don't you want to go to the hospital? Because you don't want anyone to find you?"

"That, and my visitor visa expires in two weeks."

"Do you have travel insurance?"

"No." Even if I wanted to be fixed, I couldn't afford it.

O'Dea sighed. "Well, we need to get that wrist seen to, no question about it. I'll explain you're my client here on business and that you got jumped by thugs. We'll sort out the medical costs later."

"I don't want to be found." The idea of Micah and the others finding me shoved me further toward passing out.

"We'll also make sure they know how important your privacy is. Plus, I hate to burst your bubble but no one over thirty will know who you are."

"Not true," I muttered sullenly. "We had fans of all ages."

"Mostly teens though. I know your demographic, Skylar. I researched you."

I shrugged and then winced as pain radiated down my arm to my wrist.

O'Dea noticed and scowled. "Hospital."

"And I have no say in this?" My voice sounded shrill with fear.

"You do realize you have a swollen eye, a swollen cheek, split lip, a possibly broken wrist, and some vile little fucker who *will* get his comeuppance just tried to rape you. But you got away. You're made of stern stuff, Skylar, so buck up and start facing reality." He raised an eyebrow at my visible indignation. "You can be pissed off at me all you want, but I'm trying to keep you awake by talking to you and it's working. Now . . . are you going to pull on your big-girl panties or go back to making bad life decisions?"

I glared at him with my good eye. "Fine. Hospital. I'll add it to the list to tell the doctor."

"What?"

"Of injuries. Eye, ribs, wrist, and now this insistent, condescending pain in my ass."

DESPITE SUGGESTING OTHERWISE, O'DEA MADE me tell the absolute truth about what happened. After an X-ray of my wrist, tests, and blood and urine samples, the hospital did call the police and I found myself explaining to two police officers that I had been sleeping rough in my tent in a cemetery. That the boys had followed me back there to steal my guitar. I gave more detail about the almost rape than I had to O'Dea, confused when he abruptly slammed out of the private room we were in.

"It's only natural," the female police officer, Officer Calton, said when she saw my bemused expression. "Your boyfriend will be feeling a different kind of anger than you are."

"He's not my boyfriend. He's my . . ." I shrugged. "He's trying to sign me to his record label."

She nodded and then went on about numbers for a counselor. They finished up their questioning, said they'd check out the cemetery to see if my attacker "Johnny" was there. By the time I'd given them detailed descriptions of the boys, the doctor returned with X-rays of my wrist—it was fractured. He put it in a cast, something I knew would worry me in the morning, but I was so exhausted from the attack, my brain was too foggy to care. By that point O'Dea had returned, watching the process with a permanent dark scowl on his face.

The doctor stared at me with a furrowed brow. "Now that I know you've been sleeping in a tent, Skylar, I'm a little worried about your overall health. You're slightly underweight and that might not be enough for concern normally, but considering how you've been living, I am concerned about possible malnourishment. I'm pushing your blood work through so we should get results in twenty-four hours. I'd feel better if we kept you here overnight and put you on a vitamin and hydration drip."

Panic suffused me at the thought of being stuck in the hospital overnight. "I don't need that. I'm fine, honest. I drink lots of water."

"Do you have somewhere warm to stay tonight?"

"I'll make sure my client has someplace safe to stay," O'Dea chipped in and then proceeded to lie. "I had no idea she was homeless."

The police took O'Dea's number since I didn't have one and told us they would be in touch. "Your guitar is one of a kind and the boys don't know it. As soon as they try to sell it, it'll make it easier to find them."

I nodded, hoping I'd get my guitar back in one piece.

"And I'll be in touch with your results," the doctor said, still not pleased I'd refused to stay overnight. "We'll talk."

Once we got out of there, I was on pain meds and a little out of it as O'Dea drove us into the city. As my eyes drifted closed, he said, "I'm sorry."

"For what?" I mumbled.

"For not shaking your foolish head out of your arse and getting you off the streets. None of this would have happened if I'd tried harder."

"I was warned," I yawned. "They told me something like this could happen. I thought I knew better. I thought I was smarter than them."

"And now?"

"I don't know. I don't know what I'm doing. Can I just sleep first?"

He was silent a moment. Then, "Aye, Skylar, you can sleep first."

My last thought before I drifted off was how strange and scary it was to be Skylar again.

seven

Pain.

It was the first thing I felt. Horrible, restless pain originating from my left wrist. The pain seeped into my subconscious and I floated out of a dreamless state. My eyes reluctantly tried to open and panic momentarily seized hold of me when my left one struggled with the action.

When my vision cleared and I took in the airy white room around me, I grew more alarmed and scrambled upwards in the bed I was in, only to cry out when I pressed down on my left hand. I raised it, everything coming back to me as I saw the cast around my wrist.

I was attacked last night.

It hadn't been a dream.

Images of Johnny bearing down on me, his spittle hitting my face, made my chest constrict with anxiety. I shook my head, trying to shake out the memory, reminding myself I was safe.

My head throbbed, the ache no doubt coming from my swollen eye. Glancing around, my head felt heavy on my shoulders. I was in a bedroom. The walls were white, the carpet a soft gray. Gray curtains were drawn across the window and the bed covers were a soft gray too. The only color in the room was in a beautiful, somewhat abstract, framed print of a pretty girl's face. The artist had painted the lines and motifs that framed her face in hot pinks and turquoise.

I remembered O'Dea taking me to the hospital. I even remembered getting back in his car once we were done. But that was it.

Where the hell was I?

My body ached all over, like I'd been in a car accident. I swung out of bed, relieved to see I was still in my jeans and T-shirt. The thought of O'Dea undressing me for bed was more than I could take.

As I stood, dizziness knocked me back on my ass again and I took a couple of seconds to gather myself. When I felt my head clear, I got back on my feet and slowly made my way toward the door. Stepping out of the bedroom, I found myself looking into a small but perfectly formed open-plan living space. The kitchen was modern with traditional influences—slate-gray, shaker-style cabinets, thick oak countertops, and glossy, lemon-yellow, brick-style tiles as a backsplash. It had a large range cooker with a fancy chimney cooker hood. There was also an island with more counter space, lemon-yellow stools, and beautiful drop ceiling lights with copper shades.

The sitting area had a soft gray corner sofa, a TV mounted on the wall, and a yellow button-back chair.

Beside the chair were French doors that led out onto a balcony. I immediately moved toward it, opening the doors and feeling the chilled wind whip through my hair as I stepped out in my bare feet.

We were on the River Clyde. I knew that from the walks I'd taken down there. On the opposite river bank was a huge rusty-red corrugated iron building that looked like a warehouse. There were more industrial-type units on either side of it. To the left of those was what looked like a couple of apartment buildings and next to that a church.

Stepping in out of the cold, I shut the doors and looked back around the beautiful little apartment. Where the hell was I?

As if on cue, a door slammed down the hall. Footsteps padded toward the living space and my heart started pounding.

I let out a shaky breath, not sure I felt relief or the opposite, as O'Dea appeared. He stopped short at the sight of me, drinking me in from head to foot. Finally, after I'd been subjected to his visual assessment, he asked, "How are you feeling?"

"Like I went a couple of rounds with a creepy Glaswegian kid."

"I put your painkillers in the cupboard." He headed into the kitchen and that's when I noted the carrier bag in his hand.

"So . . . any chance you're going to tell me where I am or are you enjoying discombobulating me?" I took one small step toward him.

Whatever he heard in my voice made him stop in his tracks. He frowned at me. "You don't remember getting here?"

I shook my head.

He frowned harder. "I explained last night but you were pretty out of it. This," he gestured around the room, "is a one-bed flat that belongs to the record label. We own a few flats in this building so we have places to put up our artists. The record label's building is about a twenty-minute walk down the river bank from here."

For some weird reason, I felt utter relief that I wasn't in O'Dea's apartment. It was bad enough that he pretty much blackmailed me in exchange for his help. I didn't want his charity. He'd made it clear that this was only business between us and I'd prefer it to remain that way.

"Discombobulating." He looked impressed. "Big word. Glad to see what's left of your faculties are still intact."

"What's *left* of my faculties?"

"You're a multimillionaire, Skylar, and you've been sleeping on the streets. That doesn't exactly say you're in possession of *all* your faculties. Now eat something before taking the painkillers," he said as he reached into a cupboard and pulled out a little white bag I assumed my meds were in. Then he turned back to the carrier bag he'd put on the counter and began pulling out groceries, including milk and eggs. "Do you like omelet?"

I could try to kill him, or I could eat. Choices, choices.

I hadn't had an omelet in a while and killing him would be messy. "Omelet's fine. Although I take mine with a pinch less condescension."

He shrugged out of the smart wool blazer he wore and threw it over the back of the couch. Gesturing toward it, he said, "Sit."

I made a face but still light-headed, I sat. Watching him as he moved around the kitchen, I felt a begrudging gratefulness despite his patronizing aloofness. Even though this was just business, he had helped me out last night. And the bed I'd slept in must've been like a cloud because as far as I could remember, I hadn't dreamt at all. I'd fallen into a deep sleep. For the first time in weeks I hadn't been woken up by birdsong and bitter cold temperatures. I'd been warm and safe. Because of him.

"Thanks."

O'Dea shot me a look as he pulled out a mixing bowl from a cupboard on the island. "Did you promise to audition for me?"

"I did."

"When you made that promise, I didn't know your wrist was broken."

"Fractured. A hairline fracture." I didn't have to add, "Your point?" My tone did that for me.

He shrugged. "Same thing. The doctor says it could take up to a month, maybe more, until your cast can come off. That means it's going to be weeks before you're ready to play the guitar again."

Watching as he poured cream cheese into the mixing bowl along with some herbs, annoyed that he hadn't asked if I liked cream cheese, I tried to keep the disdain out of my voice. "And?"

"You're going to audition today. Acapella. It might even be better this way. If you can impress me without actual music, then I know I'm onto something good."

I was quiet a moment, trying to calm myself. Still, my words came out like they were soaked in battery acid. "What the fuck is wrong with you?"

O'Dea didn't flinch as he put butter on a hot pan and then proceeded to beat eggs into the herby, cheesy mixture. Not looking up at me, he replied blandly, "I'm a businessman, Skylar. This is business. I'm not giving you time to wallow over what happened to you or to overthink our agreement. We'll get the audition out of the way and then we can go from there."

"You're not even going to give me a day to rest? I feel like I've been hit by a Mack Truck and I'm pretty sure I look like it took the time to reverse and flatten me afterward."

"I'm sure you do," he responded in his annoyingly calm voice.

"You know your sympathy is truly overwhelming."

"Are you always this sarcastic?"

"I'm not auditioning for you today."

"You'll feel better once you've eaten. And you *are* auditioning for me today." He looked over at me with that familiar hardness etching his features. He didn't deserve such beautiful eyes. They belonged to a man who was warm and charming. Not this cold ass. "There will be plenty of time for you to rest once we know where you and I stand. It's better for everyone if we get this audition over with."

"Better for you, you mean."

"No." He sighed. "Skylar, if I don't want to sign you, you'll need to go home. If I do want to sign you, we'll need to discuss what happens from there. Better to come to an understanding quickly, considering your visa is about to expire."

"I'm not going home." I was horrified he'd even suggest it.

"Like I said, audition first."

Butterflies woke in my belly as my mind whirled. What would I do? I had no money. Of course, I could get access to money but that would mean alerting Adam who would alert Gayle who would alert the band. They would come for me and I'd *have* to let them. There was absolutely no way I could go back to living on the streets. I suddenly believed it would eventually kill me.

I had wanted to hide. I didn't want to die.

"Stop thinking so hard," O'Dea said, pushing a plate over the counter toward one of the stools. My stomach grumbled and as if tethered to the plate of hot food, I had no other choice but to go to it.

O'Dea pushed a glass of fresh orange juice toward me too, and still standing began eating his own omelet.

It was delicious.

"I'd give you more but the doc suggested we increase your food intake incrementally. So we're using Autumn's omelet recipe."

"Autumn?"

"My sister. She likes to cook. She's taught me a thing or two."

Oh. Somehow it seemed odd to me that O'Dea had family. He seemed like the kind of man who was a lone wolf.

"I ate," I said. "I wasn't starving myself. I just couldn't eat well because I had to eat cheap."

He nodded, like he understood. He didn't understand. No one could unless they'd been in my situation.

"The omelet is good," I offered reluctantly when the silence felt too heavy.

But it was followed by more silence, the only sounds between us that of cutlery on plates and the soft sipping sounds of us drinking. I could barely finish the omelet, not used to eating something so substantial in the morning. O'Dea's brows pinched together as he took my plate, but he didn't say anything.

"I need a shower."

"There's an en suite in the bedroom. Fresh towels, soap, shampoo and conditioner in there too." He reached into the carrier bag on the counter and pulled out a brand-new electric toothbrush and tube of toothpaste. He offered them and feeling a little unbalanced by the gesture, I took them. "There's a hair dryer in the bathroom as well. Your backpack is in the bedroom."

I nodded, not quite able to thank him again after the last attempt.

"I'll be out here when you're done. We'll get straight to the audition."

And suddenly I didn't care about thanking him. Throwing him a look of disgust, I disappeared into the bedroom and slammed the door behind me.

Unfortunately, a few minutes later, I had to come out of the room again. I found him sitting on the couch, drinking coffee, and scrolling through something on his phone. O'Dea looked up at me with an eyebrow quirk. I hated that eyebrow quirk.

I lifted my wrist with the cast. "I need something to cover this."

Without saying a word, he got up, put his coffee and phone down on the island, and rummaged through one of the large drawers beside the range. He turned around with cling-film in his hands and gestured me to come to him with an odious curl of his finger. Internally huffing, I strode over to him and held out my wrist.

"This place is pretty well stocked," I grumbled.

"We like to make sure every need is catered to."

I harrumphed.

Then O'Dea triple-wrapped my cast with such gentleness, it stunned me silent.

I was still standing holding out my arm while he put the cling-film away. I frowned at his back, puzzled by his complexity. That is until he turned around and gave me that eyebrow again.

Just like that I was back to being annoyed and desperate to get out of his company.

My building resentment toward him only increased the moment I saw my reflection in the bathroom mirror.

How the hell could he look at me like this and demand that I audition?

Bluish bruising covered my puffed-up, swollen eye and upper cheek. My lower lip was swollen on one side where it had split. And underneath the injuries, my cheekbones cut sharply against my pale skin. The shoulders of my T-shirt hung down on my arms because my shoulders were too small for it.

I looked like a battered waif.

Skylar Finch was no more.

My intent had been to let her go. Let her disappear. Instead it looked like I'd starved and beaten her out of existence. If I let it, the shame and guilt would overwhelm me.

So I couldn't let it.

It was better to turn that anger toward Killian O'Dea. The heartless A&R executive.

However, as I awkwardly showered with one hand, enjoying the coconut-scented shower gel and the expensive brand shampoo and conditioner, my anger momentarily faded away. My stomach felt comfortably full, the power shower was freaking amazing, and despite my resentment toward the Scot out in the living room, I couldn't deny that I felt safe.

In pain, but safe.

I hadn't thought that I'd felt *unsafe* sleeping in that cemetery, probably because I never imagined I'd get attacked. Yet, I realized the whole time I *had* felt like I was always on the edge of peril. The weather had scared me.

But now I didn't feel afraid.

I think I resented O'Dea for that too. That a man like him could make me feel safe. It reminded me of Micah. Of having a man make me feel safe and yet horribly used at the same time.

By the time, I got out of the shower, I was exhausted and wanted nothing more than to drop down in that beautiful king-sized bed and sleep the rest of the day. I used the toothbrush he gave me, first wincing at the painful stretch against my cut lips when I opened my mouth too wide, and then flinching against the vibration of the bristles. It had been so long since I'd used an electric toothbrush, it felt uncomfortably weird against my teeth. I had to dab fresh blood from my lip afterward.

But once I'd changed into clean underwear, jeans, and a hoodie, I'd made the decision that O'Dea was right. We'd struck a bargain and it was time to suck it up and fulfill my end of it.

He was on the phone when I stepped out. He gave me another head-to-toe once-over before he said, "We'll discuss it when I get into the office. I have to go." He hung up without saying goodbye. "You look marginally better."

"I look like shit." I shrugged and sat on the sofa. "Let's get this over with. What do you want to hear?"

He sat down in the button-back chair looking ridiculously too tall and masculine for it. "All of it."

"You've already heard a few of my songs."

"I want to hear them again. But I also want to hear something new." At my silence he continued, "Why don't you start with the one about the moon and the stars."

O'Dea referred to my song "Ghost." It was one of my more upbeat melodies.

Looking away from him, out of the French doors to the river below, I prepared to sing. It felt weird starting the song straight into the lyrics because I loved my intro on the guitar to this one. This song, like quite a few I'd written over the past eighteen months, was a collision of perky sound and melancholic lyrics. "Ghost" had a folky, countrified riff and that was obviously difficult to capture without my guitar.

Still, I opened my mouth and began to sing, surprised my voice came out clear and true, despite the battering I'd taken the night before.

"The plane landed in Rome
And I shook off the past,
Oh, I hope it'll last.
Then I hopped on a train to take me
From my name.
Oh, it's gone now.

"Yeah, I'm a ghost,
Drifting coast to coast.

"I slept under the stars
Trying to make them my friends.
But just like a cleanse

They all wanted my amends.
So, I left them behind me
And turned to the moon.
For less gloom, yeah.

"'Cause now I'm a ghost,
Drifting coast to coast.

"The moon took me to Berlin
Where we started a fight
With the stars about light
'Cause they tried to shed some
Over all of the past
That I'd buried in Rome.
Oh, stop forcing me home!

"'Cause now I'm a ghost,
Drifting coast to coast.
Yeah, I'm a ghost,
I don't wanna go home.
What is home,
But a grave left in Rome.

"I settled down in Glasgow
With the moon on my side.
And the stars they all died,
Withered under my will.
They couldn't stand the chill.
But I can, yeah.

"You know I'm a ghost,

I'm not misdiagnosed.
Yeah, I'm a ghost,
I'm not misdiagnosed.
You know I'm a ghost,
And I ain't ever going home."

Without my guitar, my music, the song seemed short and ended awkwardly. I flushed, feeling vulnerable in a way I never felt when I was performing on the streets.

O'Dea gave me nothing. He merely demanded, "Another."

And so I sang another.

"Are we done yet?" I asked as soon as I finished.

"I want to hear something I haven't heard. Something even more real than all the others."

My stomach flipped at the thought. "Those two were pretty personal."

"I want more."

Butterflies raged in my stomach, the song I felt was the most personal coming to mind. I wanted the audition over and I knew instinctively that this was the song that would end it. It wasn't just the lyrics, it was the melody. I'd never once written a song and not questioned how great it was. There was always something about it that I wanted to perfect. But not this song. This song came from somewhere so deep inside me, it *was* me. The acoustic version was exactly how I wanted it to be, and I even knew how I wanted every aspect of it to sound with a band. I'd finished writing it only a few nights ago when my existence as one of the invisible had still felt like my only option.

Maybe I should have sung another, one of the songs I hadn't quite finished. But O'Dea wanted to know what kind of artist I was right now, and this was me. Fucked-up, little old me.

"This one's called 'In the Wind' . . ."

"No, I didn't understand then
That your soul was part of mine and
When yours faded out
Mine broke down to dust.

"Oh, it blew into the wind and
I can't find all the pieces
That used to be me—"

"I can't," I broke off, my voice cracking with emotion that embarrassed me. I covered my face with my good hand, flinching as my fingers touched the painful mess of my eye. Hiding from him, I tried to control my breathing, hating that he got to see me like this.

There was utter silence in the small apartment.

Then O'Dea cleared his throat and I heard the chair protest under his movement. "You need rest."

Astonished at his soft words, I removed my hand from my face and stared up at him now standing as if to leave.

He stared at the floor, seeming unable to meet my gaze.

"I *need* my guitar," I whispered.

O'Dea's dark gaze flew to mine and I saw the puzzlement there.

"My mom gave it to me," I reiterated.

Understanding dawned on his face. Everyone knew what happened to my mom.

"You need rest," he repeated, proving that he could feel empathy after all. "Take today to get yourself together. Sleep, rest. Whatever. I put some fresh soup in the fridge so all you have to do is heat it up. There's also plenty of water in there. Your painkillers are in the cupboard. I've left you what you need for tonight. I'll bring the rest with me tomorrow."

I scowled. "You don't trust me with painkillers?" At his silence, I huffed. "Nurse Goddamned Ratched. You know what, screw your apparent ability to not be a patronizing pain in my ass. You just fuck it up by reverting to instinct. So let's just do this." I indicated the seat he'd stood up from. "I want this over with."

And before he could reply, I started singing again.

"No, I didn't understand then
That your soul was part of mine and
When yours faded out
Mine broke down to dust."

Memories flooded me as I stared unseeing out the window, the lyrics, the music in my head, the feelings becoming everything until I forgot where I was and who I was with. I wasn't singing to O'Dea. I was singing to her.

"Oh, it blew into the wind and
I can't find all the pieces
That used to be me,
They're lost in a sea.

"So I wander all alone now,
Numb in my remoteness,
Content to be
Lost in this sea.

"Just a whisper on a wave,
A lost ship that can't be saved.

And it's all that I deserve.

"Ah, ah, ah.

"Oh, I wish that I had told you
All the truths locked inside me,
Instead of cutting you out
Like a knife through our lives.

"So afraid that I would fail you
With these years that I'd lied through,
And now it's too late
To tell you I'm sorry.

"I can hear your voice in my head.
Absolution that was never said.
Fingers sifting through wind,
Trying to pluck out the dust.

"It catches in the light,
Familiar fragments full of fight,
But they're always out of reach.

"Ah, ah, ah.

"No, I didn't understand then
That your soul was part of mine and
When yours faded out
Mine broke down to dust.

"It catches in the light,

Familiar fragments full of fight,
But they're always out of reach.

"Ah, ah, ah."

When I finished, O'Dea was sitting on the chair, his elbows braced on his knees. He was staring at the floor, like he was lost in thought. Then he looked up at me and my breath caught at the million heartbreaking emotions roiling in his gaze.

And then they were gone, as if they'd never been there.

"That's all I have so far," I whispered, so confused by him. "No more songs."

His expression was unreadable. "Your visitor's visa is about to run out."

Bewildered by the response, I could only nod.

"You've no money."

I tensed.

"You've run away from your identity, from your life in the band, in the US. You've no family to speak of, and you abandoned your friends."

The man was the soul of sensitivity. "Your point?"

"My point is that you don't have many options. I think you were living in some naive fantasy that you could keep running from your problems and live a relatively peaceful life as a homeless person. Somehow, miraculously, you survived unscathed for five months. But last night you were given a giant fucking look at the reality and dangers of homelessness. I wish it hadn't happened that way, but there was never any other way it was going to end. And it has ended, am I right?"

"So, do you get, like, a bonus at the end of every day if you say a hundred patronizing things in a twenty-four-hour period or something?"

He ignored me. "You can't go back to sleeping rough."

"I think I got that, thanks." I waved my cast at him.

"So . . . it's either call your old manager, your band—"

"Not an option," I snapped.

O'Dea smirked. "Then I'm all you've got. And I'm no fucking Mother Teresa. I'm in the business of making money, Miss Finch. You've already proven you're good at making it. And from what I heard today and have heard you playing when you busk, I think the world hasn't even seen a fraction of what you can do."

There was really nothing to do but glare and hope that he withered under it.

"I'll let you stay here in this flat free of charge, give you a weekly stipend for clothes, groceries, a new guitar. You can heal up here. But all of it in exchange for a record contract. A one-album deal, that's all I ask. When you're healed up, you'll be straight into the studio to record."

The thought made my stomach pitch. "I don't want to be famous again."

"Tough shit. There is no being famous again. You *are* famous. And you've got more talent in your pinkie finger than most do in their entire being. And that talent deserves more of a platform than standing on a street busking. It's a goddamned insult to all those people out there trying to make the big time. I don't care what it is you're running from. I care that you sort yourself out and make some music again. Music that matters. Music that will heal you."

I bristled. "I've made music that matters. I've got the fan mail to prove it."

"Your music in Tellurian did its job. It was catchy, appealing, and teenagers related. But your voice is meant for something else. The songs you just sang to me . . . those are songs that will really make people *feel*. It's vulnerable and brutally honest and that's the stuff that resonates with people. People want songs that make them feel good, but they also just want songs that me them *feel*, even if it breaks their fucking heart. You've been through a lot, Skylar. Even if I couldn't read a newspaper, I'd know that by listening to those songs you sang.

"Two years ago, you were a leader on social media and the lead singer of a pop-rock band that teens and college freshman loved. I'm not asking you to go back to that. I'm asking you to become an artist in your own right. If you don't want the social media exposure, we'll have someone else run that stuff for you. And we'll do what we can to minimize the tabloid exposure. It will be hard at first considering your disappearance, but once it dies down, we can make it so you're not hounded. It is possible."

"It doesn't matter whether they hound me or not. I hate the fame. I hate the touring. I hate it all."

"No." His expression hardened. "You don't. Something awful happened to you. It messed you up good but if you don't get smart, you're going to ruin your life over it. Do you think you're the only person in the world who has ever lost someone they loved? Get a grip. It's time to move on. Someone who spends her days singing in the street doesn't 'hate *all* of it.'"

"Well," I sputtered, unable to argue with that. So I lied. "I'm still locked into a contract."

A glimmer of triumph lightened his countenance. "I've already checked into Tellurian. You told the band you were quitting before you left. Your old contract had come to an end so the band replaced you with a new lead singer and they signed a new contract. Your old label has no legal hold over you and definitely not as a solo artist."

That the band had replaced me was not news to me. I'd seen it on the cover of a tabloid I couldn't avoid when I first started traveling across Europe. Still, O'Dea didn't know that, and he'd dropped the news with all the sensitivity of a joke during a death sentence. The girl they'd replaced me with, Macy, looked somewhat like me, my once-rainbow hair and all.

"If it makes you feel better, their sales aren't as high as they were when they had you," O'Dea offered.

Disgusted, I replied, "No, that doesn't make me feel better."

He grew quiet. It didn't last. His impatience took over whatever decency he had. "So . . . what's it going to be? On the streets with no guitar and no way of making money? Or access your own money to get home and let them all know where you are?"

"You would really kick me out on the streets right now?"

"I'm a businessman, Skylar. Not a philanthropist."

"That's not an answer."

He shrugged.

I bit my lip to stop myself from calling him every ugly name I could think of. I choked out, "Can I think about it? Give me the night to think about it."

O'Dea nodded. "Think on this too. If you sign that contract, you'll be signing an addendum that states that in order to fully fulfill your obligations within the contract, you agree to consult with a nutritionist to get your weight back up to where it needs to be, to a thorough health check, and to seeing a therapist once a week."

My lips parted at the audacity of his demands. "Are you kidding me?"

Exasperation colored his reply. "No one decides to go hungry and sleep on the streets, running away from their life because they're mentally well, Skylar. You need to speak to someone and you need to sort out your shit. If only so we can balance out the album. We want songs that make people feel. We don't want an entire album that makes them want to kill themselves."

I really, *really* hated him. "I'm not seeing a therapist."

"There's no shame in seeing a therapist."

"Then you go see one."

"*I* don't need a therapist."

"Oh, I beg to differ. You're a control freak. You're awful."

"I want you to be physically and mentally healthy. How does that make me awful?" He strode toward me and I leaned back into the couch away from him. But all he did was pick up his jacket and shrug into it. "You might not realize it, but the songs you're writing are an attempt to heal. I merely want to speed up that process."

I didn't know how to respond without involving violence.

"You have tonight."

I watched him walk away, my brain whirring. "Wait!" I called out.

He stopped and looked back over his shoulder at me.

"If I'm going to think about this, I want no bullshit between us. You say I wouldn't have to deal with the tabloid stuff, that you'll try to minimize it?"

"Of course."

"You're lying."

"I am?"

"There's no guarantee just because I'm a good singer with a couple songs that you like that I'll be a success for you. No one comes after someone this hard based merely on those two facts. But as soon as you worked out who I was, it was the game-changer . . . you knew you had to have me."

He turned fully to face me.

"A good voice . . ." I began to tick off his checklist with the fingers of my right hand as I stood. "Good songs, experience, and the kicker . . . a tabloid frenzy that will make my solo launch spectacular. You know I'll be everywhere when I emerge back into the public. It's the kind of publicity money can't buy."

He sighed. "You're right."

"So, you admit it?"

"Aye, I admit it. Lead singer of successful band disappears off the face of the planet after the authorities fail to find the men who murdered her mother and stepfather. She emerges two years later with a new look and a new sound. You'll be the only thing anyone is talking about when the first single debuts."

He said it so dispassionately but at least he was honest. There hadn't been a lot of that in my life. And I offered him honesty in return. "I don't like you."

"You don't need to like me. You need to learn to trust that I will make this album a success."

"I might trust that if you keep things up-front from now on."

He shrugged. "It seems you're smart enough to know when I am and when I'm not, so I don't see that being a problem."

"True. But still. I want your word."

"Fine. Honesty at all times."

"Okay. Then I'll think about it."

eight

Two years ago
Billings, Montana

We were back. Playing the home crowd. The Pub Station no less, and it wasn't our first time. This was our fourth year playing the iconic music venue we'd dreamed of playing as kids.

I sat in the private dressing room, glad our manager Gayle loved me enough to always demand a separate dressing room for me from the guys. We were in each other's faces nonstop and sometimes it was nice to get some alone time.

The walls hummed and throbbed with the dull sound of live music. Talking Trees, an alt-rock band from Arkansas, was our opening act in our US tour. Billings was our last stop. We would take a break. I'd hole myself up somewhere away from the guys, attempting to claw back my sanity before our European tour kicked off in six weeks.

Six weeks and I'd have to do this all over again. But at least in Europe there were hotel rooms and space instead of a tour bus I couldn't be alone in.

Fuck, I could barely get myself up out of this chair. The guys hated if I stayed in the dressing room on my own right up until the show. "The guys"—Micah, Brandon, and Austin. Micah was our lead guitarist, Brandon our drummer, and Austin our bassist. I could play guitar and the piano but Gayle decided my voice was at its best live when I only had to concentrate on singing, so I only played guitar on one track during our set. I wasn't sure I agreed that was fair, but what did it matter at this point?

I stared glumly at my reflection, hating myself. Hating that I could be this unhappy when I had exactly what I wanted in life. When I saw other people pitying themselves when they had wealth and fame, it made me want to puke. They were the kinds of people who deserved someone sending them a card every day with an insulting reminder that they needed a better grasp on reality.

I did not want to be one of the many insipid morons I'd met over the years in this business. There were worse things in life than being stuck in a job that made you absolutely miserable. Like having a nonexistent relationship with the mother who raised you by herself, the mom who used to be your best friend.

I hadn't called them. Mom or my stepdad Bryan. I hadn't called them when we got to Billings. Micah, Austin, and Brandon, they were all going home to see their families after the show. To stay with them a while.

Yet, I had no clue what I was going to do. The last time I saw my mom was a year ago. The last time I'd stayed with her was eighteen months ago, and the last time I talked to her was six weeks ago. And even then, I couldn't get off the phone fast enough. We texted. I avoided her calls all the time.

Guilt suffused me. Was she even still proud of me?

I certainly looked the part, didn't I? My rainbow hair was twisted up into two high buns above my ears and I wore my red velvet blazer with gold buttons over my favorite black Metric shirt. I'd paired them with a tight black satin miniskirt with fishnets and black Doc Martens. I wore three rings on each hand, my wrists jingled with bracelets, and my bold makeup was done to perfection.

Beneath my foundation were dark circles only weeks of uninterrupted sleep would get rid of.

I stared at my phone, knowing I should call my mom.

Last year when we finished our album tour in Billings, I'd lied to Mom and told her I needed to get away from the guys. I'd spent my six-week break in Paris instead of at home, bleeding money at a five-star hotel where I locked myself in a suite the entire time.

See: Woe-is-fucking-me with my room service and three million thread count Egyptian cotton sheets.

"Let me guess, you're thinking about your mom and why you haven't called her yet?"

I glanced up from my phone and stared at Micah in the mirror reflection. He stood in the doorway. When I didn't reply, he shut the door and walked over. His hair was mussed, his cheeks flushed.

I knew that look.

Tensing with anger and disappointment I should really be beyond by now, I winced when he leaned down and wrapped an arm around me so he could nuzzle my neck. "You need to talk to your mom," he murmured, pressing a sweet kiss behind my ear.

I glared at him in the mirror, stiff in his embrace. "You smell of pot and cheap perfume."

Micah rested his chin on my shoulder. My strange eyes tangled with his gorgeous green ones. Green rimmed with red from the pot. Still, he was so beautiful. All golden skin, tall, lanky, lean muscular frame, and thick, dark blond hair he only had to run his fingers through to style. He was a pretty, bad-boy musician, and he had the whole act down pat.

"Groupie," he muttered, his voice rumbling in my ear. He sounded sad.

How was it possible to hate someone I loved this much?

My eyes moved from his to take in the whole package we created together.

The two of us were a social media sensation: #Miclar

Because of Micah's inability to not flirt with me anytime we got interviewed . . . or shit, anytime we were on the goddamned stage together, fans and the media jumped on our connection. They wanted us to become a couple, always disappointed when we turned up in tabloid photos with other people. A couple? Us?

I snorted at the idea.

We were a train wreck as a couple.

Depressing, really, since we loved each other.

Staring at him, I suddenly saw him five years ago as my seventeen-year-old best friend. We'd been friends since middle school, started a band when we were fourteen, and had been working our asses off to make the big time. It was all we talked about. All we ever wanted.

But at seventeen, beyond our dreams for the band, there were feelings of jealousy and hurt anytime the other dated someone else. Until Micah's feelings exploded all over me one night and he told me he loved me. I cared too much to lie to him so I'd returned the sentiment. However, I'd also admitted that I was afraid a relationship would hurt the band. Micah agreed. We put the band first and it worked because we got a record deal three months later. Our first album came out eight months after that.

And the hurt and jealousy and resentment simmered all the while until one night three years ago, we slept together after a terrible shouting match in my hotel room in Berlin. Afterward I was freaked out, still not sure we weren't a mistake as a couple, so worried that we'd blow our shot just as we'd started to see success. We argued and I told him we couldn't be together. But the hell of it was that as soon as I walked away from him, I realized what a moronic thing it was to put a band before this person I loved.

So I'd gone to him to apologize, to give our relationship a real shot and . . . and I'd found him fucking a groupie in his hotel room.

He'd been punishing me with cheap flings ever since, and for a while, I'd punished him right back. It only made me miserable and lonely. Trying to find something real with someone else had proven difficult.

Until Max.

How could I still love Micah after that? I hated him but I was pretty sure I hated him because I still loved him too.

He kissed my cheek, a soft brush of his lips on a path to my mine. His arm tightened around me. "I love you so much," he groaned as if in pain.

I jerked away, shoving his arm off me. "No, you don't. The only person you love is yourself."

Micah straightened, shoving his hands into the pockets of his jeans. "Not true." Hurt blazed in his eyes.

That was the problem with my best frenemy. Sometimes he was vicious in an argument and other times he had the ability to make me feel like I'd kicked a puppy. I huffed in exasperation. "You just had sex with a groupie and then came in here to tell me you love me. Do you not see anything wrong with that?"

"One thing hasn't got anything to do with the other. She was a faceless fuck. You're the heartless bitch that torments my goddamned soul."

And there he was. Vicious. I winced, looking away.

"I'm sorry," he whispered. "I don't know why I said that."

Because we were a mess. We were the kind of mess there was no fixing.

I pushed the dressing room stool back from the table and stood up, pulling the hem of my skirt down. "We're on soon."

"I'm sorry about Max," he said. "I fucked up. I've tried to tell him the truth."

Max was the lead singer of Talking Trees. We began dating eight months ago and I got his band on this tour with us. He was sweet and artistic and quiet. Being around him was soothing and safe and he had this ability to calm my mind to all the crazy stuff that came with fame. He was the kind of guy who I knew with certainty would never let the fame part compromise the art. I didn't know if I'd been in love with him, but I was happier with him than I had been in a while.

Until Micah started his drama, filling Max's head with insecurities about us. The final nail in the coffin was Micah kissing me and making out to Max that it was mutual. Even believing me, that I'd pushed Micah off, Max still broke up with me, sick and tired of the drama. And who could blame him?

So now I was stuck on tour with my ex-boyfriend because Micah was a giant man-child.

"It's not about Max anymore." I brushed past him, heading for the door when his next words drew me to a stop.

"You think I don't see how sad you are, but I do. I know you better than anyone, Sky."

I knew he knew . . . and that was why I really hated him. Angry tears flooded my eyes as I glanced back at him. "Do you even care?"

He sighed, expression regretful but resolute. "Honestly, I'm afraid of what it means for the band, so I try not to."

My chest ached at his selfishness.

I turned to leave when my cell suddenly blared to life. Planning on ignoring it, I opened the door to leave when I was abruptly halted by two men in suits blocking the way.

They wore resigned expressions that made my stomach

plummet. "Skylar Finch?" the tallest of the two said, flashing me his police badge. "I'm Detective Rawlings, this is Detective Brant. May we come in?"

Wondering what the hell had happened, I stumbled back, silently gesturing for them to come into the room. They frowned at the sight of Micah, who'd positioned himself protectively at my side.

"Perhaps we should speak alone, Miss Finch," Detective Rawlings suggested softly.

The way they were looking at me . . . like they had news they weren't looking forward to imparting.

"You can say what you have to in front of Micah."

"Then . . . Miss Finch, I'm afraid we have some bad news . . ."

The detective spoke but in retrospect, I can't remember his exact words, something about "your mother," "stepfather," "armed robbery," "shot," "too late." "Gone." "I'm sorry." "Come with us."

Perspective.

For some strange reason, it was the only thing I could think of in that moment.

I was being punished for not having perspective.

nine

Glasgow, Scotland
Present day

O'Dea stared at me, holding the fruit cup and Danish pastry he'd brought with him hostage.

It was only pure physical exhaustion that caused me to find sleep the night before. After O'Dea had left, my brain felt like a hive of bees had been let loose inside it. I kept going over and over my options. Memories I'd worked so hard to bury were coming back to the surface. It was his fault.

I glared at the Scot. He was pushing me to move on, no matter what. That was a difficult concept for me to grasp because up until a couple of days ago, I'd completely given up on my old life. I didn't care at the time how that made me seem because it meant I didn't have to make difficult decisions anymore. That was freeing.

However, as much as I hated to admit it, O'Dea had held a mirror up to my behavior. It was clear he did not approve of the fact that I hadn't stayed in the US to face my grief. And for some reason I couldn't understand, that bothered me. I didn't want to think of myself as a coward. I'd never thought of myself as a coward before.

I just . . . I was trying to survive. Sometimes pain was just too much, you know.

Weren't we all just trying to survive?

"Well?" He stared at me impatiently.

As much as I feared fame, as unhappy as it had made me in the past, it was my only option at this point. After six months of no new leads in finding the armed robbers who had broken into my mom's house and shot her and Bryan, I decided I was done with that life.

I hadn't seen Micah, Austin, or Brandon since, and that was eighteen months ago. Facing them was a worse prospect than losing respect for myself at this point.

They were too much a reminder of my selfishness, of my stupidity and regret.

If I signed this contract with O'Dea, if I released an album with him, Gayle would definitely reach out. The guys would too. I wasn't sure about Micah. There was a possibility he would never forgive me for disappearing. Or the letter and voicemail I'd left with Gayle so they wouldn't report me as missing.

"I want creative control over the album," I demanded. O'Dea's eyes warmed and were far too appealing in that moment, so I continued before he could respond. "I also want it in the contract that I don't have to talk to the media about my family. And that I get to choose which media outlets I talk to at all. Also, if my manager or band members try to get in touch, I will need you to field that interaction, as in make sure that they aren't allowed to interact with me at all."

He sighed, sounding exasperated by the notion. "The world is going to come buzzing back around as soon as we announce this solo return. I can make sure the topic of your family is strictly prohibited by interviewers, but I can't guarantee they won't try to broach the subject with you anyway. Also, there is no way I'm putting it in a contract that you get to pick and choose media outlets. That would be legally allowing you the choice not to pick *any*. Furthermore, keeping closemouthed about your family and your disappearance from Tellurian and the public eye will only incite the media's interest."

I opened my mouth to argue and he held up a hand to stop me. "But . . . I can keep your old management, your record label, and your band at bay." O'Dea scratched his chin in thought. "Don't you have an aunt?"

"Pen?" I shook my head, surprised he knew about my mom's little sister since I had a nonexistent relationship with the last living member of my family. "Pen won't be a problem. She didn't even come home for the funeral. I doubt she cares about my disappearance. She's not really all that big into facing reality."

"Family trait, it seems."

I grimaced. "Well, I walked into that one."

He smirked. "What about the nutritionist and therapist?"

"There's no point in me going to a therapist if I don't want to." I shrugged. "I've got to want to. First rule of therapy."

"No therapy, no deal."

"Well, that's your prerogative." I stared him down, refusing to budge on the subject.

"Skylar."

"O'Dea."

He narrowed his eyes. "Fine. No therapy."

Delighted, I pushed. "And I *do* get to choose media outlets. I promise that I will choose some."

"A promise isn't good enough."

"It will have to be. I'm not signing that contract unless it states I get to choose media outlets."

Killian turned red with frustration. "Fine!"

Triumphant, my expression was overtly condescending. "I could see how painful that was to let me wrest away control from you. Maybe *you* really should see a therapist. An obsessive need to control the people around you is cause for concern."

He ignored my teasing and said, "My suggestion came only from the genuine belief that it would help you."

"There you go acting all noble, taking the sarcasm out of my sails."

"Not even a hurricane could knock the sarcasm out of you."

I nodded. "You're learning."

"So, we have a deal?"

"And what about Gayle? Will she be a problem?"

"Like your label, you're only under contract with Gayle as part of Tellurian. We can find you new management if you want, or we can ask Gayle to manage you as a solo artist."

"No. If I'm going to hell again, I want a new tour guide. Fresh eyes and all."

"So much melodrama." He shook his head. "New management. Fine. We'll get a contract written up."

I gestured to him, puzzled. "I thought there would be more excitement. If not actual jumping up and down, perhaps a lengthier smirk, a maniacal laugh, a proverbial sinister twist of an oversized imaginary mustache. You disappoint me, O'Dea."

He stared blandly at me. "I'm squeeing on the inside."

Amused despite myself, I smiled and then winced at the sting from my lip.

O'Dea's gaze lowered to my mouth before rising to assess the rest of my face. "At least the swelling in your eye and cheek has gone down."

"True, but the bruising still makes me look like a watercolor painting."

"It'll fade. Which takes us to the next order of business. You need new clothes and a trip to the hairdresser."

The thought of stepping out into the public looking like this made me shudder. "Unless you want people to think I'm your battered wife, I think we better put a delay on the whole hair salon business."

"Charmaine is coming to you. Tomorrow at noon. A haircut will make you feel more human and Charmaine knows how to be discreet." He frowned. "But no rainbow hair."

"If I want rainbow hair, I'll get rainbow hair, okay. I don't, but if I wanted it, I would."

"Can I assume you're going to be this difficult about everything?"

"Can I assume you're not going to stop being a giant pain in my ass anytime soon?"

"Nutritionist," he said, ignoring me. "My sister Autumn will be by tomorrow morning before Charmaine gets here. She'll be letting her friend Brenna into the apartment. Brenna's a nutritionist and she'll be handling your dietary needs. Day after tomorrow, I have you booked into a private clinic for a health check. I've got a makeup artist booked for Friday morning. She'll do your makeup so the bruises are hidden and then we're going shopping for new clothes."

Dazed, it took me a moment to find words. "You made appointments already? You assumed I'd say yes? And shopping? *You're* taking me shopping?"

"We'll have a personal shopper with us. But yes. And yes to your first question." He gave me a quick, humorless grin. "I always get what I want."

"Oh, really? Do you want a swift kick to the junk? Because I see that in your imminent future."

He squinted as if he was considering it. "Nope," he finally shook his head, "can't say that I do. Not one of my kinks."

I raised an eyebrow. "He jokes."

"I'm giving you today to rest." He pushed the fruit cup and pastry toward me. "There are some DVDs in the hall cupboard if you get bored. I'll be back tonight with groceries but I have to get back to the office now. I see you've already found the washer/dryer so you'll make do for clothes until Friday?"

I hated to ask, but . . ."I only have one pair of jeans. The other pair got ruined." Grass stains. I tried not to flinch as an image of Johnny holding me down flashed before my eyes.

I blinked it away, taking a deep breath.

O'Dea didn't notice my distress. "I'll ask Autumn to bring you a new pair tomorrow. Size?"

I tore open the fruit cup, playing with it in my hands so I didn't have to look at him. "Um, I used to be a four but I'm probably between a two and a zero now."

"UK size?"

"Oh right. Then I'm between a six and a four. I used to be a UK eight."

O'Dea was silent so long, I glanced up at him.

His expression was grim with understanding. "Brenna will get your weight and strength back up before you know it."

Pride pricked, I scoffed, "Pity doesn't suit you, O'Dea."

"Funny. Because *self-pity* doesn't suit you." And on that irritating parting shot, he left the apartment. I almost threw the pastry at the doorway he'd been standing in but he wasn't worth the loss.

I MUST HAVE BEEN TRULY exhausted because, despite having so much to worry about, I slept after I ate. And I mean I *slept*.

The next thing I knew I was blinking open my eyes to the feel of being rocked and a familiar masculine voice calling my name. When the blurring cleared from my hazy eyes, I tensed in bed at the sight of O'Dea sitting on it next to me. His frown disappeared as I became more cognizant.

"What time is it?"

"Seven o'clock. You slept all day?"

I pushed myself up and O'Dea abruptly stood from the bed. "I guess so."

"I put some food in the fridge. Dinner is ready."

"Dinner?" I shoved off the duvet and got up, the room spinning a little.

"You okay?" he asked, and I felt his warm hand grasp my arm to steady me.

"Got up too fast." I grimaced. "I guess the attack took more out of me than I thought."

O'Dea let me go and shook his head, something like anger tightening his features. "It's not just the attack. It's months of sleeping rough. You've exhausted yourself. And never mind what damage you've done to your back sleeping on a cold ground for weeks on end."

Rolling my eyes, I followed him into the kitchen. "Can you not lecture me right now?"

He threw me a look over his shoulder but refrained from answering. He slid onto one of the stools at the counter and dug into a plate of food. He was staying for dinner?

I stepped closer to the plate next to his, my stomach gurgling in hungry protest at the sight of the steamed salmon, baby potatoes, and mound of salad. Food. Real food.

"You cooked?" I asked as I gingerly got onto the stool next to him. My body was so stiff that the aches and pains distracted me from how close we sat together.

"You were sleeping when I got in with the groceries. I'd have to cook my own dinner anyway so . . ." He shrugged, not looking at me.

Confused by his contradictory nature, I studied him, curious. "Do you always look after your artists like this? So personally?"

"Only the ones who can't look after themselves."

And there he was. "I can look after myself."

O'Dea grunted. "Oh aye, and a bang-up job you've been doing so far." He pointed to my plate with his fork. "Start eating."

"You are so bossy," I grumbled but did as I was bid because *I* wanted to.

The food tasted so fresh, I couldn't help a little moan of satisfaction.

"Good?" he asked, sounding amused.

I nodded and swallowed. "Everything I've had in the past year has been fried or processed. I used to be an incredibly healthy eater. I had to be. We toured a lot. You need strength and energy for that."

"You don't think you need strength and energy to survive homelessness?"

"Of course you do. But unfortunately, fast food is cheaper than salads and a home-cooked meal. I ate what I could afford."

He nodded, getting my point.

For a little while we ate in silence. To my surprise, it was. . . . well, it was a comfortable silence. Which suggested I couldn't care less what O'Dea thought of me. I always used to care what people thought about me. Too much. You can't do fame when you care that much because the public will destroy you. Even when most of the comments were positive, it was the negative that stuck with me. Ate at me. And then there were the posts that were filled with vitriol.

The worst incident was on Instagram. I posted a photo of Max and me together. Austin had taken it and I'd loved it. We were all hanging out in a hotel room and I was sitting on Max's lap while we tried to play my guitar together. Austin had snapped a photo of us laughing into each other's faces. We looked in love.

At first the photo got a lot of likes, a lot of love.

But Micah decided to post a photo of himself sitting solo with his guitar, looking forlorn. I didn't know if it was deliberate or if he wasn't thinking, but the fans saw it as a response to my photo with Max. The comments on my photo turned nasty fast.

I was a heart-breaking bitch.

I should burn in hell.

I should kill myself for being such a bitch.

Why people thought it was okay to post things online that they would never dream of saying to someone in real life, I didn't know.

But back then, having my life become public property wore on me.

It made me depressed.

"I don't care as much now," I said.

O'Dea looked over at me. He swallowed the bite he'd taken and asked, "About?"

"What people think. I used to care too much. Maybe the publicity stuff won't be so bad now that I don't care." It would help me to think so.

He was quiet a moment as his gaze returned to his plate. And then he delivered a swift verbal punch to the gut. "If you didn't care as much what people think, you'd be ready to face your band."

I glowered at him, anger making my skin flush hot. "I meant about people I don't know."

"Well," his expression remained aloof, indifferent, "I guess we'll find out soon enough."

Any gratitude I'd been feeling toward him for the dinner turned to dust in my mouth. I pushed my half-eaten plate away and slid off the stool.

He sighed. "Where are you going? You haven't finished eating. You need to eat, Skylar."

"Eat shit and die." I slammed the bedroom door behind me and leaned back against it, trying to calm down.

Loneliness overwhelmed me. A horrendous, black, gaping hole of complete aloneness appeared, readying to swallow me.

I slid down the door, feeling tears burn in my nose.

All the time sleeping in that cemetery I hadn't felt this alone.

Crap.

I swiped at a tear that escaped.

Maybe I really did need to see a therapist.

Okay, there was no maybe about it. I wasn't stupid. I knew I was messed up about everything. But I was so scared.

So scared that if I started to talk to someone about everything, the guilt would become too much to bear.

A gentle knock on my door made me suck in a breath.

"Skylar?"

I ignored him.

I hated him.

O'Dea sighed. He was always sighing. Like I was an exasperating child he'd been burdened with. "I'm leaving so you can come out of the bedroom and finish your dinner."

I snorted. What a martyr.

"Skylar . . . I'm s- . . ."

Tensing, my eyes widened. Was he . . . was he going to apologize?

"I'm . . . fuck." He blew out an angry-sounding breath. "I'll be back tomorrow and I expect you to be civil." His footsteps thudded down the hallway and then the door slammed shut.

In the wake of his departure, I ventured back out into the kitchen where my dinner was waiting. His sat almost finished.

I shot a dirty look in the direction of the hallway. What a dick. "Martyr," I muttered. But my anger toward him didn't stop me from finishing the meal he'd cooked. In fact, I cleared both the plates and for the first time in a long time, I went to bed feeling satisfyingly full.

Pissed off.

But satisfyingly full.

ten

It was odd to not wake up with birds chirping around me. I actually missed the early wake-up call. However, the next morning I didn't need my nature alarm. After all the sleeping I'd done the previous day, I woke up around five thirty.

I showered, nearly slipped and fell trying to get out of the bathtub with only one good hand, and got ready for the day as best as I could. My bruising was turning that ghastly yellow color, which meant it was healing but it also made me look like there was something amiss with my red blood cells and thus probably dying.

Putting the hair dryer down after a vigorous one-handed blow-dry, I considered my hair. I'd always kept it long because Micah asked me to. The rainbow colors were Gayle's idea. She wanted me to look "adorably alternative." I didn't mind. Back then, I would have done anything to make the band work.

All of the dye had grown out. My hair hung down to my bra strap, lifeless. I was naturally blonde, kind of medium tone, but it always seemed a little boring, which was why I didn't mind throwing all the color at it.

I fingered the ends, contemplating.

And suddenly I knew what I'd ask the hairstylist to do.

To my surprise, I felt a twinge of excitement about it. Like it mattered. It didn't matter.

"Maybe it does," I murmured to myself. "Maybe it's all part of moving on."

Moving on.

That sounded exhausting.

A little while later I was in the sitting room watching a morning television show, eating buttered toast (it had never tasted so good!) and drinking English breakfast tea when I heard the lock turn in the apartment door.

I tensed, readying myself for another encounter (and possible altercation) with O'Dea. But the footsteps walking down the hall weren't his. It sounded like a pair of heels clacking along the floorboards.

And I was right.

Staring up over my shoulder, I froze with a piece of toast to my mouth at the sight of the beautiful young woman standing in my doorway. "Who the hell are you?"

She blinded me with a stunning white-toothed smile. "I'm Autumn." She lifted her hands in which were a ton of shopping bags. "And I bring lots of goodies!"

Ah. Okay. This was O'Dea's sister. I ate the toast, getting to my feet. Her eyes widened a little as she took me in. "I know. I'm a mess," I mumbled around the toast.

Autumn's perfectly shaped eyebrows drew together. "You're just . . . Killian told me what they did to you but . . . those little fuckers!"

I grinned because the word sounded so odd coming out of her mouth. She had a melodic accent much like Killian's. Lilting and charming and a little well-to-do. That, along with her shining auburn hair curled into waves, her perfectly manicured nails, wrinkle-free shirt, blazer, and cigarette trousers, and four-inch stiletto sandals, she was all class.

Her makeup looked like it had been applied by an artist.

Big, warm, gorgeous brown eyes—exactly like Killian's—stared at me, framed with thick lashes that seemed to go on forever. Were those real?

Of course O'Dea's sister was gorgeous. That family had *good* genes.

"If you think I look bad, you should see the other guy," I joked.

"Killian said you were a smart arse. But I won't joke about this, Skylar." Autumn strolled toward me, studying me, as she promptly dropped all the shopping bags on the floor at our feet. "Those little fuckers deserve a long stint in prison for doing this to you."

I thought about the one called Johnny who I kept seeing every time I closed my eyes at night.

And his friend, who I could've forgiven because he'd saved me, if he hadn't run off with my goddamned Taylor. "I agree."

Sympathy shined in Autumn's eyes as she assessed my face. "Once the bruising fades and Brenna gets your weight back up, you'll be good as new. Beautiful as ever."

I snorted. I wasn't beautiful. I had an interesting face and unusual eyes but no one could ever say I was beautiful. Micah used to, but that was different. Beauty was in the eye of the beholder and all that crap.

"Enough of that," she tutted at my wordless disagreement. "Look at your eyes, for Christ's sake. And those lips!"

I squirmed, hating compliments. "My eyes . . . heterochromia." I had one hazel eye and one gray-blue eye. "They're weird. Austin used to say 'Here, girl!' when he wanted to talk to me. Like I was husky. I have a bump in the bridge of my nose. And my lips? Too big for my face."

"Maybe right now they are because your face is too wee but once you put on some weight, you'll be back to your lovely self. And Austin, whoever he is, is an arsehole for referring to you as a dog."

"My bandmate. He's like a brother."

"Brothers are always charming that way." She gestured to the shopping bags. "I brought you quite a few pairs of jeans and some shirts in both the sizes Killian gave me. I also got you some new underwear and socks."

My pride was pricked. "You didn't have to do that."

"It's no big deal. I used Killian's credit card."

"Oh, well then, let's see what you got."

She laughed and put her purse down on the counter. "Okay, we have some time before Brenna gets here." She grabbed up the bags, all of them, and strode into the bedroom.

I stared after her. Was she was seriously going to stay in there with me while I tried on the clothes?

"You coming?"

I guessed that was a yes. Feeling uncomfortable about undressing in front of a stranger, I walked slowly into the bedroom. She'd thrown the bags on the bed and was emptying them.

"Um, I can handle it from here."

"Won't you need a hand? The cast?"

"Oh, I'll be fine. I can dress myself."

"But it'll be quicker with my help."

"Look, you seem very nice—so nice, in fact, I think you should get a DNA test to make sure you and O'Dea are actually related—but I don't know you that well and I'm a little uncomfortable stripping to my underwear in front of a stranger." Weird, it hadn't bothered me so much at the swim center, but that was different. I never saw those people again. I didn't know them.

Signing this contract with O'Dea implied that Autumn would inevitably be around more. I didn't want to be in her company knowing she'd seen my scrawny ass at its worst.

Huh. I guess I did still care, I thought, not happy about that realization.

"Oh." She shook her head, her auburn tresses bouncing like a shampoo ad around her shoulders. "Of course. I'm sorry. I . . . I can be a little too enthusiastic and I don't think. I just . . ." She fingered a cute Ralph Lauren tee she'd bought me. Wow. When she shopped, she *shopped*. "I want to be helpful."

More curious about her and O'Dea than I wanted to admit, I found myself taking a step toward her. "Are you O'Dea's PA or something?"

She frowned at me. "Why don't you call him Killian?"

Because it was too personal. He wasn't *that* to me. He was the guy corralling me into the fame pen again. I shrugged. "So, you're his PA?"

"No. I'm between jobs at the moment. When Killian asked me to help out, I jumped at the idea. He told me a little about your story and I," she bit her lip, "you deserve to get your life back on track, Skylar. Anything I can do to help . . . you know I'm here."

"But you don't even know me."

Her eyes dimmed with sadness. "I . . . I kind of know what you're going through. Not totally . . . but I lost my parents a long time ago."

O'Dea had lost his parents? "I'm sorry."

"I didn't know them so well. I was only six. Killian was eleven."

"I'm sorry," I repeated. Truly sorry. "I get it."

"Well." She gave me a shaky smile. "Here I am. And I want to help."

More curious than ever, I eyed the clothes, trying to sound casual as I asked, "So . . . does O'Dea do this with all his new artists? Send his sister to look after them, cook them meals, buy them clothes?"

"No." Something in her tone brought my gaze back to her. She was staring at me speculatively, a little smile playing around the corners of her mouth. "He doesn't."

My breath caught. Clearing my throat, I gestured to the bed. "You did all this in a day?"

Autumn laughed. "Oh, I am a champion shopper. Killian told me he hired a personal shopper for you and I promptly made him cancel that appointment. Now, I don't know your taste or what suits you best but you pick what you like out of this stuff and then when your weight is back to normal, I'll take you shopping. We'll need to get an everyday wardrobe with some nicer pieces thrown in just in case. Don't worry about the album and promotional photography. Killian will bring in a stylist with amazing choices for you for that."

I tried not to hyperventilate at the thought. "Let's just concentrate on this stuff."

"Okay, well, I'll wait outside. You got any orange juice?"

"In the fridge."

"You want some?"

"Sure."

I waited for her to close the door behind her before I turned and looked to the bed. Exhaling slowly, I reached for the hem of my shirt.

This was it.

Everything was changing again.

IT WASN'T A SURPRISE THAT Autumn had great taste. Some

of the stuff was a little too preppy for my tastes, but for the most part, she'd intuitively surmised that the rocker girl in me still existed. I had a lot of new chilled-out black slogan tees and a couple of new pairs of jeans. To my relief, I fit into the size UK six, which meant I only needed to get back up one size to feel healthy again.

All I used to wear was skinny jeans because I'd liked showing off that I had an ass and hips. But since those were temporarily on leave, I didn't exactly *suit* my skinny jeans. Because of all the walking I'd done, my calves were muscular but my thighs were too lean. Somehow Autumn had thought that through too. When I'd seen the boot-cut Levi's in the bag, I'd been bemused. But then she explained that they'd be more flattering for my current shape. And she was right. She was kind of a genius.

"You can go back to your skinny jeans when Brenna gets a little more meat on you."

By the time Brenna came to the apartment, I felt almost stylish again. Well, you know, except for the bruising and crazy hair.

Brenna was in her late thirties. She and Autumn had met when Autumn was doing a degree in food science. Brenna had been a guest lecturer. Autumn didn't finish the degree but she made a friend for life in Brenna despite their age difference.

Tall, slender, with short dark hair, Brenna had glowing copper skin that made her look younger than her age, and maybe that had something to do with healthy eating. More than likely. I was a great believer in the benefits of good diet and exercise.

"How I'd usually start is asking you to keep a food journal for a week and we'd go from there, correcting where we needed to," Brenna said. "However, I understand that this is a different situation. So, if you're comfortable to speak about this in front of Autumn, can you talk to me about your eating habits over the last few months?"

She was standing across the island from me, sipping tea, and I got that she was trying not to be interrogative. Autumn sat next to me on a stool.

"I can go," Autumn assured me.

"It's fine. I . . . uh . . . I know a lot of people feel shame about being homeless but my circumstances were different. I chose it. No one else I met chose it. I know people would argue that drug addicts, alcoholics, they all indirectly chose it, but you can't say that. No one knows what it's like for them. I know the people that I spoke to . . . well, if they'd had it in them to fight their addictions, they wouldn't be on the streets." I flushed a little, realizing I'd gone off topic. "Anyway, I, uh . . . I ate cheap. I tried to eat breakfast every day, although there were some days I didn't. But mostly I ate breakfast. It was usually a banana and a bacon roll. The banana for protein and the bacon roll filled me up. And it was cheap. Lunch was sporadic. Some days I'd have one, other days not. Usually it would be a sandwich that was going off that day so it was on sale. Tuna, chicken, whatever they had. Most of the time, I waited to have an early dinner instead. Fish and chips mostly. Burger. Fries. Fast food stuff. Cheap. But," and here was where I admitted how I'd fallen down, "I couldn't stomach it in the last few weeks. That stuff is filled with grease and I . . . it started to nauseate me."

Brenna frowned. "Is that when you began to really notice weight loss?"

"Yeah. I mean, I was losing a little because when I wasn't busking, I walked. I backpacked through Europe so that's when I noticed my jeans were getting a little loose. But yeah, I guess the last few months it changed from turning fat to muscle to dropping a dress size."

"And drinking habits?"

"No alcohol," I said immediately. "I needed my wits about

me, which meant no being drunk and no spending money on unnecessary shit. I drank water. Nothing else."

"And did you get plenty of water?"

"A couple of liters a day. It was all I could afford."

"Better than nothing." She nodded, her gaze direct as she put her mug on the counter. "It's not too bad, actually. I think that you're small-boned with high cheekbones anyway, so any weight loss like this is going to look worse than it is."

"I . . ." I stumbled, pondering whether I should admit this or not. But it was playing on my mind so . . ."I missed my period this month. And I'm definitely not pregnant."

Autumn tensed beside me.

Brenna nodded. "Okay, that's not unusual and it's actually more likely to do with malnutrition. It might even be stress related. You've been through a lot. Autumn said you have a health-check appointment, so be sure to mention it and also that you're seeing a nutritionist. Once we get the nutrients that you need back into your body, we'll see if everything returns to normal."

"I'll get my period back?"

"That's the hope." She pulled a folder out of the bag she'd brought with her and flipped it open. "So, I have a few questions." From there she asked me about my weight history, current and past medical history, family medical history, food allergies or intolerances, my likes and dislikes, my eating, sleeping, and exercise habits, past weight-loss attempts, and my emotional and social ties to food. I'd never had a problem with my weight before. I had a good metabolism and I was young, so it had never been a concern. Plus, I actually enjoyed eating healthy food. And, I reiterated to her what I had told O'Dea, that to keep up my strength for touring, a healthy diet had been a necessity. Brenna was happy to hear it and even more so when I told her what my diet used to be like.

"Then this should be easier for you than it is for most of my clients. We're going to dose you up a little more heavily on nutrients to begin with, and some calorie-dense, high-protein foods to get your weight back up. Peanut butter is going to be your new best friend."

Brenna had also brought a scale with her, connected to an app on her phone, and she'd made me step on it. Not only had she taken my weight, she'd measured me. My BMI was under so she wanted that back up in the healthy zone. She would be measuring and weighing me every week too.

By the time Brenna left, I was feeling more than a little overwhelmed. Autumn now had a grocery list in her hand and I'd downed a green smoothie filled with kale, banana, coconut milk, and peanut butter. I didn't mind the taste, which was good because Brenna made me promise I'd have two smoothies a day on top of the meal plan she'd devised.

"I'll go out and get all of this," Autumn said, waving the list at me after we'd said goodbye to Brenna.

I watched as Autumn threw her phone in her purse and grabbed the keys to the apartment. O'Dea had texted her a few times to check on things. Control freak. As his sister prepared to leave, I got this sudden feeling of claustrophobia. It tightened my chest. And suddenly staying here alone felt like a worse idea than going out in public with a bruised-up face. "Hey," I burst out, "can I come with you?"

She looked surprised. "What about your bruising?"

"You know," I glanced out of the patio doors to the river outside, "I'm willing to put up with the stares if it means getting a little fresh air. I feel like I've been in this apartment forever."

"Of course. You're not a prisoner. Hey," she dug through her purse, "I have my makeup with me." She pulled out a cosmetics bag that had to take up all the room in her purse. "I can do your makeup if you want. Cover up the bruises?"

Relief washed over me. "I'd like that."

And that's how I found myself feeling pampered as Autumn took great joy in doing my makeup. She also twisted my hair into a messy, stylish bun. When I looked in the mirror, I barely recognized myself. The makeup softened my angles so my face somehow looked fuller.

It made me want to cry.

O'Dea's sister saw the shimmer of wet in my eyes and clutched my shoulder. "You did what you had to do, Skylar. But it's time to start taking care of yourself again."

Angry at myself, confused, questioning every decision I'd made in the last eighteen months, I stood. "Let's go." It came out harsher than I meant.

We were silent as we left the apartment, Autumn seeming unsure of me now. "It feels weird," I said, trying to break the awkwardness as we got in the elevator. "I can't remember O'Dea bringing me here, so I've felt like I was floating in a box over the Clyde. It's weird to be in a building I don't remember walking into."

"Killian said you were pretty out of it."

"You two seem close?" The question slipped out before I could stop it.

"Well, that's what happens when you only have each other. My uncle James isn't the most affectionate man in the world," she said dryly. "I don't know how Killian can work for him. I'd have killed him by now."

"O'Dea works for your uncle?"

"Yeah. Uncle James owns the label."

That I did not know. "So, O'Dea is in line to take over?"

Autumn sneered, "Only if Killian lives up to James's exacting standards."

And suddenly everything made sense. "And I'm betting there's nothing O'Dea wants more than to run that label one day."

"And he deserves to. He's brought in more money for that label in the last five years than anyone. Does my uncle acknowledge that? No. He makes Killian jump through a never-ending cycle of hoops. Nothing my brother does is ever good enough."

Clearly, I wasn't the only one whose family was a sore point.

As if he'd heard us talking, O'Dea called Autumn as we stepped out into the fresh air. It was cold but Autumn had her car so I'd only put on a blazer she'd bought me. It was remarkably similar to the one she wore. I sucked in the fresh air, letting the cold breeze wash over me. My skin prickled to delicious life under its crisp caress.

"Everything went great," Autumn said into her phone as she led me over to a white Range Rover. If I remembered correctly, O'Dea drove a Sport. Autumn's was the smaller Evoque. Apparently, they were fans.

The car beeped and I managed to pull myself up into the passenger seat with my good arm as Autumn got into the driver side.

"I'm taking Skylar to the store for food . . . We're getting everything on the list Brenna gave us . . . because she needs fresh air . . ." She sighed. "She's fine . . . makeup . . . *my* makeup . . . Aren't you busy? . . . We're fine . . . Fine . . . okay, okay . . . Sainsbury's . . . Yes, that one . . . Okay, we'll see you there. Bye." She hung up and shot me a look. "Killian is meeting us at the store."

"God, he is a control freak."

Autumn's face pinched with annoyance as she started the engine. "My brother is not a control freak. He's worried about you."

Oh yeah, sure. "Really? He's so worried that he told me if I didn't agree to sign to his label, I'd be back out on the streets."

"He said that?"

"I asked him if that's what he meant and he didn't deny it. He said he was businessman, not a philanthropist."

Autumn tutted. "That man. Seriously. He didn't mean that," she assured me. "He'll probably kill me for telling you this, but there's a big softie underneath that intimidating façade."

"Oh yeah, he's a giant teddy bear."

She laughed at my sarcasm. "You'll see."

No, I wouldn't. All I'd ever see in Killian O'Dea was the man who forced me back into a life I loathed.

eleven

"Do you know how proud I am of you?"

I grinned at my mom. "It's all you. You never stopped believing."

"She sure didn't." Bryan wrapped his arm around Mom and pulled her into his side for a kiss, making her giggle like a little girl.

He made her happy, so I decided not to ruin the moment by reminding him that he *never believed in me. Still, while my mom wasn't looking, I shot him a dirty look and he gave me a warning one in return.*

When he and Mom got serious a couple of years ago, Micah and I were getting serious about making our band a success. We knew we had something great and my mom had been our biggest supporter. My dad died when I was a baby, so it had always been just me and Mom. And there was no one who believed in me more than my mother. She'd been my best friend for so long. I think if I hadn't been so consumed with the idea of making Tellurian a success, I probably would have had a much harder time adjusting to the idea of Bryan.

As it was, he began to complain all the time to my mom about the money and energy she put in to helping a bunch of kids chase an "unrealistic dream." He only backed off when it became a real sticking point in their relationship. And by that, I mean they almost broke up. However, the resentment simmered between the two of us. I could never really, truly like him. But I was civil for my mom's sake.

Lately, however, my dislike for him was worsening. Ever since Tellurian's debut single hit number one on the US Billboard, Bryan had become our biggest fan.

Asshole.

"I can't believe I watched my baby on The Tonight Show *last night." Mom untangled herself from Bryan to come and hug me for the hundredth time. I laughed, breathing in the familiar floral scent of Miss Dior, her favorite perfume. I wrapped my arms around her slender waist and held on tight.*

I'd been traveling the US for a while and was only back in Billings because we were playing The Pub Station for the first time that night. I planned to spend every second I could with my mom. The band's success was more than I could have dreamt of, but I had no idea how much I'd miss my mother.

Mom pulled back to grin at me. "I got cake."

"Cake is always good."

"Not just any cake. It's an eighteenth birthday cake. 'Cause I missed it." She pouted. "I can't believe I missed my baby turning eighteen."

"I know." I stared at her, drinking in her oh-so-familiar pretty face. "I miss you."

Tears shimmered in her blue eyes. "Oh, baby girl, you have no idea how much I miss you. But I am so happy you got everything you ever wanted."

Not everything, I thought. Micah and I had decided not to be together for the sake of the band, but he liked to torture me daily. Flirting with me, touching me, shadowing me. And then he'd go and blow off his pent-up frustration with a groupie.

Oh yeah, he was loving the groupies.

That's why I lost my virginity to a teen drama series heartthrob at a stranger's house party in LA instead of losing it to the boy I was in love with.

It hurt so bad, I had to throw the thought away before I burst into tears.

I stood in the small living room of the house I'd grown up in and decided not to be so selfish as to dwell on Micah right now. I was home. Mom deserved my attention because Micah got more than his fair share of it.

"What do you want to do today?" I asked. "I'm all yours."

Mom grinned. "I was thinking we could go ice skating."

Joy filled me. "Really?"

Ice skating had been our thing. Every birthday, no matter what other plans I had, my mom and I went ice skating. We couldn't afford a lot growing up since it was only Mom for so long, which meant things other people took for granted were a treat for me. Stupid stuff like going to the movies, to the swimming pool, and ice skating.

So ice skating became our thing.

"I'd love that."

"And it's . . ." She smiled over her shoulder at Bryan. "It's just you and me."

Shocked, I looked at Bryan for confirmation. One of the other things that annoyed me was that even before Tellurian took off, I didn't get to spend alone time with Mom once Bryan was in the picture. He insinuated himself into everything. Including my birthdays with Mom.

"You two go, catch up, have fun." He promptly sat down on the couch and reached for the remote. "I'm going to be here watching the sports channel uninterrupted."

Mom reached down to kiss his temple but my attention was drawn to the television, to the sight of me and the band on the entertainment news. Bryan turned the volume up.

The gorgeous female presenter stood in front of a digital screen where a clip of me and the band on The Tonight Show *was playing.*

"And the band Tellurian are trending on social media after their appearance on The Tonight Show. *Or more specifically, the lead singer Skylar Finch and lead guitarist Micah Murphy are trending. Fans of the band have been sent into a social media spin when the chemistry between the two bandmates spilled into their interview on the show."*

I frowned as it cut to a clip from last night.

"I was going to ask you about that," Mom murmured as she slid an arm across my shoulder.

I slumped into her, unable to tear my eyes away.

"You look beautiful, Sky," Bryan murmured. "Doesn't she look beautiful, Angie?"

"She does indeed." Mom gave me a squeeze but I was focused on the interview.

"So, I can't help but notice that you two look cozier than the rest of the band," the host said with his usual dry mischief, gesturing toward Micah and me.

Micah had his arm along the back of the sofa where I sat, his long fingers resting on my shoulder. He was also pressed as close to me as he could get. Austin and Brandon sat casually at the end of the couch.

Prepared for questions about our relationship statuses, I'd opened my mouth to say, "We've all known each other a long time, we're so comfortable with each other," when Micah said, "Wouldn't you cozy up to Skylar if you could?"

Shit.

I shot a look at my mom who watched the TV with a small smile playing on her lips.

The host had jumped right on it. "So, you two are a couple?"

"No," I'd laughed, wishing I could shove my bandmate off me. And that's when I gave him my rehearsed line.

Of which Micah followed up with, "Some of us are more comfortable with each other than others." The audience oohed as the host raised an eyebrow.

Thankfully, Brandon broke in with a joke to deflect and we got off the subject.

But that was all it took.

Because now we were trending and on entertainment news.

"Jesus," I huffed, pulling my phone out of my ass pocket.

My heart raced when I saw how many notifications my personal profiles now had on Twitter and Instagram. We were trending. #Miclar

Witty.

I was used to the band profile having tons of notifications, but this was worse. There were photos of us from different gigs everywhere that fans had taken, all of them of Micah cozying up to me on the stage. Basically, fans were saying they knew all along we were together, and how amazing it was.

It all seemed so infantile and stupid but they were going crazy for it.

My chest felt tight.

For the past year, we'd been in the public eye but it had only been about our music.

This felt . . . I didn't like it. I wasn't prepared for how invasive it felt. Like I was standing naked on stage.

"Honey, you okay?" Mom asked.

She couldn't know. She'd sacrificed so much for me financially, and emotionally in her relationship with Bryan, to help make my dream come true. As far as she was concerned, everything was always better than okay.

I grinned, gesturing with my phone. "It'll sell more records."

She laughed, relieved. "True. Now grab your stuff—we're going skating. And girl talk."

"Sure." I chuckled, shooting a look at Bryan before I left.

He was staring at me in a way I'd never seen before. Like I was suddenly a curiosity instead of a drain on his relationship with Mom. That's what fame seemed to do. It made everyone see me differently—

A loud clatter shook me out of the memory and I looked around, dazed, feeling my heart beating too hard in my chest.

I was in a salon, surrounded by strangers, as a woman called Charmaine blow-dried my hair.

Charmaine had chatted away to me from the moment I'd sat down but as soon as she began blow-drying my hair, she'd stopped talking and my mind had been allowed to wander. For some reason, it wandered to that memory from so long ago.

I frowned, remembering the day after. There had been paparazzi waiting at the band entrance to The Pub Station, trying to get past our security as they shouted at Micah and me, asking if we were a couple.

Why was this so fascinating?

It had freaked me out and Micah had tried to comfort me, but I was mad at him for making what was between us public.

He'd come to regret it too because from that moment on, the fans' obsession with us as a couple, like we were a freaking epic love story playing out for their entertainment, compelled the tabloids to come after us. Suddenly, I found myself front page of a tabloid magazine in cut-off jeans, an old shirt, and sunglasses as I made a trip to the grocery store. But there was an unidentified guy with me so it was big news because who was he? Where was Micah? How did Micah feel about this unidentified guy?

From there, it escalated. If someone took an unflattering photo, I found myself on the front page with a red circle around my belly. Was I pregnant? Was it Micah's? What did this mean for the band?

Or I'd be in an article for a teen magazine with a picture of me in the airport blown up with arrows pointing at my skin with the headline, "Even pop-rock sensation Skylar Finch has her bad skin days!"

Everyone had an opinion about everything. My music, my voice, my looks, my clothes, and the people I chose to spend time with. Every post on social media, every article in a magazine, and every tiring interview we had to give.

I started to feel like I didn't own my life. After a while, ironically, I felt like *I* was disappearing.

"Can I get you more water?" A junior stylist appeared at my side as soon as Charmaine switched off the hair dryer.

I shook my head, thankful for the interruption from my gloomy thoughts. "I'm fine, thanks."

The trip to the salon had been a little overwhelming. Like everything lately. But after Killian met Autumn and me at the grocery store, I'd said that I wanted more than a hair trim. He'd repeated that he didn't think dying my hair rainbow colors and going back to my old look was a good direction for my solo launch; I said that I had no intention of doing that but I knew what I wanted, and it would take more than a quick house call from a hairstylist.

So he'd called Charmaine and she booked me into her salon. It was clear she'd put a lot of money into the business. The shiny, white-tiled floor sparkled with embedded silver crystals and the main walls were a soft gray, while partition walls were a deep, dark pinkish-red color. The chairs were modern, square white leather, and the mirrors were all floor to ceiling with chunky white frames. It was cool contemporary with a splash of drama. It also said "you'll pay a small fortune to get your hair cut here but it'll be worth it."

Autumn drove, begging me to wonder what she used to do for a job.

"This was a great idea," Charmaine said as she took her scissors to my hair. I watched as my new layered look came together, and I had to agree. "It really suits your face shape."

When she was done, I marveled at the difference a haircut could make.

I'd boldly asked Charmaine to cut most of it off. Now my hair was cut short at the nape and fell in an A-line cut to just below my chin. It felt healthy and full, sharp and modern. She'd also added ash-blonde highlights to give it more dimension.

The sharpness of the cut served to soften the angles of my face.

"All done." Charmaine held up a mirror so I could see how she'd cut it shorter at the back than at the front. I loved it.

"It's great, thank you." I gave her a genuine smile.

"Let's show Autumn."

She helped me out of the cape, brushing excess hair off my nape, and then I followed her out into the front where Autumn was drinking herbal tea and reading a magazine. She glanced up and immediately froze.

"Is that a good or bad deer-in-the-headlights look?" I asked.

Autumn promptly set her tea and magazine on the coffee table and got up to stride over to me for a better look. Her eyes brightened before she broke out into a huge smile. "It's perfect! Absolutely perfect."

I smiled, feeling a little shy about it. "I just . . . I wanted a big change."

"It was the right move. God," she assessed my face, "you've got great bone structure."

"Doesn't she? I love when someone is willing to take a risk like this. It usually pays off."

"You did a great job," Autumn acknowledged. "Thank you. Killian will be pleased."

Charmaine gave her a wolfish grin. "Anything to please Killian."

"Ugh." Autumn made a face. "Charmaine, please."

"Your brother is sexy. Deal with it."

She rolled her eyes and looped her arm through mine to lead me out of the salon. "I'll tell him you said so."

"Please do!" she called after us.

I waved at her over my shoulder in thanks, wondering about payment. I wondered it out loud to Autumn as we got in her car.

"Oh, Killian will pay for it. Charmaine will send him an invoice."

I nodded and sat listening to Autumn gush over my new hair and the outfits she could now see me in because of it. When she finally took a breath, I asked, "What did you do for a living before . . . this?"

"Oh." Her face fell. "Well, I tried to set up a catering company with my ex-boyfriend. He was supposed to run the company, manage all the business stuff, and I would do the cooking and baking. But he stole my money and created an investment portfolio with it. Because I didn't stipulate legally what the money was for when I authorized the transfer of funds to him, I have no proof that he stole the money. I could have taken him to court but it would have been lengthy and stressful. Killian was mad I didn't do it."

"No wonder. I'm sorry."

"Oh, it's okay." She smiled brightly. "I'm over it. I just started seeing someone new and he's . . . different. A gentleman through and through. We've gone on three dates and he hasn't even pushed for sex yet. And he has more money than me, so I know he's not after that."

"I'm glad." And I was. Autumn was sweet. She wore her heart on her sleeve. She deserved someone who would be gentle with it.

"Plus, Killian took care of Barry. My ex," she explained.

"How so?"

"He ruined him. I don't know the hows and I don't want to know." She shot me a pained look. "You know how people say karma will get you . . . well, if you treat *me* badly, Killian is the karma that gets you."

An ache streaked across my chest, so deep that I lifted my good hand to soothe it away. It was jealousy, I realized, shocked. What must it be like to have someone care about you that fiercely? To have someone like O'Dea, who was cold with everyone else, treat you like you were all that mattered?

Once upon a time, my mom had been that person. My fierce protector.

I closed my eyes tight. She kept invading my thoughts, breaking through.

"Talk about something else," I insisted, needing a distraction. "Anything."

"Oh." Autumn's brows pinched together in worry, but she said, "I saw these amazing Kurt Geiger platforms for you. Do you wear heels?"

My smile was grim but relieved. "How high are they?"

"WELL?" AUTUMN ASKED.

She'd driven me back to the apartment and insisted on waiting for O'Dea to come over so she could see his reaction to my transformation.

If I wasn't mistaken, he'd stumbled a little when he first saw me as he walked into the living area of the apartment, so I know the haircut took him by surprise. Good surprise or bad surprise, I didn't know, because he'd immediately started making himself a coffee with only a casual "hello" thrown our way.

Autumn stood in the middle of the sitting room with her arms crossed over her chest, watching him impatiently as he moved around the kitchen. I sat on the sofa, not acknowledging the flare of agitation I felt at his lack of response. I stared out at the river, pretending I couldn't care less what he thought.

And I couldn't care less!

He was an ass.

"Well what?" he asked, coming around the island with his coffee.

His sister gestured at me. "Skylar's hair."

"It's fine."

Her eyes narrowed. "*Fine?*"

O'Dea expelled one of his exasperated sighs. "Autumn, Skylar and I have work to do."

She glared at him. "Fine."

The glare melted from her face, softening to a sweet smile as she bent down to press a kiss to my temple.

The affectionate gesture startled me and I couldn't help but smile at her in return. "I'll see you later. Call me if you need anything?"

"Call you how?" O'Dea stepped forward with a scowl.

"I gave her a phone, big brother." She kissed his cheek. "Brenna wants to check in with her, and it might be good for Skylar to start checking in with the world again."

She'd suggested I ease myself into googling the band members so I wouldn't be caught unawares later. But the thought made my stomach clench. Moreover, I didn't want to tell her because the phone was thoughtful, but the idea of being reachable, being "tagged" by a cell phone again made me squirm.

"And did you check if Skylar was ready for a phone?" O'Dea asked, surprising me with the considerate thought.

"If Skylar is ready? Or if *you're* ready for Skylar to have the independence of a phone?"

"Skylar is sitting right here," I muttered.

O'Dea heard me. "Do you want a phone?"

I shrugged, still not wanting to hurt Autumn's feelings.

"She doesn't want a phone," he surmised. "Give me the phone."

"Killian," Autumn huffed. "She's right. You're being controlling."

"I'm not. Skylar doesn't want the phone."

"Skylar?"

I gave her a regretful shake of my head. "I'm not ready for the cell. Sorry."

"Why didn't you say something?"

"Because it was sweet of you. I didn't want to hurt your feelings."

"You should be honored, Autumn," O'Dea said. "She doesn't care if she hurts *my* feelings."

I smirked. "That's because you have none."

We stared at each other, as if daring the other to look away.

"*Okay*." Laughter trembled in Autumn's voice. "I'm going to go. Skylar, give the phone to Killian. He paid for it anyway." And then she was striding out, her heels clacking down the hallway. "Ooh, Killian, you brought your Taylor! Have fun!"

And then the door slammed shut.

Expression quizzical, I sat up. "Your Taylor?"

He threw back the rest of his coffee, putting the mug down on the counter. Without meeting my eyes, he turned away to walk down the hall. "You can't play," he called out, "but I can. And we have an album to write."

When he returned, he had a guitar case in hand. He put it up on the island and opened it. I stood to get a better look, my fingers itching to play it, but instead of taking out the guitar, O'Dea pulled out papers.

"The contract." He handed it over to me. "I canceled the makeup artist since Autumn took care of that." He indicated my face.

"I've set up interviews with a few managers in the morning." He held out a small folder for me to take. "All three are in there. Their credentials, everything. Talk to them. Get a feel for them. Make a decision. Once that's done, you hand the chosen one that." He tapped the top of the contract. "He or she will make sure you're taken care of before you sign it."

"I know how it works." I dropped the papers on the counter by the guitar. "So, I'm just supposed to pick a manager in one day?"

"No, I'll give you the weekend to think about it."

How was I supposed to do this? Gayle had been my manager since I was sixteen years old. I trusted her. "Magnanimous of you."

"I'd prefer it if we could get through the day without the sarcasm."

I stared incredulously as he pulled a Taylor Dreadnought out of its case. Okay, he had great taste in guitars. So what? "Since when do label execs write albums?" The answer was never. "Don't you have a producer who could work with me?"

"*I* used to be a music producer at the label." He strolled over to the sofa with the guitar.

A producer before he was an exec? He didn't seem old enough to have accumulated all that experience. "How old are you?" I sat down on the chair across from him.

"Thirty."

Six years older than me. He'd packed in a lot in a short time. "If you've been an A&R executive for five years, then you were a pretty young producer."

"I haven't been an A&R executive for five years."

I frowned. "But Autumn said you've brought in a lot of successful new artists in the last five years."

"I have. As a producer. I worked for Skyscraper and several other labels, depending on who the artist was. But my goal has always been A&R at Skyscraper. I got that job eighteen months ago." There was a bitter note to his tone and it reminded me of what Autumn said about their uncle making Killian jump through hoops.

"Your uncle's a bit of a hardass, huh?"

Surprise flared in his eyes for a second but was immediately flattened by understanding. "Autumn."

"She told me about your uncle. That he's the label head."

"Aye."

"And that he's hard on you."

O'Dea's features grew taut with the subject. "He expects the best, that's all. And so do I. Let's get to work."

Okay. Got it. Subject off-limits. "I'll get my notebook."

When I returned, he held his hand out for it.

"You're joking, right?"

"Well, I'm assuming you've written the sheet music in there?"

"I have." I'd also written really personal shit in there. "Point?"

"I'll need it." O'Dea gave me his intense, focused stare. "To play because you can't."

I flipped through the notebook until I found the sheet music to one of my unfinished songs. I ripped it out and handed it to him. "I've been working on this one."

He nodded but looked less than pleased as I sat down with the notebook open, ready to write. "You ever going to trust me?"

"Doing this," I gestured between us, "is trust."

He didn't respond but I guessed he was satisfied because he glanced at the paper, put it down, and strummed the guitar to tune it. My gaze followed the way his long, masculine fingers plucked at the strings and I felt a little flutter low in my belly.

It was a feeling I hadn't felt in a long time.

Flushing, I looked away.

I'd always had a thing about a guy's hands, especially watching them play guitar. When Micah found out, he teased me about it.

"Does that get you hot?" He'd grinned, tickling the guitar strings. "Does it make you feel good?"

"Kicking you in the nuts will make me feel better." I'd laughed, throwing my notebook at him. "I'm never telling you anything again."

"How about this?" Micah had stood up, doing a complicated riff as he walked over to me. His green eyes danced with amusement and longing. He got down on his knees in front of me and made me laugh harder as he played a Spanish serenade. "A serenade for my señorita," he'd cracked.

God, I love you, *I'd thought, impulsively leaning in to press a kiss to his lips.*

When I'd pulled back, he'd seemed stunned. And then he grinned. "It does *get you hot."*

"Skylar? Skylar?"

I blinked, coming back to the apartment, to Killian. "Yeah, what?"

His eyebrows drew together. "Where did you go?"

"To a place that's gone."

After a moment of study, he smirked. "You *are* a writer."

"Then let's write."

Without looking at the paper I'd given him again, O'Dea played my half-written tune. I was so impressed I almost missed my cue.

"Hey, baby, go home,
Stop holding me down
'Cause you'll keep holding me down for life.

"Your toxic love seeped into my blood,
Twisted kiss drowning me in its mud,
But I need to breathe tonight.

"You know it's true, I loved you.
You know it's true, I needed you.
"And what is worse I let you love, love, love
Me till you'd fucked the love right out of me."

O'Dea stopped playing and stared, scrutinizing me. I shifted, uncomfortable with that gaze that seemed to see too much. "That's all I've got so far. What do you think?"

"It works. I like that a lot of your lyrics are a little dark juxtaposed with upbeat tunes."

"You know I was thinking this one could have a kind of electro-pop, synth-pop sound to it. Like Sia, Halsey. That kind of feel."

"Is that how you envision the album?"

"O'Dea, let's be serious. I don't know how to envision an album I don't want. I can, however, envision songs. That's how I envision this song."

His lips pinched together at the reminder I was doing something I didn't want to do. As usual he didn't acknowledge it. He settled into his guitar. "Again. This time cut the first 'Me' from the second-to-last line of the chorus. It doesn't fit."

We did it again. And the bastard was right.

"It works," I agreed. Begrudgingly.

"Is it about Micah Murphy? The song?"

My breath caught, even though it wasn't really a surprise that he'd guessed correctly. "Is that going to be part of this? You want to know what's behind the lyrics?"

"You can tell me as much as you'd like. But if you want me playing go-between with you and your band when the news breaks of your return, maybe I should know exactly what I'm getting in between."

"Nothing as far as I'm concerned."

"And as far as he's concerned?"

"I wouldn't know anymore."

"But there was something? The tabloids were right?"

"We weren't good for each other," I offered. "We brought out the worst in each other. I let him . . . I let him manipulate me too long. And I retaliated too much." I flinched, shocked I'd said that all out loud. And to him of all people.

"Writing helps." O'Dea shocked me even more with his response. "I know you think you're running away from what happened. I know you won't go to therapy. But maybe this is your therapy." He nodded to the notebook in my hand. "You're doing something about it, even if you don't think you are."

I didn't know how to reply. It was almost kind. No. It *was* kind to reassure me I wasn't as big of a coward as I was starting to feel these days.

"And it makes for great music."

And there he was!

I made a face at him and thankfully it broke the intensity between us.

"The next verse . . ." I tapped my pen against my notebook.

"Hey, baby, I'm gone ,
I'm trying to right all our wrongs,
So don't come looking for me tonight."

I sang the words directly into O'Dea's eyes and when I was finished, I couldn't help feel curious about the intensity of his gaze as he watched me. What the hell went on in his head? It was a mystery. Finally, he said, "Pen."

After I threw it over to him, he scribbled on the piece of paper

I'd given him, filling in the music for the new verse.

"Your wicked games are out of my head,
I uncovered all the lies you ever said,
And now I'm free for life."

O'Dea raised an eyebrow. "You write fast."

"Sometimes. Sometimes it comes to you. You know exactly what you want to say. When I first started writing this one, I'd just left for Europe. I didn't know what I wanted to say. Now I do."

He threw the pen back to me. "Better write it down."

As I scribbled down the words, he asked, "And is that how you really feel? Or is it how you wished you felt?"

And for some reason—maybe it was the magic of songwriting—I answered honestly as I stared at the words. "It's how I feel with three thousand miles between us."

How I would feel if I ever had to face Micah again was a totally different story.

"And then into the chorus," I said before O'Dea could respond.

"Repeat of the first?"

"Yeah."

All too soon, I forgot why we were writing together. I forgot about the album that loomed over my head like a giant, hungry eagle.

Instead I enjoyed the process. I enjoyed writing music with someone smart, someone who seemed to get my music, and everything else drifted away. We even laughed together and worse . . . we *agreed* all the time.

The sound of my stomach rumbling broke the spell.

"Shit, what time is it?" O'Dea's eyes widened at the sight of the sun dipping below the buildings across the Clyde.

"We've been at this for hours."

"You need to eat." He put down his guitar and strode into the kitchen. "What have we got?"

"I have a meal plan, remember."

"Where is it?"

"In the drawer to your left." I watched him, bewildered. Was he going to cook my dinner?

It became clear as he studied the meal plan and then pulled out the ingredients from the fridge and cupboards that he was. Watching him do this quickened my heart rate.

His phone buzzed as he chopped up vegetables for a stir fry. "One second." He pulled it out of his pocket and then cursed when he saw the caller ID. "Hey," he answered, sounding a little breathless. "Aye, I know, I just remembered. I . . . no, I'll be there . . . Don't . . . I know . . . Look, we'll talk about it later. I'll see you soon." He hung up and actually looked regretful. "I forgot I have a dinner tonight that I can't miss."

Oh.

Okay.

Shit. That was not disappointment I was feeling. It was not!

This was O'Dea, for God's sake. He was not the man to incite my disappointment. Ever. He couldn't be. It wasn't allowed. *I* wouldn't allow it. Reality check, please!

Just because we did the whole songwriting thing well together did not a friendship make. "Go. I can make my own dinner."

"But your cast . . ."

"I'll manage." I got up to take over. "Seriously. Go."

His expression turned remote again. "I'll leave my guitar. I'll be back tomorrow after the manager interviews. Remember to read that folder." He pointed to it on the counter. "I'd tell you who I recommend but I'm afraid you'll deliberately not choose the person to spite me."

I made a face.

"Okay." He grabbed his keys. "I'll see you tomorrow."

I mused over all this time he was dedicating to me. Where were his other artists in all this?

"I'll be here," I muttered.

He'd disappeared down the hall and I waited to hear the bang of the front door closing behind him. I didn't. Instead I heard his footsteps coming back and looked up from the vegetables. O'Dea stood in the doorway, studying me intensely.

It made me squirm. "What?"

"The hair looks good."

He was gone before I could reply. I stared warily at the spot he'd been standing in moments before, hating that I cared that he liked my hair.

twelve

"What do you mean you aren't choosing any of them?"

I was unmoved by O'Dea's frustration. "Just as it sounds. I'm not choosing any of those people to be my manager."

As promised, he had given me the entire weekend to mull it over, but I'd known from the moment the last guy walked out of my apartment that I wouldn't be choosing a new manager. It required too much trust. Plus, this person would be in my life a lot and I was already overwhelmed by O'Dea, Autumn, and Brenna after eighteen months of being alone.

O'Dea glowered at me as I finished my breakfast. "Does this mean you're not signing the contract?"

I nodded over my shoulder to the couch. "It's there. Signed."

He looked even more pissed off. "Please tell me you did not sign a major record deal without the advice and guidance of a manager."

"Yes. I'm a moron." I rolled my eyes at his melodrama. "O'Dea, this is the fifth one of these I've signed and I actually read them before I sign them. I know what a legit contract should look like.

Okay? Or are you trying to tell me that you're planning to screw me over?"

"Of course not." He looked peeved. "I just want to know why you don't want a manager."

"I can manage myself."

He seemed to contemplate this as I finished my omelet and hopped off the stool. I was about to attempt to rinse the plate one-handed before putting it in the dishwasher when he took it out of my hand and nudged me out of the way.

I refused to acknowledge the way my skin prickled at his nearness.

"Thanks," I muttered, finding a safe distance on the other side of the island.

"So . . . What did you get up to yesterday?"

I smirked at his back. The question was asked far too casually.

Yesterday was the first day he and I hadn't seen each other since I moved into the apartment. Autumn had stopped by for some lunch but the rest of the day I got to spend reading. The Friday after my interviews with the managers, O'Dea had taken me to my health check. I'd also explained how important dental health was to me and he'd gotten me an appointment after the health check with his dentist. The nurse at the first appointment had taken much the same tests they'd taken at the hospital, but she also threw in an STD test. I wanted to tell her it was pointless, but the truth was the last person I had sex with was Micah and there was more than a possibility the manwhore might have passed something on to me.

As for my dental appointment, it wasn't too bad. I'd been vigilant about my teeth while I was homeless.

After the dental appointment, O'Dea had asked me if there was anything else I needed before he returned to the office, and

I said that I was out of books to read. We stopped at a bookstore and he disappeared while I mused over what to buy.

As I was deciding between two fantasy books, he returned holding a bag with the bookstore logo on it and handed it to me. "An e-reader. We'll set you up an account and you can download what you like."

"You need a credit card for that," I'd argued as I followed him out of the store.

"I'll give you mine."

I'd scowled. "No, you've already spent too much."

"The company has." He'd opened the passenger door to his car for me. "I need to get back to the office. Get in."

I'd scooted in, feeling uncomfortable about taking the money for this when it hadn't bothered me that he was feeding and clothing me. "I have money," I'd muttered as he drove away.

"That you can't access without alerting everyone of your whereabouts. You ready for that yet?"

No. No, I wasn't. "I'll pay you back."

So, I'd spent two hours the day before trying to decide what I wanted to read on my e-reader, and except for lunch with Autumn, I'd spent the day devouring two books.

Saturday was spent writing with O'Dea again. We mostly tweaked the couple of finished songs I'd written. Like last time, it was a lot more fun than I cared to admit out loud.

"I had lunch with Autumn," I answered his question.

He stuck my plate and a couple of mugs from the sink into the dishwasher and turned to me. He leaned back against the kitchen counter, his arms crossed over his chest. "Aye, she told me. What else?"

"I'm sorry, um, when did you become my prison warden?"

"It's only a question."

"It sounds like an interrogation."

He cocked his head, eyes narrowed in suspicion. "Why don't you want to tell me what you were up to yesterday?"

I laughed at the ridiculousness of the conversation. "O'Dea, I read two books yesterday. That is the extent of the excitement that was experienced in this apartment."

"So why evade?"

"I'm not! You're . . . you really are acting like I'm in prison here."

"You know you can come and go as you please, but until the idiot who put you in hospital is caught, I do worry about you wandering around on your own. Which is what you did yesterday."

Confused, I shook my head. "What are you talking about?"

"I bumped into Callum, your neighbor on the second floor, as I was coming up here this morning. He's a graphic artist for the label."

"Okay."

My response made him glower. "You met him yesterday."

"I did?"

"Skylar . . ."

I met a Callum yesterday? I wracked my brain trying to—"*Oh*. The guy with the beard?" I'd taken a brief walk down the riverbank for some fresh air in the morning. When I was coming back into the apartment building, a guy with a beard had held the door open for me. I hadn't thought anything of the encounter because we'd merely smiled at each other and said hello.

"Aye, the guy with the beard."

I scowled at his annoyed tone. "Why are you acting like I'm hiding something from you?"

"Because you are. I asked you what you did yesterday and you omitted that you spent time with a bloody stranger and told him who you are. For someone who is trying to keep a low profile while we write this album, it surprised me, that's all."

"What the hell are you talking about? I took a walk down to the river. I needed fresh air. When I came back, the guy with the beard held the door open for me and we exchanged hellos. End of story. Why are your panties in such a twist, O'Dea?"

"That was it. That was all that was said?"

I wanted to slap that suspicious look off his face. "I'm not exactly in the mood for making new friends, so yeah . . . that was it. And don't ask me again because I don't appreciate being treated like a liar."

After a moment's contemplation, O'Dea sighed and uncrossed his arms. "Shit. He must have recognized you. I passed him on the way into the building this morning and he asked me when Skylar Finch moved in."

Panic suffused me. "What?"

O'Dea's expression softened. "Hey, don't worry. I warned him not to open his mouth."

"You trust that he won't?" I went to reach for a glass of water and my hand shook so badly, I had to wrap it around the glass to stop it. The idea of the paparazzi turning up at the apartment terrified me.

O'Dea's strong hand covered mine around the glass. His warm fingertips were calloused from playing the guitar. The act itself was surprising enough but the fierceness blazing from his eyes took my breath away. "He won't tell anyone, Skylar," he promised. "You're safe here."

With my heart racing for an entirely new reason, I couldn't tear my eyes from his as I nodded. "Okay."

As if he'd just realized what he'd done, O'Dea let go of my hand around the glass as if it had scalded him and abruptly moved back to his side of the island. That bland mask came down over his face again. "I need to be in the office today, but I've cleared my schedule for the next few days so we can work on the album here. We will, however, eventually have to take this to the label to start recording."

"I know." I nodded, unable to meet his eyes.

"What . . . will you be okay today?" he asked, sounding unsure.

I snorted. "O'Dea, I've been taking care of myself a long time. I'll be fine for a day, just like I was fine yesterday."

"Aye, well . . ." He slid an old-fashioned flip phone across the island, drawing my questioning gaze. "It's only a phone. No internet. I've programmed my number and Autumn's number in it. You need anything, you call."

I reached for it. The man kept surprising me. "Thanks. You have other artists you're trying to pull in?" I asked, desperate to remind myself that's all I was to this man. An artist on his label. That he'd forced my hand with his own cold ambition.

"It's more complicated than that. I oversee the entire department."

"Your card says executive, not A&R director."

His lips pinched together for a moment. "I'm not technically the director. A man named Kenny Smith is the director and has been since the label opened thirty years ago. He's . . . grown out of touch with the industry."

"He's lazy," I surmised.

"That too."

Indignant, I said, "So you're doing his job while he gets the title, the money, and the credit?"

"It's the oldest story in the book."

"But surely your uncle must see it?"

Anger tightened his features but he didn't respond. I could

see the muscle in his jaw twitching as he reached for his car keys. "I better get going."

Disappointed at the way he could shut down on me, I found myself instantly retreating. I flipped open the old cell, pretending to be interested in it.

I felt his gaze. "Last chance to tell me if you need anything before I go."

I shook my head, not looking at him. "I don't need anyone."

The air in the room seemed to physically shift, like his reaction to my Freudian slip caused it to thin. He waited for me to look at him and as much as I wanted to withstand his stare, I was compelled to draw my head up.

His expression was hard and he opened his mouth, as if to say something, but then stopped himself.

Feeling almost light-headed with the tension, I sought to break it. "If you're worried I might talk to the mailman, don't be. I've got nothing coming in the post."

O'Dea decided to take offense at my joke. "For the last time, you're not a prisoner."

And suddenly not in the mood to pretend this guy was my friend, I curled my upper lip in disdain and referred to how we'd ended up here in the first place. "You sure about that?"

His answer was to march out of the apartment and slam the front door with such force, the impact shuddered the walls.

THE FIRST TIME THE CELL made a noise that day, it was a text from Autumn.

How does Thai food sound tonight? Xo

Worried that she was feeling compelled to babysit me, and not really wanting to spend time with anyone whose big brother was making them spend time with me, I blew her off.

Not hungry. Maybe some other time.

To which she replied:

Well, of course you're not hungry now. It's only 2pm. I'll be over at 7pm. Thai or not to Thai? Xo

I smirked. Apparently, there was no getting rid of her.

To Thai. Thx.

She'd sent me a smiley face and something else that only came up as a question mark on my cell. I guessed it didn't have the software update for the new emojis.

The cell went off a few hours later; this time it was ringing and the caller ID said "Killian."

I thought about not answering it, but that was childish and honestly, the thought of continuing this little game of who can piss the other off more exhausted me.

"O'Dea," I answered.

He seemed to hesitate a moment before he said, "I just got off the phone with the police. They still haven't found the boys. Or your guitar."

Disappointment flooded me as I suddenly realized I might never get my beloved Taylor back. My throat closed tight at the thought.

"Skylar?"

I cleared it, trying to push the sob that was closing it back down. "Yeah, I heard you."

He was so quiet I thought maybe he'd hung up. I was about to do the same when he said, "They're sending a sketch artist over to the flat."

I felt somewhat relieved that the police weren't giving up. "Okay. When?"

"The artist will be there in an hour. Her name is Shelley."

The fact that they were sending someone over so soon made

me even more hopeful that they might catch the little pricks. "Got it."

"Call if—"

"I need anything," I finished wryly. "I know."

"Right." He hung up without saying goodbye.

"Ass," I mumbled, throwing the cell across the floor out of reach.

It was hard to get back into my book anticipating the arrival of the sketch artist. And Shelley, a petite brunette with big round blue eyes, turned up at my door not too long later. I didn't know what I was expecting from a police sketch artist but it wasn't Shelley. Her hair was cut pixie short and she had piercings all along the cuff of her right ear. Her lip was pierced and her entire right arm was covered in colorful tattoos.

Despite having the appearance of an extrovert, Shelley seemed shy, almost nervous, and I wondered if she recognized me. The entire time I described the boys to her, I worried about her telling someone she'd sketched for Skylar Finch. As soon as she left, I called O'Dea.

"What's wrong?" he answered, sounding concerned.

For a moment, it threw me. "Is that how you always answer your phone?"

I could practically feel him shifting in agitation. "Skylar?"

"Shelley . . . I think she recognized me. What if—"

"Part of her job is strict confidentiality. She won't—she *can't*—say a word."

"Okay. You're sure?"

"Do you think you'll ever be ready for the world to find you?"

Nope.

"I need time. You promised me that at least."

"And it's a promise I intend to keep." He hung up.

"Ugh!" I shook the cell, desperate to throw it across the room again. The guy really needed to learn to civilly finish a conversation.

thirteen

The gentle acoustic filled the apartment and I closed my eyes against the sight of O'Dea expertly playing his Taylor. He distracted me from the music.

And the music was good.

When he finished, I opened my eyes, unable to help the surprise in my voice. "It's really good."

He shot me a smug look. "Ever the shock."

"Well . . . it is shocking," I admitted from my seat on the floor. I was leaning against the chair while O'Dea took his usual spot on the couch.

We were on week three of working on the album. It had been a little tense between us at first but as the songwriting wore on, everything else melted away, including our exasperation with one another. We worked late and O'Dea cooked while I sung lyrics to him that he yayed or nayed.

It felt like we existed on some lonely part of the planet where there was only music and creativity. I couldn't describe it, but as the days passed, as I poured my heart out into the music, I felt something ease from my chest. At night when he left, I felt a melancholy I didn't want to explore.

Together we'd pieced the songs together but most of the melodies came from me and O'Dea tweaked here and there.

This was the first time he'd said outright, "No, none of that works, let's try this."

And his was better. A lot better. I couldn't even hide how impressed I was, even though it would inflate his already bloated ego.

"You want to try it with the lyrics?"

I picked up my notes. "Go for it."

He played the intro chords and then I jumped in.

"There's a girl on the corner,
Selling love for a meal.
Every kind of love,
Except the kind that's real.

"There's a boy watching over,
With a gun to his head.
Forced by the needle that
Pulls the trigger instead.

"You say
You're found and can see.
Does that include the Lost forgotten
By you and me?"

He stopped playing. "Well?"

"I already told you it works. I'm not rubbing your ego any more than that."

Something sparked in his gaze, something almost flirtatious, but he looked down at the sheet music, hiding it from me. Still, a little smirk played around his mouth.

I couldn't help but grin. He wanted to say something dirty in response to that. I'd bet my Taylor on it if I had it. Something I was learning about O'Dea as we worked together: he actually did have a sense of humor.

"You know you want to say it."

He flicked me a wicked look and I ignored the flutter in my belly. "Can we be professional, please?"

"I'm not the one who took something dirty out of what I said."

"I didn't." He shot me a deadpan look.

"O'Dea, I know you're very good at the intimidating, *no one is allowed to know what I'm thinking* gig you have going on, but I hate to burst your bubble—I'm learning your tells."

"You learn what I allow to you learn," he said arrogantly.

"And I'm learning a lot. Someone must trust me," I teased.

Looking exasperated, he gestured to the notebook in my hand. "You have lyrics to finish."

"This is all I've got." I slumped back against the legs of the chair behind me. "I told you . . . sometimes it comes, sometimes it doesn't."

Putting the Taylor down, O'Dea reached for my notebook. Instead of ripping the lyrics out like I always did, I handed him the entire notebook. Our eyes locked as he took it and my breath caught.

O'Dea lowered his thick eyelashes, masking his expression from me as he read the lyrics. "Is this about people you met on the streets?"

"Yeah. Mandy and Ham. When I met them, Mandy told me their entire life story. How her mom's boyfriend sexually abused her, her mom knew, blamed her, hit her, until Mandy ran away from home at sixteen. She had to prostitute herself to survive and got so low about it that she was ready to commit suicide. But Ham, a heroin addict, befriended her, offered her his protection." I felt so much sadness in my chest for her, it was almost too much to bear upon my own grief. "She doesn't love him but she cares about him so it's better than what she was doing. But it's still a form of prostitution. Even sadder . . . Ham doesn't see it that way. He just loves her."

"Fuck," O'Dea muttered, handing the notebook back to me. "How could anyone let that happen to their family?"

"Her mother's a bitch, that's why."

"I can think of a stronger word."

Grim, I nodded.

"Mandy took the only option she felt left open to her. Maybe she doesn't see it the way you see it."

"Oh, she does," I said, bitter about it. "She's well aware. And you know what's worse? I was kind of angry at her that she couldn't survive on her own. Because I thought that's what *I* was doing. I thought I was so smart." I shook my head in disgust. "I was a naive child."

"You survived longer than some. You did okay."

I contemplated him and I didn't know why I pushed it, why I asked. Maybe I wanted to argue, maybe I wanted a reminder that we couldn't be friends. "Be honest. You think I was a spoiled brat making a mockery of something real and horrible that other people have no way out of."

Irritation flickered in his dark eyes. "I think you did what you needed to survive."

"But the point is that it wasn't my only option."

"Wasn't it? I'm not talking about surviving homelessness, Skylar. I'm saying, I think you did what you needed to do to *survive*."

Understanding he meant surviving my mother's death, tears burned in my throat and I had to look away. If he kept looking at me like that, I would burst into tears. So I continued to prod, to push. "Autumn said you lost your parents."

When no reply was forthcoming, I knew I'd gotten what I wanted. I looked up, expecting to meet his cold, blank mask but I found something different. I found him scrutinizing me, assessing me, and I didn't know what it meant.

And then he shocked the hell out of me. "Autumn is my half-sister. Not that I think of her as anything but my sister, full stop. Her dad, Peter O'Dea, adopted me when he married my mum. My real dad has been in and out of prison since I was a baby. As far as I'm concerned, Peter was my dad.

"Our lives changed when I was eleven and Autumn was only six. We were on a family holiday. My parents booked a helicopter ride but Autumn wouldn't get on it. She screamed and cried anytime we tried to get her in the thing. Dad didn't want to lose the booking and told me and Mum to go for the ride while he watched Autumn. But Autumn wanted *me* to stay with her. She howled anytime I tried to let her go.

"Finally," he paused, his throat moving like he was struggling to swallow. I held my breath, hanging on every word. "I told Mum and Dad to go on the ride. That I'd stay with Autumn at the booking office. The operator promised to watch us, that we'd be fine, and so off they went." His lips thinned, as if the memory was nothing more than merely distasteful. But his chest, moving with shallow breaths, betrayed him. "The helicopter crashed. It was the last time we saw them. My uncle sued the operator for negligence and Autumn and I won a lot of money in compensation. He managed it for us, invested it well, and we received it when we turned eighteen. That's why Autumn has what she has without needing a job.

Of course, my uncle gloats about it, as if he wants our thanks for providing us with something we'd give away in a heartbeat if it meant having our parents back."

Grief for him, for Autumn, swelled in my throat and I blinked away the tears, instinctively knowing he wouldn't want that from me. But my own emotions, ones that had been bubbling closer and closer to the surface for weeks, attempted to overwhelm me.

Why had O'Dea shared this with me?

Now I felt like I owed him. Yet there was something freeing in that. Like I had no choice but to talk, to tell him, because it was a debt to be repaid.

"I wasn't close to my stepfather."

O'Dea shook himself out of his thoughts. "Oh?" he said carefully.

The thought of Bryan still filled me with resentment, which was horrible. It only compounded my guilt. "It had been me and Mom all of our lives. My dad died when I was a baby. He was in the army and was killed in action. Mom really loved him so she wasn't interested in getting into another relationship for a long time. She dedicated her life to raising me, and I think she thought she had to make up for my dad's absence. Anything I wanted, any dream I had, was hers to give me. Even if she couldn't afford it, she found a way. My ballet phase. My tae kwon do phase. My photography phase. The art phase. The typewriter phase. My guitar and piano phase. The ones that stuck. I was thirteen when Micah and I decided we were good enough to put a band together. My mom was behind us from the beginning, just as she had been with all my phases. But I think she knew this wasn't a phase. She saved money to buy me my first guitar, drove us to crappy gigs, paid to get us a slot at a recording booth. My dream was her dream.

"And then Bryan came into the picture a year later. He thought we were a bunch of stupid kids. He made me feel guilty about spending the little money that Mom had. They were in a relationship for two years before they moved in together. He made her happy, but it annoyed her that he couldn't support me like she did. It put her in the middle. They almost split up because of it. But then we got our record deal, they got married, and suddenly the bastard always knew we'd come through.'"

"It sounds like you didn't like him very much."

Suddenly, the memory I tried so hard to keep at bay pushed up and out.

"You're here but you're not really here." Mom suddenly burst into my bedroom suite.

After a disastrous gig in Glasgow, I asked Gayle to find me somewhere secluded to get away from Micah. She'd sent me to a summerhouse on the inner Oslo fjords in Norway. Finally, when I couldn't escape my mom's persistent questioning, I came home. To the house I'd bought my mom. A huge six-bedroom home on the outskirts of Billings with spectacular views. It was so big, I had my own suite. I'd naively assumed I could hide in it for the last two weeks before we went back to the recording studio to put together the new album.

Apparently, Mom had had enough.

"You ever heard of knocking?"

"Don't." She shook her head, anger flushing her pretty face. "Don't do that. I am worried sick about you and you keep acting like nothing is going on."

Distressed that I was causing her worry when that was the opposite of what I wanted, I got off the bed and walked over to her. I pasted a weary smile on my face. "Mom, I swear I'm just tired. I'm just . . . recharging the batteries before I head back to work."

Mom studied me intently. And then decided, "You're lying."

"Mom," I huffed.

"I know you're lying. You're avoiding me. You don't return my calls. You're never here . . . I'm shocked that you turned up. And I thought that meant you wanted to stop shutting me out and talk. But you've holed up in here the entire time."

"Mom, I'm not shutting you out."

"Is it drugs?"

My eyes widened. "No. Do you not know me at all?"

She shrugged. "The paper mentioned something about drugs."

Anger roared through me. "My mom. My own mother? Are you shitting me? You're listening to that made-up crap?"

"Well, my own daughter won't talk to me so what else am I supposed to think?" she yelled.

"Not believe the tabloids like a moron."

"Don't you talk to me like that, young lady. You're not a rock star in this house! Show some fucking respect!"

I blinked in horror. My mom had never screamed at me like that. Ever.

She shuddered, tears gleaming in her eyes as she realized it too. "I feel like I'm losing you," she whispered.

I wanted to cry. I wanted to tell her it wasn't her. I wanted to wrap my arms around her and sob and scream and tell her I was lonely. That I was lonely and miserable. That all her sacrifices were for nothing. That I'd pushed the boy I loved away for absolutely nothing. That I'd failed. That I couldn't handle the fame.

That I wanted her to forgive me for railroading her life only to fail her and everyone close to me who mattered.

But I didn't.

I choked down my loneliness.

I reminded myself that Micah, Brandon, and Austin were relying on me. That my mom was comfortable financially for the first time ever and that she was relying on me to keep her that way.

I was just having a bad few months. I'd get over it.

"You're not losing me, Mom. I'm just tired."

My bedroom door almost cracked off its hinges, she slammed it so hard on her way out.

I locked myself in my bathroom, turned on the shower to muffle the sound, and I cried.

When I eventually pulled myself together, I looked out the window to see her car pulling out of the drive. Hating that I was relieved, I wandered downstairs for something to eat.

In that moment, I hadn't thought I could feel much worse about myself. But as I sat at the island on a stool eating a sandwich, my mother's husband appeared. I automatically tensed, assuming I was about to receive a lecture.

He slid onto the stool right next to mine. He wore too much cologne. I dropped the sandwich, suddenly not so hungry.

"Your mom is upset."

"I'm just tired." I was getting bored of my own lie.

"I know." He said and pointed to my sandwich. "You going to finish that?"

I shoved the plate toward him. He took a bite, eyeing me. I frowned at his perusal.

He swallowed and said, "I've been trying to tell your mom that you're tired. She doesn't get what the touring must be like for you."

I was no longer shocked by Bryan's turnaround. He liked the nice house and the nice cars. Bryan liked telling people his stepdaughter was Skylar Finch.

I didn't get it. I didn't get why this was the guy my mom finally chose. My mom was amazing. She was beautiful and smart and funny. Now that I was a little older, I had eyes enough to see that Bryan was a good-looking guy but that wasn't enough. He knew he was good-looking and not in the charming, cocky way Micah knew he was gorgeous.

I couldn't put my finger on it. There was something so false about him and I didn't know why my mom couldn't see it.

"Thanks, I guess," I muttered.

"I won't tell her that it's because you hate the life," he slipped in, giving me a knowing smirk.

My heart pounded. "What?"

"She has wondered about it out loud. If the reason you're avoiding her is because you got what you wanted only to discover that you don't want it after all. But don't worry. I said that was ridiculous. You wouldn't obsess about making the band a success, take all your mom's money and time, nearly destroy her relationship with me in the process, and finally give her all the nice things she deserves only to turn around and say you don't want it anymore. You wouldn't fail her like that." He brushed the crumbs off his fingers and smiled at me.

Hateful. Fucking. Bastard.

"There's one thing I know about you, Skylar. You love your mom more than anything. You'll stay in the band, make it work, as long as she's happy."

I eyed the butter knife. How much money would it take to get me off felony charges? No, Skylar, stabbing your stepfather would be bad.

"Sacrifice is never easy. I'm worried about you. I'm worried you're lonely."

His concerned tone brought my gaze back to his.

"I care about you, Sky. I don't want you to be lonely in this. You can talk to me." He leaned forward and his eyes dipped to my mouth.

What the fuck?

No?

No . . .

His hand rested on my thigh.

Blood pounded in my ears as I looked down at the sight of my stepfather's hand on my leg. His fingers splayed on the inside of my thigh and he began to caress me.

Nausea made me sway, like I had motion sickness.

"You have no idea how beautiful you've gotten. You're so special, Sky." He slid his hand further up my thigh. "Hold on to that. And hold on to knowing I'm here if you need me. Let me be here for you."

The son of . . . that mother-fucking . . .

I ripped his hand off me, pushing off the stool so fast, I almost fell. I backed up away from him and saw the flash of contained anger in his eyes.

"What . . . You . . ."

"No, Sky, whatever you're making up in your head, stop." His face hardened. "I was just comforting you. Like a dad. Don't upset your mother more than you already have."

I glared at O'Dea, having regurgitated the memory as if I didn't have a choice but to get it out of me. "I never told her."

Anger and sympathy mixed in his gaze. "Did he try anything again?"

I shook my head. "I never went back. I was so messed up, I kept second-guessing what had happened . . . But in the end, I knew. We both knew what he'd been trying to start that day. He was a sleazebag and I let her stay with him. I didn't tell her what he was really like."

O'Dea slipped off the couch onto the floor, sitting with his back to the sofa, one knee bent, the other stretched out so that our legs brushed. "Do you think you were afraid she wouldn't believe you?"

"No." My lips trembled; tears burned in my eyes. "That's the horrible thing. I know she would have. I . . . I was so messed up, Killian. I was drowning and I shut out everyone who could save me. And it just all sounds so fucking stupid now, you know. What did any of that matter compared to masked gunmen breaking into her home and murdering her and her husband? And for what? A painting I'd invested three quarters of a million dollars in because Adam, my finance guy, said I should invest my money where I could. That's what they were there for. A painting. Along with some jewelry, some cash. But the police said that the painting was the target." I shook my head at the insanity of it. "I pushed her away because I didn't want to admit that I was failing. And then my fame, my money, got her killed."

Killian let go a shuddering breath, his voice hoarse as he said my name in sympathy.

"What would you have done? Could you stay and face that? I couldn't."

"Skylar, I still wake up some days and I can't breathe for how angry I am at myself for not getting into that helicopter. Mum would still be alive. Autumn would have had a loving mother instead of the cold, exacting bastard of an uncle who raised us. But as hard as it is to believe it sometimes, I'm not to blame for what happened to my parents. And neither are you."

"I'm a coward," I admitted. "I ran away from the truth, I ran away from her death, and now I'm running away from facing the people I've hurt."

"You thought you were protecting your mum. And now you need some time. You're too hard on yourself."

We shared a long look as my breathing grew steadily calmer. Finally, I asked, "Did you tell me about your parents so I would tell you about my mom?"

"Your songs." He reached out for my notebook. "There's a lot of pain in them. These things can turn to poison if you leave them inside to fester."

I felt myself drowning again, this time in Killian O'Dea's eyes. "That would be a yes, then."

His response was a noncommittal shrug.

"So, do you always play part-time therapist with your artists?"

His smile was wry. I wanted to trace my fingers along his lips to feel it. "You're the first."

"Well, you should know I'm feeling vulnerable and defensive right now. I might need you to be a prick so I have an excuse for being mean and sarcastic to you."

He grinned. A full-out grin that made my breath catch. "I don't feel like being a prick today."

"Of course, you don't. Contrary bastard."

He chuckled, a rich, deep sound that tugged an answering smile from me.

Warmth passed between us, a sweet warmth that was so unexpected, I could do nothing but stare at him. How had this man become my confidant?

Killian cleared his throat. "We should . . . we should get back to writing. If you're good to?"

I nodded. "Yeah. Of course."

We buried the moment in songwriting. We worked through the evening, only stopping for food breaks, and we didn't discuss the past anymore. As it neared midnight, I felt a desperation. I knew when he left, I'd be alone with the past I'd unburied today.

I'd grieved for six months when I lost my mom, losing my mind at the idea of her dying the way she did.

But I had never allowed myself to grieve for the way our relationship was before she died. I didn't allow myself to think about letting her die in a house with a man who had sought to betray her and possibly already had with other women.

Now it was out there.

Waiting for me to deal with as soon as Killian left.

"You know," he placed his Taylor back in the guitar case, not looking at me, "I'm shattered. It's probably not that safe for me to drive home exhausted. Would you mind if I slept on the couch?"

Relief loosened the tension in my shoulders. "Sure. Of course."

He found some extra blankets and a pillow in the linen cupboard and set up the couch as a bed while I stood awkwardly watching. Even though having him here was a comfort, I still would have to close the bedroom door behind me and be alone with my thoughts.

"You know, I usually watch a little TV before bed," I lied.

The way he looked at me . . . I swear this guy could see right through me. He nodded. "All right."

And that's how I found myself watching episodes of *Boardwalk Empire* with Killian. Neither of us had seen it before and we got hooked fast.

In fact, it was the last thing I remember. Being curled up on the couch while Killian sat on the floor with his back against it.

When I woke up the next morning, I was magically in my own bed in an empty apartment.

fourteen

O'Dea didn't come around for a couple of days.

And just like that, he went back to being O'Dea, not Killian. Not because I was mad at him for disappearing after I'd let down my walls. In fact, I was glad for the space. It allowed me to process everything I'd brought out into the open.

"Your songs . . . There's so much pain in them. These things can turn to poison if you leave them inside to fester."

O'Dea was right. And the fact that he was willing to open up to me about his own parents' death told me how much he wanted me to work through my issues. He wasn't a man who allowed himself to be vulnerable to anyone but his sister. I was sure of that. But he'd been vulnerable to me in a seemingly self-sacrificing act. How much of it was because he genuinely wanted to help me and how much was about making sure his artist was mentally healthy by the time the album dropped, I wasn't sure.

My gut told me it was a little of both.

I wasn't mad at O'Dea. I'd needed to open up regarding that moment with Bryan, to reveal my guilt over not telling my mom about it or anything else. It didn't mean the guilt was gone, but it had settled to a manageable level as though all it had wanted was for me to face it head-on.

Definitely not mad at O'Dea. But his disappearing act reminded me who we were to each other and calling him by his surname felt like mental armor.

"You okay?" Autumn asked as we wandered through a department store.

After three days in the apartment processing, I needed a breather, so I'd called Autumn and she'd suggested a little retail therapy. I didn't care what we did, as long as I got out for a while.

"My wrist is itchy," I complained honestly, lifting up my cast. "I'm desperate to get this thing off."

She wrinkled her nose. "I broke my ankle when I was fourteen. Skiing trip with the school. I hated the cast. It made me miserable. Killian had just started his second year at uni and he missed out on all the first-semester partying to look after me."

Oh God, I didn't want to know that. "Which uni did he go to?" *Damn your own curiosity, Finch.*

"Glasgow." She gave me a sad smile. "He wanted to stay at home so he could look after me."

"Your uncle really didn't parent you at all?"

She walked around a perfume display and stopped in front of me, lowering her voice. "He kept informed of our grades at school, our extracurricular stuff, and the moment we showed any sign of weakness, a B instead of an A, a lost football match for Killian, a failed audition at the Royal Conservatoire for me, and he would castigate us for what felt like days."

A bottle of Miss Dior caught my eye and I thought of how amazingly supportive my mom had been about everything. When I came home with a bad grade, she never made me feel like a failure.

"Jesus, he sounds like a piece of work."

"You have no idea." Autumn threaded her arm through mine and led me toward the stairs. "Anything else, he had absolutely no interest in our lives whatsoever."

"What's the Royal Conservatoire?"

"Of Scotland," she replied. "I was thirteen when I applied for their junior modern ballet program."

I smiled at the imagery. "I took ballet when I was six for a year. I was useless. I didn't know you were a ballerina."

She grimaced. "Yes, but not an exceptional one, I'm afraid. Which was why I never got into the Conservatoire here. It's in the top five in the world for performing art schools."

"Did you stop dancing after the audition?"

Sadness flickered in her eyes. "When I didn't get in to RCS, my uncle refused to pay for any more dance classes. Or anything to do with dance. What was the point if I wasn't going to be the best?"

I felt my skin flush hot with anger on her behalf. I hadn't even met their uncle, but my level of dislike for him was growing by the day. And I'd just signed to his goddamned label.

"Your uncle sounds like a man with a very tiny dick."

Autumn burst into surprised laughter, stopping us near the exit to the department store. Her body shook mine as she laughed until tears pooled in the corner of her eyes. Finally, she wiped at them, her giggles slowing. She beamed at me. "Thanks, Skylar."

I smiled at her. "For what?"

"For making me laugh when I told you that story. There are a small handful of people in the world who know that story, and not once has it ever ended with me in fits of laughter."

I squeezed her elbow with my good hand. "What can I say? I have a gift."

The bitter wind hit us as we strolled back out onto Buchanan

Street and I was glad for the winter coat O'Dea had bought me a few weeks ago. Autumn and I huddled into each other as we walked toward Argyle Street, my gaze drawn to the guy busking a few feet from us.

He was pretty good.

A twinge of longing caused an ache in my chest.

"Do you miss it?" Autumn asked as we passed him.

"Busking?"

"Yes."

I nodded. "It was simple."

"Killian told me you're reluctant to get back into the music business. Something about hating the fame part of it all."

"He did, huh?"

I felt her scrutinizing me. "He thinks it's fear after all the horrible publicity surrounding your parents' murders." Her voice was gentle, as if she was afraid to mention it, but I still flinched.

Murder.

I still couldn't wrap my head around that.

My mom and Bryan were *murdered*.

And the bastards who did it were still out there somewhere.

"Your brother believes what he wants to believe," I said, bitter.

"He thinks if you really weren't interested in a music career, you would have found another way. That you had other options. Don't you think there's a possibility he's right?"

"I don't know," I admitted dully. "When I was in the band, my complicated relationship with Micah put us in the eye of a storm we couldn't escape. Maybe if things between us had been less messy, if fans hadn't picked up on it, the fame would have been different. But I don't know that. All I know is that I had everything I thought I wanted and I was desperately unhappy." I gave her a sad shrug. "Does that mean I will be again? I don't know. So, I guess I was less afraid to take that risk than I was to face the guys. They were my family too and I . . . I abandoned them. I wasn't ready to face them yet, so I agreed to do things O'Dea's way and hope that it pans out okay."

"You're angry at Killian," she murmured.

"No, I'm not. What was he supposed to do? Let me live in that apartment, feed me, clothe me, all for nothing? I was a stranger. He offered me an alternative to living on the streets and I accepted it. Now I'm here on a work visa instead of being kicked out of the country, I have travel insurance, a place to stay, and time to sort things out. In exchange for something that frankly scares the shit out of me. I'm not mad at him. I resent him a little," I huffed, "but I'm not mad. I'm just . . ."

"You're just . . . ?"

I shook my head, not sure how to finish the sentence.

"My brother will help you through this, Skylar, you have to know that." Autumn gave me big, sincere puppy eyes and I almost laughed. It was so obvious that she wanted me to like O'Dea. It became even more obvious when she continued, "He's highly competitive. Very ambitious. And I'm not blind to his faults. I know he can be ruthless. And cold. But our uncle, our upbringing, made him that way.

"Nothing was ever good enough and while I didn't care as long as I had Killian, my brother needed someone too. He was like a parent to me, so I've always had that kind of support and love in my life. But Killian lost his when our parents died. He didn't have someone older to protect and love him. His dad is a criminal who has spent more time in prison than out—he's currently behind bars—and my uncle . . .

"For the longest time, Killian wanted James to love him, to be there when life got hard. But when he realized that wasn't going to happen, Killian strove to prove something to him. He's brought more success to that label in the years he's worked there than the label has seen in its entire thirty years. Do you think my uncle acknowledges that? Never. And as much as I try to convince Killian otherwise, all that does is drive him to do better, to get that elusive pat on the shoulder.

"It's never coming." She looked desolate. "And I don't want my brother to lose himself trying."

"Like Sisyphus," I murmured, feeling bleak for O'Dea. "Rolling that damn boulder up a hill only for it to roll back down, an eternity of futility."

"Exactly. But in my brother's case, one of these days, that boulder is going to roll back down and flatten him."

Feeling as if a weight had been placed on my shoulders, I sighed heavily. "Why are you telling me this, Autumn? I doubt very much that O'Dea would be happy you've told me something so personal about him."

She drew to a stop outside a shoe store, strangers passing in my peripheral like blurs. She seemed to plead with me with her eyes. "You're right. Killian would be so angry at me, which is why I'm going to ask you not to repeat any of this. But I'm worried about you both. I'm worried what happens when the tabloids come knocking because we know they will, Skylar. I'm worried for you and for my brother. And I don't want you to hate him."

"I don't hate him."

"Not now, you don't," she said, sounding almost prophetic.

Confused, I shook my head. "Why? Why does it matter if I hate him?"

Autumn exhaled slowly, shakily. "Because he's not acting like himself. He hasn't been acting like himself for weeks."

Something fluttered in my chest. I didn't know if it was panic or something worse. Like excitement. "And you think that has something to do with me?"

With a little smirk of knowing, Autumn turned and began walking again. "The timing is interesting."

"We haven't spoken in days," I argued, but I did it knowing that deep down we hadn't spoken in days because we had connected that night in the apartment. I suspected that freaked O'Dea out. No wonder. It would be the height of stupidity to explore that connection.

"Busker Girl?" a familiar voice called out before Autumn could reply.

The voice drew my gaze to the entrance of Argyle Arcade. Sitting on her own, shivering in a hoodie and sleeping bag was Mandy.

I moved toward her without even thinking about it, ignoring Autumn's questioning voice as she followed me.

"Hey," I said softly, not hiding my accent. "How's it going?"

She grinned at me with those yellowing teeth. "Right as rain. So ye dropped the fake accent . . ." Her gaze flickered to Autumn and narrowed a little. "Got yerself a rich sponsor?"

"This is my friend." I knelt, looking around. "No Ham?"

"Nah. I gave him the heave-ho."

"I'm sorry."

"Don't be. It was time." She shivered, huddling into herself. "The man's gonnae kill himself. I dinnae want to be there when he does." Her eyes dropped to my cast. "What happened to ye, then?"

"Little prick tried to steal my guitar."

Her expression turned admonishing. "I always worried about ye, Busker Girl."

"You were right to. But I'm okay now."

"Good. One less thing to worry about." She coughed, deep and racking. It sounded like the chill had wrapped itself around her rib cage.

Feeling overwhelming sadness and concern for her, I stood and turned to Autumn who looked confused and distressed. "How much cash have you got?" I murmured under my breath.

"There's a cash machine," she whispered. "How much do you need?"

It was offered without hesitation. A wave of affection for this woman hit me so hard, it took me a minute to answer. "I'll pay you back," I promised.

"How much do you need?"

"A hundred?" I wanted to say more but I also didn't want to take advantage.

She nodded and walked away, and I turned back to Mandy. "How's life been treating you?"

Her eyes followed Autumn. "Who's the lassie? Bonnie thing. She could be a model." Envy soaked her words.

"She's a friend. A good one. Good person."

"Really?" Mandy turned back to look up at me. "Good-looking and good person dinnae usually go hand in hand."

"My, what a cynic you are."

"Aye, well," she cocked her head, assessing me, "ye're actually a bonnie girl too, now that ye've got some meat to you. And I know *you're* a good person."

"Am I?" I frowned. Because I'd deliberately not thought about the poor souls I'd left behind on the streets. It made me feel powerless on top of all the other emotions I was trying to manage.

"What? Bonnie, or a good person?" she teased.

I laughed. "I guess I'm neither."

"Modesty doesnae suit ye."

My grin felt forced. I was anxious for her and concerned she wouldn't take what I was about to offer.

Autumn came back to my side and turned into me so she was facing away from Mandy. She murmured, "Three hundred," and slipped the cash into my hand.

Surprised, I whipped my head around to look her in the eye. *Are you sure?*

She saw the question and nodded, squeezing my hand around the money.

Thank you.

I shrugged out of my coat, bending down to wrap it around Mandy. She smelled of stale sweat and bad breath, but I didn't flinch.

"What are ye doing?" she asked.

"Take it." I grabbed her hand with my good one and curled her fist around the money. "Three hundred," I whispered. "Get yourself into a hostel. And now that you're away from Ham, get yourself to Shelter Scotland or to someone who can help you find your feet, Mandy."

I moved to pull my hand away but she grabbed onto me. "Good person," she declared.

Tears burned in my eyes and I pulled back abruptly, standing, trying not to shiver now that I had no coat. "Take care of yourself."

She slipped her arms into my coat, grinning. "*You* worry about yerself, Busker Girl. I'll be all right."

I waved as Autumn and I walked away. My friend—and I decided she most definitely was my friend—put her arm around my shoulders and declared, "We need to get you a bloody coat, pronto."

WE WERE IN A STORE where I was trying on a lovely and very stylish wool coat when Autumn's cell rang.

"It's Killian," she said before answering. "Hey, big bro. What's up?" She eyed me, giving me a thumbs-up as I turned to let her see the coat from all sides. "Coat shopping. Skylar gave hers away to a homeless person . . . yes." She grinned. "I did say that . . . Someone she knew . . . Well, she was homeless for a while, Killian, it isn't shocking she made some friends."

I laughed under my breath, slipping out of the coat to try another on.

"Because she was cold . . . I know that means now *Skylar* is cold, that's why we're buying her a replacement coat."

I threw her an amused grin at the sound of laughter in her words.

"She was cold for less than five minutes . . . I can send you a photo to prove she's perfectly okay, if that will help? . . . No, I'm not taking the piss out of you . . . No . . . fine . . . Killian, why are you calling?"

I studied myself in a nearby mirror and made a face at my reflection. When I looked over at Autumn, she was shaking her head too. I studied it in the mirror. It made me look like I was dressing up in my mother's clothes.

"Really?"

Something about the seriousness of her tone drew my gaze back to her.

"When? . . . Okay, I'll let her know . . . Bye." She hung up and stared at me in so much concern my mind began to whir with questions. Had someone found out about me? Did the guys know where I was? Did the press? "What's going on?"

"Killian's lawyer called. They found the boys who attacked you. The police need you to come in and ID them."

I felt a weird mixture of relief and anger. Relief because my location was apparently still a mystery to the outside world but anger because I didn't want to have to face those boys again, especially Johnny. But I knew I had to. "When?"

"Killian's texting me the number you've to call. They'll give you the details."

For some stupid reason, I felt hurt that Killian hadn't called me himself. Clearly, he had no intention of being there for me for anything personal anymore. I knew that it was the smart thing for him to do but . . .

No, never mind. No buts.

"Okay." I blew out a breath. "Guess I better buy a coat."

"I liked the wool one," she offered, gently tugging at the one I was currently wearing. "This is a no."

"I'm going to pay you back. For everything," I assured her as I shrugged out of it.

"It's all out of the company credit card," she replied. "So you don't have to. I know accessing your money means letting certain people know where you are."

We grabbed the coat we'd both liked and walked to the till to pay for it. As we stood at the cash desk, waiting to be served, I said, "If I haven't told you before, I'm really glad I met you, Autumn O'Dea."

She grinned, nudging me with her shoulder, "Back at ya, Finch."

fifteen

Officer Calton asked me to meet her at the police station the next day where they were holding the boys before officially charging them.

Without needing to ask, Autumn guessed I might want some company while facing the kid who tried to rape me. As crazy as my life had been these last few weeks, it had been a good thing because I really didn't have much time to dwell on the attack in the cemetery. Of course, the cast did its best to be a constant reminder, and there were moments when I closed my eyes at night and I could still feel the weight of Johnny's body bearing down on me. When I was feeling particularly grim, I couldn't help but imagine what might have happened if his friend hadn't saved me.

I'd been one of the lucky ones. I eyed my cast, grateful that my worst wounds from the attack were physical. Although I was still carrying around a hefty amount of anger.

The door to the apartment opened that morning and I stood, ready to go. I frowned as I listened to the footsteps walking down the hall. They were too heavy for Autumn.

O'Dea appeared in the doorway, wearing a black double-breasted wool coat. He had a black scarf tucked into it like a cravat and was holding leather gloves.

I sucked in a breath, resenting the flutter in my lower belly.

"What are you doing here?"

His eyes roamed over me, too long, too intense, until I felt myself squirm. I was wearing indigo bootleg jeans, my new fitted blue wool coat, and heeled boots that Autumn decided I had to have. The only mar on what I thought was a pretty nice outfit was my cast. "O'Dea."

He stepped closer, those dark eyes focused on my face. "You've put on weight."

I had.

Brenna had been weighing me every week for the past month. My BMI was healthy again and to my everlasting relief, I got my period two days ago.

"That was the plan," I answered dryly.

"Good."

Good? That was it? Okay. I guess it was "good." Exasperated, I sighed. "What are you doing here, O'Dea?"

He scowled. "Taking you to the station. I thought that was obvious."

"I thought Autumn was taking me." I grabbed my purse and keys from the side table, brushing by him, pretending not to notice the clean smell of soap and a hint of spicy aftershave, or what it made me feel. He smelled good—who cared?

O'Dea followed. "Well, I'm taking you. Problem?"

"Nope."

It felt like a problem once we were stuck in the elevator though. Awkwardness that hadn't been there between us before made me shift from one foot to the other in discomfort.

"I guess you're mad at me for some reason?"

I threw him a befuddled look. "I am?"

He threw back that bland stare of his, like nothing I did affected him. "Last time we spoke, I'd graduated to Killian. Now I'm back to O'Dea. And now the silent treatment."

Hating his perceptiveness, I made a face. "I have no idea what you're talking about. And I'm not giving you the silent treatment. I'm nervous because I'm about to face the boy who tried to rape me and the one who stole my goddamned guitar."

O'Dea flinched at the word "rape" and then his expression turned hard. "You'll get your guitar back."

"He sold it," I said bitterly. Officer Calton had told me the boy they'd picked up was called Douglas Inch and they hadn't found the guitar in his possession. The obvious conclusion was that the little shit had sold it.

"We'll get it back."

I didn't share his out-of-character optimism, so I said nothing.

He opened his car door for me and I got in, murmuring thanks as he gently closed it. When he got in on the driver's side, however, he slammed his.

"Problem?"

He cut me an impatient look and I felt a little gleeful that it had taken me less than a minute to wipe out his blank countenance. "You tell me."

"O'Dea, I'm not mad at you. Why would I be mad at you?"

"Because I've been busy with work lately."

"Well, how sane of me to be mad at you for working hard."

His lips twitched at my sarcasm. "So . . . you're not mad?"

"Like I said . . . I'm . . . I'm just a little nervous."

"They can't touch you. They won't even know you're there when you ID them."

I nodded, but that didn't make me feel any better.

The ride to the station was quiet, but this time O'Dea didn't hold it against me. Officer Calton came out to greet us when we arrived.

"I didn't want to say this on the phone, but we actually only have Douglas Inch here at the station. Jonathan Welsh is currently in the hospital. You'll have to ID him from a photograph."

I frowned in confusion. "What is he doing in the hospital?"

"Both boys had been attacked when we picked them up. Mr. Inch's injuries were minor but Welsh's were considerable. He's got a broken femur, collarbone, and a few broken ribs."

"What happened?"

Calton shrugged, like we were talking about afternoon tea and not serious assault. "This isn't their first offense. They've been in and out of juvie for years. And word is that they got on the wrong side of the McCrurys."

"The who?"

"Well-known Glasgow gang," O'Dea answered for her.

"Oh." The vengeful part of me was glad. Karma *was* a bitch after all.

"This way," Calton said, and we followed her into a barren office. She rounded a desk and opened a folder, pushing it toward me.

I turned it around and found myself staring at a photograph of Johnny.

"Johnny, let's go."

"No before I teach this bitch a lesson."

I flinched, hearing my breath shudder as I remembered clawing the ground to get away from him.

"Miss Finch?"

Suddenly O'Dea was beside me, his arm pressed against mine. I looked up at him and this time, he wasn't hiding his emotions.

Concern and anger seethed in his dark eyes. "Skylar?"

I nodded. "It's him."

"To clarify, Miss Finch," Calton said, drawing my gaze reluctantly back to hers. "You're identifying Jonathan Welsh as the man who attempted to rape you."

"Yes." Then I let myself think about something I hadn't allowed myself to before because it scared me too much. "Does this mean it will go to trial?"

That the world would find out?

"If he pleads guilty, it won't go to trial. But his defense might talk him into a trial. There is evidence but not so much that a defense lawyer might not chance his arm in court. You know you can ask your lawyer about all this."

"Yes," Killian stated. "I mean, *we* already did."

We had? Obviously, Killian had thought to ask his lawyer, but I hadn't. I'd been too busy recovering and adjusting to my new life to really think about it. All I'd wanted was justice. I hadn't wanted to dwell on how I'd get it.

My mind whirred. What a mess. I felt numb as she took us to a room with a two-way mirror and they brought in Douglas Inch.

I didn't know what I expected to feel when I saw him. He had bad bruising on his left cheek and eye and a split lip, but otherwise he was intact. I felt a bizarre mixture of gratitude and fury toward him. "That's him." I looked at Calton as she nodded. "I don't think he's a bad kid, you know. Just a moron."

"Agreed." She nodded. "We'll see if we can get him to fess up, find that guitar of yours."

"That would be appreciated." I felt a little shaky and light-headed, like my blood sugar had dropped. "We done?"

"We'll be in touch."

As soon as we got outside the police station, I leaned against the wall for support, sucking in air like there had been none inside.

I felt O'Dea's hand on my back. "Skylar?" He sounded worried.

I waved away his worry with my good hand.

His hand pressed deeper. "There won't be a trial," he murmured in my ear. "I'll make sure of it."

Confused, I looked at him, my breath stuttering at finding his face so close to mine. "What do you mean?" I whispered.

Determination hardened his gaze. "It *won't* go to trial. I know people who can be very convincing when they want to be."

"I don't understand."

"You don't need to." He surprised me further by grabbing my hand and leading me back to his car. "You just need to know that I won't let this situation become a public media circus for you."

"You know what's freaking me out?" I said as he opened the door for me.

"What?"

I met his gaze. "I believe you."

sixteen

A few days later, after being shadowed by Autumn almost twenty-four/seven since that day at the police station, I took a walk along the River Clyde on my own. It was mid-October now, the air was brisk, crisp and fresh, and filled my lungs in a way that made me feel a little light-headed. But in a good way.

All wrapped up, I didn't mind the cold. It got as cold as this back in Billings at this time of year.

I meandered down the street along the riverbank, ignoring the itch in my cast. The irritation was getting increasingly worse, which meant it was healing. It didn't hurt anymore, not unless I accidentally put too much pressure on it. The cast was due to come off in two days and I couldn't wait.

My curiosity compelled me to take a fifteen-minute walk down Stobcross Road to the building that housed Skyscraper Records. The name had its obvious imagery but the building was nowhere near as tall as a skyscraper, only moderately tall and made entirely of glass. It looked like it housed more than Skyscraper Records. There were a few company names etched on the side of the large entrance door.

I hadn't ventured down this way before, afraid of bumping into O'Dea, so I hadn't realized how close the label was to the Hydro. The sight of it in the distance felt like a spear through my memories. I wrapped my arms around myself, shivering but not from the cold, as I remembered the last time my band played at Glasgow's busiest event venue . . .

Glasgow, 2014
SSE Hydro

There is nothing quite like the feeling of thousands of fans singing your lyrics back to you. Sometimes it felt so big, I thought my chest might explode.

I wished it was only this for us.

Standing on a massive stage, staring out into a huge arena, I was sweat-soaked, adrenaline coursing through my body. Our light show made it hard to see anything but a sea of figures in front of me, and up on the seated stands I could see the shadow of thousands of them. It still blew my mind that all these people had come to hear us play.

The first time we played Glasgow, we'd played The Barrowland. We'd all been psyched but extremely nervous to play the renowned Barrowland Ballroom where so many legendary rock bands had played. The Barras, that's what the locals called it. Just to play Glasgow, the city of music, was amazing. It had been so special.

But now we were selling out *arenas* in Glasgow.

Epic.

And I wished as I sang my heart out with the crowd, striding from one end of the stage to the next, that all the other shit would disappear because *this* was what made me happy.

"Well, you turn my insides and make them outsides,
You string out my bones like bunting.
Splatter my heart and call it art,
And art is meant for the world to see.
Public property with an admission fee."

They sang my song of hatred of the paparazzi back at me with as much ferocity as I sang it to them. There were moments, only ever offstage, where I resented our fans. If it weren't for the phenomenon they'd swept us up into, the tabloids wouldn't care what the hell we did with our lives. But because the fans cared, the tabloids knew we'd sell magazines and bring them those online hits they wanted.

The funny thing was that every time I sang this song, one of our biggest-selling singles to date, the fans sang it back to me like they cared how much I hurt. And any resentment I felt melted away.

The thrum of the music vibrated through me as I ended the song on its huge note. My chest heaved with breathlessness as the amps' growls died out and the cheers from the crowd came at us like a windblast. Their shouts and whistles, the clapping and stamping of their feet became a heartbeat that found rhythm with mine.

"Thank you, Glasgow!" I yelled into the mic. "You guys are the best fans in the world. We love visiting this beautiful city. I don't know if we've ever been any place where music is as appreciated as it is here."

They cheered harder like I knew they would and I grinned, wiping sweat from my forehead. "We've got one last song for you and then I'm sorry to say we have to go." The crowd screamed harder at the lie. We were traditionalists and they knew it. We'd finish up, leave the stage, and then at their pounding demand, come back on for our encore.

The lights had dimmed behind me so the stagehand who came

out with a stool could barely be seen. When he was gone, a spotlight lit the stool he'd set center stage for me. My Taylor leaned against it, plugged into the amp. And the mic stand was now in front of it.

"Well, guys, we're going to say goodbye the only way we know how." I put the mic onto the stand, slipped onto the stool, grabbed my guitar, and did it all unable to look at Micah.

I'd been dreading this song since we'd walked onstage tonight.

We'd been having a good day. The guys and I were exhausted because this was the end of our European tour, but we'd decided to head out and take photos in Glasgow for our social media pages. It was a fun day.

Until a new headline hit the tabloids.

Someone had snapped a photo of me and Jay Preston kissing outside a bar in Berlin a few nights ago. Jay was the drummer of a Canadian rock band and we'd both been playing the city at the same time, different venues. Our bands met in a bar and while Micah got drunk and left with some groupie, I'd gotten drunk and left with Jay.

I hadn't expected anyone would find out about it, but once again there I was, plastered all over the internet.

Our fans had viciously attacked me on Instagram for breaking Micah's heart again. They did the same to him anytime he was photographed with another girl.

I'd worried that when we stepped onstage that night, there might be some shouts about it from the crowds, but the incident didn't exist for them.

Unfortunately, the incident existed for Micah.

He'd gone quiet when we were out doing tourist stuff and I was grateful for the sullen response, and for the fans who stopped us on the street for photos and autographs, making it even harder for him to say anything to me about it.

But then I got back to my hotel room and hadn't even been

in there five minutes when I heard the knock on the door. It was Micah. And he was pissed.

I could still hear him shouting at me, tears in his eyes. "Jay Preston! Jay fucking Preston?"

It was so unfair. He did this every time. He could go off with groupies and I didn't say a word, I suffered in silence, but God forbid I let another man touch me.

Micah was born in the wrong goddamned century.

"I hate you!" he raged, shaking his hands like he wanted to wrap them around my throat. "I hate that you do this to me!"

"Me to you? What about your groupies, Micah?" I'd said, trying to stay calm. I never wanted to be that rock star who screamed like a banshee in her hotel room and caused scenes. "You whore yourself out all the time. I don't. That doesn't mean I don't *need* someone sometimes."

"I'm right here." He pounded his chest breathlessly. "Take me. I'm all yours."

"Until you decide I've hurt your feelings and you go stick it in someone else to spite me."

His face mottled with frustration. "How many times do I have to explain? If I'd known you were coming to work things out, I never would have been with her. I can't even remember her fucking—"

The door to my hotel room blew open, cutting him off. Gayle waved a keycard as she glared at Micah. Austin and Brandon were right behind her. "The entire hotel can hear you."

"Come on." Austin grabbed Micah's arm.

"We're talking." Micah shook him off.

"I swear to God, man, you better let him walk you out of here because if you don't, I'm going to fucking beat that pretty face to a pulp," Brandon warned.

Micah lifted his chin defiantly. "Try it."

"You think I won't." Brandon strode over to him. Our drummer was a big guy and although they'd never gotten into a serious physical fight before, he'd easily subdued Micah on the rare occasion our guitarist got a little aggressive when drunk. Brandon cut me a worried look before turning back to Micah. The anger slammed back down over his expression. "I hear you come at her like that again and I will fucking end you. You hear me?"

Micah's head whipped back like Brandon had actually hit him. "I would never hurt her."

Brandon snorted. "You do it all the time. And if you're not careful, it's going to rip this band apart. Now get out of Skylar's room before I physically remove you from it. And I swear to God, man, stay out of her business. She gets enough shit from the press and the fans. She doesn't need your immature ass in her face about it too."

"You need to stay out of this," Micah warned.

"Enough." Gayle sighed, crossing her arms over her chest. "Is this what it's like when I'm not here?"

Austin shook his head. "No, we're fine. It's just been one of those days."

"Well, I'm officially worried."

"Don't be." Micah shrugged off Austin's grip. "We're fine." He stormed out of my room without looking back at me.

Brandon rubbed my shoulder affectionately. "You okay?"

I was shaken but what was new? "I'll be fine."

But I wasn't. These days I never was. And now I had to finish our set, like always, with the love song that I'd written about Micah. A love song he knew I'd written about him.

It was also the only song the band didn't play with me. I did it solo.

I took a shaky breath, exhaled, and strummed the opening chords.

"Under my bed there's a box
Filled with these things
My heart has saved.
A photograph of a young man,
Wearing green and a face of the brave.

"And beneath that there's
A case my mother bought
That she couldn't afford.
Inside, a CD of a song
That made me realize what I was meant for.

"Somehow one day, one rainy day,
This boy found himself in that box.
Somehow one day, one rainy day,
He smiled his way into my thoughts.

"I think of those moments I've kept
Hidden and safe
Beneath my old bed.
And wonder if you ever knew
They say all the things
My mouth never said.

"Somehow one day, one rainy day,
I fell for a smile I can't have.
And yesterday, yesterday we found,
We found ourselves on different paths.

"Under my bed there's a box
Filled with these things

My heart has saved.
And even though we said goodbye
I can't help but keep hold to my faith.

"That out there on some rainy day,
In some other time,
On some other plane.
Our love is waiting for us,
To give us a chance without all this pain.

"Somehow one day, one rainy day,
A girl and a boy will collide.
But this time, this time they'll stay
Tied as they brave the landslide."

There was an unexpected hush as the last chord sang from my guitar, but then I felt him.

I turned my head from the mic, confusion furrowing my brow at the sight of Micah standing guitarless by the stool. This wasn't part of our show.

I opened my mouth to say his name but it turned into a gasp as he clasped my face in his hands and bent down to crush his mouth over mine.

The arena filled with the deafening boom of screams and catcalls as he kissed me with passion. But I knew those kisses. I'd tasted them before. They were Micah's angry kisses.

And all I could think, all I could fear, was how this was going to be all over entertainment news tomorrow. I couldn't push him off or get mad at him in front of the fans because it would only make things worse.

Instead I let him kiss me. When he finally let me up for air, he didn't let go of my face. He had this smug, triumphant gleam in his eyes that fought with the anger. "Thanks for the reminder."

I put my hand over the mic so the crowd couldn't hear. "What reminder?"

"That no matter how many morons you fuck, you'll always be mine." He kissed my forehead, setting the crowd off even harder, and I swear it took everything in me not to throw my beloved Taylor at his back as he walked offstage.

I fought for composure, turning to the crowd with a shaky smile. Sliding the mic into the stand, I slipped off the stool. "That's all from us tonight, Glasgow. We'll see you soon!"

The yells that accompanied us offstage were different. They were even more explosive, fueled by Micah's little performance. I met Brandon's gaze as we walked offstage and he appeared ready to murder Micah.

"You okay?"

I shook my head. "Let me deal with it."

"What the hell was that?" Gayle cried as we gathered in the wings, the thrum of the crowd growing more frenzied. "Is this something that's been added to the show that I didn't know about?"

I bet our manager was glad she'd decided to join us for the last leg of our European tour. She was going to be even happier when she heard what I had to say.

I glowered at Micah who stared back at me defiantly. "What the fuck was that?"

He shrugged. "Giving them a show."

"Do you realize that you've stirred all that tabloid shit up even worse?" I yelled to be heard. "Do you even care?"

"Look, we need to get back out there," Austin interrupted.

"Yeah, we do. And now thanks to this idiot, I have to go out there and pretend that I don't want to rip his face off!"

"Oh, come on, Skylar, it was just a kiss!" he yelled.

Brandon moved toward him but I clamped my hand on his arm to stop him. I stepped forward with deathly seriousness. "I am not yours. I don't belong to you."

"Tell yourself whatever you need to hear." His eyes burned in anguish. "But we both know the truth, and being apart is ridiculous bullshit!"

"No, it's my choice. And you know what else is my choice? Whether I stay with this band or not."

"Wait, what?" Gayle looked panicked.

"Yeah, you heard me. You sort out your shit, Micah, or I walk."

Everyone stared at each other.

"Guys, you need to get back out there!" the stage manager shouted.

"Well?"

"Fine!" Micah bullied past me and stormed up the stage steps.

I shared an exhausted look with the boys and we hurried after him.

As soon as I hit those lights, I plastered on a big smile and waved for the crowd. We immediately broke into the song that had exploded us into the stratosphere when it became the lead song on the soundtrack to a huge teen dystopian movie. Usually when I sang it, I plugged into how I felt sitting in the movies that first time, hearing our song on the end credits of a box-office hit. It was the kind of moment I clung to, to remind myself there were moments where all the stuff I hated about my life seemed almost worth it.

That night I could barely focus on the lyrics, let alone that feeling.

I got through it, trying not to buckle under the weight of failure. Not only did I hate this life I was so sure I'd wanted, but I was failing at it. Because of a toxic teen romance. We were a fucking cliché.

The relief was unreal as I walked off that stage. I shot past everyone, heading straight for my dressing room.

It hadn't even closed behind me when it burst open and Micah stormed in.

"Are you kidding me with this?" I hissed.

"I'm only here to say one thing. Don't threaten the band because of us. It's an empty threat."

"Meaning?"

"You would never quit the band because it isn't in you to give up." His expression softened. "It's one of the things I admire most about you."

I shook my head, feeling an overwhelming sadness embrace me. "I might give up. If it begins to hurt too much."

Micah immediately looked ashamed. "I fucked up," he whispered. "Again. I . . . I get stuck in my own head and I don't think. I didn't think. I . . . I pissed all over you like a big dumb dog. And I messed up."

I nodded, my anger softening at his apology. "You promise this is behind us? That this won't happen again?"

After a moment's hesitation, he nodded and turned to leave. But then he had to look back over his shoulder at me. "I'll never stop loving you, even if you never stop punishing me for that night."

As soon as he walked out, my whole body sagged. I slid down the wall, pulling my knees into my chest. My head buzzed like always with the sound of the crowd. I went to bed after gigs and that's all I could hear as physical exhaustion drove me into sleep. Sometimes the crowd was all I could hear when I woke up the next morning too.

And now, whispering through the chaotic hum of the crowd, I could hear Micah's whisper repeating over and over, "I'll never stop loving you. I'll never stop loving you. I'll never stop loving you."

The messed-up thing was, as much as it hurt, I knew it would hurt worse if he ever actually did stop loving me.

I wanted to call my mom and tell her all about it. But then I'd remembered the time she sold her car and bought this cheap little thing that kept breaking down and making her late for work. And she did that so she could pay for me and Micah to go to California with the band for this spotlight competition we auditioned for. We got to play for a real label. We were only fifteen.

We didn't win a record contract.

But she never stopped having faith. Brandon's parents were so mad about it, they sold his drums and said we couldn't practice in his basement anymore.

So my mom worked overtime for three months while we all got part-time jobs after school. And between us and Mom, we saved enough to buy new drums for Brandon. She also stopped parking her crappy car in the garage and let us soundproof it so we'd have a place to practice.

I remembered her yelling at Bryan that he could pack his stuff and leave if he wasn't prepared to support me. He did leave. She cried for days. I didn't like the guy, but I was never so relieved as I was when he came back.

Still, she'd almost lost the one man she'd fallen for since my dad died, and it would've been my fault.

Every hardship, every month we struggled to pay the bills, it was because of me.

All our conversations, our planning, my guitar and singing lessons, everything was about me.

About my dream.

Three years of struggle because I wanted to be the lead singer in a professional rock band.

And we did it.

Only for me to no longer want it.

How could I tell her that? And how could we talk now without her realizing that I was miserable? This was my mom, my best friend. She'd know. She'd *know*.

Worse still, she had a good life now. I bought her a beautiful big house, an SUV, she had no mortgage, and a monthly stipend I paid into her account. I had plenty of money and a great financial adviser that invested it, but I knew my mom . . . if I left the band, she'd go back to worrying about money.

I didn't want that for her.

I didn't want Bryan to say "I told you so" and for her to have to hide the disappointment she felt at my failure.

And then there was Micah. I'd sacrificed our love for our band and now we were so messed up, there was no fixing us. I *couldn't* hate this life after choosing it over him.

It was too much. I wasn't thinking clearly, I—

The door to my dressing room opened and Gayle poked her head in. She frowned at the sight of me on the floor and stepped in, closing the door behind her. "I'm worried, Skylar. What's going on? What do you need?"

"I need a break," I blurted. "I need to be alone for a while."

"Where do you want to go?" She pulled her phone out.

"Somewhere quiet. Secluded."

"And that's all you need?"

I felt her anxiety and hurried to assure her. "I'm not leaving the band, Gayle. I just need a break."

A break would help. I'd feel better after time apart from the guys.

But the next morning as my phone exploded with notifications, including missed call after missed call from my mom, I knew a break wouldn't help. My anger toward Micah was building and building as I stared at the multiple photos, taken from different angles, of him kissing me on stage. They were all over the internet. The fans loved it.

I stared at one particular shot, taken from someone close to the stage.

It looked like something from a movie. Micah kissed me with so much longing that an ache for him pierced my lividness.

But only momentarily.

Because it might look like a kiss of pure longing, but I'd tasted it. Tasted his petty wrath and immaturity in that kiss.

And I wondered what this life we'd chosen would be like if Micah and I could break this toxic bond between us.

Then I hightailed it to a summerhouse in Norway, hoping some space would make me feel less crazy about everything.

Glasgow, Scotland
Present day

I GLANCED AWAY FROM THE Hydro, from the memories there. Just a few weeks after hiding out in Norway, I'd returned home to my mom and had that stupid argument with her only for her creepy husband to come on to me.

Instead of the guilt I usually felt, anger suffused me.

I never saw it coming. Not once had Bryan ever made overtures toward me. Looking back, I remember he'd compliment me more than he used to but I thought he was being a douchey sycophant.

It was his fault I felt this guilt. He'd put me in the untenable position of either having to break my mother's heart and gain her anger, or keep the secret from her. I chose wrong.

The secret tore us apart anyway.

"'Oh, I wish that I had told you, all the truths locked inside me, instead of cutting you out, like a knife through our lives,'" I sang softly under my breath. Tears burned in my eyes.

There was no going back, I realized.

All these months of hiding, some crazy part of me held onto some hope that I could go back and fix everything. But I couldn't. She was gone and there would never be any closure. The only way to get through that, I thought, sucking in a shuddering breath, was to believe with every bit of light left within me that my mom died knowing I loved her. That I loved her the best. Always.

Tears fell slowly down my cheeks and I let them. I had months of tears locked inside me. I would no longer be afraid of releasing them.

Bracing my head down and into the wind, I walked slowly back toward my apartment. I knew it wasn't really my apartment but rather a haven. A place where I think I was finally ready to heal.

seventeen

As soon as I let myself into the apartment, I knew someone was there.

I froze at the threshold. "O'Dea?" I called.

"In here," his deep voice rumbled from the front of the apartment.

Relaxing, I closed the door behind me and wandered down the hall to find him. His coat and scarf lay draped over the couch and he was standing in the kitchen drinking coffee.

"What are you doing here?" My eyes landed on the guitar case lying on the island and my heart sped up. "Is that . . . ?"

O'Dea studied me as he put his coffee mug down. "The police returned it. They wanted to release it to you but I convinced Calton you didn't need to make another trip to the station."

A well of emotion churned deep in my gut as I walked over to the case. My hand trembled as I took my time unlatching one side, then the other. And then my breath faltered as I opened it and found my Taylor lying inside, right where I'd left it. Grasping the neck, I lifted it out carefully. O'Dea saw me struggling to turn it one-handed for inspection and stepped in to help me. I took in every inch of it as he held it up for me.

There wasn't a scratch on it.

I focused on the personalization etched on the back along the curve of the body.

"Music is the outburst of the soul" and your soul is beautiful, my darling. Love you always, Mom.

And it hit me with the force of a car knocking me off my feet. She had known. When my words failed me, my music spoke, and it told her everything she needed to know.

She'd known I was unhappy and all she'd wanted was for me to say it out loud so she could help me. I *knew* it.

I could feel my throat closing with the need to keep the mass of emotion inside of me from exploding out in front of O'Dea. I didn't want to have a meltdown in front of him.

"I need a minute," I managed to whisper and hurried into the bedroom.

My body shuddered as I tried to lock the feelings down. I'd made the decision to let all the tears out whenever they wanted but not here, not in front of him.

"Music is the outburst of the soul" and your soul is beautiful, my darling. Love you always, Mom.

No, no, no, no! I squeezed my arms around myself but I couldn't stop it. The sob got past my throat but I clamped my mouth shut, holding it in.

My heart was pounding so hard, the blood whooshing in my ears deafened me. That's why I didn't hear the door open and nearly jumped out of my skin at the touch of O'Dea's hand on my shoulder. I whirled around, taking in his unsure, uncomfortable expression.

"I'm okay," I said, sounding *not* okay at all. "I'm okay, I'm okay." My voice grew shakier and shakier with each claim and I felt it coming again. *God, get out, leave me!* I wanted to scream. "Please, I'm o—" but I wasn't okay.

She would have forgiven me. I knew it.

My mom would have forgiven me, so why couldn't I forgive myself?

The sobs racked my body. I couldn't hold them off any longer.

"Fuck, Skylar," I heard O'Dea whisper.

I held up my hand to ward him off, but he gently knocked it out of the way and then my cheek was pressed to his hard, warm chest. His strong arms bound tight around me.

It was permission to let go.

So I did.

I cried, wrapped up in his strength, wondering if the tears would ever stop now that I'd *really* let them loose.

IT WAS BECOMING FAMILIAR TO wake up in bed momentarily confused about how I'd gotten there. It was still light out, daylight streaming in through the open curtains.

The last thing I remembered was sobbing in Killian's arms.

Ah, shit.

He was Killian again.

Why did he have to be such a complicated asshole? *Just pick a personality*, I grumbled to myself as I got up and wandered into the bathroom.

My face was splotchy and my eyes swollen from crying so hard. Using my good hand, I splashed water on my face, not caring about my makeup since it had already bled off with the tears.

Feeling exhausted from my emotional release, I wandered back out into the living area, stumbling to a stop at the sight of Killian sitting on the couch, typing something on his phone.

I'd expected to be alone.

"You're up," he said, his eyes assessing if I was going to have another meltdown.

"Yeah." I looked away, embarrassed. The clock on the oven told me I'd only been out for an hour or so. "Coffee?" I asked, shuffling into the kitchen.

"Aye, sure." He got up and slid onto the stool across from me as I set up the coffee machine. Keeping my back to him was rude after his kindness, so I turned around and met his gaze.

"You're still here?"

He shrugged. "Wanted to make sure you were okay."

I frowned. "You're not going to try to put me in therapy, are you?"

"Depends. Do you think you need it?"

I sighed. Heavily. "Killian . . ."

He tensed at his name and something I didn't quite understand flickered in his gaze before he banished it.

"I . . . I'm dealing with things my own way. I'm getting there. I actually think my music got there before I did."

Killian nodded like he understood. "'Music is an outburst of the soul.' Frederick Delius."

"Mom knew it was one of my favorite quotes."

"And very true."

"Yeah."

"*Are* you okay?"

I gave him a weary smile. "I've decided I'm going to try to forgive myself for not telling her about how I felt about the band and about what happened with Bryan. I know that she would've forgiven me. That's who she was. That's why I adored her."

"And her . . . her death?" he asked.

The quiet rage that lived in me simmered. "I don't think there's ever a way to get over that. If it had been an illness or an accident, I might have been able to one day. But they shot her in the head because she had the audacity to wake up while they were robbing her. My mom was murdered. She and her husband were *murdered.*" My voice cracked on the word. "And the people who did it have not been brought to justice and I don't know if they ever will be. I think I just have to . . ." I sucked in a shuddering breath. "I have to learn to live with that anger. Find a way to manage it. I can't let them ruin my life like they ruined hers."

Killian eyes gleamed with empathy. "I think you're right." The coffee machine beeped. When I handed him a mug and raised mine to take a sip, he asked, "And the band?"

I knew what he was asking. Was I ready to face them? Face the world? "Today was a big day. I feel like I've been walking around with this giant knot in my stomach and today it got a little smaller. Let's just go with that for now."

He was silent while he processed and then finally said, "Take all the time you need."

We were quiet as we sipped our coffees. My Taylor was now propped against the wall at the couch, the guitar case closed beside it. I stared at it lovingly. "Killian."

"Yes?"

"Thank you."

When I got no response, I pried my gaze off my guitar. My breath caught at the softness that warmed his dark eyes. God, I could drown in his eyes when he looked at me like that. They made my already tired limbs feel like jelly.

"You're going to be okay, Skylar," he pronounced. And he said it like he really meant it.

And for the first time in two years, I believed I might be.

THE BUZZING OF THE CAST saw was unpleasant to say the least. I kept trying not to flinch, worried the doctor was going to cut my damn wrist off, even though I knew that wouldn't happen. Finally, the doctor was done and she left to see to another patient while the nurse took a pair of scissors to cut through the padding. He told me I could slip my arm out.

Killian stood off to my side. I shot him a look, nervous about the state of my wrist and how long it was going to take until I could get my guitar back in my hands. He looked emotionless and stoic as he gave me a nod of encouragement, but I was starting to realize that was his mask for the rest of the world. Like being homeless had been mine.

I sucked in a breath, nodded back, and then turned to look at my wrist as I gingerly slipped out my hand. I wrinkled my nose at the sight. It smelled. Yuck. And it looked tiny and damaged.

When I tried to bend it, it stiffly refused. "What the . . . ?" I glared up at the nurse like it was his fault.

He gave me a patient smile. "The doctor told ye it would take time for the stiffness to ease."

I frowned.

Killian seemed to read my impatient mind. "Give it time."

"And the way it looks?" I didn't want to draw attention to the smell by asking about that.

"Yer wrist has been inactive for weeks. It'll get back to normal over time. Don't scrub at it to clean it." The nurse addressed the smell for me so I guessed that was normal. "All the skin we shed that we don't ever see or think about has gotten trapped in yer cast and on yer skin this past month. I know ye'll want to scrub it clean but the skin is very sensitive at the moment. Take a warm shower and the extra skin will slowly come off."

I looked up at Killian. "I've never felt sexier than I do right now."

As if he couldn't help himself, he flashed me a rare grin, and suddenly I couldn't give a shit about my gross wrist.

When I turned back to the nurse, he was grinning at me too. "I can give it a little clean with a baby wipe now, if ye'd like?"

"Oh, I'd like. While you're at it, you could put the cast back on so I don't scare your other patients with my zombie wrist?"

He chuckled and rolled his stool across the room to look through a drawer. He returned with the baby wipes and took my hand to give it a gentle clean. My fingers tingled to life and I felt a keen urge to make the wrist move. I wanted to play my Taylor. These past two days I'd been eyeing it like I was starving and it was a giant, juicy chicken wing.

It was such a relief to have it home with me again.

"All done." The nurse dropped the baby wipes in a nearby bin as he held onto my hand and gave me a reassuring smile. "Ye'll be zombie-wrist no more before ye know it."

I extricated my hand from his. "Well, thanks to you and the doc for trying your best not to make cutting into my wrist with a saw any scarier than it had to be."

"Ye're welcome." He reached for me as I moved to push up off the hospital bed. "Careful with that wrist."

"I've got her." Killian held my arm as he stared at the nurse, his expression unyielding and the nurse's bemused. The nurse hesitated and then removed his hand from my arm and stepped back.

"Thanks again." I grabbed my purse with my good hand as Killian led me out of the room.

Staring at my unsightly wrist, I wrinkled my nose. "I need a shower."

"Now?"

"Yeah. That a problem?"

He seemed perturbed. "I was planning on taking you to the

label today."

Suddenly all the good, girly feelings I was experiencing fled. Reality hit. "Oh. Big day for me, huh."

Before my appointment at the hospital, Killian's lawyer called to say the boys had confessed to attacking me and stealing the guitar. Douglas Inch was pleading guilty to theft, and Jonathan Welsh was pleading guilty to assault and attempted sexual assault, which meant there would be no trial. Killian's lawyer would be in touch to let us know what sentence they got. It was a relief to know there was going to be justice without me having to face a trial, but it was a lot to digest.

Then my cast came off.

And now Killian wanted me at the label.

"If it's too much . . . ?"

No, no, it wasn't. It was exactly the splash of cold reality I needed. Killian and I . . . yes, I knew that we had become friends. There was no denying that. But he was also the guy railroading my future.

Suffice it to say my feelings for him were extremely complicated.

"No, that sounds fine. I *would* like to shower first though." We approached his Range Rover.

"Okay, we'll stop at the apartment. Maybe we should grab some lunch?" He pulled open the passenger door for me and held my elbow as I tentatively placed my weight on my wrist by gripping the inside door handle. I stopped, wincing at the stiffness, and then I bore down on the seat with my good hand and slid into the car. Killian smirked at my furrowed brow. "Give it time."

"Say that to me again and I'm going to find violent ways to work out the stiffness in my wrist."

The bastard hesitated and I saw the flicker of the devil in his eyes. He'd had a dirty thought and was stifling a retort. It didn't take a genius to guess what kind of dirty retort he'd wanted to make. "Ugh."

He chuckled as he shut the door and hurried around to the driver's side.

We stopped at a sandwich place and grabbed food to take back to the apartment. Killian ate while I showered. The doctor had been in to see me before the nurse removed the cast and had prescribed painkillers for when my wrist inevitably began to feel uncomfortable. But he'd also told me that I needed to work out the stiffness, using my wrist as much as possible for light tasks. He'd told me the guitar was out of the question for a couple of weeks, which was not the news I wanted to hear. I was determined to get my wrist strong again, fast.

I washed my hair, wincing in discomfort as I forced my wrist to help out with the task.

By the time I blow-dried my hair, styled it, did my makeup, and got dressed, my damn wrist had swelled and was throbbing.

Killian eyed me from a stool at the island as I strode out my bedroom with a face like thunder. "Problem?"

I waved my wrist at him in agitation. "Look at it. A couple of menial tasks and it's gone from an underfed Dr. Banner to the Incredible Hulk."

His lips curled at the corners and he pushed my sandwich along the countertop toward me. "Eat. Then you can take a couple of painkillers."

I did as he suggested and while I ate, he talked about what I was to expect at the label.

"It's merely an introduction. I want you to meet the staff who are going to be working on the album with us, let you go into the booth, get a feel for it. We're not doing anything official today. I'd like to wait until we can get you in the booth with your guitar. I want this album to be authentic."

"Okay," I agreed, ignoring the angry butterflies waking up in my belly.

It had felt like I'd been living in this apartment for longer than five weeks. It felt like Killian and I had been writing the album together for longer than five weeks. It had been a suspended moment in time for me, living in a bubble where I was safe, healing, and bonding with Autumn and Killian in a way I hadn't let myself connect with people in so long.

Now reality wanted to burst that bubble.

When we pulled up to the building that housed Skyscraper Records, I felt stuck. Physically stuck in Killian's car. He walked around the hood to the passenger side to open the door for me.

I had no choice but to get out.

"Is your wrist still sore?" Killian frowned as he held the glass door to the building open for me.

I nodded, taking in the large reception area. Marble floors, contemporary furniture, all white leather and steel. It was cold. I shivered.

"Skylar?"

"Let's do this, O'Dea." I was so locked up in my own thoughts, my voice sounded far away even to my ears.

"O'Dea?" I thought I heard him mumble but I was too busy making eye contact with the big guy with the scar across his cheek who stood by the bank of elevators. He wore a smart black suit that strained across his epic biceps.

"Sir." He nodded at Killian, stepping aside to let us pass.

The blood rushed in my ears as soon as we stepped into the open elevator.

"Skylar?"

"Hmm?"

"I'm only going to ask this once more. Are you okay?"

I glanced up at him without really looking at him. "I'm fine."

"If you're worried about my staff recognizing you, they already know about you. They signed a confidentiality agreement. No one from my office will leak your whereabouts to the press."

That was something, at least.

The elevator doors opened before I could respond and then I jolted a little at the feel of his hand on my lower back as he led me out into a huge open-plan office filled with people. *This* room wasn't cold. There were music posters and artwork decorating *every* available space on the walls. The reception desk was directly across from the elevator.

"Mr. O'Dea," the young man behind the reception desk greeted us without a smile. I reckoned it was because Killian wasn't a smiley guy and the receptionist knew it.

"Justin, this is Skylar. Skylar, Justin is our receptionist."

"Nice to meet you." He held out his hand across the desk and I shook it, still feeling dazed. "May I offer you a drink? Water? Tea, coffee? We have hot chocolate."

"I'm fine, thanks."

"Is Oliver in the recording studio?" Killian asked. "I want to start the tour there."

"Let me check." Justin picked up the phone and pressed a button. After a second he said, "Ollie, Mr. O'Dea is here with Miss Finch and would like to know if you're happy for them to come see you first? . . . Great, I'll let him know." He hung up and nodded. "Booth Two is free."

"Good. Tell Eve she's needed."

"Mr. O'Dea, I'm here!" A young woman of Asian descent scooted around the reception desk from our right. She grinned as she skidded to a stop in front of us. Her dark hair was piled high into a messy bun and she wore thick-framed, green cat-eye glasses that sparkled with a few strategically placed crystals. Her Killers T-shirt hung off one shoulder and was short at the hem on the opposite side, showing a glimmer of her pale waist. She'd matched the casual tee with skinny jeans with turn-ups and a pair of battered green Converse.

She looked about sixteen but had to be older.

"I heard you'd arrived," she said a little breathlessly, like she'd run from one end of the floor to the other. I suspected she might have.

Killian gestured to her. "Skylar, this is Eve, my assistant. She'll be happy to help you with anything you need."

"Hi." I stuck out my hand and her eyes lit up as she shook it, holding it in both of hers. "Nice to meet you."

"You too." She refused to let go of my hand. "I promised myself I wouldn't fangirl but your music was the soundtrack of my life for a while there."

A complicated flush of delight and agitation traveled through me. It was the greatest compliment in the world but also a horrible reminder that I was no longer just Skylar: Busker Girl. I was definitely, one hundred percent, Skylar Finch again.

I gave her what I hoped was a warm smile. "That means a lot. Thanks."

"Eve," Killian warned, and the smile fell off her face as she dropped my hand.

"I didn't mean to be forward. I'm sorry."

I shot Killian a quelling look and fell into step beside Eve as her boss led us down a hallway on the left side of reception, taking us past a bunch of closed doors. "You're fine," I promised her.

She gave me a grateful smile.

The silence among the three of us felt awkward, and I needed to distract myself so I wouldn't faint from my overwhelming emotions. "How old are you, Eve?"

"Twenty-one. I graduated from Glasgow Uni this summer and was lucky enough to get this job."

"What's the goal?" I hoped I didn't sound interrogative. I just needed her to keep talking, keep distracting me.

"Goal?"

"Producing, A&R, publicist . . . ?"

"Oh. A&R. I love music." Her hands fluttered in front of her body in nervous excitement. "It would be, like, absolute heaven to spend my days finding raw talent and then watching it grow into something mature and successful. I mean, like, imagine being the person who found Tellurian. Music is what matters, you know. It's the soundtrack to every important moment in life. *Your* music helped me through so much my last year at high school and then uni. My parents' divorce. The guy I lost my virginity to breaking up with me and then sleeping with a girl in my dorm the very next day. My turtle dying. All of it."

I smiled at the pained look Killian threw me. So his assistant was a "wear your heart on your sleeve" type of girl. She couldn't have been more his opposite.

I loved it.

"I'm sorry you went through all that," I told her. "But it means a lot that my music helped."

"Oh, it did. You were the soul of that band. Macy has a good voice but it doesn't have that thing that makes you *feel* what she's singing, plus the songwriting isn't nearly as good. It's no wonder their sales aren't great."

The mention of my band and their new lead singer made the breath catch in my throat and Killian whipped around, halting us. He glared at Eve. "You want to keep your job, keep your mouth shut. Get Skylar and me a coffee and meet us at Booth Two."

Two bright splotches of pink appeared on her cheeks and her dark eyes widened as they glimmered with embarrassed tears. She turned and darted back down the hallway as if the hounds of hell were nipping at her feet.

I turned to Killian.

"She knows better than to get familiar with the artists," he said defensively.

"*I* asked her the questions." I shook my head, grateful for this reminder. "You can be such a dick, O'Dea."

He walked away, hiding his expression as he said over his shoulder, "Try to watch your language while you're here. Oliver's waiting."

Oliver turned out to be the recording studio manager. He was a big guy in his late forties who sported a very impressive beard. He wouldn't have looked out of place on *Sons of Anarchy*.

After we exchanged greetings, he shot a questioning look between Killian and me, seeming to sense the current chill between us. Killian ignored him and let me into the sound booth so I could get a feel for it. Memories flooded in as I stood inside, staring out at Killian and Oliver on the other side of the glass.

Recording with the band felt like a lifetime ago. As I looked around, I could see them on the other side of the glass, watching me work on the vocals. Brandon couldn't sing but Austin and Micah could, so sometimes they were in the booth with me doing backing vocals. Their deep laughter filled my ears. I could almost feel Brandon hugging me and telling me, "good job, Sky."

I didn't know what I felt for Micah anymore, but I was absolute in my feelings for Austin and Brandon. I missed them. I missed them so much it hurt.

Once upon a time, they were my family. They were sometimes

the only thing holding me together when we were out doing all the publicity and marketing shit that I hated.

How would I be able to do this without them?

My chest tightened, and I felt like the glass wall was closing in on me. By the time I hurried to the door, Killian was already there, pulling it open.

"Skylar?" He reached for me but I pushed past him, needing air.

As I threw open the studio door, I collided with Eve and gasped as hot coffee soaked the front of my cashmere sweater.

"Oh my God, I'm so sorry!" Eve's hands flailed above my chest, as two now-empty coffee cups rolled at our feet.

"You okay?" Killian grabbed my shoulder, turning me toward him.

I pulled the sweater away from my body. "I'm fine. The sweater shielded me from the worst of its heat."

"I'm so sorry, I'm so sorry, Mr. O'Dea."

"Eve," I put a hand on her shoulder, trying to calm her, "*I* collided with *you*." And the collision had stopped what had felt like the beginning of a panic attack. "We're good."

She still looked slightly terrified of Killian, so I glared at him, trying to communicate with my eyes that he needed to reassure her. His lips pinched together for a moment but then he offered, "Eve, it wasn't your fault."

His assistant immediately relaxed.

"Do you have a spare T-shirt Skylar can borrow?"

She winced regretfully. "No, sir . . . oh, but you do!"

And that's how I found myself following Killian and his assistant to his office at the farthest end of the floor. It wasn't a huge space but it had a great view over the Clyde. He waited outside while Eve rummaged through a cabinet.

"This should do." She pulled out a Biffy Clyro tee from the

bottom drawer.

I took it and waited for her to leave before I looked around the office. My curiosity got the best of me as I wandered around, taking in the framed newspaper articles on his wall. They depicted moments of success for the bands he'd worked with at the label. His desk was sparse with only an iMac, a phone, a few pens, and a photo of him and Autumn. I smiled, picking up the photograph. I loved how much he loved his sister. They were sitting together at a table at some function, both looking glamorous—him in a tux, Autumn all dolled up. His arm was around her, her cheek pressed to his, and while he didn't share her big, beaming smile, his eyes were warm with affection.

I brushed my fingers over his face. What must it be like to be loved by him? I imagined it a heady thing, winning the love of a man who offered it so sparingly.

Blinking out of the dangerous thought, I put the photo back where I found it, reminding myself I was supposed to be getting changed, not nosing through his stuff.

My wrist protested as I pulled my sweater over my head. I was just reaching for Killian's tee when his office door opened. "Are you read—"

We both froze.

Me in my bra and jeans.

His lips parted, not even hiding that he was taking in every inch of me. I flushed all over.

Killian cursed under his breath and then slammed his office door shut so no one would see me from the hall while finally turning his back to me. He sounded hoarse when he spoke. "Sorry. I thought you'd be dressed by now."

"My wrist was hurting," I lied. "I needed a minute."

That was all it took to make him move. Suddenly he was in

front of me, grabbing the tee out of my hands. "What are you doing?" I tried to cover myself.

Killian gave me an impatient look. "It's not anything I haven't seen before. Lift your arms."

"I can put the tee on myself."

"The longer you argue, the longer I see you half-naked. I'm a man who appreciates the female form, so I don't mind. I can do this all day."

Grunting, I lifted my arms, my annoyance with him lessening as he carefully pulled it down over my head and then gently placed my arms through the short sleeves. He shrugged it down slowly, as if savoring those moments of naked skin.

My breath caught as his fingers brushed the sides of my breasts and my eyes flew to his as he pulled the T-shirt down excruciatingly slowly, caressing my skin with it. Those dark eyes smoldered.

Then somehow, we were standing closer, our bodies almost touching. Excitement tingled between my legs and I felt my nipples peak against the fabric of my bra.

A flush crested Killian's cheeks and his chest rose and fell in shallow breaths.

I forgot everything.

Where I was.

Who I was.

Who he was.

All I could think about was the way my skin prickled to electrified life under his touch. I wanted him to kiss me. I wanted him to push me up against his desk, rip my jeans off, and thrust into me.

My breath shuddered at the thought and Killian's eyes blazed even hotter, as if he'd been able to read my mind.

"Sir, Mr. Byrne would like to speak with you!" Eve's voice called through the door and shattered the moment.

Killian stumbled back. His hands dropped from my waist, allowing the T-shirt to fall.

I tried to catch my breath as he whirled away from me. "Just . . . Just a second," he called back.

"Killian . . ."

He glanced over his shoulder at me, his expression unreadable. "I'm Killian again?"

Confused, I blinked. "What?"

Exhaling heavily, he shook his head. "Nothing." Then his nostrils flared as he stared at me. I glanced down at myself. His T-shirt drowned me. It also smelled of him, which was very bad because I really needed to stop thinking of Killian and sex in the same sentence, and wearing his scent was not helping. "I look ridiculous." But I didn't think Killian thought I looked ridiculous at all.

He wore the same look Micah wore when some other guy showed an interest in me.

Possessive.

Oh boy, we needed to get out of his office, pronto. "You mind if I knot it?"

He frowned, shaking his head as if shaking away thoughts. Possibly dirty thoughts. No. *Probably* dirty thoughts. "What?"

"Knot it." I grabbed the hem and pulled it tight against my belly with the excess material at the back.

"Oh. Aye, sure."

I put the knot in the back, feeling slightly less ridiculous. Killian was staring at the small expanse of skin I'd revealed in doing so. My hands trembled with the desire to reach out to him, so I forced myself to look away. "Can I leave my sweater in here?"

He cleared his throat. "Of course."

I only looked up again when I heard him open the office door.

When I stepped out, I found Eve standing nervously beside

an older man with dark hair and gray eyes. He was a little shorter than Killian but still looked fit and strong for his age, distinguished in his expensive three-piece suit.

He wore a look of disapproval and I'd soon discover that this man wore a *perpetual* look of disapproval.

"Killian." He eyed him coldly.

"James." Killian nodded just as coolly. He turned to me, gesturing me forward. "Skylar, I'd like you to meet the head of the label, James Byrne. My uncle."

eighteen

James Byrne pierced me with his chilly gaze.

I knew it was probably best to be polite since he was Killian's uncle, but that's exactly why I didn't want to be. From everything I'd learned so far, I did not like this man.

So I stayed silent.

As did he.

Finally, he looked back at Killian. "A word. My office."

He followed his uncle, shooting me a frown over his shoulder as they walked about fifteen steps to a door that had James's name on it. When they stepped inside, I noticed a door across the hall that bore the name "Kenny Smith." Hmm. Wasn't that the guy getting all the credit for Killian's work?

I tried to shrug off my irritation, telling myself these were not my problems.

"He's hardly ever here," Eve whispered, drawing my attention back to her. "I wonder what he wants."

I wondered that too.

The phone on Eve's desk rang and she hurried to pick it up.

"Good afternoon, Skyscraper Records, Mr. O'Dea's office, how may I help?" She listened for a second, then looked up at me and rolled her eyes. "No, I'm afraid Mr. O'Dea is unavailable at the moment . . . Yes . . . Yes, I did say that because Mr. O'Dea was unavailable then too . . . I did pass along your message . . . I did . . . yes, I will again. Thanks for calling." She hung up with a beleaguered sigh.

"Problem?"

"Ugh, yeah." She leaned over the table toward me and dropped her voice. "That was Yasmin. Mr. O'Dea's ex-girlfriend."

I didn't know why that information made me feel cold considering I knew a man like O'Dea wasn't a virgin. I guess I'd assumed that he was more a player than a guy who would have a girlfriend.

"They broke up last week and she's been calling nonstop. Guess someone doesn't know when to give up."

They broke up last week. They broke up last week.

"I've only been here a few months, but Sarah in marketing told me that Mr. O'Dea's one of those serial monogamist types. She said he's been in, like, five relationships in the past two and a half years. She says it always ends because Mr. O'Dea's never out of the office. Although he has been lately, so we all thought maybe the whole Yasmin relationship was working out after all, but then he told me not to take any calls from her anymore so we're all intrigued about the disappearances." She suddenly straightened, looking concerned. "I'm sorry. I shouldn't have said all that to you. Oh my God, I'm terrible at this job."

I managed a weak little laugh, even though an unexpected and painful wound had been inflicted. "I'm not going to repeat that. But—and I don't mean this to be a bitch, this is friendly advice—I wouldn't gossip about your boss to any of his artists anymore. It might get back to him, and you seem pretty enthusiastic about wanting to work here."

"I am." Eve's eyes rounded with intensity. "But I have this filter problem and I talk too much."

"You'll learn with experience."

But would I? Or was I fated to continually put my feelings somewhere they didn't belong? Like in a man I thought was my friend, despite all the shit between us, only to discover that I knew very little about him. And most of what I'd learned had come from his sister.

Not telling me about a girlfriend . . . What must she have thought he was doing those late nights at my apartment? Why didn't he ever mention her? Was it because she mattered so little, or because I mattered so little?

Fuck.

How the hell did everything get so twisted up? I wrapped my arms around my waist, ignoring the throb in my wrist. I wanted to go. I needed to be alone to process this new information.

However, I had to stand there as Killian emerged from his uncle's office wearing that damn blank mask I hated so much. His uncle followed him out and they drew to a stop in front of us.

James flicked a look at Eve. "I need a coffee, girl."

No please, no thank you. No use of her name. It's not like I hadn't been around people in powerful jobs who thought it was okay to treat others like their servants. It annoyed me then and it annoyed me now. I bristled as Eve scurried off to do his bidding.

"So you're the ex-pop-rock princess my company is spending all the money on."

Wow.

Nice.

The thought of the apartment, the clothes on my back, all the food that had helped me get healthy again, suddenly made me feel vulnerable. Like I was stripped naked in front of this guy. Because it was *his* money that had helped me. Not Killian's. I hadn't minded it when I'd thought otherwise, but being faced with the truth made me feel small. I'd been taking this man's money and he didn't look happy about it. Why should he?

"I'm going to pay you back," I said. Riotous butterflies flurried to life at the thought of accessing my money, but in that moment, I thought being beholden to him instead of Killian was worse than my band finding out where I was.

"If your album does well, you will." He dragged his gaze down my body and back up again. "You'll need to dress better."

Screw you, ass—

"There was a coffee spillage," Killian explained. "We had to find something for Skylar to change into."

James flicked his nephew a look before turning back to me. "This boy," he gestured to his nephew and I swear my fingers almost sprouted claws at him calling Killian *boy*, "thinks you'll be an impressive addition to the label. I see the merit in it, considering the free publicity, but since he won't let me hear any of your music yet, I'm a bit skeptical."

Choking on my annoyance, I couldn't speak for fear of what I'd say.

He raised an eyebrow and shot Killian an amused look. "You better make sure her music is more interesting than she is."

Annoyance flickered over Killian's face and James appeared surprised by it. "Something I said?"

"No. It's been a big morning for Skylar. A lot going on. She's done this before, James. She'll be fine."

James harrumphed and then turned his attention back to me. "Nothing to say?"

I felt like I was in front of my school principal. God, this man was the most condescending prick I'd met in a long time. "Do you always greet your artists this way?" It slipped out before I could stop it.

"In what way?"

"Interrogative. Condescending." I couldn't be stopped. It was that word *boy*.

He pressed his lips together in displeasure. "I'm your boss. Not the other way around."

"But surely it's your policy to keep your artists happy? Not make them feel like they're about to get detention."

"Only when my artists are making me money and not bleeding me dry." He cocked his head, narrowing his nasty gaze on me. "Has it always been your policy to be rude to your label head, Miss Finch?"

"Actually, my current policy is to give zero fucks."

Killian exhaled a shuddering sigh, rubbing a hand over his head like he couldn't believe I'd said that.

James gave his nephew a look filled with such disdain, a lesser man would have buckled under it. "I hope you know what you're doing, boy."

Oh, if he called him *boy* in that snotty tone one more time!

He marched away before I could say anything, hopefully to exit the building and relieve us of his toxic personality. How did someone like him make a business out of music? Janet Wheeler, the head of Tellurian's label, was unbelievably passionate about music. Yes, she had a business degree, but her passion was ultimately what drove her.

But James . . . that guy was all coldhearted, soulless business. And you did not make a label successful by talking to your artists like they were crap on your shoe!

"Can you believe that guy?" I gestured toward the empty hall.

"That guy," Killian bit out between clenched teeth, "is my boss and your label head. What the hell were you thinking?"

Surprised by his anger, it took me a second to respond. I sputtered out, "You're mad at me? God, if that guy called you *boy* one more time, I was going to push him out of a window."

Killian blinked as if he wasn't expecting that response at all.

"He's an asshole."

His face darkened. "Right now, *he's* not the asshole. This is my job, Skylar, and you made me look incompetent in front of my boss. Was it deliberate? Are you trying to sabotage this and get out of our deal?"

That he would even ask that floored me. Hurt on top of the hurt I'd already been experiencing over the news that there was a Yasmin made me feel even smaller than his uncle had. I hated feeling small. "No. I just . . . I didn't like him."

"Well, sometimes we have to work with people we don't like," he said pointedly.

That sucker punch knocked the breath out of me. Hurt didn't cover how I felt. It obliterated my sarcasm shields, leaving me entirely defenseless. The only option left was to retreat until I could reboot them.

"You know, I think we should finish the tour another time." I turned away, unable to look at him. "My wrist is making me irritable."

"You think?" he snapped. He disappeared into his office, returning a couple seconds later with my sweater. I took it from him, careful not to touch him, and hugged it into my chest as I marched ahead down the hallway toward reception.

Before we turned the corner, a door burst open on my left and I nearly collided with the young woman who came out of it.

"Oh, sorry." She smiled apologetically up at me and then froze as our eyes met.

Confusion and shock drew me to a halt.

It was Shelley, the police sketch artist.

What the . . .

She threw Killian a look over my shoulder and whatever she saw sent her scurrying away from us.

Shelley worked for him, not for the police?

I stumbled forward, my mind whirring. What did that mean? That Killian found those boys before the police—

Oh my God.

I was vaguely aware of someone calling goodbye to us as we stepped into the elevator, but I wasn't paying attention to anything other than my current realization. As soon as the elevator doors closed behind us, I whirled on him.

"Did you have those boys beaten up before you turned them over to the police?"

Killian stared ahead, refusing to look at me.

"Killian?"

He glanced down at me out of the corner of his eyes, apparently bored. "Well, I'm a dick, right? Dicks do those kinds of things."

I ignored his jab and pressed, "How? How did you get to them first?"

Shrugging like our conversation didn't matter, he replied, "We found them through Shelley's drawings. My birth father has connections. He owed me one, so he had them interrogated. They were a bit more thorough than the police and they fessed up."

"That's why Welsh was in worse shape than the other kid."

Did he care beyond obligatory moral outrage that I'd been attacked? Was that why? I needed to know. And if he did, how could he be such a goddamned bastard to me now if he cared about me? It was as if that sexually tense moment in his office had never happened.

"Why?"

We stepped out of the elevator and Killian said goodbye to the burly security guard before guiding me to the exit. He didn't answer me as we walked out. It wasn't until we stopped at his car that he asked, "Why what?"

Impatience itched in my fingers but I stayed calm. "Why? Why did you do that?"

"To teach the little shit a lesson he wouldn't forget."

Which suggested he cared. So why was he acting like this? "Did you also persuade those boys to plead guilty? Is that how you knew it wouldn't go to trial?"

"The McCrurys promised they would make them disappear if they didn't plead guilty."

"The connections your dad has . . . it's that gang you mentioned?"

"Aye."

I knew from the little I'd gleaned that he and his father had no relationship to speak of. So wasn't it a pretty big deal that he'd gone to the man for me? "So . . ." I felt vulnerable asking but I needed to know. "What? You did all that because he hurt me?"

Killian took in a deep breath, gazing down the street. The muscle in his jaw ticked a second before he replied, "I did it to make sure the publicity goes the way we want it."

I didn't believe him. "You didn't need to have the shit kicked out of that boy to do that."

His head whipped back around and he scowled at me. "Are you mad I did that?"

"No." I wasn't exactly Miss Perfect. My moral compass was a little skewed these days. Those boys had followed, intimidated, and stolen from me, and one of them had tried to rape me like it was his God-given right. I wasn't broken up that someone had meted out payback. It was doubtful a short stint in prison would stop him from doing the same to another woman. But maybe fear would. Right or wrong, that's how I felt.

And I was confused. Because I felt utterly safe in the knowledge that Killian would do apparently anything to protect me. Yet at the same time, he was completely incapable of protecting me from himself and his casual callousness. "I'm confused," I offered honestly.

"There's no need to be confused. I take my job seriously. I want this album to be a success and to do that, I need to control every aspect of it, including the PR."

He really wanted to hide behind that lie? Really? I pushed. "So, it was only about our deal?"

Finally, the mask slipped and he glared at me in warning. "What the hell else would it be about?"

Was this nastiness because of my treatment of his uncle? This inability to admit the truth? "Oh, I don't know, O'Dea, maybe something involving your heart. Or at least your dick. Or are you too pissed to admit that? Because you don't forgive me for using the F-word in front of your uncle."

Not missing a beat, he scoffed, "To forgive, there usually has to be an apology first."

As if! "I won't apologize for how I dealt with your uncle. He talks to you like you're five. It's bad enough he does it anyway, but he should not talk to you like that in front of your artists."

Anger flushed across the crest of his cheeks. "My relationship with my uncle is none of your business. You and I . . . we're not friends. Artist," he pointed sternly at me and then jerked his thumb towards himself, "label. I've done a lot for you and all I expect in return is for you to hold up your end of the bargain with a modicum of professionalism."

I felt winded again, this time like he'd barreled into me with enough force to expel the breath from my body.

Tears of frustration were desperate to fall, but I curled my fists and fought the emotion. I let my disappointment and resentment flood me. How dare he? How dare he pretend like there was no connection between us? That I'd made it all up in my head.

Or maybe I had. Because I didn't know this man standing in front of me at all.

Whatever he saw in my expression caused his features to harden.

I couldn't look at him a second longer.

Turning around, I braced against the cold wind and marched away.

Sounding exasperated, he called, "Where are you going?"

"I can walk back!" I yelled over my shoulder.

"You signed a contract, Skylar."

The pointed reminder made me stop and whirl around. I hoped he withered under the intensity of my glare. "I did. I did sign a contract. And that's a promise I intend to keep. But just because you regret your past kindnesses to me—and whatever the hell was about to happen in your office—doesn't mean I have to stick around so you can erase those moments with cruelty. That *wasn't* in the contract." I walked away before I could see his reaction.

However, I heard the regret in his tone as he called my name. "Skylar."

I didn't want his regret. I didn't want anything from him anymore. I'd spent too many years of my life loving a boy who could be kind one second and cruel the next. No way was I putting myself through that with Killian. Micah had been a boy. Killian was a man. Where Micah's words were like bee stings, Killian's were like a knife.

"Skylar!"

I ignored him, turning the corner around the neighboring

building and out of sight. I was so lost in my tumultuous thoughts, I reached the apartment having little memory of actually walking there. As I unlocked the building's main entrance, my phone rang. Pulling it out of the ass pocket of my jeans, my chest squeezed at the sight of Killian's name on the screen.

I declined the call.

As I got in the elevator, my cell binged, telling me I had a voicemail.

I wasn't sure I wanted to hear anything he had to say, but unfortunately the compulsion to ignore it wasn't as strong as the need to hear it. I hoped what he had to say was cold and unfeeling so I could solidify my hatred for him.

I dumped my stuff on the couch, took a breath, and clicked on the button to listen to my voicemail.

"It's me." The mere sound of his voice in my ear caused a sharp ache in my chest. "You're right. I crossed a line and I'm sorry. You didn't deserve that. My uncle tends to bring out the worst in me. It's no excuse, I know." He sighed. "But we also need to remember what we're doing here, Skylar. This is business. Somewhere along the way, we forgot that. I shouldn't be defending you unless it's in direct relation to your career, and you shouldn't be defending me, full stop. It can't be that way between us. I think it would do us both well to remember that."

I slumped on the couch, feeling disappointment and heartache. Companions I knew well. There was something between us. Something completely undeniable, but he was going to try to deny it anyway for the sake of both our careers.

Didn't that sound familiar? I winced, running my fingers through my hair and groaning. That's what I'd done to Micah.

Is this how he'd felt?

Rejected, gutted, made to feel like he wasn't worth the complication?

Guilt I'd already been feeling suddenly magnified.

The truth was although I felt guilty for choosing our band over our relationship, only for me to not want to be in the band, I also blamed Micah. He'd made it easy for me not to choose him by sleeping around and manipulating me and playing all sorts of games. And I still blamed him for that . . . but I realized now that I'd started it.

Micah didn't have family like the rest of the band. He'd lived with a couple of different foster families in town. At thirteen he eventually moved in with the Ryans, a foster family who had two of their own kids and were caring for two others before Micah arrived. He stayed with them right through high school, but they weren't a family. They really only had time for the younger kids in their care. Micah was a paycheck and he was allowed to do as he pleased.

I was too young to understand what that did to him. Not having a family to place any kind of worth on him. I knew he had abandonment issues, I just hadn't realized how much my choosing the band over him must have fucked with his head on top of that.

"Oh, Micah," I whispered, tears slipping loose. I had so much to apologize for.

It was shitty that it took someone doing the same thing to me for me to truly comprehend how much I'd screwed over my best friend.

Shit.

I pulled out my cell and texted Killian back.

You're right.

nineteen

Killian didn't text back.

In fact, I didn't hear anything from him the next day. Or the one after.

I felt alone again.

And like the apartment was closing in on me. I tried to distract myself with TV and books, but that didn't work. I attempted to do the one thing that always distracted me: I picked up my damn guitar.

It was too soon.

My wrist throbbed like a motherfucker and I could do nothing but stare at the TV and let the pain settle down. But all that did was lead me to overthink everything. I couldn't believe I'd compared what Killian was doing to what I'd done to Micah. There was no way I felt for Killian what Micah felt for me.

I wasn't in love with Killian. I barely knew the guy.

There was some other weird reason why he could hurt my feelings like no other and why finding out he had an unmentioned girlfriend felt like betrayal.

I had a crush.

That was it.

I had a crush because he was an attractive, brooding bastard with a hot accent.

I could get over a crush.

Especially a misplaced crush on a man whose words cut to the quick. A man who pretty much used my issues against me to get me to sign a record deal.

C'mon, let's face it: Killian O'Dea was the devil, and it was totally messed up to have developed feelings for the guy.

I'd get over it.

But I'd need some distraction to do that.

So I called his sister.

"Ooh, cast-free!" Autumn smiled at the sight of my wrist as she walked into the apartment an hour later. The difference between her and her brother always surprised me. Their childhood had made Killian closed-off and a cold, ambitious dipshit. Yet, Autumn was open and positive and full of light. She hadn't let the world change her. In a way, she was one of the strongest people I'd ever met. I admired that about her.

That's why I noticed the way her smile didn't reach her eyes. Autumn's smiles always reached her eyes.

I frowned, standing up from the couch as she strode into the kitchen to put the kettle on. "Everything okay?"

She didn't look at me. "Yes, why?"

"Nothing. You just . . . you seem . . . off?"

Puttering around the kitchen, she chuckled, "I said three words. How can you tell if I'm off?"

"You're right." I shrugged. "I'm the one who's off."

Autumn whirled around from grabbing milk out of the fridge. "You're not the only one. I was so glad you called. Killian had me running around doing errands and my God, is that man in a shitty mood." She shook her head in exasperation as she poured milk into our tea. "I had to have a word with him. If other people want to let him talk to them like that, they can. But no way in hell does he talk to me like that."

"Good for you."

"Any idea what's wrong with him?"

"Nope."

"Brothers," she muttered, holding out a mug toward me. As she did so, her sleeve rose up her forearm, revealing a ring of dark bruises that looked like finger marks.

Ugly suspicion took hold. I was a glass-half-empty kind of gal, you know. I took the mug and Autumn dropped her arm out of sight, ignoring my questioning gaze.

Not wanting to scare her off, but feeling my heart rate quicken as worry took root, I sat on the couch as she slid onto a stool at the island.

"So, how's the boyfriend? What was his name again?"

Was that too obvious?

Autumn looked down into her mug, her expression withdrawn. Again, something highly unusual for her. "Darren. We broke up."

Why? Because he was leaving bruises on her? Fury heated my blood at the mere thought of anyone hurting Autumn. How could anyone hurt Autumn? She was the sweetest, kindest person on the planet. "Oh." I struggled to keep emotion out of my tone. "What happened?"

"It didn't work out."

"That's too bad. Why not?"

"Just didn't." She slammed the mug down on the island. "I don't want to talk about it."

Autumn didn't want to talk about it? Okay. There was definitely something going on. Autumn wanted to talk about everything!

"How's the album going?" She changed the subject.

"Hmm?"

She smirked. "The album? You know, that thing you and Killian have been working on night and day?"

"Oh. Right. Um . . . yeah, well, I can't start recording until the wrist is healed enough to play guitar." I waved it at her. "I tried yesterday and it brought on a world of pain."

Her eyes brightened with sympathy. "If you were in pain, you should have called."

"Thanks, but there's nothing to do about it but take some painkillers and keep doing the wrist exercises the physio told me to do."

"True." She stood, kicked off her boots, and curled up on the chair across from me. "So, you went to the label. You met Uncle James."

"Ah, you heard about that."

"Eve told me." Autumn grinned. "She also couldn't stop talking about how she embarrassed herself by fangirling over you. But she was very proud that she curbed the urge to tell you that you have the most amazing eyes and were so nice. Girl-crush alert."

I laughed at Autumn's teasing. "She's a sweet kid."

My friend smiled at me quizzically. "Kid? Eve's twenty-one. She's only a few years younger than you."

"She seemed really young. Or maybe I'm an old twenty-four-year-old. I didn't mean to sound condescending. Eve's nice."

"I know. I hired her." She grinned mischievously.

I burst out laughing. "I knew O'Dea couldn't have hired her."

"Well, the man needs to lighten up. I thought Eve would do the trick."

"Have I told you lately that I love you?"

Autumn chuckled. "It's so much fun to finally have someone

who enjoys irritating my brother as much as I do."

"You were never friendly with his girlfriends?" The question popped out before I could filter it.

If she was surprised by it, she didn't let on. "Not really. Killian chooses to be in relationships with shallow, insipid women because he knows he'll never get attached to someone like that. That's why his relationships never last. He's a workaholic. It always comes first."

"Is that why he and Yasmin broke up?"

"He told you about Yasmin? Oh, good. I didn't mention her because *he* hadn't mentioned her and I didn't think she was important. Which was true because it ended. He said she was getting clingy, so he broke it off." She gazed at me with a knowing gleam in her eyes. "However, I'm pretty sure *she* wasn't the reason he broke up with her."

At Autumn's insinuation that *I* was somehow the reason, I decided, just like I'd decided with her brother, that I was done beating around the bush. "He didn't break up with her because of me. We're putting out an album together. I'm his golden ticket. Nothing else."

Her expression fell. "Okay, I'm not liking how bitter you sound." Understanding dawned on her expression. "And Killian is walking around snapping at everyone like a wounded animal. What happened between you two?"

Just like that, my anger spewed out of me. "I let myself be vulnerable with him. Told him shit I haven't told anyone. I made the mistake of thinking we were friends." I twisted my lips in distaste. "He informed me otherwise, and he wasn't nice about it."

Fuck.

I regretted the words as soon as they were out of my mouth. "I shouldn't have said that to you. Christ. You're his sister. I shouldn't have said that."

Anger flushed Autumn's cheeks. "What is wrong with him? I could slap him silly sometimes!"

Oh no, no, no. "Autumn, don't say that. And don't say anything to your brother. You're the only person he really cares about. If he thought I was trying to turn you against him, he'd hate me."

She raised an eyebrow. "And would you care?"

Thankfully, her cell rang before I had to answer that. It lay on the island and she had her feet tucked under her so I stood up to get it for her.

"Leave it," she said, trying to untangle herself.

But I was already up.

DARREN

Calling

I held up the phone to her, suddenly no longer distracted from the suspicious bruising on her forearm. "The ex?"

Her expression tightened and I saw the flash of something I really did not like in her dark eyes. "Ignore it. I'll talk to him later."

The phone rang off in my hand anyway.

Then it rang again.

I stared at her as she stared at the phone, growing paler by the second. Eventually Darren stopped calling. But then it started ringing immediately again.

"If you two have split up, why is he calling you so persistently?"

She swallowed hard. "Oh, he left some of his stuff at my place. We need to arrange for him to collect it."

Autumn O'Dea needed a lesson in how to lie.

Her phone buzzed and a message from Darren popped up.

If you don't pick up . . .

Damn! I was only getting the preview. Was that a threatening message?

"Give me the phone."

"What does his text say?"

Autumn frowned. "Nosy much?"

Okay, something was wrong. My gut told me so.

Reading my expression, she looked past me and into the kitchen. "Is that the time? Wow. I . . . uh . . . I told Killian I'd come into the office to give him an opinion on . . . on something." She got up and put her mug on the island before scrambling to get her boots back on.

She didn't look at me the entire time.

"Autumn . . ."

"You'll call if you need me?" She kissed my cheek, not meeting my eyes, and was out of the apartment within seconds.

Shit.

I gazed across the room at my cell.

There was nothing on this earth that could compel me to call Killian.

Except fear for his little sister's safety.

What if I was wrong though? I bit my lip. What if my gut was wrong that some guy she'd dumped for manhandling her didn't know how to back off? Killian had proven he was willing to get his hands dirty to protect someone, and I was sure whatever he dealt out on Autumn's behalf would be a hundred times worse.

If I didn't make him aware that there was possibly something to be worried about, and then this guy did turn out to be dangerous, I'd never forgive myself.

And honestly, I knew I was right.

Autumn was acting jumpy, the bruising, the persistent calling, the possibly threatening text . . .

Screw it. I crossed the room and grabbed my cell. My hands shook a little as I pressed speed dial and held the cell up to my ear.

It rang.

He was ignoring me?

I didn't know why that surprised or hurt me, but it freaking did. Scrolling through my contacts, I dialed his office.

"Good morning, Skyscraper Records, Mr. O'Dea's office, how may I help?" Eve answered on the second ring.

"Eve, it's Skylar. I need to speak to O'Dea."

"Oh, hi, Skylar," her voice got a little high-pitched with excitement. "It's great to hear from you."

"Uh, thanks, you too."

There was an awkward silence.

"So . . . Is O'Dea there?"

"Oh. Right. Oh . . . well . . . uh . . . Mr. O'Dea is busy. I'll let him know you called."

I was being Yasmined? He was actually Yasmining me!

Oh hell no. I said goodbye to Eve, shoved on my boots, grabbed my coat and scarf out of the closet, and locked the apartment on my way out. Indignation that he was being so immature fueled me and I got to the label in record time. No pun intended.

The big guy with the scar stopped me at the bank of elevators. "No ID, no entry."

Sighing in irritation, I glanced back at the main reception to the woman sitting at the front desk. "Would you call up to Justin at Skyscraper Records to get him to confirm that Mr. O'Dea is expecting me?" I bluffed. "The name is Skylar."

Luckily, Justin must have assumed he'd missed the memo because he confirmed and the big guy let me pass.

However, as soon as I stepped off that elevator, Justin gave me a strained smile. "Miss Finch, it turns out that Mr. O'Dea—hey!" he yelled after me as I veered to the left, heading down the corridor toward Killian's office. I hurried my steps, hoping to get there before Justin stopped me.

Eve looked up from her desk as I barreled into view. "Oh, Skylar. You're here . . . Oh, well, he doesn't want to be disturbed!" She squeaked as I passed her and pushed open his office door so hard, it slammed open and back into the wall.

"What the—" Killian's wide eyes shot to me. He had his phone pressed to his ear. "I'm sorry, Xander, I'm going to have to call you back."

I stood staring at him, arms crossed in defiance as he glared at me while hanging up.

"I'm sorry, Mr. O'Dea, she slipped right by me," Eve said breathlessly at my back.

"It's fine, Eve." He waved at her impatiently. "Close the door, please."

I stepped out of the way so she could reach in and do as asked.

Killian raised an eyebrow in that pompous way that got on my nerves. "You call this professional? Always with the drama."

I didn't flinch at the insinuation. I was no longer going to let him get to me. And well, to be fair, it had been kind of a dramatic entrance. "Well, I couldn't be sure if you were ignoring me and this can't wait."

"I wasn't ignoring you." He stood and rounded the desk. He sat casually on it, crossing his ankles. "I was on a conference call. So now that you have my attention, what is so important that it couldn't wait?"

"Autumn."

Killian stood up off the desk at the mention of his sister's name. "What about her?" His concern for her made me not want to hate him.

"You know she broke up with that guy."

"Darren? Aye, she told me yesterday."

I let out a shaky breath. "This might sound crazy, but I know it's not. Autumn came to see me today and I noticed bruising all around her forearm. It looked like finger grips. Like someone had grabbed her. Hard."

Her brother's face instantly darkened.

"I'm a pessimist. I think of worst-case scenarios all the time, right? So I ask her about the guy, trying to feel her out."

"And?"

"She tells me they've broken up so I tried to put the bruising to the back of my head. But she's closed off, and shifty, and we both know that's not Autumn. Your sister is usually an open freaking book. I know every detail of how she lost her virginity, for God's sake."

He winced.

"Not the point, sorry. Point is, she was acting strange and not like herself. And then that guy, Darren, starts calling her cell. She told me to ignore it. But he calls two times more right at the back. Persistent fucker. And she got paler and paler each time he called. Then there was the text. I didn't get to see it all but what I did see had a threatening air to it. And, O'Dea, she tried to hide it but she looked afraid."

I'd heard the phrase "stormy expression" before, but I'd never really seen it in action until that moment. Killian looked ready to strike Darren down with lightning bolts from his eyes.

He paced the room in agitation.

"There is a chance I'm wrong, right? Of course, there is. But my gut is telling me something is going on and I thought if some guy is harassing Autumn, it needs to stop."

"Oh, I'll take care of it." His voice rumbled with dark retribution.

And I didn't care that if I was right and this guy was screwing around with Autumn that Killian would make him pay. A few years ago, I would've condemned vengeance. But something had happened to me when I realized my mother's murderers were probably going to escape justice. I no longer saw the world quite so black and white. There was a darkness in me now.

Just as I'd felt protected knowing that Killian had Welsh threatened so he couldn't hurt me anymore, I was okay with him doing the same to protect Autumn, Autumn who was better than the two of us combined. She deserved to be protected from the darker parts of human nature.

"I know you'll take care of it. That's why I came straight to you."

Our gazes locked and for a moment, the anger mirrored in our expressions changed to something more complicated, deeper—something that drew us together even as we stood with the entire office between us.

Affinity.

He and I were so alike in so many ways.

I guess I hadn't realized quite so much until that moment.

"Thank you," his voice was hoarse, "for telling me."

I had to clear my throat of the emotion bubbling up out of me. "Well," I dropped my gaze as I turned to open the door, "I care about Autumn."

THE NEXT MORNING I WAS pulled out of sleep by a loud banging noise.

It took me a minute to realize someone was banging on my apartment door. Groaning, stumbling out of bed, I pulled on the silk robe Autumn had bought me and yanked open my bedroom door, forgetting in my sleeplike state about the fragility of my wrist.

"Fuck," I hissed, rubbing it gently.

The banging continued.

"Who is it?!" I yelled, beyond irritated.

"Skylar, open the door!" Autumn called.

Worry yanked me out of my fog and I hurried down the hall. Autumn had obviously opened the door with her key but couldn't get past the security chain.

As soon as I removed it, she shoved open the door and I had to skitter out of the way. She blew past me, thundering down the hall. I shut the apartment door and followed her into the living area.

"What's up?" I asked tentatively, because I was beginning to think Killian had told her about my suspicions.

She whirled, her lovely auburn hair spiraling around her before settling flawlessly across her shoulders. Seriously, how did it do that?

"You told him," she huffed, drawing me out of my sleepy thoughts.

"Huh?" I pretended ignorance.

"Skylar, this isn't a game."

I tensed. "What happened?"

"What you must have known would happen. He interrogated me, I can't lie to him, and so he tracked down Darren and got into a bloody fight."

Worry shot through me. "Is he okay?"

"No, Killian beat the shit out of him."

"I'm not talking about Darren," I cried. "I couldn't care less if your manhandling, stalkery ex-boyfriend got what was coming to him. Is Killian okay?"

"My brother is fine. A neighbor called the police but Darren, surprise, surprise, refused to press charges." She crossed her arms over her chest and studied me like she'd never seen me before. "You guessed correctly, okay. Darren became controlling. He slapped me during an argument and when I tried to leave, he wouldn't let go of my arm. I screamed bloody murder and he let me go. He lives in a flat with thin walls apparently. He tried to apologize but obviously, I broke up with him. He was calling me constantly and he was saying things that were . . . unsettling."

"Stalker-like things?"

"Yes. But . . . I knew if I told Killian, he'd do this and worse. That's why I didn't tell him and even though I knew you knew something was up, I never would've thought you'd team up with Killian, let alone be okay with him going after Darren."

"You told me yourself that Killian has gone after anyone who has hurt you in the past."

"Yes, usually by going after their career or giving them a stern, threatening, wordy warning by using his father's connection to the criminal bloody underworld. But no one has ever physically hurt me before until now, and I knew he'd react physically in return. And that's not okay. And I can't believe you encouraged it! That's not justice, Skylar. It's revenge!"

I scowled at her in disbelief. "And all the other stuff he's done to protect you isn't an eye for an eye? Of course it is, Autumn. Just because he didn't use his fists doesn't mean it wasn't revenge. There are no gray areas with revenge. And you know what, I don't see him putting the fear of God into a guy who hit you and was set on harassing you as revenge. It was a threat, and it's one that will save you from living in fear from some nutjob. So, yeah, I'm okay with that."

She deflated a little but I winced at the look in her eye. At the pity. "Shelley at the label told me about the 'police' sketch. And I know that boy who attacked you ended up in hospital. I can only imagine that Killian's dad had something to do with it. He hates his father but he wields the man like a bloody battle-ax whenever it suits him. How can you be okay with that?"

I flushed, knowing deep down that she was right to question

me, but angry that she would. "Because that 'boy' followed me until he had me all alone, broke my wrist, and held me to the ground with every intention of raping me. I fought back but if that boy who was with him hadn't stepped in, he would have raped me. I wouldn't have been able to stop him on my own. The way Darren made you feel frightened and powerless . . . imagine that and then magnify it by a million."

Tears gleamed in her eyes before she dropped her gaze.

"I left the States when they told me they'd run out of leads in my mother's murder. The guys who did it weren't a couple of idiots off the streets. They were organized, masked gunmen, after a painting I wish I'd never bought, and they left no trace of themselves. Like ghosts. The only lead we had was that painting, and it's never shown up in the public art world. So I have to live with the fact that I'll likely never get justice for my mom and Bryan. And that kind of anger does something to a person. What Jonathan Welsh did to me only compounded it. I don't want that to ever happen to you."

Her eyes flew up to mine and her tears slipped free.

"You befriended me, no questions asked. I wasn't some project of your brother's you needed to help with. You *wanted* to help me. And you have, Autumn. I spent eighteen months disappearing because it was easier to be invisible than to face all the shit that had happened. But you helped bring me back. And it's hard and it's every day, but I am healing." I let out a shaky breath. "You're important to me. I would do anything to help Killian make sure that life never changes you the way it has changed me and the way it has changed him. *Anything*. Even if that makes me a bad guy."

She nodded, wiping the tears from her cheeks as she walked toward me. "You're not a bad guy, Skylar. Neither is my brother. You're both just . . ." Her lips trembled and more tears spilled down her face. "You're both lost. And me too. But it's a different kind of lost. I'll find my way, I know I will. But I'm scared for you and Killian. I'm scared that what you both need is each other, and you're going to mess up so badly, you'll be worse off than ever."

I listened to her heels clack on the floorboards as she walked away. I heard the front door close behind her.

Only then did I let my own tears fall.

twenty

Have you ever been in a car with someone and the silence between you is so excruciatingly awkward, an image of opening the door and throwing yourself out of the moving vehicle plays over and over in your head?

If so, you'll know exactly how I was feeling as Killian drove us through Glasgow to a place unknown. He'd called and asked me to have lunch with him. He said, "We need to talk."

That could've meant anything, so I was feeling a little nervous as I got into his car. We shared a hello and then I saw the bruising on his knuckles as he drove away.

"That must've been a helluva punch," I observed.

"Believe me, I wanted to do worse." His bruised hand clenched around the steering wheel.

"Autumn actually didn't tell me what the extent of the damage was."

"Swollen eye, broken nose. Nothing he won't recover from."

"Your sister said someone called the cops. How did you get Darren to drop charges against you?"

He shrugged. "I'm persuasive. And anyway . . . he's a coward who thought he'd found someone he could manipulate in my sister. When she proved him wrong by breaking up with him, he tried to scare her into doing what he wanted. As soon as he realized he'd messed with the wrong sister, he practically pissed his trousers." He shook his head. "Autumn knows how to fucking pick them."

Feeling indignant on my friend's behalf, I snapped, "It's not her fault guys have been assholes to her."

Killian threw me an impatient look. "I didn't say it was. She's openhearted and too trusting for her own good. Unfortunately, she's had the bad luck of meeting only men who want to take advantage of that."

"Well, hopefully, next time will be different."

"It needs to be," he replied. "I'm afraid meeting another arsehole might change her."

"You won't let that happen."

This time his lips parted in surprise when he looked at me. Killian O'Dea was many things, including imperfect, but I believed in his love for his sister. That belief seemed to unsettle him and it was the last thing said between us until ten minutes later (it felt like ten hours!) when my curiosity prompted me to ask where we were going.

"Jaconelli's. It's a favorite of Autumn's. She thought you might like it. It's kind of a fifties American diner throwback."

"Okay."

And there was that damn silence again. When were we going to "talk"?

Killian cleared his throat. "It was in the film *Trainspotting*."

"Huh?"

"Jaconelli's. It was in *Trainspotting*." He gave me a brief, questioning look before returning his attention to the road. "Don't tell me you haven't seen *Trainspotting*?"

"Nope, I have not."

"Please tell me you've at least heard of it?"

I chuckled at his disbelief. "I've heard of it. Ewan McGregor, right?"

"Oh, well, if it's got Ewan McGregor in it, of course you've heard of it."

I sniffed haughtily at his sarcasm. "I know it's based on an Irvine Welsh novel."

His lips twitched. "That's something at least. Maybe I'll forgive you for having not seen the film."

"I thought it was set in Edinburgh?"

"It is. Little known fact: most of the scenes were shot in Glasgow."

I smiled. I liked him like this. Chatting about nonsense. This was how he was when we were songwriting. My smile disappeared as I remembered his unkindness at the label. It was like he became a completely different person as soon as we walked into that place.

Just like that, silence fell between us again.

Five minutes later Killian parked off the main road in Maryhill but walked us back toward it. It was a typical fall day here, the rain falling hard and fast and slickening the sidewalks. It would all have been a mass of gray if not for the many vehicles passing by, the typical red sandstone architecture, cigarette stubs, and the multicolored blobs of chewing gum and trash that had cemented itself to the sidewalk over the years.

I'd never been to this part of Glasgow before and tried to take in as much as I could from beneath my umbrella. It seemed to be a busy thoroughfare for the city, with lots of traffic passing through. Businesses stood arm and arm below red sandstone apartments and offices. We strolled past stores on the street and stopped beneath a white sign that said Café D'Jaconelli. It was still early for lunch, so when we walked in, lowering our dripping umbrellas—or "brollies," as Autumn called them—there were a couple of booths open.

I saw exactly what Killian meant by a fifties American diner throwback. The red-leather booths along one side of the wall, the curving stainless steel counter with the ice cream and old-fashioned candy jars behind it, and the essential jukebox in the back.

It was cozy and smelled amazing.

Killian gave me a searching look.

"I like it," I assured him.

"The food is good," he promised, and gestured for me to follow him to the empty booth by the jukebox. Drops of water that had lashed in under his umbrella glistened on his wool coat and I couldn't help but admire the breadth and strength of his shoulders. He had what I'd call a swimmer's build, which made sense because Autumn told me Killian swam every morning before work. It was a part of his life I wasn't privy to: his workout routine. I guess I wasn't privy to much of his personal life at all. And doubtful ever would be.

I slid into the booth opposite him, right next to the silent jukebox, grateful I'd be able to hear him when we eventually got around to our talk.

We ordered, and although I wanted a cheeseburger, I was trying to stick to Brenna's recommended meal plans. She had me eating a whole lot of kale and fish and other healthy, protein-packed stuff and since my weight and energy levels were back to normal, I didn't want to mess with it. So I ordered a baked potato with tuna and a salad.

"You're being good?" he asked, surprised. "This place has the best burgers."

"And it's very tempting, but my meal plan is working for me.

I feel great."

He nodded and didn't press any further. Killian ordered an omelet and a salad after that and I had to wonder if it was in deference to me so I didn't get lunch envy.

"You wanted to talk?" I asked after the waitress left.

He nodded. Then sighed. Then shifted as if uncomfortable. This progressed to him playing with the tongs of the sugar cube bowl. Finally, he glanced around the diner, back at me, and then back to the tongs. I'd never seen him so unsure and I realized why as soon as he opened his mouth.

"I spoke to Autumn. She, uh . . ." His eyes flicked up to mine and then back down to the table. "She said that you told her . . ." He exhaled slowly and again lifted his gaze. There was a quiet intensity in his dark eyes that held me captive. "I hurt you. You told me some very personal things. I acted like a friend and then I was hurtful at the label. I hurt you."

I didn't reply. My expression said it all. *Yes, you hurt me.*

Regret softened his gaze. "I don't like that I hurt you, Skylar. I'm sorry."

Grateful for his apology, I replied, "I forgive you. I'm sorry for being rude to your uncle but not for his sake. For yours."

Killian smirked. "Well, I forgive you. And if you must know, I want to punch him every time he calls me *boy*."

I grinned. "I knew it."

The smirk fell; the warmth bled from his expression. "I acted like an arsehole because of him. It's not the first time. It's just the first time anyone has called me out on it."

Since he was being so honest, I decided to test the boundaries of that honesty. "Why do you need to prove yourself to him?"

Anger flashed across his face. "It's not about proving myself. It's about beating him. He's held the fact that he took Autumn and me into his home over our heads for years. Every failure was our own but every success belonged to him. I want to surpass him. I want him to know that everything we have we have because we *earned* it. That we're better than him. That we don't need him."

God, I truly disliked James Byrne. "He holds the fact that he took in two kids over their heads? So what? He had one tiny bone of decency in his body and that makes you forever in his debt? Fuck that."

Killian's eyes danced at my anger.

I realized I'd cursed quite loudly. "Sorry. It's just . . . you don't see it."

"See what?"

"Why he calls you *boy* when you became a man long before other boys had to. You became a man the moment you realized you were all that Autumn had left."

His eyes flared and he sank into the booth like I'd knocked him off balance.

I nodded. "You did, Killian. You've been a parent since you were eleven years old. You're not perfect. We both know that. But you're one of the most passionate, determined men I've ever met. And your uncle, who is a typical bully, calls you *boy* because he knows you're more of a man than he'll ever be. You're there for your sister to protect her, love her, in a way he's probably never been there for anyone. And he knows what you've done for that label and I have a feeling it scares him. Maybe you tap into his insecurities. Maybe he's afraid you *will* surpass him because he knows you can, and so he does what he can to make you feel small and worthless—knowing it affects you makes him feel powerful again." It all came out in a rush of sympathetic frustration.

And Killian stared at me with an open awe I'd never expected to see on his face. He was so closed off, so good at hiding positive emotions, I thought I felt my heart skip a beat at the naked warmth in his eyes.

"I . . . that makes sense." He sounded winded by the realization.

The waitress appeared with our food, breaking our gazes.

I felt a little off-balance, my skin flushed. After the way he'd treated me at the label, I'd promised myself I was over my crush. Yet all it took for me to forget that vow was an apology and those dark eyes melting like chocolate as he stared at me.

I wanted Killian O'Dea.

I couldn't help myself.

I was tethered to him somehow and I didn't think I'd be able to cut myself loose so easily.

"Skylar?"

I loved the way his deep, accented voice wrapped around my name. "Aye?" I teased, trying to break the electric tension between us.

He didn't smile. He appeared unsure before he said, "I didn't *just* want to apologize for the way I treated you. I wanted to reiterate something."

And just like that, the warmth disappeared. I got a sinking feeling in my stomach and dropped the tomato I'd been about to shove in my mouth. I knew what was coming.

"I won't pretend when you confided in me I did that merely to help get you where you needed to be mentally for the album. You needed someone to talk to, and I genuinely wanted to be that person."

I cleared my throat of the disappointment beginning to clog it. "I appreciate that."

Killian's expression turned almost pleading. "But I . . . I can't be your friend anymore. I think we both know that it was crossing a line into territory that would only confuse things. We can't complicate our business relationship. Things are going to be stressful for you at first and you don't need any extra pressure. And I'm . . . You may be right about my uncle, but *I* still need to be the best. My job is my passion and I can't risk it. Not . . ." He broke off, looking away.

Not for me.

The few times I'd been vulnerable with Killian, I'd felt safe. It had been a purging of emotion so intense, I was drowning in it, and it had been like Killian was there to pull me to the surface.

But this time I only felt naked and cold and alone.

I needed him to think him choosing career over whatever it was between us wasn't a big deal. I needed him to think I didn't care.

That I had other things on my mind.

"You're right," I finally responded, grateful that my voice came out strong, my tone neutral. "A lot is about to happen and I need to be focused."

He assessed me carefully and I gazed at him, seemingly unconcerned. When I was about to throw the salt shaker at him to get him to stop looking at me like a wounded animal, Killian nodded. "Good."

How could it be so easy for him?

Was it only physical attraction for him? Was that why? Did he not feel the pull between us, like there was a cord that drew us together despite our resistance?

Was that all in my head?

I stabbed some salad with my fork, unable to look at him. "So, what's next?"

"Next?"

"With the album?"

"Well, how's the wrist?"

"Not quite ready. I tried playing and I was in pain for the rest of the day."

"I'm sorry to hear that." He sounded so formal.

"Yes, it was quite taxing," I teased in an uppity voice.

He gave me an unimpressed sigh. "In the meantime, I've put together a PR and marketing team. We should arrange a meeting with them. See how we can find ways to handle the inevitable circus when the news of your return hits. And then we can look at how to make sure, once the initial interest fades, that your publicity is career-focused. We don't want your personal life becoming tabloid fodder again."

"Yeah, it would be good if we avoided that."

"I'll arrange the meeting, then? You're ready for that?"

I didn't know if I'd ever be ready for it, but this was happening whether I wanted it to or not. I stared at the man partly to blame for that, wishing I could hate him. "I should probably start checking in on the world, right?"

"How do you mean?"

"Before I sit down in a room with a bunch of people to discuss protecting my personal life, I should probably google a thing or two about the current state of my ex-band." The thought made the food in my stomach churn unpleasantly.

Killian couldn't mask his concern for me, and my patience slipped. "I don't mean to be a bitch, but if we're *not* going to be friends, you can't look at me like that anymore."

For a second his expression turned hard, but then it was gone, that signature blank façade slackening his features. "Fine. I'll get you a laptop. You can google to your heart's content. Just don't come running to me when it messes with your head before you're ready to deal with it."

"Oh, I won't." I gave him a tight smile. *"O'Dea."*

Killian stared at me apparently emotionless . . . but the little tick of muscle in his jaw gave his frustration away.

It was a tiny balm to my own.

twenty-one

When a day passed and Killian still hadn't gotten me access to a laptop, I began to suspect he was deliberately avoiding doing so. I could've hounded him about it and he would've brought me a borrowed one, but I wasn't sure I was ready to start opening all those wounds. Maybe he understood that better than I did.

Yet, when another day passed with another failed attempt to play my guitar, I started to feel stir-crazy. It had only been two days—and there had been days in the past eighteen months that I hadn't spoken a word to anyone—but I was used to speaking to Killian almost every day, and if not him, then Autumn.

How mad at me was she? The thought of losing her friendship made me feel sick, so I finally got up the nerve to text her.

I didn't mean 2 go behind ur back 2 O'Dea. I was worried abt u.

While I waited for a response, I read a book but I read the same paragraph fifteen times before my phone finally binged in response.

I'm not mad. Just embarrassed. Also I'm worried about you . . .

Oh no. Did we have to have another open conversation about how her brother and I were planning to ignore our attraction . . . because *awkward.*

But my phone binged before I could respond.

. . . You text in abbreviation? Skylar, I'm shocked. Really. Maybe you should see a text therapist. Xx

I grinned, absolutely relieved she was joking with me.

Me: I know. It's a problem. I've tried rehab bt it didn't stick.

Autumn: Why would you miss the 'u' from 'but'? It's one letter! Lazy much??

Me: I cld b mo lzy . . .

Autumn: It's sad that I understood what that meant. Xx

Me: So wht u doin?

Autumn: Trying to decide what I want to do with my future.

Me: Heavy. Dya wanna take a break from the heavy?

Autumn: What did you have in mind?

Me: Anythg tht will get me out of this apt.

There was no response for a minute or two, but finally she replied.

Autumn: Have you ever been to King Tut's?

I felt a flush of excitement at the thought. King Tut's Wah Wah Hut was one of Glasgow's cult music venues. It was where Alan McGee discovered Oasis. Blur, Biffy Clyro, Radiohead, Kings of Leon—they'd all played there. New bands and old still played the venue. The guys and I had wanted to see it for ourselves when we played Glasgow, but we never got the chance.

Me: No so don't dangle that carrot unless u mean 2 let me eat it!

Autumn: LMAO. Would I do that to you?

Me: Possibly . . .

Autumn: A friend bought tickets to see this guy I've never heard of but she has to work now. I googled the guy—Saul Crowe—and he's really good. Do you want to come with me? It's tonight at 8pm. Xx

Me: 100%!

Autumn: Okay, great! I'm actually not in the city today so I'll just get back in time for the gig. Can you meet me there at 7:45pm?

Me: Not a problem. See u then! Can't W8T!

Autumn: Too many abbreviations!!!!!! Xx

I laughed and replied:

Me: xx is an abbreviation for kiss, kiss.

Autumn: Well, it sounds creepy as kiss, kiss . . . xx

Me: True. x

Autumn: Aw, I got a kiss from Skylar! I feel special. Xx

Me: :p

I TOOK A CAB TO St. Vincent Street that evening because I had no idea how to get to King Tut's from the apartment. When the cab driver dropped me off, I was slightly confused. We were on a wide sloping street in the commercial part of the city. Opposite me was a glass office building, but behind me was a row of typical Georgian townhouses that had been converted into business premises and apartments. Lights below a large bay window of one lit up the big King Tut's signage beneath it.

Huh. Not at all what I'd expected.

Apparently, King Tut's was an inconspicuous basement bar.

I shivered in the cold November air, hugging myself as I watched two young couples walk down the steps to the entrance. Not really knowing what to wear and sick of jeans after twenty months of wearing them, I'd chosen a casual but formfitting black dress Autumn had talked me into buying a few weeks ago. It had a scooped neck that bared my collarbone and dipped low in the back, three-quarter-length sleeves, and it hugged my thighs to a couple of inches above the knee. Paired with my black tights and wedged black boots, it wasn't overly revealing but it had a casual sexiness that made me feel good.

It'd been a while since I felt good about my body, but I'd

gotten my hips and ass back over the last six weeks and I wanted to celebrate it. Yay for peanut butter!

However, I hadn't wanted to overheat in the venue so I'd only thrown on my blazer and a scarf and was consequently freaking cold waiting outside for Autumn. Then I realized she hadn't specified where we would meet. Inside or out?

Me: I'm outside. U here yet?

After what felt like forever because of the aforementioned chill, my phone binged.

Autumn: I'm inside. At a booth in the bar. You'll see me as soon as you come in. xx

Thank God. Hurrying down the steps, I pushed open the door, desperate for some heat in my bones. I might have a beer. It had been a long time since I'd had a beer.

Anticipation and excitement were things I thought long dead so the giddiness of stepping into a famous music venue, looking forward to grabbing a beer and listening to good music with a friend was so sweet, it almost made me want to cry.

I walked up a couple of steps and opened the door into the inner bar. The smell of stale beer and bar food hit me and I smiled as I stepped further into the room to search for Autumn. The space was small—a row of booths along the back wall, a bar opposite it, and at the far end double doors that I assumed led up to the event room. It was covered in music memorabilia—photographs and posters—and had the kind of well-worn appearance that reminded me of an aging legendary rock star who could dress whatever fucking way he liked because he was a goddamned legend.

I liked it immediately.

Where was Autumn to share this moment with me? Hmm.

I was looking for red hair so it took me a moment to see *him* instead.

His head was bent over his phone as he sat at a booth on his own, a half-filled pint of lager in front of him.

Killian?

My heart rate sped up and I suddenly felt self-conscious in my dress.

Autumn never said her brother was joining us, the little sneak. I shot a look at the bar, wondering if she was there, and made eye contact with a tall, good-looking bartender. He had a scruffy beard and broad shoulders. He was lean and wiry and his overall appearance was "music aficionado who could give a shit." He gave me a crooked smile and I returned it with a small one of my own, confused as to where my friend was and why Killian was here. I reluctantly drew my gaze back to him and our eyes immediately connected.

He held me still with that intense focus and I tried to catch the breath he always managed to knock out of me.

Business associates and nothing more.

Right.

Newcomers accidentally knocked into me with an apology, and I stumbled out of the eye lock with Killian. Okay. So he was here. That was fine. Autumn would be our buffer.

I pasted a small, not-too-friendly smile on as I strode across the bar, shrugging out of my blazer and scarf. I threw them onto the cracked leather bench seat before sliding in. "Hey." When I looked at him again, he was dragging his gaze up my body in a way that sent a delicious shiver down my spine.

"Hi. I wasn't expecting you."

I shook my head. "No, Autumn didn't say you'd be here either."

Killian tensed and then comprehension slackened his expression. "She wouldn't," he muttered, touching the screen on his phone. "Or would she?"

"Wouldn't she what?"

Instead of answering me, he put his phone to his ear and I could hear it dialing. I heard a click and the faint sound of a woman's voice answering.

"Autumn, you are planning to be here tonight, right?"

She wasn't here? What? "She just texted and told me she was here."

His jaw clenched and then his expression darkened at whatever she said on the other end of the line. "Right . . . so this just happened to come up at the last minute? . . . So why did you tell Skylar you were here already? . . . Right . . . aye . . . sure . . . You and I will talk about this later." He hung up on her and threw his phone on the table.

Starting to put two and two together, I shifted in my seat, feeling the urge to bolt. "She's not coming?"

"No." He glared but I knew it wasn't *at* me. "She said she had a friend emergency and was needed elsewhere. She lied to you about being here because she thought you wouldn't come in if you knew it was me waiting for you."

Liar, liar, pants on fire.

This was a setup.

And we both knew it.

Fuuuuuuck.

"Well, she's wrong," I cracked, trying to defuse the situation. "Not even you could keep me from seeing King Tut's for the first time."

His gaze softened. "You've never been here before?"

I shook my head, grinning like a fangirl. "I'm pretty excited."

"Aye." He smiled and then glanced around. "I suppose it has that thing."

"What thing?"

"That air of anticipation. Magic has happened here. People come in wondering if they're going to be lucky enough to witness a magic moment."

"Yeah," I agreed, stroking my fingers across the air in front of me. "You can feel it. The guys and I would've loved to play here, but we weren't cool enough."

Killian's lips twitched. "Coolness is in the eye of the beholder."

"Or something like that." I grinned.

We shared a warm look and the tension between us increased tenfold. I could only assume it was because we were doing something that didn't involve work, and this felt . . . Well, in this dress it felt like a date, which was so far beyond what we'd agreed to, it wasn't funny.

"You don't have to stay with me. I don't need a babysitter."

He shook his head. "I want to hear this Crowe guy."

Okay, then. I was definitely going to need a beer to get through this.

"I'm going to get a drink." I grabbed my purse and was moving to slide out of the booth when Killian got up first.

"I'll get it. What would you like?"

"Uh . . ." I looked past him to the bar, hoping to see a list of beers. "What do they have? What are you drinking?"

"King Tut's Lager. It's brewed in Glasgow."

Ooh. "Well, I have to have that, then. Half a pint though." I made a gesture with my finger and thumb. "I'm only little."

Killian's eyes flickered down what he could see of my body and I thought I saw a flush high on his cheeks. But the lighting was low so I couldn't be certain. He cleared his throat and turned away with a muttered, "Right."

My cheeks felt hot and I put a hand to one as I watched him walk over to the bar. The place wasn't too packed, but it was possible everyone was already in the venue waiting for the band. I could hear the soft thrum of music and guessed it must've been the opening act. Although eager to get up there, I really needed a drink before I had to stand next to Killian in a darkened room.

God, he had an ass on him.

He wasn't wearing his usual uniform of black suit trousers and shirt that fit him like a glove and showcased his lean, strong physique. He was wearing dark jeans that cupped his muscular ass and a red plaid shirt over a Kaleo T-shirt. He looked good in red. He usually wore darker colors but the red made his hair look blacker, his skin more golden. Dressed like that—indie, relaxed—he looked younger.

I felt more than a tingle of heat between my legs as I studied him standing at the bar. His rugged, sharp profile was somehow more familiar to me than any other person's profile on the planet. I imagined walking up beside him, sliding my hands down his fine ass and reaching up on my tiptoes to press a kiss to his neck. Breathe in the scent of soap, spicy aftershave, and Killian. Run my tongue along the rim of his ear. Feel his heavy, warm heat lean back into me, the rumble of his groan vibrating through me—

Oh, fuck.

I shook off the thought, knowing my cheeks were probably rosy red. My whole body was left needy and wanting. I crossed my legs under the table and looked anywhere but at Killian, hoping my peaked nipples weren't visible through my bra and way-too clingy dress.

My gaze landed on a booth a few down from ours because there was a group of young women laughing and shooting hungry looks at the bar.

At Killian.

A roar of possessiveness I didn't know I was capable of shot through me as I watched them. In fact, I think they were eyeing him *and* the bartender.

To be fair, they were both very juicy eye candy.

But Killian was *my* eye candy!

Shit.

I slumped back in my seat.

No, he wasn't.

And I shouldn't want him to be.

What a clusterfuck.

"Here." Killian was suddenly back and pushing a half pint of lager toward me.

The smell of hops filled my nostrils as I reached for it, unable to look him in the eye for fear he'd see my sexual frustration. "Thanks."

He slid back into his side of the booth and I could feel him staring as he reached for his own pint. "Crowe will be coming on soon."

"Right." I took a drink, thinking he was politely telling me to hurry up.

"You okay?"

"Sure."

"Is that why you're not looking at me?"

Reluctantly, I met his gaze. "I'm looking at you." *God, Skylar, act normal!* I gave him a crooked smile that was meant to be teasing and probably looked panicked. "And I'm not the only one."

Shit, why did I say that?

Why would you draw attention to the pretty girls eyeing him?

Moron!

He quirked that damnable eyebrow. "Sorry?"

Well, you've done it now. "The girls behind you. They were watching you at the bar."

Killian didn't say anything. He stared at me inscrutably. I was beginning to consider rolling myself out of the booth when he said, "The bartender asked if we were here together."

My gaze flew to the hot bartender right as he looked up from pulling a pint. He offered me another small smile.

I looked at Killian. "What did you say?"

"Well, he didn't ask in what way we were here together, so I told him 'aye.' He drew his own conclusions. I'm sure you could clear it up if you were that way inclined," he drawled casually before taking a sip of beer.

But his eyes never left mine, and there was nothing casual about the way he was looking at me.

I felt a deep, throbbing tug low in my belly and had to pull my gaze from his or I was going to launch myself across the booth.

"I'm not that way inclined," I mumbled, and sipped the lager.

Liking the taste, I took a bigger pull.

"Skylar?"

Oh God, why did I have to love the way he said my name? I cleared my throat. "Uh, yeah?"

His eyes roamed over my face as if he was searching for something, and then he shook his head. "Nothing." He then took a huge swallow of lager and as I watched his Adam's apple move with the gulp, I imagined running my tongue over it.

Oh, hell.

What was the matter with me?

Usually, I could keep my wayward thoughts about Killian O'Dea suppressed. They were there but deep, deep in the back of my mind.

Was it this place? Was this venue turning me on?

"Skylar?"

"Hmm?" I drew my eyes back to his face.

His features were so taut, he looked almost angry. But his eyes were hot, not hard. "What are you thinking?" he asked.

My breath puffed out and I couldn't help but admit, "You don't want to know."

We shared a frustrated look and then tore our gazes from each other. Why would Autumn do this to us? It was her fault. We'd been alone together a lot and had been very able to ignore the sexual tension between us.

So why was it so freaking hard now?

I blamed him. Usually he was a master at hiding his emotions, but he was looking at me like he wanted to see me naked.

"Maybe we should go in." I threw back the rest of the pint, feeling it slosh unpleasantly in my stomach.

"Another beer to take in with us?" He slid out first.

To get through the next ninety minutes alone with Killian? Probably not a bad idea.

Once he'd bought us fresh pints, Killian led me through the double doors at the back of the bar. The walls were timber clad and painted a shiny white. Posters covered most of them. But it was the stairs that made me stop.

I grinned and looked up at Killian who smiled back down at me. "The Steps of Fame."

Every step had a year painted on it, and next to it the artists who had played King Tut's that year.

"1993, Oasis, The Verve," I mumbled as we slowly walked up. "1997, No Doubt . . . 1999, Biffy Clyro." I nudged him. "One of your favorites."

He pointed as we walked up to 2004.

I shook my head in awe. "Kasabian. The Killers. Oh man, this place is like porn for music lovers."

Killian laughed. "Weird analogy but okay."

I giggled as he pushed open a door at the top of the stairs and we were hit by the loud thrum of an amp growling.

The room was tiny. When they said King Tut's was an intimate venue, they weren't kidding. If you got stuck at the door, you wouldn't see the band because the small stage was tucked at the far right of the room.

We walked farther in, the room not too crowded since Saul Crowe was still an up-and-comer. He was younger than I was expecting, maybe nineteen or twenty, with a mop of thick, curly blond hair and a baby face. He was sitting on a stool with a guitar in hand. He had a mouth organ resting around his neck and a pedal attached to a single drum at his feet.

The amp purred behind him. Behind that, painted on the walls was King Tut's Wah Wah Hut signage.

We stood in among the smallish crowd where I could see.

"I, uh, wrote this next song when I was fifteen and going through some shit," he mumbled into the mic.

As he shifted on his stool getting ready to play, I felt Killian lean into me. My breath caught.

His own hot breath whispered across my ear. "Do you want to play here?"

Surprise flashed through me, momentarily distracting me from how ridiculously sexy it was having him whisper in my ear. "What?"

He smirked at my shocked expression. "I can get you booked here."

My heart pounded at the thought as my gaze flew back to the small stage. I looked back at him like he might be Santa Claus in disguise. "Really?"

Killian's eyes were soft, too soft, too warm on me. "If it'll make you happy."

What . . . ?

The sound of the mouth organ pierced the room, jolting us

out of our intense staring match.

The kid was good.

Then he sang in a growling, heavy rock voice that was a complete surprise. The kid was better than good. He was excellent. And a momentary distraction from the man beside me.

But only momentary.

Because after an upbeat rock song with a hard country-folk edge, he played a beautiful acoustic ballad.

Not merely beautiful.

Sexy.

How a nineteen- or twenty-year-old kid had the experience to speak of love and attraction the way he did, I didn't know, but as he sang of "running his tongue down her spine" and "his little death from her moonlit kisses," I stopped thinking about how impressed I was with him.

And started thinking about what it would feel like to have Killian run his tongue down *my* spine.

To feel those strong, beautiful hands gripping my hips, strumming my nipples like he delicately plucked the strings of his Taylor . . .

My chest rose and fell in shallow breaths, aware of everything about him as he stood in the dark beside me. His breathing sounded shallow too; he emanated hot tension. He shifted from one foot to the other, as if restless.

He lifted his glass to take another drink and his arm brushed against mine, sending an overreaction of sensation, a prickle of goosebumps along my skin.

After song five, I knew I needed to get away from Killian or I was going to ruin everything by throwing myself at him. I bravely made contact by nudging him and he frowned down at me.

I mimicked the act of drinking and then hurried out and

down to the bar.

Having a floor between us really helped.

I almost collapsed against the bar in relief and exhaustion.

The bartender chuckled as he wandered down the quiet bar toward me. "Bad date?"

No, the absolute opposite of a bad date. "No. Just too warm. Can I have a half pint of the King Tut's Lager?"

"Ye sure can." He pulled a pint and then looked up at me quizzically. "Ye know, I've been trying tae place ye all night, thinking we've met before."

I tensed, not needing to deal with being recognized on top of my out-of-control attraction to a man I couldn't have. I wrinkled my nose in confusion. "Oh. I don't think so."

"No, but then ye started talking and it hit me." He came back down the bar with my pint and leaned over, studying my face. "Ye look a bit like that singer who disappeared off the face of the planet."

I decided to head him off at the pass. "Skylar Finch, right?" I gave him what I hoped was a teasing smile along with a roll of my eyes.

"Ah, ye get that a lot, do ye?" He grinned flirtatiously.

"I do. All I need is the rainbow hair."

His eyes took in my own now-short, light blonde hair. "Nah, yours is good. My opinion?" He leaned closer, blue eyes dancing. "Ye'er way hotter than Skylar Finch."

I wanted to burst out laughing but instead gave him a pleased smile. "I've heard that too."

He chuckled and straightened up, so I handed him money for my drink. He took it but brushed his fingers over mine. "Do ye have tae go back up or can ye stay and talk tae me a while?"

Deciding he was a much safer option than Killian, I agreed to stay. I let him flirt with me while I drank my lager, feeling loose and a bit tipsy. He asked me questions I couldn't answer without giving away the truth, so I danced around them coyly, which in retrospect came off a lot like flirting.

And that's how Killian found me.

I didn't hear him come into the bar because of the music and I was laughing at something the bartender said. But I felt him as soon as he got within two yards.

Killian's hard gaze flicked between me and the bartender as he strode over to us and put his empty pint glass on the bar top with a calmness I saw through. He stared at me with a mix of annoyance, want, and incredulity.

I didn't know how to untangle myself from his eyes.

I never could.

Especially when they smoldered.

I'd hung out at parties with Hollywood actors and charismatic rockers but I'd never met a man who actually *smoldered* until Killian O'Dea.

"We need to leave." He sounded so cold, so completely at odds with his expression.

And I knew he was right. Whatever Autumn was trying to do here had worked, and it was dangerous. I nodded and pushed my nearly empty glass away. I said goodbye to the bartender who didn't hide his disappointment that I was leaving.

Killian rounded the bar, placed a possessive hand on my lower back, and gently pushed me forward.

"Put your blazer on," he commanded as he held the door open for me.

"I'm not cold." And I wasn't. I was burning hot. Part alcohol, part utter sexual frustration.

"You might not feel it but it's cold."

We hurried up the steps and I saw the light of an available taxi in the distance. Rather than put on my blazer, I prioritized getting home and away from Killian O'Dea and threw out my hand.

"I'll be fine," I said, releasing a long breath of relief as the taxi indicated it was pulling over for me. I gave Killian a quick look that didn't land on any particular part of him. "Thanks for tonight." I marched over to the taxi and pulled the door open. I'd put my foot in to slide inside and was pulling the door closed when I felt resistance.

Killian.

He nodded to me. "Get in."

Confused, I let go of the door and slid along the back seat, watching as he got in beside me and slammed the cab door. He rattled off my address to the driver and stared stonily ahead.

"What are you doing?" I whispered.

"Making sure you get home all right."

I didn't reply.

I stared out the window at the passing lights of the city in the dark and tried not to think about the man beside me. But the more I tried not to think about him, the more I thought about him.

I'd never experienced this kind of heightened attraction before. I knew it existed between me and Killian. It was there during the songwriting and it was definitely there in his office that day. However, we'd both had tight control over it.

But now it was like I'd lost hold of the reins and whatever I was feeling was so big, it was spilling out all over Killian. Or maybe it was the opposite. Maybe it was him who had lost control and was making me careen all over the place. And now it was like he could sense my body's reaction, sense that my breasts felt tight and swollen, that my nipples were two stiff peaks against my bra, and there was a ready, hot slickness between my legs.

I'd never wanted anyone the way I wanted Killian right then. Not even Micah.

The longing was so sharp, it brought tears of frustration to my eyes.

I blinked them away, grateful to see the streetlights reflecting off the dark waters of the Clyde and the sight of my building a short distance away.

"I'll pay," Killian muttered.

Even if I paid, he was still paying because the money I had was from the borrowed allowance he provided me.

Shouldn't that be a cold reminder of what he is to you, Skylar?

But it wasn't.

Shit.

As soon as the cab pulled up to my building, I muttered a thanks to the driver and a goodbye to Killian. I slammed the door behind me and got out, shock freezing me on the sidewalk as I watched Killian emerge from the cab too.

The driver pulled off, leaving us staring at each other on the street.

Fierce need burned in Killian's eyes.

Almost pleading.

Longing.

Mirrored desperate want.

I guessed we were both done fighting this, then.

A deep thrill moved through my lower belly and that slick heat got a whole lot slicker and hotter between my legs.

We fell into step beside each other and I unlocked the main door with shaking hands. He held it open for me and I moved past him, my breasts brushing against his chest. His breathing faltered, as did my own. When we stepped into the elevator, the oxygen seemed to thin. All you could hear was our shallow breaths.

My fingers itched to reach for him, but I held onto some restraint, even though the urge to rip off his shirt was extremely powerful.

I trembled so hard to get the key in the apartment door that Killian covered my hands with his and helped me. For a moment we stood there, his hand wrapped around mine, the heat of his body at my back. I wanted to ask what the hell we were doing, thinking, but I was afraid it would shatter this. That it would make us overthink ourselves out of it.

And I didn't want to think.

I wanted to feel.

I pushed the door open and strode into the apartment, dropping my purse and key on the side table as I passed it, listening as he closed and locked the door behind us and followed me into the sitting room. Standing with my back to him, feeling him everywhere as if he were wrapped around me, even though he was on the other side of the room, I gazed out at the dark river.

As soon as I turned around, everything would change.

I had a moment of hesitation and then, "Skylar?"

And that was all it took. Him saying my damn name in that sexy as fuck voice.

I whirled around, letting exactly how much I wanted him blaze from my eyes. His hands clenched at his sides and his nostrils flared.

Then we rushed each other. Our bodies collided seconds before our mouths did.

It wasn't a sweet romance-movie kiss.

It was lips, tongue, *need*.

Killian's hand fisted the short strands of my hair as he held my head to his; my fingers bit into his biceps. I grasped onto him for what was nothing short of a ravaging.

The kiss tasted of longing, frustration, desperation, and

punishment. A punishment of each other for having feelings we knew we shouldn't have.

I whimpered against his tongue as his other hand gripped my ass hard to pull me against his thick erection.

The sound made Killian grind his hips harder into me. He ripped his mouth from mine to ask on a groan, squeezing my ass, "Where the hell did this arse come from?"

I laughed, reaching for his face, wanting his lips back. "I grew it just for you."

His chuckle rumbled in my mouth as we kissed harder, the need inside me flaring toward combustion.

I needed him inside me.

I didn't want foreplay. Or to be teased and stretched and taunted.

I wanted to be filled. Overwhelmingly filled. I wanted him inside me. Now.

Fumbling for the button on his jeans, I made that very clear.

Then we were on the floor, hands pawing and ripping while lips and tongues found any naked spot they could find. I'd frantically shoved Killian's shirt off but before I could get to his T-shirt, he was pushing the hem of my dress up. His longer fingers curled around the elastic waist of my tights and he tugged so wildly, I heard them tear.

Neither of us cared as he yanked them and my underwear down my thighs. They got caught around my boots and Killian cursed as he managed to yank one boot off along with the torn leg of my tights and underwear.

But as he struggled with the other, my patience fled. "Fuck it," I panted. "Just get inside me. Killian, now."

Whether it was my saying his name or my pleading or both, he abandoned the other shoe and moved back over me. His kisses were even hungrier as I fumbled to pull the zipper down on his jeans.

He slipped his hands between my legs, sliding his fingers into me. The wet he found there made him grunt into my mouth. He tore his lips from mine and my chest rose and fell in frenzied breaths as he stared into my eyes with more hunger than any man ever had.

And the fact that it was Killian looking at me like that only increased my desire.

"You're soaked." His face hardened with need and he sat up straddling me, the movement forcing my hands to fall to my sides. I watched him, watched his shaking hands, all composure gone, as he tugged out his wallet from his back pocket, flipped it open impatiently, and removed a foil package.

Anticipation made me squirm beneath him as he threw away the wallet and tugged the zipper on his jeans down the rest of the way. He never broke eye contact as he shoved down his jeans and boxers just far enough to release his thick, swollen erection. It saluted me as he tore open the condom packet.

My fingers clawed the carpet beneath me. Every second he took felt like torture. But to be fair, he rolled that condom on in record time and fell between my legs, his elbows braced on either side of my head as he kissed me.

I let my legs fall open, wide, and as he nudged against me, I moaned into his mouth only to break the kiss to beg. "Killian."

He pushed into me. Hard.

My desire eased his way considerably but he was big, thick, and that overwhelming fullness I'd been desperate for shot electric sparks of pleasure down my spine.

I needed more.

"Killian," I breathed, sliding my hands down his ass, pushing his jeans further out of the way so I could curl my fingers into his silken, hard muscle.

"Fuck, Skylar," he growled, his head bowing into my neck as he pushed up onto his hands and moved his hips.

If everything was out of control before, it turned to animal chaos. Everything we were, wanted, and needed, centered around the hot, fast, hard drive of him inside me. My hips rose in shallow thrusts to meet his, my cries filling his ears as his groans filled mine.

I held onto him so fiercely, I probably left bruises.

The tension inside me tightened, tightened, tightened every time he pulled out and slammed back in. So full. So overwhelmingly full.

It was bliss.

Coiling bliss.

"I'm close," I gasped.

He reached for my thigh, wrapping his big hand around it, and pulled it up against his hip, changing the angle of his thrust.

The tension inside shattered, lights flickering behind my eyes as I flew to some before unknown physical nirvana. I think I might have screamed.

It rolled through me, my inner muscles rippling and squeezing around Killian. His hips pounded faster against me and then momentarily stilled before he cried out my name, his grip on my thigh bruising as his hips jerked with the swell and throb of his release.

As his climax shuddered through him, he let go of my thigh and slumped over me. I felt his warm, heavy weight and closed my eyes, enjoying the sweetest, most contented satisfaction I'd ever felt.

Our labored breathing filled the apartment.

My heart was thumping so hard.

Finally, the blood rushing in my ears calmed and I became fully cognizant of our situation.

I was sprawled on the living room floor with Killian on top of me, between my legs, still inside me. My dress was pushed up around my waist, my underwear and ripped tights were stuck around my right ankle because I was still wearing a shoe, and Killian was still fully dressed.

It had been frantic.

Animalistic.

A base need to have him inside me after weeks of foreplay.

And it had been the best sex I'd ever had.

So I lay there hoping he wasn't going to ruin it by letting reality intrude.

Finally, Killian lifted his head so our lips were inches from each other's. He wore the amused, soft look of a man who had been deeply satisfied. It made my lips twitch with relief.

"Well, we're definitely doing that again."

Laughter bubbled out of me, making me shake beneath him. We grinned at each other as I replied, "Yeah, we are."

twenty-two

"Blame it on the dress."

I rolled my head to the side to stare at Killian incredulously. "Seriously? It was the dress?"

We'd graduated from the living room floor to my bed. I'd changed into a tank top and fresh underwear while Killian cleaned up in the bathroom.

When he came out, his eyes drank in the sight of me sitting on the bed waiting for him. He lingered on my bare legs and then shucked off his shoes. The T-shirt followed, and I got all warm and tingly again as he removed his jeans. I'd felt his lean muscle while holding on to him for dear life as he moved inside me, but *seeing* it made my girly bits very happy.

Although broad-shouldered, he wasn't bulky muscle. I knew that. But I hadn't anticipated how defined his physique would be. That six-pack. Dear God, I might swoon. That came from more than swimming. The man had to work out every day to look like that.

"Enjoying the view?" Killian asked, smirking as he clambered over me and onto the other side of the bed. He laid back on my pillows, one arm stretched above his head, and watched me.

It was weird how comfortable this was.

I'd stretched out beside him. "I am. I'm also waiting for you to start freaking out. What happened to that tight control of yours?"

That's when he said, "Blame it on the dress."

"Seriously? It was the dress?"

"It was the dress." He nodded, completely unabashed.

I wrinkled my nose. "God, even smart men can be so easily undone by a dress."

He studied me, suddenly serious. "Only if it's on the right woman."

Stupidly pleased by that, I bit my lip to stop my huge grin.

Killian's eyes dropped to my mouth and darkened.

"So, you saw me in the dress and all your rules and ideas about us went out the window?"

He scrubbed a hand down his face and let it drop limply at his side. He looked resigned. "I can't fight how I feel about you anymore. Clearly. It's fucking exhausting anyway."

Butterflies fluttered in my belly. I wanted to ask him what exactly he felt, but I wasn't brave enough. Instead I teased, "And how long have you been planning to seduce me with your eye smolder?"

His lips twitched. "Eye smolder?"

"Yes. Eye smolder." I turned onto my side, bracing my elbow on the bed and my hand on my head. "You smoldered me."

"I didn't know that was one of my special powers."

"Well, it is."

"I didn't plan on anything. You know I didn't."

"I guess what I really mean is . . . how long have you wanted to throw me on the floor and fuck my brains out?"

His brows drew together. "Is that what I did?"

"Don't worry, I liked it. Or did my almighty orgasm not make that clear?"

He flashed me a wicked grin. "No, that was very clear. And I don't know. I don't know when admiring you, your music, turned into something else."

I nodded because I understood. "I don't know when it turned into this either. But it happened. And you haven't looked at me blankly and told me it can't happen again . . . so what now?"

"Do you want me to say that?"

"No. I want it to happen again," I admitted. "I feel . . ." How much did I say without scaring him away?

Killian reached out and drew his fingertips softly down my cheek to trace my lips. "You feel?"

I held his gaze and whispered, "I *feel*."

He squeezed his eyes closed briefly and then sat up, sliding his hand around the nape of my neck to pull me to him. This time his kiss was soft, lush, and so sweet, I found myself melting into him. I wrapped my arms around his shoulders and shifted so I was straddling him. He wrapped his arm around my back, pulling me flush to his body. I luxuriated in the joy of being held against the solid, strong weight of him.

We kissed. Learning every curve of each other's lips, every dance of our tongues, our taste.

It was the first time in forever that I didn't feel alone.

"What are we doing?" I panted as we finally broke for breath. I leaned my forehead against his and closed my eyes, sending a wish out to the universe that this moment could last forever.

"I don't know," he answered, giving my waist a squeeze. "I only know I don't want to stop."

"But the . . ." I didn't want to mention the album. I didn't want the reminder of our bargain.

"We could keep it a secret." He pulled back so I had to look into his eyes. "See each other in secret until the album is out and the dust settles. Then no one will give a fuck if we're seeing each other. My uncle won't care as long as we're making the label money. And I'm not famous, Skylar. Your fans won't care."

He was looking that far ahead? This really wasn't just sex to him? The question tumbled out of my mouth before I could stop it.

Killian frowned at me in displeasure. "Do you really think I'm the kind of man who would risk my career and yours for a simple fuck?"

I shifted on his lap, feeling the evidence of his desire. "Attraction can be a powerful thing. And I know about Yasmin and your many nonstarter relationships."

His scowl deepened to a glower. "Who told you about Yasmin?"

"More to the point," I loosened my hold on him, "why didn't you tell me about her?"

His grip on me tightened, pulling me back into him. "Because it was a casual relationship that didn't mean anything and didn't go anywhere."

"And you didn't want me to know you had a girlfriend?"

"I didn't want you to worry that there was a woman waiting for me to come home when I wanted you to be in the moment with me, working on your songs. And she wasn't waiting on me to come home because we never lived together." His hand tightened around my nape, his expression fierce. "I broke it off with her when I realized that the first person I thought of every morning when I woke up was the same person I thought of last before I went to sleep."

Realization made me melt into him. "I knew you cared about me."

"What I feel is a little stronger than that, Skylar." He stared at me with pure need. "You're mine."

A thrill shot through me, tingles and heat prickling my skin. I shook my head, holding staunchly to my independence. "Micah used to say that too, but I don't belong to anyone."

He let out a low growl, like a freaking caveman, and flipped me onto my back, pressing me into the bed. "If you were *his,* my dick wouldn't have been inside you thirty minutes ago. You're *mine*, Skylar Finch. I think somehow I've always felt like you were mine. That's why I didn't go after Jonathan Welsh myself because I would have killed him," he hissed. "Killed him for hurting you."

"Killian . . ." I shook my head, feeling unsure, confused, wondering why a part of me wanted to scream in revolt while another was howling with exultation.

"And I'm yours," he softened, brushing his mouth gently over mine. "Yours."

Mine.

Hadn't I thought that before? Hadn't I thought that in the bar when those girls were eyeing what was mine?

I slid my hands up his shoulders to clasp his familiar face. My feelings for him were complicated. I had feelings I didn't want to acknowledge because they would ruin the bliss of being with him like this. Of having Killian O'Dea look at me like I meant the world to him.

A man who did not love easily.

And he wanted to belong to me.

"You're mine," I agreed. "I'm yours."

Killian kissed me hungrily in answer. A kiss that led to us shedding our clothes so he could slide inside me slowly and deeply. We took our time. We touched and stroked and kissed.

While he moved inside me, he stared deep into my eyes, and although the words were never said . . . I felt loved.

SO ATTUNED TO KILLIAN, I knew even in sleep when he was pulling away from me. The bed moved and the sound of rustling filtered into my conscience.

I blinked slowly, my eyelids feeling heavy like I hadn't had enough sleep, and I turned my head on the pillow to see Killian sitting on the bed in his jeans, tugging on his shoes.

Light filtered into the room through the split in the curtains.

Was he not going to wake me?

Did he regret last night and had decided to sneak out?

I groaned sleepily and sat up, not about to let him have the satisfaction of hightailing it out of the apartment without an awkward confrontation.

He looked over his shoulder at me and smiled softly. It made my tense muscles relax. "I was trying not to wake you."

I pushed my fingers through my hair to get it out of my face. "What time is it?"

Killian stood and rounded the bed to pick up his T-shirt. "Back of eight."

Hearing the disgruntled tone, I couldn't help but grin. "Have I fucked with your schedule, Mr. O'Dea?"

He gave me a wicked grin that I was quickly growing addicted to and then tugged his T-shirt over his head. "Quite literally."

"What time do you usually get up in the morning?"

He hesitated, as if unsure about telling me. Then, "Five."

Horrified, I gaped. "Why?"

Killian chuckled. "I like to swim and then hit the gym before my day starts."

"I knew it." I eyed him as he came toward me. "No man has a body like yours without working for it."

"Aye, well, some of us aren't lucky enough to wake up as sexy as you without having to work for it." He braced his hands on the bed in front of me, his dark eyes dancing. I was at the point of squirming under such intense focus when he murmured, "You have the most extraordinary eyes. The first time you really looked at me, I was stunned."

I smiled, feeling stupidly giddy at the idea that even as a homeless waif, I'd had the power to stun Killian O'Dea. "I never would've guessed that."

"Well, it's true. I knew you had different-colored eyes because when I was researching you, there were a few internet articles about it. But you can't truly appreciate how beautiful they are until they're staring back at you." He smoldered. "Or how good it feels to gaze into them as you come around my cock."

I flushed. "Good morning to you."

"Morning."

"And as to your other point, I do have to work hard to look good. It takes skill to eat as much peanut butter as I have to get my ass back."

His beautiful eyes dropped to my mouth. "The effort is much appreciated."

My hand shot up between us as he leaned in to kiss me. He raised an eyebrow. "I haven't brushed my teeth."

"Move your hand, Skylar."

"Nope." I slid out of the bed, blowing past him so quickly he barely had time to blink.

I heard his chuckle as I dashed into the bathroom and grabbed my toothbrush. Once I'd brushed, I came back out with a sheepish smile.

Killian was waiting for me, arms crossed over his chest. "You're very weird."

"Uh, something you knew before you threw me to the carpet and fucked my brains out."

"You keep describing it like that and I'm sensing you're not going to let me forget it went down like that anytime soon."

I sauntered over to him and he grabbed me by the waist, hauling me up against his chest. Without my heeled wedges, I felt short in his arms. I looked up at him with a playful smile. "Why would I want you or I to ever forget that it went down like that? It was the hottest thing that's ever happened to me."

He wore a smug, pleased look. "Me too."

His answer made me feel smug and pleased too. "Yeah?"

"Aye," he muttered, bending his head.

This time I let him kiss me. It started out sweet, lazy, but I made the mistake of moaning and Killian's hold on me tightened. His kiss grew hungry and I found myself stumbling back into the wall as he pressed the entire length of his body against mine.

Heat and need flushed through me and I slid my hands under his T-shirt, pushing it up, desperate to feel his warm skin against mine. He took the hint and drew it over his head and threw it away. He caressed my stomach under my tank, the rough calluses on his fingertips making me shiver, and then he dipped them beneath my underwear, zeroing in on my clit.

I gasped into his mouth as he played me, my hips undulating against his touch. "Shit, you need to stop," I pleaded. "No condoms."

We'd used the only two he had in his wallet last night.

"I don't need a condom for what I want to do to you," he murmured thickly in my ear and then lowered himself to his haunches, his eyes on mine. They darkened as I sucked in a breath of excitement.

I bit my lip, my chest rising and falling quickly, sharply, as he curled his fingers into my underwear and pulled them down my legs. I stepped out of them, growing wet with anticipation, and he clasped the back of my calves, caressing me all the way back up to my inner thighs. He pressed them open and I widened my stance for him.

"Take your top off," he demanded, his voice hoarse with need. "I want to see all of you."

I grabbed the hem of the tank top and pulled it over my head. My breasts had filled out as I'd put weight back on, but I'd never be a big girl. Apparently, that didn't matter to Killian, who stared at my nakedness like I was the sexiest thing he'd ever seen.

He got on his knees, his fingertips tickling my inner thighs as he leaned in to drop a sweet kiss on my stomach. "Do you know how gorgeous you are?"

I felt a ripple of need just below where he'd kissed and reached for his head, running my fingers through his hair as he peppered kisses down my belly toward where I wanted his mouth most. "Killian," I heard myself pleading.

He turned his cheek against my skin and I felt him smile.

"What are you grinning about down there?" I tugged gently on his hair and he leaned back to look up at me with mischief in his eyes.

"You've not got one submissive bone in your body . . . until the promise of an orgasm. If only I'd known that sooner."

I looked up at the ceiling and spoke to an imaginary god, "How can he be this irritating and sexy at the same time?"

Killian's answer was to yank my leg over his shoulder and press his mouth to my sex. The sharp movement made me let go of his head for purchase against the wall.

And then nothing else mattered but the feel of his tongue as he licked and sucked my clit until I was gasping his name and begging for more.

When he slid his fingers inside me, the tension, already stretched to breaking, snapped into shattering bliss. I cried out as my orgasm rolled through me like a tidal wave, my hips shuddering against his mouth as he continued to lick me through it.

My body sagged against the wall as Killian got to his feet, his cheeks flushed as he stared at me with hungry eyes. His hands rested on my waist for a second and then traveled upward to cup my naked breasts as we gazed at one another, mine full of awe, his full of need. He squeezed my breasts and I let out an exhalation that surprised me. How could I want him again so soon? His head bent to my chest and he wrapped his hot mouth around my nipple and sucked.

"Gah . . ." I held onto him as he took his time kissing, licking, and sucking at my breasts. Finally, he pressed his body into mine and rested his forehead to my shoulder, breathing heavily.

I could feel his hard-on digging into my stomach.

I reached between us for the zipper on his jeans and he lifted his head. His eyes searched mine, as if seeking an answer to an unspoken question. I yanked his zipper down and he grabbed my hand. "You don't have to."

The fact that he would say so, that he wasn't looking for reciprocation after he'd gone down on me, made my heart swell. "I want to," I promised.

He caught my chin between his forefinger and thumb, his voice low. "Still . . . I only ever want to give with you. I don't want you to feel like I'm ever taking from you."

It was a moment that could ruin this feeling between us if I let it because I saw the sincerity in his eyes, and I realized that he truly had no idea how much he was planning to take from me as soon as that damn album launched.

It hurt my heart. So much.

But there was a much bigger piece of my heart that had quickly grown addicted to this. To being with him. To feeling more alive than I had in years. I couldn't let that go. I wanted this feeling to last forever.

I replied, "Don't you think making you feel good makes me feel good?" I pushed my hand under his boxers and fisted his steely hot length.

Killian hissed in pleasure, falling immediately into my touch and quickly reaching for the wall to brace his hands on either side of my head.

I wanted him to be distracted all day by the memory of me on my knees with his dick in my mouth. I wanted to have power over him like he had power over me.

He tensed when I let go of him to yank his jeans and boxers down; I lowered myself in front of him. "Skylar," he rasped as his eyes flared.

And then he was groaning my name over and over, rocking his hips with building desire as I licked and sucked him. Watching him pant, his face contorted with raw lust, made me so turned on my own hips undulated.

"I'm going to come," he warned on a groan and I slipped him out of my mouth to fist him through his orgasm.

"Skylar, fuck!" He came all over my breasts and I felt my lower belly ripple in a mini-orgasm.

Sex-fogged desperation still clung to me as Killian came down from his climax. I got to my feet, reaching for him, for his mouth.

He kissed me hungrily, falling into me as I leaned back against the wall and took hold of his wrist, pulling it from the wall at my head and leading his hand between my legs.

He immediately slipped his fingers inside me and I gripped his waist for support, rocking against the thrusts of his fingers. "I've got you," he muttered, "I've got you."

It took very little time for my orgasm to shatter through me.

We slumped against each other, limbs loose with satisfaction. After a moment of trying to catch our breaths, I felt his soft lips pepper kisses along my shoulder, all the way up my neck to my ear. "I think we both need a shower."

"You'll be late."

"Do you think I care?" His hands roamed down my waist like he couldn't not touch me. "I now have the memory of you on your knees with my cock on your mouth. Whenever I want to, I can have that image in my head. That's more than worth being late to the fucking office."

I chuckled. Men were so easy. I dragged my fingernails softly down his muscled back. "Let's not make you any later. We gotta shower."

The hot water poured down over us and we took time exploring each other as we cleaned ourselves up. I asked tentatively, "Should I see about going on the pill?"

"Definitely," Killian said.

I hated to broach it but a smart woman always should . . ."I hate to, um, mention it . . . but well, I took those tests when I got that health check and I got my all-clear—"

"I'll get checked," he cut me off and then kissed me softly.

"Okay, good."

Afterward, I slipped into a pair of jeans and a T-shirt, following Killian out into the living room where he'd left his phone. "You sure you can't stay for a quick breakfast?"

He looked up from his cell. "Wish I could but I have three missed calls and a bunch of emails to look at."

"Okay. Let me walk you out."

When we got to the door, I had just taken off the chain when he pulled me into his arms. "I'll call you later," he promised.

Realizing he was worried I was worried, I smiled. "I know you leaving for work doesn't mean anything."

"So, we're okay?"

"We're more than okay."

"And you're all right with us keeping this a secret for now? Even from my sister?"

I slid my hands around his shoulders. "I think it's kind of hot."

"Don't get me started again, you insatiable wench."

I laughed, loving this side of him more than I thought possible. "No promises."

We were smiling when we reached for a kiss and that made us laugh. I can't explain how amazing a feeling it was to be laughing between kisses with Killian O'Dea.

"I have to go," he groaned, reaching for the door handle.

"Uh-uh, one more." I drew him back to my mouth as he opened the door and licked my tongue against his.

Just like that, the kiss got out of control as we fell against the hallway wall and hungrily devoured each other.

It was only the sound of a throat clearing that stopped us.

We tensed against each other.

Oh, fuck.

Breaking the kiss, we turned to face the intruder.

Autumn stood in the open doorway with two Starbucks cups in her hands, grinning at us with more than a hint of triumphant happiness.

twenty-three

"Well," Killian looked between me and his sister and then ducked by her, "I have to get to work."

My hands flew to my hips in amused indignation. "That's right, you leave when it gets hard."

Mischief curved his mouth into a grin. He started to respond with something I knew was going to be dirty.

"Don't say it!" I cut him off before he could.

He gave a huff of laughter and leaned back in to give me a quick kiss on the lips. "I'll be back tonight."

And then he was gone.

Leaving me to deal with telling his sister. I slammed the door and she smiled at me like the cat who got the cream. "It's not fair." I marched down the hall, reaching in to shut my bedroom door because the room smelled of sex.

"What's not fair?" Autumn followed me into the living area.

"All he has to do is smile at me." I threw a hand up in exasperation. "And I'm ready to sacrifice my firstborn for him. Do you think he might actually be the devil?"

"Uh . . . I think I want to know what happened—but spare me too much detail. He is my brother."

But I wasn't really listening. I was musing over the addiction I had for him. "I think it's because he doesn't smile a lot. It gets me off that I make him smile and laugh. Is that sick?"

Autumn gave a sympathetic smile. "I think it's *love*."

My heart jolted at the very idea of it. "Autumn, it's not like that, it's—"

"If you're about to tell me that you're fuck buddies, I don't want to know."

I felt the urge to screw with her a little like she did with us last night, but it would break her sentimental heart too much so I quelled the impulse. "No, we're definitely more than that. The truth is we don't know what we are. We care about each other. We're attracted to each other. That's what we do know."

She shook her head, chuckling as she slid onto a stool to sip her coffee. She pushed the other cup toward me. "I came over here ready to face your wrath for setting you up like that last night." She shimmied giddily on her stool. "But it worked."

I sat beside her. "Yes, it did work. But you need to gloat on the inside because we're keeping what's happening between us a secret. And it's imperative that you don't tell anyone about us."

I felt the air chill and all the joy fled from Killian's sister's face. "You're kidding me?"

Confused by her reaction, I hesitantly shook my head.

"I don't think that's a good idea."

"Why not?"

Her eyes widened. She looked at me like I was a moron. "Because Killian needs to realize that you're more important than anything else or your relationship will never work."

My stomach dropped at the cold splash of reality she was

delivering. Was it necessary? I didn't think so! "Autumn—"

"No. This is a bad idea, Skylar. Tell him you can't keep your relationship in the dark. Fuck his career!"

I blinked, taken aback by such vehemence, and I felt a mix of sadness and anger as I stared into her disappointment. "It's not just about *his* career." I found myself getting defensive. "What do you think the tabloids will do when they find out I'm sleeping with the nephew of the head of my new label? They'll have a goddamned field day with that information. Skylar Finch returns after her mysterious disappearance and she brings a new romantic drama with her. The fans are going to be pissed as it is that I disappeared on them without any updates on my well-being—do you think they'll forgive me for doing that if I return to the limelight with someone who isn't *Micah* on my arm?"

"Screw your fans," she huffed. "Screw my uncle. Screw Killian's ambition! What does any of that nonsense matter in the long run?"

Her blowing off my concerns as if they weren't valid hurt. "You can say that . . . not knowing what it's like to have the whole world judging you for every life choice you make. Do you know how exhausting it is to not only have to think about how *you* feel about something or someone, but to have to factor in your band, your manager, your label, and millions of fans? To have to think about how a newspaper might spin a single decision? To have to plan it this way and that in the hopes that you spoon-feed it to them in a way that reflects best upon you? It was making me crazy. It made me into someone I no longer recognized."

She reached for my arm in comfort and then leveled me with her next words. "Which is exactly why Killian needs to realize now, rather than later, that *you* are more important. You know what I'm talking about, Skylar."

I pulled away, clenching my jaw to stop myself from railing

in fury at her for bringing it up. I didn't want to hear it. Struggling for calm, I finally replied, "Don't. Autumn . . . please don't." I looked at her. Pleaded with her. "We aren't *there* yet. And I woke up happy this morning. Actually happy. Not numb. Not surviving. Not healing. Not moving on. Just *happy*. I can't remember the last time I felt truly happy."

Autumn studied me a second. Then she slumped in defeat. "Well, I can't argue with that, can I?"

"I'm hoping not."

"Fine." She sighed. "I . . . Killian isn't the only one who cares about you. I want you to be happy. I want my brother to be happy and I've never seen him behave this way with a woman. You *do* make him smile more, you know."

Relieved, I grinned. "I know."

We were silent a moment as I enjoyed our truce and sipped at my coffee.

And then Autumn said, "Killian told me you need a laptop. If you're not too exhausted by whatever happened last night—you've still to tell me, FYI—do you want to go buy one today? Because I was thinking that if you're getting a laptop, you may as well upgrade that brick you call a phone."

Suddenly the idea of googling the band and Micah put a knot in my stomach. That was information that would one hundred percent ruin my happy. I didn't want to ruin my happy.

It was selfish, self-indulgent, and the opposite of the kind of person I wanted to be, so I promised myself two days. Two days of enjoying Killian, and then I'd return to the reality of moving on.

"Let's leave it for a few days."

"HAVE YOU HAD SEX WITH anyone famous?"

Killian lay on my bed in nothing but his boxers and gave me a low-lidded, dry look. It was hot. Okay, to be fair, everything about him was hot. "You know, in some cultures they call what we just did sex."

I huffed. "I meant with someone other than me."

I saw the curiosity in his eyes. "Are you trying to ask me if I have a thing for famous people?"

Chuckling at the ridiculousness of that, I shook my head. "No. I merely wondered, since you're in the music business, if you'd 'shagged' someone famous."

"Don't say shagged," he said, laughter in his voice.

"I won't. But you should. It sounds so much sexier in your accent."

"Have I shagged a famous person other than you?"

"Mmm?" I was sitting up, turned into him, reveling in the intimacy of being with him like this after another round of amazing sex. I'd spent the day messing around on my guitar. I couldn't play too much too often, but I was getting somewhere, and that, along with the abundance of endorphins released during two nights of epic sex, made me feel better than I had in a long time. Killian had left the office early and arrived at my apartment with Thai food. We'd talked while we ate and then not too long later jumped each other.

"No. I was either working with them or knew there was a possibility I could end up working with them." He reached out and curled a hand around my thigh. "It's usually a bad idea to mix business with pleasure."

"I have heard that somewhere," I teased. "So you're saying you've been in a position where it was an option for you to sleep with your label's artists? Someone has tried to get you in the sack?"

He shrugged arrogantly. "Tried and failed."

I fluttered my eyelashes in ridicule of his sexy obnoxiousness.

"I managed to lay Killian O'Dea. I *do* feel special."

He attempted to tickle me in punishment and I laughed, struggling to get away from him. But his strong arms banded around me and he tugged me down beside him, tucking me into his side. "You need to start working out or it's going to be really easy to win every play fight with you."

"I'm thinking about working out again. I used to have a personal trainer." I lifted my wrist. "It's getting better. We had all that sex, I played the guitar, and it's only twinging a little."

Killian gently held my wrist to his mouth. He pressed a reverent kiss to it that made my heart swell.

Romantic bastard.

What was he doing to me?

Then he disarmed me further. "Did you only ever date famous men?"

It was only fair that I respond since he did. I shrugged against him. "I didn't actually date a lot. Micah caused too much drama about it."

"Aye, manipulative little shit."

That was true, but I still didn't like Killian insulting him. Not wanting him to misconstrue my defense of Micah as anything but years of friendship, I stayed quiet.

"You were photographed with famous guys in the tabloids," he pressed hesitantly. "None of that was real?"

"Some. Max."

"Max Carter? From Talking Trees?"

"You *did* research me, huh?" I teased. "Yes. Max. And it was real. I'm not saying we were in love but we cared about each other."

"What happened?"

"Micah happened," I said, my bitterness hard to miss. "Max knew Micah was filling his head with nonsense about us to try and make him crazy insecure. Max was too smart for that. But he was also a very cool guy. Non-confrontational, laid-back, a zero-drama kind of guy. And he couldn't handle the Micah twenty-four / seven drama. So he broke up with me."

"Then you're better off without him."

I smiled. "I just had multiple orgasms. I'm well aware I'm better off without him."

Killian grunted and caressed my arm.

"Mostly I had flings though," I continued. "Jay Preston."

"From Cabin Fever?"

"Yes. And Danny Alexander."

I felt his gaze and turned my head on his shoulder to look up at him. He was surprised. "The superhero-movies guy? He's what? Twenty years older than you?"

I wrinkled my nose. "Don't sound so judgy. I was drunk. And it happened in the bathroom of the VIP section in a nightclub. Very romantic."

His lips tightened.

"You're judging me."

"Just . . . spare me the actual details."

I didn't particularly think that was detailed. *Caveman*. "Okay. I'll spare you the Spence Holloway details, then."

"That name is vaguely familiar."

"Supporting actor in that dystopian movie."

"Your big-break song?"

"That's the one. We got to meet the cast at an awards show. I was lonely. He was there."

He gave me a squeeze. "Is that all of them, then?"

Nope. There was one more. But it was kind of a painful memory. I snuggled deeper into him and laid my hand on his chest so I could feel his heart beneath my palm. "Not long after the first album dropped, I turned eighteen. Micah and I had decided before the band even took off that we wouldn't pursue a relationship with one another for the sake of the band. We were struggling with it. And I was starting to think it was bullshit. That no band was worth not being with the guy I loved. I got the feeling he felt the same way, and when he gave me this stupidly expensive bracelet for my birthday, I believed it meant something.

"That night we had plans to go to a party we'd been invited to. It was at the actor Jack James' Malibu beach house. We thought we'd made it." I gave a huff of laughter but I wasn't really amused by the memory of how naive I'd been. "I got all dressed up but decided I wanted Micah and I to work things out . . . maybe go as a couple. So, I dropped by the apartment he was staying in with the guys and I found him screwing the brains out of some girl. Something that became a regular pattern in our relationship. I'd make myself vulnerable and he'd fuck someone else. He'd make himself vulnerable and I'd punish him for the many times he'd fucked someone else. We were toxic to each other.

"Anyway, I went to that party heartbroken. Naturally, I got wasted." The memory was still a pressing weight of regret on my chest. "I ended up losing my virginity to *Mike Roth*. The guy from that teen drama set in Boston where everyone is ridiculously beautiful and rich. Anyway, he got off, didn't get me off, got off me, and left me in a stranger's bedroom like I was a common prostitute."

I'd felt worthless. And so goddamned alone.

Killian's arm tightened around me and I felt his lips brush my forehead.

"I know I shouldn't because it wasn't his fault, but I blamed Micah for that too."

"I'm sorry, Skylar. I wish it hadn't been that way for you."

"Long time ago now." It was also time to shake it off.

"Did you and Micah ever . . . ?" Killian prompted, sounding like he needed to know as much as he didn't *want* to know.

"About a year later. Despite my not-so-nice experience with Roth, I gave Spence a shot. It was marginally better. But Micah found out and lost his shit. We argued. It turned into sex. But afterward I was still hurt about the groupies and I said that sex didn't change anything. I was horrible. I hurt him. Really badly," I whispered the last in regret. "It took me less than a day to decide I'd made a terrible mistake, that I needed to stop punishing him, and get over it. A fresh start together. But when I went to tell him, he was screwing a groupie. She actually asked for my autograph while he was inside her."

"He sounds like a walking STD."

I snorted. "He *did* like to spread the love around. He blamed that on me. Apparently, it was his way of coping with not getting to be with the one he loved."

"So you slept with him just the once, then?"

I was silent a moment as worry began to percolate. Was Killian concerned about my feelings for Micah? That I might still have some? Was that what all the questions were about?

This was the moment I could choose to lie so as not to plant some stupid seed of doubt in his mind. But I'd lied to my mom. I'd lied to everybody. And lying screwed everything up. "He was the last person I slept with before you. Before I left the States, I called Gayle and the band together and I told them I was quitting. They were devastated but supportive. Later that night, Micah came to me. He said he was terrified that my leaving the band meant he wouldn't see me again. We ended up . . . well . . . you know. The worst thing was it was almost as bad as my time with Roth. I felt so detached from it because I knew I was only doing it because I felt like I owed him a debt. I left the States the next day."

"Jesus, Skylar," Killian muttered.

I tensed, sensing judgment. "I know it was horrible to do that to him."

"That's not . . . I'm upset for *you.*" He lifted my chin, forcing me to look at him. "Micah should have known you were in no position to be thinking clearly about anything, let alone a relationship with him."

"Maybe. But I'm not the type of person to blame someone else for not protecting me from myself. My actions are my own."

"I still blame him," he grumbled.

I laughed and relaxed back into his body. After a little while of sweet, silent contemplation between us, I cracked a grin and asked, "So how and when did you lose *your* virginity?"

"A long time ago."

I smacked him playfully. "No fair. Details."

He chuckled. "Fine. I was fourteen."

"Holy shit. Why is it guys are always so young?"

"Not all guys," he disagreed. "I had a friend at uni who lost his when he was twenty-one. We celebrated for so long after it happened, five of us ended up with alcohol poisoning."

I snorted. "Okay. So not all guys. But fourteen? Wow."

Killian shrugged. "I don't think it's the same for a guy as it is for a girl. For me, it was about being horny as hell and finding an outlet."

I wrinkled my nose. "What you're saying is that it was a form of masturbation?"

"I am not," he scoffed. "I mean it was about mutual release. It felt good. Sex was an escape from . . . reality."

"Who was the girl?" I was trying desperately not to sound jealous. Even though the scary truth was that I was jealous of any woman who had touched Killian that way. Especially one who had offered him an opportunity to disappear from his grief for a while.

"Maryanne Wright. She was gorgeous and sixteen." He scrubbed a hand over his face with a regretful sigh. "Everyone called her the town bike."

"The town bike?"

"Because every guy at school had ridden her."

"Okay, now I feel less bad about my virginity story."

"Hey, I learned some valuable lessons from Maryanne Wright."

"I'll send her a thank-you note. And should I send more to all the women who have come after her? Were they all part of your unattached, undramatic, serial monogamy philosophy?"

"Aye. If you hadn't noticed, I'm quite career-oriented."

"No, I really hadn't."

He ignored my sarcasm. "I didn't have time for girlfriends when I was a teenager. I was too busy looking after Autumn."

The truth in that gave me pause. When I was a teen, I was single-mindedly forging a path to success for my band. Getting a record contract was the extent of my worries.

Killian's was school and raising a child.

I turned into him, resting my chin on his shoulder as I traced his jaw with a whisper of my fingertips. "You're a good brother."

He frowned, concern dimming his eyes. "Autumn is drifting. She seems lost. I feel like I'm failing her."

"No," I hurried to assure him. "Killian, she would be the first person to tell you that that is not true."

He bent his head toward me and I kissed him, letting my feelings for him sink into the kiss, hoping it was a balm for his worry. I knew if it was, it was only temporary. Like a parent, Killian saw it as his full-time job to worry over his sister.

"What were your parents like?" I asked as we pulled back from the kiss.

He stared at me, seeming surprised by the question. "The only other person who's ever asked me that is Autumn."

"You don't have to answer if you don't want to." I didn't want to push him.

"It's fine," he reassured, and I sank back down to rest my head on his shoulder. "They deserve to be talked about. To be remembered. They were good parents. Pete adopted me when I was so young that I never thought of him as anything but my dad. He was a good man. You know he was a police officer?"

"No, I didn't know that."

"He was my real dad's complete opposite. He was CID."

"What's CID?"

"Criminal Investigation Department. Plainclothes detective. He went after the bad guys." He laughed softly, humorlessly. "He . . . he was my hero."

Tears burned in my eyes at the heartbreaking way he confessed that. "I'm glad you had that."

"You never knew your father?"

"No. But my mom said he was a hero too. There was an ambush. First a roadside IED that blew off his friend Mullen's leg. Everyone took cover. My dad wouldn't leave Mullen so they offered firing cover while he went back for him. But he was killed trying to drag Mullen to safety. Mullen survived. Mom said he came to visit when I was four, but I don't remember it."

"Your dad *was* a hero."

"Yeah, he was. I don't miss *him* because I didn't know him, but I've always longed for the idea of him. I missed the ghost of him. It's sad," I whispered, "that we both had heroes in our lives, only for them to be taken away from us when we needed them most."

His answer was a sweet kiss to my temple.

I nuzzled into him. "What was your mom like?"

"Brilliant." He answered immediately. "While all the other mums were giving their kids a row for coming home for dinner caked in mud, Mum was right there with us. She'd take me and a bunch of pals camping, canoeing, and hiking and all the while she'd crack rude jokes they couldn't repeat to their parents. Looking back, they weren't that rude, but they seemed so at the time."

"You had the cool mom."

"I had the cool mum." He agreed and then his voice lowered with pain. "Sometimes I wished they'd been just a little bit awful . . ."

So it wouldn't hurt so bad.

I only allowed our moment of sad affinity for a few seconds and then I distracted him, asking him when he first knew he wanted to work in the music industry.

He talked. I listened. I talked. He listened.

And that's how it was.

Easy.

Our voices drifted together into the wee hours of the morning as we talked about everything and nothing at all.

twenty-four

The sound crackled in my ear through the headphones and I heard Oliver say, "It sounds good, but you dropped that last note."

I stared at Oliver sitting at the recording deck behind the glass of the sound booth and then flicked a look at Killian. He stood next to my producer with his arms over his chest, his expression typically unreadable. I sighed. "We've been at this for three hours without a break. I'm tired."

"We've got to lay down the vocals so we have plenty of time to figure out production," Oliver reminded me.

I waited for Killian to jump in, insist on me taking a break, but he just stood there.

We'd been secretly dating for the last three weeks.

It had been bliss unlike anything I'd ever imagined.

It had also been frustrating because every time we walked into the label's offices, the man who smiled and teased and played in bed with me turned into the man who had first approached me on Buchanan Street.

Cold. Aloof. Impersonal.

Irritated, I yanked off the headphones. "I'm taking a break. Unless you want me to lose my voice." I slammed the headphones down and strode out of the booth.

Oliver swung around in his chair as I came out. "We're not trying to exhaust your voice. We have a lot to do in a short amount of time. And honestly, I didn't realize we'd been in here that long without a break."

Killian pulled out his phone and pressed a speed-dial button, all without looking at me. "Eve," he said, "we need some lunch in Studio Two for Oliver and Skylar . . ." He pulled his phone from his ear and glanced between me and my producer. "Sandwiches and soup?"

"Sounds good," Oliver replied. "Ask Eve to get me a Sprite too."

I nodded, trying not to glare at my—I actually didn't know what to call Killian. Was he my boyfriend? Right now, in this moment, I had a warmer relationship with my postman.

"That's fine. Thanks, Eve." He hung up. "I've got to catch up on some calls." He looked at Oliver. "If you need me, I'll be in my office."

I watched him leave after throwing me a vague nod of acknowledgment and I felt a now-familiar ache in my chest. We were recording the album, but so were a few of the label's other artists. As such, we all had to work around a schedule. Which meant I'd been in and out of the studio for the last two weeks. Although Killian made sure to be there for the recording, he was so cool with me, it hurt.

But then at night, back at my apartment, he was the opposite. He was loving and passionate and so attentive, it made me momentarily forget the human icicle he became at work.

That utter focus in the studio to get this album complete, and the lack of care for how tired I was or how emotional this whole thing made me, was starting to piss me off. And another thing! We always stayed at *my* apartment. I'd never set foot in his. Why wasn't I allowed into that part of his life?

There was keeping our relationship a secret.

And there was making me feel like his *dirty little secret*.

The two were mutually exclusive.

"Hey," Oliver said as I slumped into the seat next to his. "If this is too much, I can tell Killian we need to reschedule."

I twisted my mouth. "And upset *his* schedule? No, thanks. I wouldn't do that to you."

He shrugged. "I'd take the flack. Pushing artists can backfire. You're right, we can't push your voice to the point you lose it."

"It's okay. I'm okay." I took care of my throat by keeping it hydrated. I drank lots of room-temperature water all day. Plus, I was avoiding caffeine again. When I was on tour, I had a no-spicy, no-acidic foods diet and I would rest my voice as much as possible between performances. The guys bought me a whiteboard I could hang around my neck so I could still communicate with them. They got a kick out of it. "I'll probably steam tonight."

Oliver nodded, knowing I meant I'd stick my face over a bowl of boiling water with a towel over my head to steam and hydrate my vocal folds. It also got rid of any mucus in there. It was extremely sexy.

"So, O'Dea is pretty invested in this album," Oliver mused.

"Hmm?"

"I've never seen him sit in on *all* the recording sessions before."

"Well, he helped write some of it." I shrugged nonchalantly. "I suppose he thinks of it as his baby too."

"Right, right." He leaned toward me, grinning. "I secretly think he misses producing. He's the most ambitious bastard I've ever met but I wonder if he regrets moving up the ranks away from the studio."

As annoyed as I was with Killian, I didn't want to gossip about him. "He loves that job. That man has no regrets. So, which note did I drop?" I changed the subject.

We discussed the track for a while and then the door opened and Eve came hurrying in with a large brown paper bag in one hand and a cardboard cup in the other.

"Hi!" she greeted us cheerily. I smiled in return. "I bring sustenance."

"You're a lifesaver." Oliver stood and helped her unpack the food.

"Oh, and this." Eve handed me the cup. "Herbal tea, not too hot, with honey and lemon for your throat."

Pleased, I smiled. "That was thoughtful, Eve. Thank you."

"Oh, no, it's not from me. Mr. O'Dea told me to get it for you."

I inwardly harrumphed at that.

The thoughtful gesture didn't make me feel anything but agitated with him. I didn't know why. I knew he was acting this way at the office to protect our secret, but his unbelievable self-control pissed me off. Sometimes I could barely concentrate when he was in the room because I was remembering the feel of his tongue on the dimples of my lower back. Or the rumble of his laughter in my ear as he held me in bed.

How was it so easy for him to compartmentalize?

How could he stand in a room and look at me like I was a stranger while my fingers itched to grab his shirt and pull him against me?

I worried I was coming to need him more than he would ever need or want me, and that scared the shit out of me.

Eve left us to eat and Oliver sat playing on his phone as he ate his sandwich. Growing more pissed by the second, I finished mine and said, "I'm going to take a walk. I'll be back in ten."

My producer waved me off, too engrossed in whatever was on his phone to look up. Familiar with Skyscraper Records now, I strolled down the corridors until I found myself at his office. Eve looked up from her desk where she was eating her own lunch. She swallowed a bite of sandwich too fast and choked out, "Skylar?"

I gestured to Killian's door. "Is your boss in his office?"

She nodded. "I'll check if he's available."

"No need, he just called me," I lied, walking by her to knock on his door.

"Come in," Killian called.

I slipped in, closing the door behind me. When I turned to face Killian, he gazed at me with a slight frown between his brow. "Problem?"

In answer, I walked across the room, rounded his desk, and pushed his chair back so he was facing me. As I moved to climb onto his lap, he gripped my waist and resisted.

"What are you doing?" he bit out, annoyed.

I dug my hands into his shoulders. "I thought that was obvious."

Killian pushed me away and I stumbled back. "Not here."

Hurt flooded me. I narrowed my eyes as he glowered up at me. "I've never known a man to turn down sex before."

Spinning the chair away from me, he got up and stood on the other side of the desk, putting it between us. "This is my office, for Christ's sake, Skylar."

"You're telling me you've never had any afternoon nookie in your office before?"

"That's exactly what I'm telling you."

"Oh, remove the stick from your ass, O'Dea," I huffed, walking around the desk so I was standing in the middle of the room.

He remained where he was, rigid and cool. "We're supposed to be keeping our relationship a secret."

"Oh yeah, you've made that clear."

"What the hell does that mean?"

So I put it out there. "Are *we* a secret? Or am I *your* dirty secret?"

Killian stepped toward me, anger flushing his face, and I silently triumphed at the show of emotion. "And what the hell does that mean?" he repeated, his voice thick with displeasure.

"Well, I've never been to your apartment, we always do it at mine, and then there's the fact that you treat me with cold disinterest anytime we set foot in this place."

Looking baffled and increasingly annoyed, Killian ran a hand through his hair. "First, I haven't not invited you to my flat out of some arsehole reason to keep you out of my life. Your flat is a two-minute drive from the label and it makes more sense for me to come to you straight from the office. And second . . ." He took another step toward me. "We agreed that this was how it would be while we here at the label so as not to draw suspicion. I'm treating you the same way I'd treat any of my artists."

But somehow that didn't make me feel better. "It's easy for you though."

"Excuse me?"

"This is a big deal for me." I gestured around us. "Being here, recording an album. I never thought I'd be doing this again, and I've never done it alone. I have a whole ton of emotion about that and the one person I need to be there as a reminder that I'm not alone looks through me every time I meet his gaze."

He flinched but I barely registered it as I continued, shaking my head as realization hit with me the smack of disappointment. "I'm so stupid. I struggle to be in any room with you without wanting to touch you, and it's *easy* for you to push me away." Autumn was right. I never would be as important to him as his job. I shook my head, turning to leave. "I'm a fucking moron."

I'd only taken a couple of steps toward the door when I found myself spun around. Anger flushed Killian's face as he gripped my biceps and then forced me back against the wall, a framed photo protesting with a squeak behind me. I gasped, pressing my hands to his chest as he pushed the length of his body into mine.

"You think it's easy for me," he said, voice guttural, "that every time you step close to me and I smell you that I don't have to fight not to get hard remembering how it felt to fuck you the night before?" His lips almost brushed mine and my heart thudded in my chest, heat flushing through me like he'd lit a fire at my feet. "I have to fight the need to touch you every time I'm near you. The only way I know how is to detach myself completely." He grabbed my hand and slid it down his stomach to the hard-on pushing against his trousers. "Is this what you want? You want me to lose control?"

"Yes," I hissed, still furious because I'd let Autumn's worries become my worries and now they were stuck there, eating at my insecurities. I squeezed his dick, making his nostrils flare. "I don't want your control. *Ever.*"

He crushed his mouth over mine and I whimpered as his hands became wild things over my body, apparently needing to touch me everywhere. I wrapped my arms around his back and widened my legs so his hot hardness pressed where I wanted it most.

Our kisses were breathless, hungry, and wet, a complete loss of control that I relished as Killian pumped his hips against mine. We panted together as pleasure tingled down my spine from the friction of the seam of my jeans catching my clit.

"Killian," I gasped, rocking harder against him.

"Fuck," he muttered, pressing his cheek against mine. "If we don't stop," he pushed harder into me and groaned, "I'm going to come in my trousers like a callow bloody youth."

I wanted that. I turned my face, searching for his lips again.

I was distantly aware of Killian's office phone ringing as he tugged down the zip on my jeans and pushed them down. His office answering machine clicked on as he unzipped his own jeans and then the sound of an attractive American-accented female voice echoed around the room.

"Killian, it's Deena. I couldn't remember your cell but I had your office ext. saved on my phone so I hope you don't mind me calling you at work. Anyway, you told me if I was ever back in Glasgow to look you up. The label sent me to check out this kid here who's made a splash on YouTube. I'm staying at the Blythswood again. I'll be there for four nights. My number here is 07384121560. I had a lot of fun with you in January so . . . I really hope you call."

We were silent, frozen together, as the phone call acted like blast of ice on the heat between us.

I pushed against his chest to move out from under him, unable to look at him. I seethed with jealousy. I couldn't remember ever feeling such a choking, burning, ugly sensation over any of the girls Micah had been with. But the thought of Killian going to this Deena person made me want to claw out her eyes.

Killian pressed me harder into the wall and grabbed my wrists to secure them against his chest. I could feel his heart beating hard and a little too fast.

"You know I'm not going to call her," he said quietly, but with a hard edge to the words.

"I know." Yet I still couldn't meet his eyes.

"Look at me."

"I really need to get back to the studio."

He made a noise of frustration and let go of my wrists only to grip my chin. My eyes automatically met his and he studied my face, a frown marring his brow.

"What is going on? Why did you barge in here, accusing me of not needing you as much as you need me when I make it perfectly clear how I feel about you when we're alone? And why the fuck are you pushing me away because of a message left by a woman I have no intention of touching?"

I glowered at him. "You told me you never mix business with pleasure. I thought I was the exception. Turns out I'm not."

Anger flashed in his eyes. "I told you I'd never sleep with one of my artists or anyone at my label. Deena is an A&R executive from a label in New York. We met at the beginning of the year going after the same artist. I totally forgot about her until that phone call. End of story."

"Were you with Yasmin while you were screwing Deena?"

The muscle in his jaw ticked. "Are you deliberately trying to cause a fucking fight?"

I shrugged, feeling reckless and crazy and angry. And I didn't even really know why!

"No," he hissed, shoving his face in mine. "I would never do that. I'm not *him*."

I sucked in a breath. "We're not talking about him."

"I think we are because I have done nothing to deserve your jealousy or insecurities and frankly, it's pissing me off." He shoved his hands between our bodies, releasing himself from his trousers with one, while he pushed my underwear and jeans down further with the other. Heat flashed through me—a mixture of indignation and excitement. "I'm not him." He grabbed my wrists and pinned them above my head, glaring at me like he was frustrated with his desire for me when I was pissing him off this badly.

And suddenly, I felt unbearably sad for us because I'd never truly been a jealous or insecure person until Killian. And the only reason I'd feel that way is if I knew what we had wasn't going to last.

I slumped against his hold. "I was never like this with him. He never made me feel like this."

Surprise flared in his eyes for a brief second only to be clobbered by a fierceness I didn't understand until I felt the hot heat of his dick nudging between my legs.

Lust battled with my unwelcome melancholy. "Killian."

"I'm yours," he breathed harshly against my lips. "I've never been anyone's until now. Do you understand?"

I shook my head, not sure it was enough.

And then he thrust inside me, covering my mouth with his to muffle my cry.

He pumped into me, our lips parting as our breaths quickened with desire. "I'm yours," he reiterated with another thrust. "You're mine. Say it."

"Killian . . ." I let my head fall back against the wall, my eyes slamming closed as sensation took over my body. I wanted to forget my fears. I just wanted to feel him inside me because when we were like this, it felt like it was forever.

"Look at me." He gripped my nape, forcing my head up, and my eyes opened to stare into his. "I'm yours. You're mine. Say it."

When I couldn't bring myself to, he crushed his mouth over mine and fucked me harder, faster. It didn't take long for the tension inside me to snap and he swallowed my cry of release in his mouth before he broke away to rest his forehead against mine. His hips stilled and then juddered against mine as he came.

Our breaths mingled as we fought to catch them.

"I'm yours. You're mine. Say it."

The problem was I wasn't sure I really believed it now. I believed I was his. But I also believed that he truly belonged to this label more than he'd ever belong to me.

"I'm sorry I got jealous," I whispered. "This whole thing . . . the album . . . I . . . it's making me a little emotional and all over the place."

"Skylar," his voice was hard as his eyes blazed into mine, "say it. Or I'm going to bend you over my desk and spank your bare arse while I fuck you harder than you've ever been fucked."

Arousal flushed through me at the thought, fighting with indignation. Part of me would like that to play out. But it would only confuse me further. "Fine, you bastard. I'm yours."

"And I'm yours."

I dropped my gaze and he cursed under his breath before cupping my face in his hands and kissing me. It was a deep, drugging kiss, and I felt him pour himself into it until the worries eating at me were forced to the back of my mind. When he released me, his voice was thick with emotion. "I can't lose you. You have to believe that, Skylar."

Hearing the sincerity in his voice, I finally relaxed, falling against him to rest my cheek on his chest. I felt his whole body sigh with relief as he held me.

"I'm stubborn," I whispered.

"I got that."

"It might take a while for me to hear you sometimes."

"I got that too."

"I'm sorry I barged into your office and provoked you into sex."

He shook against me, laughter rumbling in his voice. "Can't say I'm especially upset about that."

We kissed again, softer, sweeter, the intensity of our passion momentarily quietened by release. As Killian gently eased out of me, I bit my lip. "Do you have something I can clean up with?"

He moved away, not caring to zip himself up as he opened the door of what I thought was a stationery cupboard.

"I didn't know you had a private restroom in here."

"Stay." He disappeared inside. When he returned, he'd put himself back to rights and had a wet washcloth in his hand.

I reached for it but he evaded me, a possessive look in his eyes as he stepped back into my body and pressed the cool cloth between my legs. He watched me as he cleaned me up. Renewed tingling sparked to life, and I flushed at how easily this man could turn me on.

He smirked as if he knew.

"Don't act so smug," I huffed. "I'm the one who got you to break your no-sex-in-the-office rule."

"True," he agreed. "But I'm the only man who makes you crazy with jealousy. I don't think either of us has the upper hand here."

It was sweet of him to reassure me, but I was still feeling the pinch of jealousy. And honestly, I didn't want to feel like the only one who got jealous. "Are you telling me that the thought of me fucking someone else doesn't make you insane with jealousy?"

His expression darkened and he suddenly slipped two thick fingers inside me. I gasped as he leaned into me, his hand moving between my legs. "I can't bear thinking about it," he admitted. "It would kill me, and I'd probably kill any bastard who touched you. But there isn't going to be someone else, Skylar. My fingers, my mouth, my cock will be the only ones pleasuring you for the rest of your life. Can I make myself any fucking clearer than that?"

Love shattered through me at the same time another orgasm did. He kissed me to soften my cry and I grabbed onto him like he was a life preserver.

God, I loved him.

I loved him so much.

The last person I'd loved with this much of my soul had died.

I clung onto him for dear life, even though I also wanted to run from how I felt.

But I didn't.

The desire to be in his arms forever was much stronger than the fear of losing him.

twenty-five

If Eve heard any of what went on in Killian's office that day, she never let on. As she was easier to read than an open book, I deduced that she hadn't heard anything suspicious. Either that or she'd suddenly grown proficient at hiding her thoughts and feelings.

We continued with the album and managed to keep our relationship private from everyone but Autumn. I did my very best to stifle my worries about our future and although he never said the words, Killian showed me every day that he loved me.

And although he obviously wasn't Mr. Touchy-Feely at the office, he also stopped being so cold and even started acting like we might be friends. If anyone thought that was weird, no one said so. Killian had invested more of his own time into this album than usual and I think everyone saw me as kind of a musical passion project for him . . . and not just . . . well, a *passion* project.

There were no more bouts of jealousy. I knew he didn't call Deena back to meet up with her because he spent every evening with me. Even if he hadn't been with me I knew in my gut that he didn't reach out to her. Despite the bargain that drew us together in the first place, I trusted Killian to never lie to me.

As our time together wore on, however, I realized that the only way I could truly get over my fear of losing Killian was to start living outside my little bubble by the River Clyde. Although we couldn't be in a relationship in the open yet, we needed to start being in a relationship while I was facing life and not pushing it aside. Otherwise we'd never really know how we could work as a couple in the real world.

I asked for that laptop and let Killian set up a PR meeting with my new team at the label.

That's how I found myself, two weeks after our interlude in his office, back at Skyscraper Records but not to record. I was sitting in a private boardroom that had a view over the river, accompanied by Killian and four strangers who would soon be planning my future.

They all stared at me expectantly and I was grateful to see Eve pop her familiar, friendly face around the door.

"Refreshments?"

"Aye, please, Eve," Killian replied congenially. I sent him an approving look. Eve was sweet. She deserved a nice boss.

Killian and the four strangers asked for coffee.

"Skylar?"

"Water, thank you."

She beamed at me and disappeared to get our drinks.

"Skylar," Killian drew my attention back to him, "I'd like you to meet Lois." He gestured to a stone-faced redhead. "She's our director of publicity."

We shared a nod of hello.

"And this is Kit." He introduced a tall, skinny guy with thick, black-framed glasses and a beard. "And Jaclyn," a curvy blonde with flushed cheeks, "our flack agents. Our publicists. And this," he nodded to a dark-skinned beauty with a short afro who stared at me intensely, "is May, our marketing coordinator."

"Nice to meet you all."

"Nice to meet you," May said, surprising me with her American accent as she reached across the table to shake my hand. "My kid sister is a huge fan."

"That's always nice to hear. You're not from around here."

"San Francisco. I did a study abroad at Glasgow University and kind of fell in love with the place. After graduation, I moved here and never looked back." It was weird but hearing a familiar accent made me feel a little less tense.

"It's easy to fall in love with this place, especially if you like music."

"True." She grinned. "I can't wait for your PR to launch so I can tell my sister I'm on your marketing team. The kid will hit the roof."

I laughed, trying not to be nervous about the "your PR to launch" part. "If you want me to sign anything for her, I can." God, I hadn't signed an autograph in so long.

"Really? Great. The new album will suffice. I can't wait to hear it."

"Which leads nicely into our first dilemma," Kit interrupted. He had a lovely southern English accent I could've listened to all day. "We," he gestured to himself and Jaclyn, "haven't heard the album yet, so we can't come up with an approach for radio and media. We can't explain or sell what we haven't heard."

"Yes, Kit, I'm aware," Killian appeared beleaguered, "and I told you the album is in postproduction. You'll hear it very soon. But this meeting isn't about that."

"No, it's about managing what will be an explosive return," Lois jumped in, "considering you disappeared off the face of the planet nearly twenty months ago. Once we have that under control, it's about managing your exposure. Killian says you want to quieten your public image. Make it more career-focused."

I nodded, ignoring the unpleasant fluttering in my chest. "Yes."

She wrinkled her nose. "Unfortunately, I'm here to tell you that is incredibly naive and possibly career suicide. We live in a platform-based society where hits, likes, and interest are cultivated by personality and personal anecdotes. The world moves much more quickly than it did even fifteen years ago. Although it's possible to grow a fan base, it's very easy for customers to become disinterested, for their attention to be drawn elsewhere. We *will* need you to nurture your fan base on social media platforms." Her condescending tone and the way she drew her eyes up and down my body made me bristle. It also made me question if Killian had explained things fully to her.

I gave her an unfiltered look of irritation. "Tellurian had nine million followers on Instagram. My personal account had just as many as that. I know the power of social media and I understand the fickle, ever-changing entertainment industry. Lois, is it?"

She nodded, pinching her lips together in obvious annoyance.

"I was the lead singer of a commercially successful band. I'm not an inexperienced young artist who loves the music but doesn't want the fame—something you clearly find irritatingly naive. I've experienced fame so I can say with absolute certainty that I love the music and I hate the fame. There are no ifs, maybes, or buts. So the condescending attitude? Get rid of it. I was a kid when our band became famous and I listened to all these people telling me I needed to share my personal life with the fans to keep them coming back for more. So, I did that, and it made me miserable giving them so much access. Do you know what happens when you give the public that kind of access? They begin to believe they have a right to you. A right to your decisions, your choices, and your opinions.

No one has a right to those things. *No one*. My deal with Killian," I flicked a look at him but his expression gave nothing away, "was that I put out a record but I stay out of the limelight unless it's directly promoting a single or the album. We're not here to negotiate. We're here to work out how to make sure Killian holds up his end of the bargain."

Lois shifted uncomfortably while May looked away, her lips twitching like she wanted to laugh. The two publicists seemed mildly affronted for their boss.

And Killian. Well, he met my gaze head-on and I saw the warmth of his respect in it.

"Skylar is correct. And we've already spoken about it. Lois has been briefed. Which means I assume that you have a plan other than trying to talk my artist out of something she has absolutely no plans of being talked out of."

Lois swallowed and her cheeks flushed with embarrassment. "Of course, Mr. O'Dea. I didn't mean to insult Miss Finch. I only wanted her to be aware of the difficulties in growing a career with that kind of constraint."

"And so you did. What's the plan?"

"Well . . . it has been a while since the tabloids have speculated on Miss Finch's disappearance from the public eye. That's partly due to the aforementioned short attention span of the public, but also because without Miss Finch, the usual tabloid frenzy set off by her relationship with band member Micah Murphy fizzled out. After Micah's stint in rehab a year ago, the partying, the groupies, has all ended. His Instagram account is pretty placid. He's not giving the tabloid anything to chew on. The band has continued on in relative peace from the tabloids, but they've also suffered a loss in sales."

None of that, thankfully, was news to me.

After telling Killian I wanted to get back online and see what had become of my band in my absence, Autumn came over to the apartment with her laptop. Killian wanted to be the one to sit with me while I opened that door to the rest of the world, but I wanted to react honestly to what I discovered. I didn't want to worry about how Killian was feeling as I looked into the guys, i.e., Micah.

Autumn and I sat at the island together as I googled Tellurian.

The top headlines that came up were old ones.

Ones that made me feel sick.

PARENTS OF POP-ROCK PRINCESS FOUND MURDERED
STAR'S FAMILY SHOT DEAD IN MULTIMILLION DOLLAR HOME
NO LEADS IN TELLURIAN MURDER CASE

I'd felt Autumn's hand on my shoulder as I stared at the bold headlines I'd avoided for so long.

"Are you all right?"

The pain was an old friend now. "I'm okay."

"Skylar, you don't have to do this."

"It's time." I typed in my name to the search engine.

The first headline made me smirk.

GONE GIRL

Where Did the Tragic Princess of Rock Go?

"Cute," I'd said dryly.

For the first six months, there were sporadic articles about my disappearance. After typing in Micah's name, I'd discovered his trip to rehab. According to the newspapers he'd checked himself in three months after I took off. He'd apparently been sober ever since. The only article about him in the last three months was regarding a college scholarship fund he'd set up in Montana for kids in foster care.

That almost made me cry with pride.

I was so happy he was doing well in his personal life. I didn't know if there was a new girl and it felt strange to now hope that there was. I was happy with someone new and I wanted him to be too.

As for the band . . . they weren't doing so well.

DID TELLURIAN'S MOJO FLEE WITH FINCH?
MACY PROVES SHE AIN'T NO TELLURIAN
TELLURIAN'S FIFTH ALBUM FAILS TO CHART THE TOP TWENTY

It made my heart hurt to see the guys fail. To know it was my fault.

And then I saw a headline from eight months prior:

BAND PLEADS FOR THE SAFE RETURN OF SKYLAR FINCH

My breath caught and I clicked on the article. I was somewhat relieved to discover that it was a case of a headline twisting the truth to get clicks. It led me to a YouTube video of an interview with MTV the band had done eight months ago.

I stared at Macy Olson sitting in the middle of my boys, where I used to sit. Whether it was her idea or not, she still wore her hair like I used to—dyed a multitude of colors. She'd curled hers though, whereas I always wore mine poker straight.

She was traditionally much prettier than I was, with a button nose, big blue eyes, round cheekbones, and full lips. She did backing vocals on a couple of tracks for us. That's how they'd found her. She was nice. I was glad they'd chosen someone nice.

"So," the MTV presenter finished up a line of questioning about the direction of the new album, "of course we have to address the elephant in the room. And that's Skylar's ongoing disappearance from the public eye. We all understand why she had to leave the band and you guys have spoken openly about your support of that decision . . . but where is she? Her fans want to know. I mean, people are genuinely worried, and if she's okay, maybe she should let her fans know she's okay. Do you know where she is?"

Austin and Brandon shared a look while Micah stared stonily at the floor. Finally, Brandon sighed. He looked exhausted and couldn't hide his worry. "Honestly, we don't know exactly where Skylar is right now. All we know is that she's taking some time off."

"So, you don't know if she's okay?" the presenter said dramatically.

"No. I guess we don't."

"If she's listening right now, what would you want to say to her?"

"That we hope she's safe. That if she's okay, she should call us. We miss and love her." Brandon's voice trembled on the last bit and he looked away, as if trying to compose himself. He seemed to fail when he said, "Can we take a break?" He got up and walked off camera.

It was the thing that broke me.

Autumn wrapped her arm around me and I leaned into her as I cried softly.

They deserved better.

The reminder brought me back to the label, to the meeting, and I glared at Lois the publicity annoyance. "We get it, you think social media is a big part of sales. And you're right. But Tellurian's sales haven't plummeted because I'm not there to help Micah play out our tragic love story for the press." I looked at Killian. "I listened to some of their new stuff yesterday. It's . . . it's not great. And I'm not blaming Macy. She has a good voice. The music, it's tired."

He nodded. "I agree. And it's not your fault."

It was kind of him to say so, but it was my fault.

I turned back to Lois. "Were you leading to something resembling a point earlier?"

May coughed to cover up a snort and Eve interrupted before Lois could follow her scowl with a verbal response. Killian's sweet assistant had brought us our drinks and some fresh doughnuts. Once she'd left, I waited for Lois to respond.

"I really am sorry if I insulted you earlier."

"Apology accepted. It will stay accepted if you'll get off your point about the importance of social media versus sales. I know it's important. I'm not disputing that. I'm just not doing it. If you want to set up a team to run social media for me, knock yourself out."

"This meeting isn't about creating a positive image through social media," Killian addressed the entire team. "The media will say whatever they have to say when Skylar returns. The album is great. I have faith that her music will do a lot of the talking for her. The reason for this meeting is to assure Skylar that this career is possible without having the paparazzi follow her every move."

"Of course. It is possible." Lois turned to me. "We looked at your previous history with the paparazzi and, as you mentioned, a lot of it centered around your relationship with Micah Murphy. Our suggestion then," she sucked in a breath, "and it is only a suggestion, is that you minimize your public appearances with Mr. Murphy. In fact, we think you shouldn't be seen in public with him at all."

It made sense.

But it still hurt.

Killian studied me with a furrowed brow, and I knew he was attempting to gauge my reaction to this advice.

"I don't have a relationship with Micah anymore," I said. "So that won't be a problem."

The rest of the meeting was a blur. The only thing I remembered about it was the way Killian watched me after they dropped the Micah suggestion.

When the four of them finally left us alone, Killian stayed where he was instead of coming to me. He asked, "What do you think?"

"Your director of publicity is more sales oriented than image oriented. She should be in marketing."

"Noted. But I wasn't asking for advice about my staff. I was asking what you think of their plans?"

"They're fine."

He frowned. "That's it? Fine?"

"Fine."

Keeping his expression clear, he pressed, "Even the part about Micah?"

"Now that you mention it, we need to talk."

"About?"

"I did a lot of googling yesterday. Which always sounds dirtier than it is, unless you're googling porn."

Amusement lit his eyes. "True."

"I'm going to contact Adam, my financial advisor. And since he's Gayle's son and Gayle's my manager, I'm going to contact her too. And she'll tell the band that I'm okay."

He got up slowly, seeming to process this as he paced for a few seconds. Finally, he turned to me. "And you couldn't have told me this before so your team could plan for this? We need to control how the press finds out about your return, Skylar."

"Gayle isn't going to tell the press. She's going to tell the boys."

"Why now? Three months ago, you signed a record deal rather than access your money and alert Gayle."

"One, I don't want to owe your uncle anything—"

"Skylar—"

"No," I cut him off. "I'm paying you back for everything and I'm paying rent for my apartment. Plus, I want to start a charity for the homeless. That's the money part of it."

"A charity?" He blinked at me in confusion. "What the—"

"But mostly I need to let Gayle and the guys know I'm okay. I don't have any other family but them." Tears of anguish burned in my eyes, and Killian froze. "Three months ago, I couldn't see past my own pain. I can now. They deserve to know I'm okay. They deserve an apology. I've been selfish for far too long. How would you feel, Killian? If you were them? If it was you I'd disappeared on?"

He studied me a moment and then let out a heavy sigh. "You're right. You need to let them know you're okay. But Micah? It wasn't my idea about you not seeing him in public, but I do think it's valid and not because of my personal feelings on the matter. He's what stirs the fans and consequently the tabloids."

"It's not about Micah—it's about all of them. And it's not about anything romantic with Micah. You know that. We've been friends since middle school. No matter the shit between us, he deserves to know I'm okay too."

His expression veered from annoyance to exasperation to concern and finally to what I gathered was understanding. "Okay. You're right. You need to do this. So you do that, and we . . . well, let's talk about this charity and how we can turn it into PR gold."

I burst into incredulous laughter. "You're incorrigible."

My stomach fluttered as he offered a smile that was nothing short of devilish. "That's show business."

I DIDN'T KNOW THEN AS I called Gayle that it would change the course my life was currently on. I only knew that I owed her the kind of apology it would take a dozen lifetimes to make good. Of course, I didn't have my old phone with my contacts in it anymore but I remembered Gayle would send our schedules and tour info via email and she always included her direct number on them.

When I logged into my email, I found all the most recent mail was junk. I was scared to scroll further down, in case I discovered the guys had tried to reach out over the last twenty-one months. I typed in Gayle's name, found an old email that caused an ache of nostalgia in my chest, and dialed her number.

I thought maybe I might throw up, and I wasn't sure I'd even be able to hear her because my heart was pounding so freaking loud.

"Gayle Abernathy," she answered. "Hello? Hello, anyone there?"

Struggling to get the words out, I forced air out of my nose instead.

"Okay, creeper, hanging up now."

"Gayle, it's me," I burst out, afraid she wouldn't answer again.

Silence reigned.

She was definitely going to hang up now.

"Skylar?" she whispered in disbelief.

"Yes. It's me."

And more silence.

"Gayle?"

"One second." I heard a door open and close in the background and then, "Where the fuck have you been?"

I flinched hearing the tremble of worry in her anger. "I'm so sorry."

"Sorry? You're sorry? I've been worried sick, kid. We thought you were dead and we couldn't put a freaking missing persons out on you because of the letter and voicemail crap you left to let us know you were taking off. The cops refused to consider it a missing-persons case because you said you were leaving indefinitely. All you had left were a couple of months and we could have declared you legally dead because you haven't touched any of your money. How did you survive without money? What have you been doing, you little brat?" She ended on a yelled sob.

My God.

Gayle never cried.

"Gayle . . . I . . . there aren't enough sorrys in the world."

She sniffled. "You bet your ass there aren't. Oh my God, Skylar. I'm so mad at you but I've never been happier to get a phone call in my life."

Tears of gratitude welled in my eyes. "I took too long."

"Yeah, you did. So why now and not then?"

"Time," I said. "That's the only answer I can give. It was like I was sleeping for a long time and now I'm finally awake, and I can't believe that I put you all through this. I woke up with a million apologies to give."

"Where are you?"

I told her. Everything. The whole sordid story. The only thing I left out was my romantic relationship with Killian, so unfortunately, she didn't get to know how good things were for me now.

Still, as she listened patiently, I felt the knot in my stomach shrink a little bit more.

NOT EVEN FIFTEEN MINUTES AFTER I hung up with Gayle, my phone rang. It was an LA number and my thumb hovered over the accept button for a few seconds as I fearfully considered who I would get on the end of the line.

Whoever it was, it wouldn't be easy.

Sucking in a shaky breath, I answered.

"Skylar?" Brandon asked, sounding disbelieving. "God, is that really you?"

"Brandon?" I slumped on the couch, closing my eyes. It felt like years and years since I'd heard his voice. "It's me."

"Fuck. Fuck, fuck, fuck. When Gayle called, I wasn't sure she was for real. It still doesn't feel real. Say something else," he demanded.

I smiled through renewed tears. "I'm so sorry."

He went silent.

"Brandon?"

"I am so angry, Sky." Tears filled his words, sending my own spilling down my cheeks. "I'm so angry with you but I'm so fucking glad to hear your voice. I was so worried you hurt yourself or someone hurt you. Why did you leave? Why couldn't you stay and let me help you?"

I sobbed uncontrollably, listening to the tears in my best friend's voice, a guy I only ever saw cry once and that was at my mother's funeral. I'd hurt Brandon. I'd hurt my family.

He let me cry, patiently waiting for me get a hold of myself.

"I'm sorry for that too." I wiped at my cheeks. "You don't need to hear that from me. You deserve an apology."

"I deserve honesty."

"You do." I nodded, even though he couldn't see me. "I wish I had a better answer than this but here is the truth: I was a fucked-up, selfish kid and it took me too long to pull my head out of my ass."

"Gayle said you were living on the streets. God, Sky, when I think what could have happened. And who is this guy? This label guy? Did he blackmail you? Because it sounds like he blackmailed you."

"How did Gayle manage to tell you so much in less than fifteen minutes?" I said, awed at her ability. I'd been on the phone with her for over an hour.

"So, it's true? He blackmailed you?"

The thought of him thinking badly of Killian caused a tightness in my chest. "No. It was complicated. Killian has helped me a lot. He gave me somewhere to stay, clothes, food, and I've been writing new music . . ."

"You have millions in the bank. Why the hell did you need to rely on this guy?"

I sucked in a breath. "Because I knew once I called Adam, he would call Gayle, and she would call you. I left it so long to come back to you all that the longer I waited, the more terrified I got at the idea of facing you. I was a coward."

"What did you think we would do?"

"Hate me," I answered immediately. "You're the only family I have left, and I treated you like crap. So yeah, I was terrified of you hating me."

Brandon was silent so long, I thought my worst fear *had* come true.

"I'm angry with you. But I could never *hate* you. I love you. You're my family. But you put me through hell, Sky. You put me through hell. Then I keep reminding myself that you were already there. In hell. That I can't possibly understand what you're going through. But I kind of do because I loved Angie too. I know it's not the same, but I lost her too. You could've come to me."

Fresh tears scored hotly down my cheeks. "But I couldn't, Brandon. It wasn't just about losing my mom and losing her the way I did. It was about Bryan and Micah and the band. I was so miserable in that life but I didn't want to let anyone down. When Mom died, it was easier to walk away from the music but not from the years I'd wasted avoiding her because of how unhappy I was."

"Gayle told me about Bryan. Why didn't you tell me? I could've helped."

"I didn't want to face it. Facing it meant telling my mom, and

I didn't want her to resent me. I did a lot of running away back then. And I kept running. However, I'm not running anymore."

"Okay." He let out a heavy exhalation. "There's so much to say and talk about, but I don't want to do it over the phone. Can I come to you? The band is on a break so I'm staying with Heather in LA. I could get on a plane today."

The thought made my stomach flip-flop but I couldn't say I wasn't going to run anymore and then do just that. "I'd like that."

twenty-six

That night Killian came over and held me while I let myself get lost in my thoughts and emotions. He didn't make me try to articulate them. He let me be.

The next morning, I got a text from Brandon to let me know he'd landed at Heathrow and would be in Glasgow by five o'clock. Killian had left early, as always, to fit in his workout and would be on his way into the office. I called him to tell him about Brandon and the line went quiet.

"You're not okay with this?" I surmised by his silence.

"You've been really lucky here, Skylar. This is a pretty laid-back city and if you have been recognized, no one cares enough to plaster it on the internet. But put you and another band member together and you're definitely going to get attention."

"He's coming to the apartment. We'll stay inside."

More silence.

"Killian, this is a good thing. If I can make peace with Brandon, with Austin, and yes, even with Micah, then I can really start to move on. And that's what you want, right?"

"Of course. You've just . . . You've come a long way. I don't want anyone derailing you."

I smiled at his overprotectiveness. "Trust that I'm strong enough to handle this now."

"I do trust that. I've always believed in you more than you've ever believed in yourself."

I love you. I struggled to hold the words back. "I'll call you when Brandon leaves."

"Maybe I should come over? Meet him."

"I think I need to do this alone."

"You call me if you need me."

"I will."

It was hard to concentrate the rest of the day. I wandered around the apartment, almost feeling like I was losing my mind. Finally, needing something to do, I sat down with my guitar and without even really expecting or meaning to, I wrote a song.

Realizing hours later that I'd barely eaten a thing, I'd gotten up to make myself a salad for dinner when my cell rang. Not recognizing the number, but seeing the Glasgow area code, I hesitated answering it. Then I realized it might be someone from Skyscraper.

"Hello?" I answered.

"Sky, I'm sorry," Brandon burst out breathlessly down the line.

His tone made my heart speed up. "For what?"

"For not telling you that Micah came with me and then took off from the hotel without me. We haven't even checked in yet. He must've stolen the bit of paper I had with your address on it because I can't find it, and I'm guessing he's on his way there now. But give me your address and I'll be right there."

The thought of seeing Micah made me more than a little nauseated. "Oh . . . Oh, okay. What should I expect here, Brandon? Is he coming here to verbally attack me?"

He sighed. "He's . . . I don't think he even knows. I think he just needs to see you. To see for himself that you're alive and you're okay. But even so, this is my fault, so give me your—"

"Excuse me, are you Brandon Kline from Tellurian? Was that Micah Murphy who just left? Oh my God, this is so cool!" a female Scottish voice in the background cut him off.

"Uh, yeah, hey," he said distractedly. "Nice to meet you."

"Can we get a selfie?"

"I'm kind of in the middle of something, guys. Later, okay. Thanks." Another heavy sigh. "Shit, Sky, sorry. Give me your address."

I felt like I had a bunch of bees buzzing around my ears. "Were you and Micah just recognized?"

"Yeah, we're not exactly easy to miss."

That was true. They were both tall, good-looking guys, and Brandon was built like a linebacker. Recent photos of them online showed Brandon with a full beard and Micah with a lot of scruff. Tattoos covered seventy percent of their bodies. Alone they drew attention; together they would definitely draw recognition.

Shit.

"Look, Gayle said you don't want the press knowing your business right now and I get that. We're not going to bring that on you. Tell me where you are and I'll come fix this."

I gave him my address.

"I'm leaving right now."

Feeling my nerves completely rattled, I paced the apartment, my heart jumping at every little sound until it was almost a relief to hear the buzzer for the downstairs door. I couldn't bring myself to go to it at first, but there was no running away anymore.

When it buzzed again, I hurried over to the intercom and hit the speaker. "Hello?"

There was a moment of silence and then the intercom crackled. "Sky?"

The sound of his voice brought back a wave of memories. Those memories felt like they belonged to another person, to another life, and the fact that I felt so adrift from those memories was achingly painful. "Micah?"

"Yeah, it's me," he breathed. "Can you let me up?"

I pressed the buzzer and stepped over to the door to remove the chain.

Resting my palm against the door, I waited, my breathing growing exponentially shallower as I waited for Micah to come up on the elevator.

Even though I heard his footsteps approaching, I still jumped at his loud knock on the door.

Fingers shaking, I unlocked and slowly opened it.

Green-gold eyes blazed into mine.

"Micah." Every inch of me hurt. It felt like . . . grief.

His own expression seemed filled with the same emotion.

And I braced, watching that grief transform to anger.

When he suddenly came at me, I tensed, unsure, only to freeze entirely as he hauled me against his chest and crushed me to him. Realizing he was hugging me and not killing me, I closed my arms around his back and held on.

He didn't smell like Micah. Micah used to smell of pot and beer. Other times of perfume and sweat. There were rare times when you could smell soap and shampoo beneath the other scents that more than hinted at his lifestyle.

But soap and shampoo were *all* I could smell now.

"Micah," I mumbled against his chest.

He squeezed me hard and then gently let go of me, only to cup my face in his hands so he could stare at my face. "I don't know whether to kill you or kiss you, Skylar Finch."

Since kissing wasn't an option and killing was not preferable, I went with neither and gently extricated myself so I could close the door.

"We have a lot to talk about," I said.

He nodded, his eyes dragging down my body and back up again. "Brandon filled me in on some."

"Why didn't you wait to come here with him?"

Micah looked at me incredulously. "Because you and I need to talk on our own. With Brandon and Austin, you left the band. With me . . . you left *me*."

"That's not true," I replied, walking away from him down the hall. I heard him following me into the apartment. Still, after all this time, Micah couldn't see past us. "Brandon and Austin were my family. They're like my brothers. I left them too."

"It's not the same." He ran a hand through his hair, absently taking in his surroundings before turning his attention back to me. His face was unshaven and somehow that added to his gorgeousness. A long time ago I only had to look at him and I'd get butterflies. Although I felt many things looking at him now, I didn't feel that attraction. His attractiveness felt like a fact rather than something that provoked a feeling in me, other than nostalgia.

Had it really been love between us or merely an infatuation?

"Where's Austin?" I feared he hated me and that's why he hadn't come.

Micah seemed irritated by the question. "He's doing *Wild*. We can't get a hold of him."

"Doing what?"

"*Wild*. You know that book. Or it might be a movie. Something that involves hiking the Pacific Crest Trail," he said. "His girlfriend, Selina, talked him into it."

I smiled at the idea of Austin doing something for a girl. Both he and Micah had been the one-night-stand kind of guys. Brandon had always been the relationship type. For a long time, none of his relationships had lasted until Heather. She was a stylist he'd began dating before my mom died. According to the media, they were now engaged.

Austin never seemed to want that. I hadn't seen anything in my googling about a girlfriend.

"Selina. Have they been together long?"

"A couple months." Micah shrugged. "Can we talk about this later and instead talk about the million fucking apologies you owe me?"

My response was immediate. "I'm sorry. I'm sorry, Micah. I'm sorry for running away. I'm sorry for punishing you through the years. I'm sorry for sleeping with you and leaving you the next day and disappearing off the face of the planet. I am sorrier than you could ever possibly know."

For a moment, he stared at me. Finally, he gestured. "Gayle said you'd been living rough. That things have been hard. But you look better than I've ever seen you. I like the hair," he said, his big puppy eyes wounded and accusing.

I fingered the short strands. "I want to tell you about it. However, I want to hear about you first. I heard you went to rehab."

His beautiful mouth twisted into a sneer. "You were keeping up with us while we were left in the dark about you?"

Apparently, his anger wasn't going away anytime soon, and I got that. I did. I indicated he should sit on the couch while I took the chair. He folded his tall body onto it and waited.

"I only recently found out. I had no access to the internet and had no desire to have access to the internet until a couple of days ago."

"You didn't care?"

"Of course, I cared. That's why I didn't check up on you. I cared so much, it was killing me. All of it was killing me and the only way I knew how to survive was to push it all away. For a while, I actually thought you were all gone. Ghosts. No . . . it was more like *I* was the ghost. Like I'd died and left your world behind. I needed it to be that way. It was the only way to get through the grief."

"You seem pretty together now. How come you can handle the grief now and you couldn't then?"

"Time," I answered as I'd answered Gayle. "And I've made friends here. Met someone who knows what it's like to lose a parent."

He beat his fist on his chest, his face red with frustration. "I could have been that friend. I grew up in the fucking foster care system, for Christ's sake, Skylar!"

I flinched but refused to turn away from his fury. "It's not the same," I said as gently as possible. "Yours is a whole other kind of pain that I can never understand. And mine . . . well, I wish you knew what it's like to have a parent love and support you but you never had that, Micah. My friend had that and understands the kind of pain *I'm* going through and the kind of anger and regret that lives inside you. That never goes away, no matter how or where or whom you move on with."

"So you let strangers help you heal? Great."

I let his anger roll over me, trying not to let it grab hold. "Isn't that what you did? When you went to rehab?"

That gave him pause. "I also went to therapy."

He'd been brave enough to do what I couldn't. "I'm glad."

"It wasn't only because you took off. Although that was the catalyst. After you left my drinking got out of control. Brandon said it was rehab or I was out of the band. I couldn't lose the band.

So I started rehab, started therapy, and it helped a lot. It made me realize how much you hurt me when we were kids when you chose the band over us."

Tears of guilt and regret blurred my vision. "I know. I'm so sorry."

"It was . . . you were, like, the first person I let myself love. I stopped loving people when I was kid because they always threw me away. But I let myself love you—I trusted that you loved me back. That *you* wouldn't throw me away."

The tears let loose.

"I'm not trying to hurt you. My therapist said I should be honest with the people in my life. You hurt me, Sky. So I punished you. Because I knew you loved me and I hated that it wasn't enough. But it was enough to inflict pain as payback." His eyes blazed with regret. "Do you forgive me?"

"I forgive you." I wiped impatiently at my tears. "Do you forgive me?"

He hesitated and then, "I want to."

The door buzzer broke the tense moment and Micah sat up, scowling. "Who's that?"

"It'll be Brandon."

"Don't let him up."

I stared incredulously at him. "Micah, he flew over five thousand miles to see me."

"You and I aren't done talking."

I was right. He still didn't get it. "It isn't always about you and me, Micah."

The petulant look on his face as I walked out to let Brandon in made me question if Micah had changed much after all. There was silence from the sitting room as I waited on Brandon coming up the elevator. It was a different feeling entirely anticipating his arrival. With Micah, I felt sick. With Brandon, I wanted to throw my arms around him as soon as I saw him.

When he appeared, so tall, all bearded, purplish circles under his eyes that told me he was jet-lagged, I rushed him.

And he caught me.

He lifted me up in a bear hug and as he whispered my name, the sob burst out of me before I could stop it.

Because it felt like coming home.

twenty-seven

It was hard to take my eyes off Brandon. He was like a bright light that captured my attention and wouldn't let go. I realized as all three of us sat in my apartment and talked that he held me captivated because I had no bad memories attached to our relationship.

When we were on tour and I was tired and lonely, he'd snuggle up with me to watch a movie on the tour bus, or he would take me out for dinner so we could unwind and pretend we were ordinary people grabbing a bite to eat. He was the one who kept Micah at bay when I'd had enough.

He was the big brother who protected me.

He was the one thing that tethered me to sanity during the craziness that was our lives.

Of course, I loved Austin too, but he was more like the little brother who made me laugh and annoyed the hell out of me.

It was different.

"Heather's pregnant." My eyes widened as Brandon shared this news. "You're going to be an aunt."

That he would offer me that made tears well in my eyes. "An

aunt! That is so cool. Congratulations. Tell Heather congrats too."

"I will." He grinned. "She's been worried about you."

"We all have," Micah said sullenly. He was standing at the French doors looking out over the Clyde and had been the entire time Brandon caught me up with his life. "It's been almost two years of worrying. Fuck. Two years. Who can believe that?"

Sobered by the raw pain in his voice, I offered, "If I'd been in a better frame of mind, it never would've gotten to that point. It makes me feel sick that I left it this long."

"You've apologized enough," Brandon said, scowling at Micah's back. "You're here and you're healthy and that's all that matters."

"Oh?" Micah whirled around. "Is it? A couple of apologies and we're okay?"

Brandon narrowed his gaze. "Three days ago, you would've given anything to hear from Skylar and know she was okay. Remember that."

"Brandon, it's fine," I soothed. "There's no way in hell I expect any of you to forgive me so quickly."

"Well, I have."

I loved him. "That's because you're an angel. The rest of us are just tellurian."

He grinned at my joke.

Micah huffed, "I'm starved," and strode into the kitchen. He pulled open the fridge, perused it, and cursed under his breath. "Still a health nut, I see." He slammed the door closed and turned to me. "Got any real food?"

I shrugged. "We could order takeout."

So that's what we did. While we waited, we talked about Austin and Selina, about Gayle, about friends in the music business. We did not touch on Macy and the band, as if we were all afraid to mention it.

And then my cell rang. It was Killian. "I need to take this," I told the guys before disappearing into my bedroom.

"Hey," I answered once I'd closed the door.

"Hi, I'm just checking in."

Despite my warm, mushy feelings for Brandon, I hadn't realized how tense I was until I heard Killian's voice. It was almost as if I could feel the solid heat of him at my back. Still, I wasn't looking forward to telling him about Micah. "We ordered some food. We're easing into it. Catching up."

"Was he glad to see you?"

"Very. It's wonderful to see him again. I've missed him."

"I know. I'm happy for you."

The soft, loving way he said that made it difficult to tell him the next part. "Micah is here too. I didn't know he was coming."

Killian was quiet on the other end.

"Killian?"

"I'm here."

"Well?"

"You'd have to face him sooner or later. At least it's happening in the privacy of the flat with Brandon there."

Then why did he sound so pissed?

"So, you're okay? We're okay?"

"Fine. I have a meeting. We'll talk later."

And he hung up, taking all my good feelings with him.

The worst of it was that I couldn't even be mad at him. I'd acted like a jealous idiot over some one-night stand while he had valid reasons for being jealous of Micah.

"Shit," I murmured under my breath.

I had to brace myself to go back out to the boys.

"Food arrived," Brandon said, taking cartons out of a carrier bag.

"I didn't even hear the buzzer."

"They didn't buzz up. They just appeared at the door," Micah said, studying me. "We paid."

"Oh, someone must have let them in while they were going out. Thanks." I walked into the kitchen, my stomach rumbling to life at the smell of the Thai food.

"Who was on the phone?" Micah asked as I helped Brandon put out plates and cutlery.

I didn't respond at first, waiting until we were standing around the island, digging into the food. Finally, I said, "It was Killian."

"The guy who signed you to the record deal here?" Brandon asked.

"Yeah."

"He a good guy?"

"How can he be?" Micah stabbed a piece of pork like he was imagining it was something or *someone* else. "Gayle said he signed you to his label after you'd gotten attacked by street thugs who stole your guitar. He used how messed up you were against you."

I squirmed, supremely uncomfortable with his version of events. "That's not true. It's complicated."

"There's nothing complicated about it. You told us you were leaving the band because this life, the fame, made you miserable. But you sign a record deal with this guy and we're supposed to believe you did that of your own volition?"

Angry, I glared at him. "You weren't here, Micah. You have no idea what you're talking about."

"And whose fault is that?"

"Hey!" Brandon waved a fork at us. "Cut it out. We're not going to do this. Eat your food and enjoy the fact that we're all alive and bar one of us who is probably getting bit by a snake as we speak, we're all together. Let's enjoy that."

Micah and I shared a look, and then nodded to Brandon. However, a wealth of anger simmered beneath the surface.

SITTING WITH MY BACK AGAINST the chair, I stared across the room at Micah in the dim light. It was midnight. Brandon had checked their luggage at the hotel before coming after Micah, so their rooms were waiting for them. But Brandon had barely been able to keep his eyes open with the jet lag so I'd helped him into my bedroom where he'd collapsed on the bed, out within seconds.

The apartment was dark except for lights under the kitchen cabinets and baseboards. Still, I could feel Micah looking at me from his sprawled position on the couch. We hadn't said a word to each other in what felt like forever.

"It's a miracle you're still awake," I whispered.

"I slept on the plane," he whispered back. "Brandon was too anxious about seeing you to sleep."

The thought made me smile.

"You don't deserve him, you know."

Hurt pierced me. "What?"

"Brandon. You don't deserve him. Neither do I. He'll love us until the end of time, no matter what shit we pull. He deserves better friends than us."

"I'm going to make it up to him. I'll never treat him like that again," I vowed.

He scoffed. "You don't know that. Let's face it, Sky—you and I are two of the most selfish, self-absorbed bastards on the planet. That's why we love each other. No one else would put up with us."

Anger burned in my gut. "You don't know me anymore."

"I know you left. I know you run. That's who you are."

"I'm not running now."

He shrugged. "So you say. Look, I'm not judging you. I'm not perfect either. I can admit that. And I'm not looking for perfect from you. I don't expect that. I never have."

"You're still angry with me."

"Of course I am. I made love to you and you skipped town the next day. For almost two years."

"As wrong as I was to do that, you get why, right?" I leaned forward, my eyes narrowed, waiting for him to show me he wasn't completely oblivious.

"Because you've always been afraid of your feelings for me."

His arrogance made me feel like I'd been punched in the stomach. "You think I left because we slept together?"

"Well, you did leave right after it."

"Yes. I did. Because I never meant for that to happen. Because it was too much to deal with on top of what I was *really* dealing with." I realized I was almost shouting and lowered my voice to a whisper. "I spent most of our fame avoiding my mother because I didn't want her to know that she'd spent all of her time and money, nearly wrecking her relationship, on a dream that as it turned out, I didn't want. And that sounds stupid now, but back then, it felt huge. I was a kid. And I wasted all that time avoiding her. All that time I can't get back because two masked gunmen broke into the house I bought her and they murdered her for a fucking painting. And two days before you and I slept together, the cops told me that although they'd keep looking, their leads had gone cold.

"Finding them," I bit out, the rage that still burned deep in my guts curdling my words, "was the only thing that kept me going when she died. And then that justice slipped out of my hands. I had nothing but my grief. I wish I could've been stronger, as strong as I feel now, but I wasn't then. I just wanted to disappear. I wanted to exist in a world where I wasn't Skylar Finch, the pop-rock princess whose mother had been shot in the head. So, no, Micah, I didn't leave because of you."

Hearing the disdain in my voice, he sat up. He looked haggard as he stared at the floor.

Silence pressed upon us but I couldn't bear to speak another word. I'd missed Micah, but perhaps I'd missed him through rose-tinted spectacles. Or maybe, finally, I was free of whatever spell he'd had me under and I could see him for who he really was. He wasn't a bad person. He'd been hurt a lot in his young life. But his aloneness, his need for self-protection, had also made him incredibly selfish and self-involved.

If he thought we were the same, then I had a lot of work ahead of me to make sure I lived my life as a better person.

"You're not in love with me anymore," he suddenly said.

My stomach flipped at the words, hating that being honest in this case was going to be painful. The last thing I wanted was to be another person who rejected and disappointed Micah. "I care about you."

"But you aren't in love with me."

I exhaled slowly, the sound shuddering in the quiet dark of the apartment. "No, I'm not. I'm sorry."

"Maybe you never were."

"I loved you. I was attracted to you. But I think . . . sometimes I think we were more addicted to the longing than to the loving."

"How do you mean?"

"As long as we were pining for each other, we didn't give ourselves a chance to be in an actual relationship where we could disappoint and hurt each other until there was no coming back. Instead we got to hold onto fantasizing about each other. The angst was more powerful than the love."

He grunted. "Or maybe it's simply that there's someone else for you now."

God, he was asking me to hurt him. "Micah—"

"Is there someone else?"

I couldn't tell him about Killian, but again, I didn't want to lie to him. "Yes."

He blew out a shaky breath. "The friend you were talking about?"

"Yes."

"And you love him? It is a him, right?"

"Yes, it's a him. And yes, I am in love with him." I sat forward as he turned his face toward the light so I saw the pain slash across it. "Micah, I'm not all those things you said. I refuse to be. And the fact that you think that of me . . . Love isn't tearing someone down to bring them to your level. Love is seeing in the person you love," my voice cracked on the emotion as I thought about Killian's belief in me, "the best possible version of who they can be."

His jaw clenched but he nodded, tears shimmering in his eyes.

"You know I'm right."

He kept nodding, swallowing hard as if trying to swallow his emotions.

"If you came here for me for yourself or for the band, I'm not going home with you."

Micah finally looked at me. "So, you're never coming home?"

I gave him a sad smile. "I *am* home."

"Shit," he exhaled shakily, drawing a hand through his hair. "I need a drink."

Concern prickled over me like a chill had blown through the room. "Don't say that."

He grimaced. "Don't worry. I'm not going to. I just . . . I have triggers, you know."

I was almost afraid to ask. "I . . . I'm a trigger?"

Micah didn't reply, but his expression spoke for him. Worry

gnawed at me and as the night wore on, I forced myself to stay awake, to watch him, until jet lag finally dragged Micah down with it. Convinced he was out and there was no way he'd leave to find that drink, I crashed out beside Brandon on my bed, so exhausted not even his snoring could keep me awake.

twenty-eight

"Sky." My body was gently shaken, leading me up out of dream world. "Sky, wake up."

I grumbled and reluctantly opened my eyes. It was still dark outside. "What time is it?" I mumbled.

Brandon's head appeared above mine. His hair was sleep-tousled but his eyes were no longer bloodshot with exhaustion. "It's seven forty-five. We're making breakfast."

"Some things do change." I watched as he strolled out of the room. "I'll be right out." I rolled over and reached for my phone on the bedside table. I'd put it on silent last night so as not to be disturbed with the guys, and I'd forgotten to switch it back on. I expected a message or a missed call from Killian but there was nothing. I did have a text from Autumn.

Killian said Micah and Brandon have come to visit. Hope all is okay? xx

I sat up and quickly texted her back.

They slept here becoz we talked so long . . . I think we'll be ok.

And I did. Brandon didn't know how to hold a grudge, even

though I'd changed his life (something I still intended to face and discuss with them) and Micah . . .

I think eventually Micah would come around.

I shuffled into the kitchen to find Micah making—"Holy crap, are you actually making us frittata?"

He gave me a boyish, pleased grin. "Yep."

"It smells amazing." I slid onto the stool across from him while Brandon puttered around making coffee. "Since when do you cook?"

He shrugged. "I helped out in the kitchen at the rehab facility. I liked it. It stuck."

"It's been great on tour." Brandon pushed a coffee toward me. "Sometimes we actually eat real food."

"Well, you should," I said. "You know how important it is to put the right stuff in your body for touring. You need energy."

They shared a look, something nostalgic and sad passing between them, and I realized that I used to say that all the time, lecturing them on the crap they put in their bodies.

Deciding it was now or never, I said, "How is Macy doing?"

They shared another look, this one a little more unreadable, and Micah plated the frittata. Brandon spoke first. "She's having a hard time. With the album not doing so great, she feels the fans are coming down on *her* for it."

"But she didn't write the album," Micah grimaced. "Austin and I did." I hesitated to say what I wanted, but Micah read my expression. "Just say it."

"Well, I had a listen to the album the other day."

"And?" Brandon asked.

"It sounds like you were trying to write songs you thought *I* might write."

"It sounds like that because it's true. We were trying not to piss off any more fans," Micah huffed, shoving a plate across the island to me.

"Thanks," I said. "Look, Tellurian is now Tellurian 2.0. It has to be different but as long as it's authentic, the fans won't care. If they do, you'll get new fans. Micah, you need to write the songs that mean something to you. And on that note, if Macy is capable, she should be involved in the writing process. She *is* singing the songs."

"You don't feel weird talking about her?" Brandon asked between bites.

I wrinkled my nose. "I didn't want to know anything about her or the band when I first took off. However, I realized when I was checking up on you guys that I'm glad you picked her. She was always nice and she has a great voice."

"It's not *your* voice though," Micah grumbled.

"No, it's hers. And you can make that work for you. Side note, does Macy really want the rainbow hair or was that Gayle's idea?"

"Gayle's idea," they said in unison.

"Then scrap it. Macy isn't me and she shouldn't be forced into trying to be me. That's part of the pressure she'll be feeling. Let her be herself. In every way."

The guys shared a look and then nodded. Micah surprised me by turning to me and offering, "Thanks, Skylar."

Tenderness for them welled inside me. "You will always be my family. I know I didn't treat you right, but I'm going to be here for you from now on, no matter what. I want you all *and* Macy to succeed because you deserve to. You've worked too hard not to."

"And you?" Brandon asked. "Are you really okay about this album you're launching?"

Unable to meet their eyes, I took a bite of food and used the time to think about how to frame my answer. "They've promised me that I don't have to take part in the social media thing and that once the big blow-up over my return happens, they'll work their asses off to make sure my private life remains out of the tabloids."

"They can't guarantee that, Sky," Micah said.

"I know. But it is possible."

Micah shook his head. "Not for you. You have a quality, charisma, it draws people to you. It's the reason the fans were obsessed with you and why the tabloids came after you."

I flushed at his description of me. "Not true. They came after us because of *our* whole angsty-love thing."

"That was part of it, but after the rehab news, they left me alone. When I'm not partying and getting wasted or pining after you, apparently I'm boring."

"Micah's right. I'm worried about you," Brandon said. "I hate to think you've been forced into something you don't want to do."

Pressure, much like anxiety, settled over my chest but I covered the discomfiting feeling with a smile. "I love you guys for caring, but it's just one album. If things blow up in my face, then I walk."

"It's one album that could have the paps hounding you for a while."

"I know."

"They'll be outside your house, your hotels, the places you shop, the restaurants you eat in. They'll try to hack your phone again, dog your friends—"

Brandon sighed, "She gets it, Micah. Stop."

"Well, I'm worried." He shrugged.

"I'm asking you not to be." I flashed him a cheeky grin and changed the subject. "This frittata rocks."

He smiled, pleased. "Yeah, I got pretty good."

"We need to get back to the hotel. All our shit is there," Brandon said. "We were talking and we thought maybe later today Micah and I could visit your record label, meet this Killian guy, and see what it's all about."

Brandon. My protective big brother.

The thought of them meeting Killian, however . . ."Oh, I'm not sure about that. They run a pretty tight schedule over there. We'd probably have to make appointments and they might not be able to fit us in while you're here."

"Sky," Brandon gave me his no-nonsense face. "We're visiting that label. No discussion."

I slumped on my stool. "Fine. I'll see what I can do."

After we finished breakfast, I walked the guys downstairs to wait on their cab with them. They shivered in the cold November air. "I hope you brought warmer clothes than that." I gestured to the shirts they wore over T-shirts.

"Uh, not really." They shared a look and chuckled.

I rolled my eyes. "I think you're both spending way too much time in LA."

"The weather *is* nice." Brandon nodded, although his eyes twinkled in a way that reminded me it wasn't the weather keeping him California.

"When do you need to get back for Heather?"

"Soon. Real soon. But I'm not leaving until I know you're okay."

"I *am* okay."

"Yeah, we'll see." His eyes flew over my shoulder. "That looks like our cab. Come here." He wrapped his arms around me, bending down to lift me into a hug. I held on, hiding my smile in his shoulder. The knot in my stomach shrunk a little bit more again. When he lowered me, he pressed a kiss to my nose. "I'm calling you in two hours."

"Okay." I grinned, feeling warm and fuzzy that not only had he forgiven me but he still intended to worry over me despite the ocean I'd put between us.

"Come here." Micah drew me into a hug. This one I went into more tentatively but when his arms banded tight around me, I couldn't help but hold him back just as tight. There was too much history and affection there not to. I felt his lips on my shoulder and tensed a little. Micah felt it and lifted his head to stare into my eyes. "I know," he said. "I get it. It's going to take me a little more time. That okay?"

Understanding he meant moving on from seeing us in a romantic light, I nodded and reached up to press a kiss to his cheek, but he turned slightly so the kiss landed on the corner of his mouth. My skin prickled with the scratch of his stubble and I jerked back.

It was hard not to drown in his mournful gaze right then, but I gently extricated myself and stepped back. "See you soon."

Micah got in the cab first so I took the opportunity to grab Brandon's hand. He frowned and leaned down to me so I could whisper, "He said last night that he needed a drink. Watch him, please."

Expression grim, he nodded. "I got his back."

I squeezed his hand in thanks and let him go. While I watched the cab pull away, I thought I saw movement in a car across the street—like someone ducking down to hide.

My pulse skipped in alarm and I squinted to get a better look. Unable to see anything, however, I had to put it down to lack of sleep and general jitteriness after such a big evening. Heading back inside my apartment, all I wanted to do was hit the hay but I knew Brandon and Micah weren't going to let up about seeing the label and meeting Killian.

I was about to call Killian when my phone binged with a text.

Autumn: Are you alone yet? Can I come over? Xx

Me: Yeah, of course.

Autumn: I'll be there in five. Xx

Wondering if she'd just been at the label and hoping she wasn't coming over because Killian was mad at me, I sucked in a breath and dialed my boyfriend's number. Because fuck it. He *was* my boyfriend.

It rang off.

So I called again.

He picked up. "I'm running out of a meeting into another, Skylar, I don't have time to talk."

He sounded pissed. "Good morning to you too. I thought you'd call."

"I've been busy."

"Too busy to see if I was all right after my band members came back into my life after a near two-year absence?"

"I gathered it went okay since they slept over."

Was that his problem? "Killian, they're like brothers to me."

"Micah isn't."

"Which is why I crashed on my bed with Brandon and Micah took the couch."

He went silent and I heard the rustle of movement and then a door closing before he practically growled down the phone. "You shared a fucking bed with one of them?"

My cheeks flushed. He made it sound like I'd done something wrong. I guess he didn't realize how much Brandon felt like family to me. "Brandon might as well be blood related, that's how much he's like a brother to me. I would never have done that if he weren't."

"He's not blood related and you did. Jesus, Skylar, you lost the fucking plot when you heard a voicemail from my one-night stand. You expect me to be okay with you sleeping in the same bed as another man?"

Feeling the situation escalate out of my control, panic fluttered in my chest. "Killian, I promise you that if you see me and Brandon together, you'll get it. You'll see we're like brother and sister."

"I take it they're not leaving anytime soon, then?"

"They want to make sure I'm okay. And to do that, they want to come to the label today and meet you."

"Fine," he answered immediately, surprising me.

"Seriously?"

"Aye, seriously. I want to meet them too."

I hesitated . . ."Are you still mad at me?"

"I don't know. How would you feel if you found out I shared a bed with another woman last night?"

The thought made me want to grind my teeth together. "If that woman was Autumn, then I'd be fine with it. Which is exactly what we're talking about here and you'll see that for yourself today."

He blew out what sounded like a beleaguered breath.

My heart clenched at the thought of him being angry with me, but I was also more than a little annoyed. "You know, it would be nice if you could put your jealousy aside to ask me if I'm okay." When there was no response, an ache flared in my chest. "Okay then, what time should we meet you?"

"One o'clock should be fine."

"See you then."

"Skylar." He stopped me as I was about to hang up. "I missed you too. I miss you whenever you're not by my side."

I closed my eyes as the panic eased but my irritation, and yes, hurt, remained.

At my silence, his voice lowered. "I'm sorry I'm a jealous prick. Are you okay?"

I slumped in relief. "Yes, I'm okay. I'll be even better when I get you alone. After I'm done kissing every inch of you, we can talk about it."

"I'm looking forward to it." I heard the desire in his words. The need. God, I wished he were with me. Unfortunately, I'd have to wait.

"Before then, I'll see you at the label."

"See you then."

I hung up, holding the phone to my chest, wishing that I was able to walk into the label at one o'clock and kiss the surliness right out of Killian O'Dea. Instead I'd have to pretend there was nothing more between us than an album. However, as soon as I got him alone, I was going to rock his world so hard, he'd forget all about being a grumpy pain in my ass.

Thankfully, keeping me from overthinking the last twenty-four hours, Autumn arrived—with coffee—not long after I hung up with Killian. After we'd settled and I told her how my night with the guys went, she shot me an apologetic look.

"I got your text while I was with Killian, so you should know he knows about the guys staying overnight."

"It's okay. I got off the phone with him. I know he wasn't happy about it, but he'll see when he meets Brandon that there's absolutely nothing like that between us."

"I really don't think it's Brandon that worries him. You've got to understand, Skylar, Killian researched you before he ever had feelings for you. He found article upon article about your romance with Micah. You guys were everywhere."

That panic returned, as I began to fear that I wouldn't be able to make Killian understand that I no longer was in love with Micah. "Those days are long gone. When I look at Micah now, I don't feel any of what I used to feel. All that's left is history, affection, and frustration that he'll always see the world from his point of view and no one else's."

"Maybe today will help, then. Killian can see you interact."

I nodded, hoping she was right. Then I studied my friend and how her perfect makeup was unable to hide the dark circles under her eyes. "You know, all we do lately is talk about me. I know I have a lot of crap going on, but that doesn't mean I get to let you off the hook. What's going on with *you*?"

Autumn threw me a tired smile. "Nothing."

"I don't believe that for a second." I had a sudden horrible thought. "Shit. Darren hasn't been bothering you, has he? You would have told us?"

She shook her head. "No, Darren is long gone."

"Then what is it? Someone new?"

"Ugh, God no." Autumn looked even more exhausted by the thought. "The last thing I need is to get into another relationship right now."

"Then what is going on with you, Autumn? You mentioned something that's been bothering me. I didn't want to push about it because I didn't think it was my place, but you're my friend and I think it *is* my place. You said a while ago that you felt like you were lost."

She grimaced. "You have so much more to deal with than me right now. We're not talking about this."

Worry suffused me. "We *are* talking about this. I'm officially concerned. What's going on?"

"I'm just *floundering*. I feel like I have no purpose. Like I'm useless."

"You are not useless. Don't ever say that."

"But what am I doing with my life? I occasionally run errands for Killian but other than that, I spend my days shopping and socializing. How dumb is that?"

"Hey," I shook my finger at her, teasing, "there are socialites with over a hundred million Instagram followers. Those millions of followers don't think *they're* dumb."

"Well, I do," Autumn huffed. "Pot meet kettle."

"Then what do you want to do about it?"

"That's the thing. I don't even know."

We sat in contemplation while I processed her concerns and tried to figure out the most helpful response. The one that came to mind was the one that would piss Killian off the most, but in this instance, I had to put his sister before our relationship. "Maybe you should get away for a while."

"Away?"

"Yeah. Go somewhere different. Somewhere you can think about you and what you want."

"Is that what you did?"

"I ran away. There's a difference. But if you want to put a less cowardly spin on what I did . . . let's say I did take off to get some perspective. And it worked. I'm not telling you to run away. I'm telling you that going somewhere, traveling, getting some distance from this city and your life here, might give you some much-needed perspective."

Autumn stared at me as if she were having a lightbulb moment. "Get away to find myself. That . . . I think you're right." She grinned suddenly. "My friend Catie invited me to this ski resort in Montana next January. I said no because the thought of skiing again after I broke my leg last time scares the crap out of me. But maybe that's what I need. To face my fears. And Montana is supposed to be beautiful."

A wave of nostalgia hit me. "It is. I'm from Montana."

Concern crossed her expression at whatever she saw in mine. "I forgot. Do you . . . do you miss it?"

I shook my head. "It's a total cliché but I guess there really are truths in clichés: home is where the heart is. There's nothing left of my heart there. Only memories. So . . . where in Montana?"

"Um, I can't remember. Some mountain ski resort. Whiterock . . . or White-something. I'll find out."

"It sounds like a plan."

She beamed at me. "I feel better already. Thank you."

I grinned and then immediately grimaced. "Just don't tell your brother it was my idea."

WE STOOD IN THE OPEN-PLAN office section of Skyscraper Records, me nervously watching Micah and Brandon as they looked around, taking everything in. Mirroring my complicated, stormy feelings, rain lashed against the windows, the dark clouds outside making the aluminum lighting in the office a glaring, harsher yellow.

I wanted the guys to be okay with what I was doing here.

Which was hilarious because I still wasn't one hundred percent sure I was okay with what we were doing here. Not the album. I was proud of the album.

Annoyed that we'd been waiting ten minutes and Killian still hadn't deigned to show up, I shot Justin at reception an impatient look. He grimaced. "Eve said he's on a conference call. He'll be out as soon as he's done."

I nodded and turned to Brandon. "What are you thinking?"

"Not a lot to think about right now." He glanced at the framed posters by the elevator. "They've signed some pretty fucking great artists lately though."

"Agreed." Micah's reluctance to admit that was obvious in the way he tucked in the corner of his mouth.

"Skylar."

Killian's voice made my skin tingle and I whirled to watch him stride past reception. He wore black suit trousers and a dark red cashmere sweater that molded to his body perfectly. After I'd told him red suited him, I noticed he wore it more often. God, it was awful not being able to walk up to him and put my arms around him. And I really needed that right then. I needed a hug from the one I loved most.

Eve followed behind him and I pasted on a professional smile. "Killian, Eve, hi. Thanks for taking time to meet Micah and Brandon."

"Not a problem." Killian nodded, giving me a thin-lipped smile before he turned to Brandon. "Brandon, it's nice to meet you. I'm Killian O'Dea."

Brandon shook his hand, eyeing him speculatively. "You too."

Sensing that was all he was going to get out of my ex-bandmate for now, Killian let go and offered the same hand to Micah. "Micah."

Micah stared at it for a second and for an awful moment, I thought he wasn't going to accept it. Finally, however, to my great relief, he reached out and took my boyfriend's hand. "I'm here to make sure no one is messing with my girl."

Killian's expression hardened and I didn't know if it was the insinuation that he would "mess" with me or Micah referring to me as his girl. I had a feeling it was both. "I'm taking good care of Skylar."

Not "we." *"I'm."*

Shit. He needed to watch that. "Yes, the team here has been wonderful," I interjected. "For instance, Eve has been very helpful."

Eve blushed and gave an adorable little wave. "Hi. I'm Eve, Killian's assistant. I'm also a *huge* fan of Tellurian."

Micah and Brandon grinned at her. "Nice to meet you." Brandon stuck out a hand and her eyes widened as she tentatively reached out to take it.

"I'm shaking Brandon Kline's hand," she whispered audibly.

Killian rubbed a hand over his mouth to cover a smile and I

thought how changed he was from the first time I stepped into this building. Eve's fangirling used to bother him. Now it amused him.

Brandon chuckled and let go of Eve's hand.

"Do you want to shake mine?" Micah offered with laughter in his voice.

"Uh-huh." Eve nodded and her expression clearly stated, "I've died and gone to heaven" as Micah shook her hand, clasping it in both of his for good measure. He gave her his flirty eyes and I swear, I thought she was going to melt in a puddle at his feet.

"You're so pretty," she blurted out, and then flushed even redder. "I mean, you're all so pretty. It's a little overwhelming." She gulped and stepped back, shooting Killian a worried look as she realized how much she'd fangirled.

Killian was too busy staring at me. *I* almost blushed at the intensity of his gaze and gave him a quick warning look before I turned away.

"So, what first?" Brandon asked.

I opened my mouth to suggest a tour but Killian cut me off. "Skylar needs to lay down vocals for a final track on the album. I think you should both sit in so you can hear for yourselves how special this album is going to be."

Before I could respond that I didn't know how comfortable I was recording solo material in front of the guys, Micah said, "Perfect. Let's do that. Eve, lead the way."

She giggled and nodded. I couldn't help but grin as Brandon and Micah fell into step on either side of her as she led them past reception. They were too charming for their own good and someone as adorable as Eve only brought out the devil in them.

When they disappeared around the corner, Killian said, "Shall we?"

I nodded and fell into step beside him. "You need to not look at me like that," I said under my breath.

His hand rested on my lower back but he maintained a professional distance. "Like what?"

"Like you want to throw me to the floor and have your way with me."

"I thought you liked that look."

"I do," I admitted. "Very much. But not when we're trying to keep our relationship a secret from people, including my ex-bandmates."

We turned the corner and saw Micah and Brandon up ahead with Eve. Micah shot us a look over his shoulder and I gave him a reassuring smile.

Once he'd turned back around, Killian replied, "It's hard to hide how I feel when your ex insists on calling you 'his girl.'"

I stopped, letting my friends disappear out of sight again. I looked up into Killian's dark eyes. "Then remind yourself that I'm not his. I'm yours."

He glanced down either end of the hall and determining we were alone, he slid his hand from my back to my ass and stepped into me. Bending his head, his lips almost touched mine and my mouth tingled in response. My breath mingled with his as a flush of arousal moved through me. "I wish we were alone," he murmured, squeezing my ass. "I had only my hand for company last night."

I smirked to cover the desire heating up between my legs. "And what did you fantasize about?"

"I didn't fantasize. I remembered." Lust gleamed in his eyes. "I replayed every touch, every lick, every bite, every fuck. Your tits in my hands as you rode me. Your ass in my hands as I rode you."

My breathing faltered. "If you don't stop talking, it'll be obvious what we were up to when we walk into that studio."

"We're not up to anything. I've barely touched you."

"And yet," I stood on tiptoe to brush my mouth against his and whisper, "I'm wet and flushed." I glanced down at his crotch. "And you, Mr. O'Dea, are sporting wood."

The haze seemed to clear from his eyes and he cursed, letting me go. Throwing me an aggravated look, he gestured down the hall. "You go. I'll catch up."

My smile was full of mischief. "You're acting like it's my fault. You started it."

I laughed at his glare and walked away, only to glance over my shoulder to find him watching me. Watching me predatorily with a promise in his gaze.

I shivered, very much looking forward to him acting on that promise.

When I reached the studio, Eve looked behind my shoulder as I stepped inside. "Where's Mr. O'Dea?"

"Oh, someone stopped to ask him something. He'll be here in a minute." I smiled at Oliver. "Hey, did Eve introduce you to the guys?"

"Aye, all intros have been made," Oliver said congenially. "You ready to lay down 'In the Wind'?"

Of all the songs the guys got to hear, it would have to be that one. I gulped, feeling nervous. "Sure."

"What's this one about?" Brandon asked. He and Micah took seats at the deck and I walked toward the booth door.

I blew out air between my lips and it sounded shaky even to my ears. "It's about my mom."

Silence fell over the booth and I pushed inside. I had to forget that the guys were here. I had to forget that everyone was here. I'd already recorded this song, but my mind wasn't in the right place and neither Killian nor I were happy with it. Hence I was back to rerecord it.

A thought struck me and I pushed open the door to tell Oliver

I didn't have my guitar when Killian walked into the studio.

With my guitar case.

How? I blinked up at him like an owl as he held it out to me. "I forgot to ask you to bring it, so I had Autumn run over with it. I hope you don't mind."

"No." I shook my head as I took it from him. "Thanks."

He placed a hand on the side of the booth, essentially blocking me from everyone else's view. He lowered his voice to whisper, "Forget we're all here. It's just you and your guitar."

Hoping I could do that, I disappeared back into the booth and got set up. I didn't look out into the studio at all. I settled on the stool, put the headphones on, made sure the mic for the guitar was set right, and I began to sing about losing my soul when I lost my mom. About letting it drift into the wind and being lost at sea.

I sang it with all the grief I'd felt the last two years.

As I finished the lyrics—"But it's always out of reach"—I looked up and locked eyes with Killian. It wasn't true anymore. Somehow, he'd helped me find my soul again. It would never be whole, but I think that's what life was about. You started out with a pure, whole soul and life took hits at it. It charred it, bruised it, and sometimes even smashed it to dust. But there were ways to hold on to it and to even piece it back together in new ways. To add patches of light to a shadowy bruise, to stitch a crack with a little thread of joy.

"Wow, that was awesome, Skylar," Oliver's voice crackled through the headphones and made me jump. "I don't think we need another run at that."

I jerked my gaze from Killian to Brandon and Micah. Brandon's eyes were wet with tears and Micah looked conflicted.

After I packed my guitar away, I ventured out of the booth only to drop the case against the wall as Brandon came at me. He wrapped his arms around me and kissed my head. "That was stunning, Sky. Fucking stunning."

I smiled and hugged him hard. "Thank you."

He pulled back, his eyes washing over me. "Music heals, yeah?"

Tears burned in my nose and I nodded. "It's definitely helping."

Reluctantly, he let me go and I gazed past him at Micah.

He glanced at Killian. "Give us the room."

Killian's expression hardened, but he looked at me for the answer.

Even though I was afraid of what Micah had to say, I nodded.

I could tell this did not make Killian happy, but he asked everyone to give us privacy. We shared a long look as he was the last to leave. I gave him a reassuring nod.

Then I waited.

Micah took a step toward me, anguish all over his face. "I didn't get it."

"Didn't get it?"

He shook his head. "I loved Angie. I miss her. It kills me what happened to her and Bryan, but I didn't get it. Until now." He gestured to the booth, his voice suddenly hoarse. "That is some song, Sky. It'd make a grown fucking man want to cry." Micah's eyes narrowed on me. "That's what you felt this whole time? That's what you were going through?"

My God.

A tear slipped down my cheek before I could stop it.

It really shouldn't have surprised me that it would take my song to finally communicate my feelings to Micah. The guy understood music more than he understood anything.

"That's how I felt up until three months ago, yes."

He scrubbed a hand over his head. "I'm sorry. I'm sorry I didn't get it."

"Don't be. I'm sorry I didn't try harder to make you understand."

"I forgive you," he burst out, striding over to grab my shoulders. "Sky, I forgive you."

Relief moved through me and I nodded, choked on my emotion. Finally, I managed, "Thank you."

We shared a sweet moment of silent understanding and then worry clouded Micah's expression. "Be careful with him."

Knowing instinctively that he was talking about Killian, I hoped I could relieve him of his concerns. "Killian cares about this album. I trust that he'll do what he can to protect it and me."

"That's not what I meant." Micah dropped his hands from my shoulders. "He's the *friend* you were talking about."

Anxious that he'd guessed right, I tensed, not knowing what to say to dissuade him.

He smirked unhappily. "It was the way you looked at him when you finished the song."

Shit. Had anyone else picked up on that?

"He cares about you too. Or at least he's possessive of you. The guy looks at me like he wants to rip my head off."

"Micah—"

"Don't lie to me, Sky. Just be careful. This is your label now and he's . . . I don't want you to get hurt."

"I won't."

"You will if he makes the same mistake as me."

"What mistake was that?"

He shrugged, looking forlorn. "I knew you were miserable and I stood by and did nothing about it because I was a selfish asshole who didn't want to lose my band."

That old hurt flared to life.

"I guess we both chose the band over each other in the end." Micah sighed. "I'm letting all that shit go and you should too. But you shouldn't ever forget. This time you pick a guy who cares more about your happiness than he does about his own. Promise me you'll do that."

A part of me loved him for saying that but another part resented him. Because I knew, deep down, it was a promise that would take me from Killian.

"Sky, promise me," he insisted.

Knowing he was right, knowing *it* was right, I whispered, "I promise."

twenty-nine

My sighs of ecstasy were short and breathless as I rose and fell over Killian. His hand caressed my right breast, his calloused fingertips causing delicious prickling sensations across them both, while his other hand held my left hip tight in his grip.

Mine lay pressed upon his hard chest as I rode him, our eyes connected the entire time our bodies were. His gaze burned with want, need, possession, as the tension tightened inside of me. I moved slowly over him, his thickness gliding in and out in teasing, languorous strokes that took us toward oblivion on an exquisitely slow roller coaster ride uphill.

"Killian," I moaned, feeling my climax edging closer. I slid my hands down his chest, my thumbs dragging over his nipples.

His expression grew tauter and he practically bared his teeth at me. "Harder," he grunted, pulling on my hip.

I shook my head, grinding down into him.

"Skylar." He squeezed my breast. "More."

"I like this." I panted as the coiling tension reached breaking point. My hips moved faster of their own accord as my body suddenly hungered for instant satisfaction now that it was so near.

Bliss shattered through me and I stilled over Killian before I shuddered around him on a broken cry of release.

The air whipped around me as I found myself flipped onto my back on the bed with my hands held at either side of my head. Killian caught the waves of my orgasm, driving into me in hard, fast thrusts. I felt the heat catch hold of the sparks of my climax until it blazed bright into another orgasm.

"Oh my God . . ." My head fell back on the pillow and I lost sight of the ferocious look on his face as he slammed into me.

"Oh fuck," he cursed gutturally. "Fuck, Skylar!" His hips stilled and then his body jerked hard as his cock throbbed and swelled inside me. I felt the warm rush of his release and his hands eased their grip on my wrists as he relaxed into me.

A too heavy but delicious weight.

I rubbed my foot along the back of his muscular calf. "You have a problem with control," I teased, my voice sounding smoky, lazy.

Killian lifted his head, his features slack with relaxation. "You fucked me the way you wanted to fuck me and I fucked you the way I wanted to fuck you. Fair is fair."

I grinned because he had a point. "Okay."

He gave me a quick, sweet kiss and then rolled off me, throwing his arms behind his head. "It's been some day."

It had been. After their visit to the record label, I said goodbye to Micah and Brandon, sad that I couldn't see them to the airport. We promised to check in with each other and they promised they'd have Austin get in touch with me as soon as he was back in the land of modern technology.

"'In the Wind' sounds amazing."

It was weird being proud of a song that was written with so much pain, but I did feel proud of it. Still, I needed Killian to know that's not how I felt anymore. "I wrote a new song yesterday."

"Aye?"

"Mmm." I turned my head on the pillow to look at him. Was there ever a time in my life when this man wasn't beautiful to me? I reached out and drew my fingertips along his jaw.

He side-eyed me curiously. "Can I hear it?"

"Yes." I sat up and shimmied off the bed. I disappeared into the bathroom for a brief cleanup, and then I sauntered out into the living room with a swing in my hips.

"You're going to sing naked?" Killian called after me, the sound of the bedclothes rustling in the background as he got up.

The apartment was warm and no one could see us up here, so I didn't see the point in putting on clothes when I was impatient to sing my song. Part of it was nervous anxiety. I wanted to do this before I lost my nerve.

I sat on the chair and crossed my bare legs with my guitar on my knee as Killian walked out of the bedroom in his boxers. At the sight of me, he lounged against the wall with his ankles crossed. Although his posture was relaxed, his expression was dark, devouring and filled with emotion. His voice was hoarse as he said, "This image of you right now will be the last thing I remember the day I die."

I smiled softly as my chest filled with love. "Yeah?"

Killian nodded, so serious. "Yes."

For not the first time, I almost blurted out that I loved him. Then I realized after I stopped myself that it didn't matter because the song I was about to sing was pretty much a love letter.

I strummed the opening chords, the sound light and upbeat. In my head, it was a melody that would crescendo with the chorus but I couldn't achieve that with my acoustic. That didn't matter in that moment.

All that mattered was singing to him.

"I was concrete standing still,
Cemented heart, bricked-over soul.
But there were cracks I couldn't see,
Through them my song called out.

"The river heard me and it came for me.

"I was cold there forged in stone,
And you were colder on your throne
Of freezing waves that flooded me out,
To free my song upon you.

"The river heard me and it came for me.
It rushed me on toward a waterfall.

"I feel the wind on my skin breathing,
My heart is beating to the feeling.
I catch my soul as I free-fall,
Then your arms close tight around me
Right before we land.

"I'm alive and it's all your fault,
Blood is pumping, burning hot.
Worse, I'm growing addicted to
Being awake, being with you.

"The river heard me and it came for me.
It rushed me on toward a waterfall.

"I feel the wind on my skin breathing,
My heart is beating to the feeling.
I catch my soul as I free-fall,
Then your arms close tight around me
Right before we land.

"You're in my heart, you're like a beat.
You're the air I drink in breaths.
You're the flood that set me free.
The waterfall I'd gladly drown in.

"I feel the wind on my skin breathing,
My heart is beating to the feeling.
I catch my soul as I free-fall,
Then your arms close tight around me
Right before we land.

"The river heard me and it came for me.
Now my song belongs to it."

My fingers almost slipped from the strings as I finished, realizing what I'd put out there. The silence that rang through the apartment didn't help with the sudden wave of uncertainty that knocked me back in the chair.

I couldn't look at him.

It was like being foggy-minded with desire, having sex, and then realizing it was a mistake as soon as it was over.

What if I'd blown it with too many feelings?

"Skylar."

Reluctantly, I drew my gaze from the floor to him. He was standing straight, no longer leaning against the wall, and my breath caught at what I found in him.

Shaking, I lowered my guitar carefully and got up to cross the room. His gaze dropped hotly down my body before coming back to my face as I halted before him.

Killian crushed me to him and kissed me breathless.

I held on for dear life, hoping the fierce desperation of his kiss meant I was not alone in my feelings. When he finally let me up for air, I said dryly, "I take it you liked the song?"

He cupped my face in his hands and whispered, "I loved it. I . . . I love you."

My knees almost gave way, the emotion that rolled over me was so powerful. My arms tightened around his back and I pressed as close as I could to him as I whispered against his lips, "Thanks for not leaving me hanging too long. There was a moment there I thought I might have to jump out the window when I thought you didn't feel the same way. I didn't really want to do that butt-naked. It's cold out."

Killian gave a slight shake of his head, his lips twitching with amusement. "I feel the same way. Never fucking doubt it."

Then I realized I hadn't actually said the words. "If you didn't get it from the song, I love you."

He grinned, rubbing his nose against mine. "I got that."

I kissed him again, pouring my heart and soul into it until Killian impatiently lifted me up into his arms. I wrapped my legs around his waist and held on as we stumbled and kissed our way back into the bedroom. He dropped me on the bed, managing the feat of climbing over me and removing his boxers at the same time.

"We need to put it on the album."

Happier than I ever thought possible, I beamed. "Really? You like it that much, huh? I can feel my ego swelling."

"Mine is swelling too," he murmured wickedly, and then kissed me as he slipped his hand between my legs.

I gasped against his mouth as his thumb caught my clit. "I'm so . . . oh God . . . so happy you liked it."

"I fucking loved it," he growled against my lips. "I want it immortalized and when it's time," he pushed his fingers inside me, working me until my hips undulated against him and my pants of need filled the bedroom, "everyone will know that Skylar Finch wrote it for me." He paused, drawing my focus from impending orgasm to his face, to his utter seriousness. "I know I don't yet, but I'll do everything in my power to try to deserve you."

And as we fell together, loving each other more honestly than we ever had before, the darkest corner of my mind whispered to me. I had to force its thoughts back into the shadows, hoping that those fears never came true.

thirty

It was still dark out when Killian's cell rang.

He groaned in his sleep beside me and made no move to reach for it.

I planned on closing my eyes and going back to sleep when it stopped, but as it rang again, my cell rang too.

What the hell?

Killian muttered something under his breath and reached across to his side of the bed to grab his phone off the table. Annoyed that we'd been so rudely awakened, especially considering our sexual shenanigans had kept us awake most of the night, I turned over and almost knocked my phone off the table trying to grab it.

"What? Lois, slow down." Killian was suddenly very awake as he sat up.

I frowned at him as I fumbled to open my phone, not liking the sound of his side of the conversation at all. Seeing Autumn's name on my screen, I refrained from unleashing my tired grumpiness on her.

"Skylar, it's me," she sounded distressed and breathless.

It made me bolt up into a sitting position too. "What is it?"

"It's all over the news."

"What's all over the news?" I asked, but as I looked at Killian, staring at me with concern and anger in his eyes, I thought maybe I already knew.

"A fan posted photos of you, Micah, and Brandon outside the flat yesterday morning on Instagram. She said she followed Micah and Brandon from their hotel and when they disappeared into, and I quote, 'a mysterious flat, I just knew in my gut something good was going down. I called a friend who brought her car and supplies and we camped out all night waiting for them to emerge from the mystery flat. We had no idea how big the climax to our ridiculous night of playing paps would be. Lo and behold, we found Skylar Fucking Finch!'"

"Holy shit." I felt my chest tightening as I practically fell out of the bed, hauling the bedsheet out from under Killian to cover myself as I hurried down the hall to the door.

"Are you okay?" Autumn asked in my ear.

I pushed the peephole cover aside and looked out, feeling marginally calmer to see the hallway was empty.

I felt a warm hand on my shoulder and spun around to find Killian. "They can't get into the building."

Still, the fear made my gut churn. "What's going to happen?"

Autumn sighed. "Is my brother there?"

"Yes."

"Put him on."

Dazed, I handed the phone over to him. He took it, appearing beyond exasperated. "Aye, I'm here," he said impatiently. "I just got off the phone with Lois. She was giving me a heads-up that the paparazzi have set up camp outside Skylar's building."

Oh fuck, oh fuck, oh fuck.

"Problem is, I'm here and I can't be seen leaving here at this time in the morning."

Oh, shit. I hadn't even thought about that. I threw my hands up in disbelief and horror and Killian caught one of them. He pulled me into him, caressing my back in soothing strokes as he listened to Autumn. "That sounds like a plan. Thank you. We'll see you soon."

"What sounds like a plan?" I asked as soon as he hung up.

"The paparazzi can't see me. This is already going to be a shitstorm without adding that on top of it. Autumn is going to come over with a security team we've used for other artists. You'll get dressed and you'll leave the apartment to draw them away so I can get out." He took hold of my biceps and bent his head to mine. "Under no circumstances are you to engage with any of the press. You keep your head down and the security team will get you out. Okay?"

My mind whirled. I felt so disoriented.

I think I'd always secretly hoped it would never actually come to this.

"And . . . and . . ." I blinked, trying to remember what I wanted to say. My lips felt numb. I brushed my fingers over them, checking that they weren't made of rubber.

"Skylar?"

I shook my head. "I, um . . . yeah . . . uh . . . where am I going? Where is this security team taking me?"

"To the label." He brushed my hair off my face. His eyebrows almost touched, he frowned so hard. "Tell me you're okay."

I couldn't.

I wasn't.

"Fuck, Skylar, *I'm* going to make this okay. We knew this would happen eventually." He wrapped his arms around me, holding me tight, and even though I held on, devastatingly his arms felt nowhere near as safe as they had the night before.

Nowhere felt safe now that *they* had found me again.

AUTUMN ARRIVED NOT TOO LONG later. I'd showered and dressed, feeling jittery and more than a little sick.

It was adrenaline.

Adrenaline spiked by fear that I was about to lose everything that had begun to make me happy.

Killian's sister, as promised, was not alone. There were two huge burly guys with her wearing dark jeans and black sports jackets. Beneath their jackets their sweaters stretched across massive muscular chests. Their expressions were mirror images of fierce calm that said "don't fucking mess with me" without actually saying anything at all.

They looked like every other professional security personnel I'd ever hired.

Not that I was hiring them. Since Adam had given me access to my accounts, I'd tried to pay Killian back for everything but he wouldn't let me. We'd argued before I got in the shower about who would pay for the security.

Again, he wouldn't let me.

I'd figure out a way to pay for this, even if I had to be sneaky about it.

I stared at Autumn standing in the living room with the security guys. She looked flushed and harried, and there was a large suitcase beside her.

I flicked a look at it, then back to her. "What happened?"

She rounded her eyes. "They swarmed me like bees as soon as they saw these guys with me." She gestured to the men.

I gave them a halfhearted wave. "Hey, I'm Skylar."

They each held out a hand one after the other to shake, introducing themselves as Rick and Angus respectively. "We have a car waiting for you outside," Angus said. "We'll get you away from here safely."

I blew out a shaky breath. "What's with the suitcase?"

"I'm packing you up." Killian strode out of the bedroom, pulling on a sweater. His hair was still wet from the shower he'd insisted we take together. I'd stood under the stream of water while he washed my hair, taking care of me, as I tried not to disappear into myself. It was hard to stay present but I needed to face this, not run away from it.

"Packing me up?"

"You can't stay here anymore now that they know where you live."

"And where am I going to stay?" I asked.

He looked at the security men, his sister, and then back to me. "We'll discuss that at the label."

"We should probably get this over with," Autumn said. "Rip it off. Like a plaster."

"Like a Band-Aid," I corrected her stupidly, like it mattered.

She smirked. "You're in Glasgow. We call them plasters here," she teased.

I couldn't bring myself to smile back. The effort to do so seemed too great. "Let's do this." I brushed by Killian to hurry to the bedroom closet. He came in after me as I was shrugging into it my coat.

He stared at me warily. "We'll get you through this. This was always going to happen, no matter how you came back into the limelight."

I bristled at how defensive he sounded, like I was blaming him for putting me in this position when I wasn't. I knew that this was always going to happen once I reached out to my old life. However, for a long time, I thought I was never going back and as awful as it made me, it was nice to think I'd never have to deal with this shit if I didn't go back.

"I know this isn't your fault."

He scowled. "Then why have you barely touched me since the news broke?"

Confused, I gestured to the bathroom. "Did we not just take a shower together?"

"Aye, where you stood like an icicle in my arms."

"What? Oh, I'm sorry. Is my paparazzi crisis cutting into your sex life?"

Fury slashed across his face and he slammed the bedroom door closed.

"Don't," he bit out, his chest rising and falling in shallow breaths. "Don't you fucking dare take this out on me. I'm trying to help you after you had Brandon and Micah come to the bloody flat and blow your cover."

"My cover?" I laughed humorlessly. "Like I'm some spy? I'm not a spy, Killian. I'm a soon-to-be disgraced ex-pop-rock star. They're never going to forgive me. No one is going to buy this album. You get that, right? When they find out that I'm safe and alive and I haven't let my fans know I'm safe and alive, they're going to annihilate me. It might have been okay if we got there first. Spun it the way we planned to. But not now."

Killian contemplated and then said calmly, "Last night you sang a song you wrote for me and we said we loved each other. And I do. I love you, Skylar. I will do whatever it takes to protect you. But do you really love me?"

Feeling winded by his need to even ask, I whispered, "You know I do."

"Then stick with me." He stepped toward me, his dark eyes pleading. "Hold it together and stick with me. Stop panicking. Take a breath. And know that I'm beside you. We will fix this. Believe me."

His soothing tone worked and I released a shaky sigh. I nodded. "Sorry. I . . . I'm out of practice handling these assholes."

He took hold of my hand and I stumbled into him. His kiss was soft and reassuring. He held my face in his palms. "Let's get this over with."

I nodded, feeling like if I could keep it together like he wanted, then maybe I really could do this.

However, nothing quite prepares you for the barrage of the paparazzi. It was not the first time I'd walked into a crowd of them, but I'd forgotten.

I'd forgotten how it was to be jostled as security tried to shove paps back, to hear camera lenses whirring in my ears, feel them knock against my shoulder, my chin, feel hands that snuck past security to grab and pull on me. All the while the cacophony of shouting and blinding flash from digital cameras discombobulated me. It was how I imagined a deer might feel, surrounded by a pack of wolves.

Hunted.

Trapped.

That's probably why it elicited fear. Even with the rational part of my brain telling me they were only paparazzi and Rick and Angus would protect me, adrenaline flooded me.

"Skylar, where have you been?"

"Are you joining Tellurian again?"

"Do you have anything to say to the fans?"

"Skylar, are you and Micah back together?"

"Skylar!"

"Skylar!"

SKYLAR!

I gripped hold of Rick's jacket as panic tightened my chest. Most of the accents shouting at me weren't even British. How the hell had the US press gotten here so fast?

Feeling my grip, Rick grew more aggressive in his efforts to forge a path for me to the car. Within seconds I was sliding into the back of an SUV with Autumn hurrying to slide in beside me. Rick slammed the door shut as soon as she was safely inside and Autumn hit the lock. Angus got in the driver's seat.

As soon as Rick moved out of the way of the door to get into the front passenger seat, the paps pulled at the door handle to get in.

"Jesus Christ," Autumn instinctively leaned toward me.

A pounding on the window at my head made me flinch into her. She grabbed my hands at the sight of the pap snapping photos of me through my window.

The SUV pulled away slowly, picking up speed as soon as we were on the road.

"You okay, ladies?" Rick glanced into the back to ask.

I nodded, feeling numb.

"I'm not." Autumn squeezed my hands, worry etched on her face. "Skylar, how do you cope?"

Well, there was the rub because as of yet, I hadn't found a coping mechanism for this that worked.

THE OFFICES OF SKYSCRAPER RECORDS felt marginally safer. Rick and Angus were hanging out downstairs with the full-time security guard. Autumn had gotten me a tea while Eve hovered over me worriedly. I'd understand why when I escaped to the restroom and saw my face in the mirror.

I looked pale and shell-shocked.

Lois, Jaclyn, and Kit sat quietly with me, Autumn, and Eve in a private office as we waited for Killian to arrive. I'd been offered something to eat and only took a banana to appease Autumn's concern when I said I wasn't hungry.

Killian blew into the room like he'd been running and headed toward me with a fierce countenance that widened my eyes. He came to an abrupt halt and I knew he'd realized that he couldn't come to me like he wanted to. We were in a room filled with people who weren't supposed to know we were together.

Frustration clouded his face before he cleared his throat and yanked out a chair on the other side of the table. "You got here okay?"

"Yes."

"It was scary, Killian," Autumn put in, still shaken. "They grabbed and pushed her and tried to get in the bloody car. I've never seen anything like that."

His expression flattened and grew cold, and I knew that meant he was having to work very hard at hiding his fury. "Well, you're safe while you're here." He looked at Lois. "Let's talk about damage control."

"Yes." She nodded, grim. She clicked on the space bar on her laptop and the action lit up a white projector screen on the far wall. The Instagram post that kicked off this morning's chaos appeared. It was the size of the entire wall so I could clearly see the photo of Micah and I kissing. Well, that's what it looked like from this angle.

Fuck me sideways.

Autumn hadn't mentioned that in her call. She winced at my expression.

I turned tentatively to look at Killian but his jaw was working as he tried to hold onto whatever emotion he was feeling. I was guessing it was anger. A lot of anger.

"It's not what you think," I said. "It's the angle it was taken at. I reached in to kiss him on the cheek and he turned so I caught the corner of his mouth. This makes way more out of it."

"It doesn't matter what the truth is," Lois replied. "Skylar, all that matters is that the public knows you're alive and well, and kissing your ex-bandmate." She clicked her laptop again and the next photo on the post appeared. It was me and Brandon hugging. Another click, another photo. All three of us smiling at each other on the sidewalk outside the apartment building. The last photo was zoomed in on my face as I looked at the car across the street. Jesus Christ, I *had* seen someone ducking down in the car.

Little fuckers.

My nails bit into my palm from clenching my fists so hard.

"This is exactly what we didn't want, I'm afraid," Lois sighed, like I'd really put her out.

Screw you, Lois.

She clicked another button and a news article came up.

SKYLAR FINCH RETURNS FROM THE GREAT UNKNOWN

Then the publicist clicked another.

FINCH IS BACK AND ALREADY LIP-LOCKING WITH MURPHY!

And another.

SKYLAR FINCH FANS DEMAND ANSWERS

Feeling light-headed, I braced myself as I asked, "What are they talking about?"

Lois looked sorry for me. "The news broke here last night,

which meant it reached the States yesterday afternoon."

"Hence the American paparazzi outside my door. They do move fast," I murmured.

"Right. Well, fans have responded on the band's social media pages and on your long-neglected personal pages. There is positive commentary but the negative commentary is there, and there's a lot of it. Controversy does of course divide the crowd."

"What are they saying?" Eve asked.

I felt like slamming my hands over my ears yet somehow managed to refrain.

"There's no need to get into the nitty-gritty," Lois said, to my relief. "What this means is that we have a challenge ahead of us. But it can be managed. I think the only way to quieten the deluge of press is to do an exclusive interview where Skylar has a chance to apologize and explain to her fans. The public in general has a short memory. We need to remind them that Skylar's mother was murdered and she had a valid reason for needing a break. I think we could definitely get *Good Morning Britain*."

The thought made me ill. The casual way she spoke about using my mother's death as my excuse. That's what this life was like. Nothing was sacred. Everything was fodder to be used first before the other guy used it. I was shaking, I was so angry. "I told you I don't want to talk about my past." I turned to Killian. "You promised."

Our eyes locked, mine pleading, his full of turmoil. "Fuck," he hissed, pushing back out of the chair to pace.

I didn't like the pacing. It suggested thinking and there was nothing to think about. We had an agreement! "Killian?"

"Skylar . . ." He stopped, bracing his hands on the back of Jaclyn's chair. "They're going to keep coming until you give them something. If we don't handle this, it could completely overshadow the launch of the album."

Feeling betrayed, I stared at him incredulously. "You said that you wanted to sign me because the initial furor would be good for the album."

"Well, reality is a bit different. I've read what they're saying." He gestured to the projector. "Your fans feel betrayed. They want answers. Without them, they're not going to support you."

"I don't owe them answers!"

"Yes, you do," he bit out. His tone caused the room to fall completely silently. "Skylar, as a collective, they've invested millions of dollars and time and emotion into *you*. You do owe them."

Rage rushed through me and I flew out of my chair so fast, it rolled back and slammed into the wall. "Your office. Now." I blew past him before he could argue, thundering down the hall and into his office.

As soon as he followed me in and closed the door, I threw up my hands in disbelief. "What happened to this morning? Everything you said to me *I* said to you! And you told me it would be okay. Suddenly we have an audience and you change your fucking tune?"

Killian held up his hands as if trying to placate a wounded animal. "I hadn't seen the news yet this morning. I hadn't seen you trending on Twitter." He winced and I wanted to smack the sympathy right off his face. "It's not good."

"It's the first day. Give it time."

"Time isn't going to help. I think we both know that. If you don't make a statement, if we don't orchestrate this down to the smallest detail, this is going to run away from us. And you've worked too hard and come too far with this album to see it fail."

And just like that, the whole explosion and invasion of my privacy felt like small change.

Because I'd realized that Killian O'Dea had lied to me for the first time.

He had no intention of protecting me from this. Of putting

me first. Not if it meant destroying the album launch and whatever chance he had of forcing his uncle to acknowledge that he was the best thing that ever happened to this label.

This time you pick a guy who cares more about your happiness than he does about his own.

The fight fled me as Micah's words came back to haunt me.

I was trapped again.

In love with a man who loved his career more than me.

Tied to a contract I couldn't get out of.

Hounded by the press.

Suffocated.

And it had been less than a day.

Last night with Killian seemed like some long-forgotten dream.

"Fine," I whispered, unable to look at him. "I'll do the interview."

He exhaled slowly in relief. "It's the right thing, Skylar. And you don't have to worry about a thing. We'll write you a script and we'll make sure we get final say over what questions the interviewer is allowed to ask."

"Okay."

He approached me and I tensed as he tucked a strand of hair behind my ear. "I promised I'll take care of you and I will."

My smile was more of a grimace but it seemed to appease him because he pressed a kiss to my lips. Stupidly I reached for something deeper that he gladly provided. I held on as I kissed him like it was the last time I ever would.

In that moment, I hated him because I still wanted him. I still loved him. It was easy to, looking into his eyes and seeing his love for me.

But like Micah, it wasn't enough.

Killian didn't love me enough.

thirty-one

I moved into a hotel.

Killian wanted me to move in with Autumn but I had money now. Money I could burn on an expensive hotel suite indefinitely.

Everyone wanted to hover, including Killian, but I wanted space to hear my own thoughts. Brandon, Micah, and Gayle all called to see how I was coping with the media storm. Micah wanted to come back over to support me, but I told him that would only make things worse.

And I finally got hold of Austin. Apologizing to him, catching up with him, was a much-needed distraction. Apparently, he'd hated every minute of the nature trail, which didn't surprise me, but he loved Selina so he'd put up with almost anything for her.

That shocked the hell out of me and I didn't mind telling him so. He said she was different. She was a college graduate he met in Berkeley who was bartending during the summer until her postgrad courses started. Her complete and utter lack of interest in him as a rock star did it for him.

"I knew when I finally won over her over, it was because *I* won her over, not the guy with the guitar. She's so fucking smart, it's frightening, Sky. She takes none of my bullshit," he'd told me with more than a hint of satisfaction.

I was glad. She sounded like exactly what he needed. I said I wanted to meet her and we made it a promise that I would.

Talking to Austin was the only joy I felt in the forty-eight hours since Skylar Finch officially belonged to the world again.

I'd been stuck in this hotel suite since yesterday afternoon with nothing but my thoughts to distract me. They weren't fun thoughts, I'll tell ya.

Throwing myself across the huge bed, I picked up the notes from Lois for my interview with one of the biggest morning talk shows in the UK. I'd agreed to it, but I'd also asked Killian for some time. He granted me three days.

"How generous," I muttered.

He'd also banned me from looking at social media. A few months ago, that would've been fine by me. The incessant buzzing that used to fill my brain back when I was in Tellurian had returned. So was the constant sharp tightness in my chest.

I was beginning to suspect it was anxiety.

It had never occurred to me before, but Mandy had anxiety and had described it to me once. I wasn't an anxious person. I didn't think I had an anxiety disorder. But now, feeling those feelings again and remembering Mandy's description, I guess I did.

It wasn't a constant thing for me—I supposed life in the spotlight was my anxiety trigger.

The physical symptoms were accompanied by the all-too-familiar feeling of impending doom. It was horrible. It was a sickness in my gut. That doom weighed on me. It made me feel brittle, like one tap would shatter me into pieces.

Back then, the only way I knew how to cope when it was bad

was to push people away, isolate myself, so I didn't have to worry about my band or family noticing that I wasn't myself. I went through periods, especially when we were touring and I was too busy to overthink, of being okay. Some days I felt almost normal. Other days were bad.

Today was a bad day.

Yesterday had sucked pretty hard too.

Thankfully, Killian couldn't be spotted coming to my hotel room late at night so I didn't have to deal with my heartbreakingly complicated feelings for the man.

It was another reason he wasn't happy I hadn't chosen to stay with his sister.

No nookie for Killian.

I sighed and flopped onto my back, glaring at the ceiling. Killian didn't care about getting laid. I knew that. I was just . . . I guess I was trying to vilify him. Make it easier.

None of this was easy, and it wasn't any less difficult being in the dark about what the fans were saying online. A few months ago, I didn't want to know. But now I *needed* to know. I reached over for the phone on my bedside table and called the concierge.

Five minutes later there was a knock at the door. I opened it to find an immaculately dressed staff member in a gorgeous skirt suit. She smiled as she held out an iPad.

"We've created a user account on one of our hotel iPads for you, Miss Finch. Should you need anything else, please don't hesitate to ask."

"Thank you." I shakily took the iPad from her and closed the door.

My gut churned.

"Here we go," I muttered to myself.

It took me a while to access my accounts because I'd forgotten a couple of passwords and had to reset them before I could log in.

My heart pounded as I opened the Twitter homepage and saw under the side bar titled "Trends for you": #FecklessFinch

Bracing myself, I clicked on the hashtag.

There was a barrage of tweets accusing me of deliberately scaring fans and then having the audacity not to speak up now that I was outed as "alive and well." People had retweeted the interview on YouTube with the band where Brandon got upset. They called me a coldhearted asshole. Fans asked why the guys had forgiven me. Someone even tweeted:

I wish the bitch had died. I'd rather mourn her than be this disappointed in her. #FecklessFinch #FuckYouFinch

Beneath it I could see people call the person out for crossing the line, but it still made me throw the iPad onto the bed. I wasn't sure how I could still be stunned by that shit, but I was. I scrubbed a hand over my face, wishing for once, just goddamned once, that a pair of ruby slippers that sparkled and glittered and took you to a magical place called *Home* really did exist.

I slid down the wall until my ass hit the carpet and I stared unseeing across the suite.

Four days ago, I was gloriously happy. I thought I *was* home.

Then I'd made one call, one phone call, and I'd lost everything. Because I *had* lost everything, hadn't I?

My cell rang, jolting me out of my miserable thoughts. I forced myself off my ass to answer it.

It was Killian.

I considered ignoring it, but that would only bring him to the hotel to check on me, and that might make things worse.

"Hey," I said, curling up in an armchair.

"Hey yourself."

I squeezed my eyes shut at the sound of his voice, savoring it.

"I wanted to check in. I wish I were there."

"I know."

"Have you eaten?"

"Yeah," I lied.

"The hotel is temporary. We'll find you somewhere else to live."

I didn't mind the hotel. "I slept in a tent in a cemetery for five months. The hotel is fine."

"How are you feeling about the interview?"

Like I want to stab you in the eyeball for making me do this. "Fine."

"Lois's notes make sense?"

"They're fine."

"Look, there was a lot to discuss yesterday so I didn't want to overload you, but we think we should move up the schedule for the album cover photo shoot. It would be nice to have it when you do your interview so fans get your apology and the promise of new music. Does tomorrow sound good?"

Is that why you really called? "Fine."

"From there, we'd like to shoot the video for 'In the Wind.'"

So you've decided that's my first single without discussing it with me? "Fine."

He was silent a moment. "Is that the only word you intend to say ever again?"

"I'm too tired to say anything else."

"Skylar, you don't know how hard it is for me to see you have to deal with this. You don't know how hard it was that the bastards surrounded you and I couldn't even comfort you afterward."

But it's not enough. "I know that." Tears burned my eyes; I blinked them away. "Hey, listen, I'm really tired. I'll see you tomorrow, yeah?"

"Of course, get some sleep. I love you."

That tightness in my chest became almost unbearable.

I hung up without saying it back.

Guilt made me feel sick to my stomach. Then I raged at myself for feeling guilty for inflicting pain on him because he'd inflicted pain on me. Unlike mine, however, I knew his wasn't intentional. Complicated bastard. I huffed and walked back over to the bed where Lois's notes were.

They had it all planned.

I read through what she wanted me to say. Anger gripped hold of my hands and crushed the papers. The iPad lay on the bed, the screen now blank. I reached over and tapped it. The horrible tweet glowered up at me. I glanced at the crumpled papers in my hand and then back to the iPad.

Killian was right. I did owe my fans an explanation and no matter if I never released another song again, that explanation would have to happen.

However, I wasn't the Skylar Finch I was back in Tellurian. I'd been seventeen when we signed our first record contract and I was only twenty-two when I lost my mom and quit the band. I'd listened to everything Gayle and our publicists advised. All of it. I did it their way. I let myself be controlled and manipulated. I didn't think Gayle or any of them meant anything by it. They were doing their jobs, trying to make us a success.

But two years of living alone, living rough, seeing how the other half lived, had changed me. Whether I wanted to admit it or not now, Killian's and Autumn's kindness toward me had also changed me.

I wanted to be stronger.

I wanted to be braver.

And most of all, I wanted to own myself again.

I was done doing it their way.

I grabbed the monogrammed notepad and pen from the bedside table and began to write furiously. I wrote everything *I* wanted to say. It was extremely personal and it was difficult to give them all of it; however, I decided that it was better I did than let other people make damaging speculations.

When I was done, I read the words over and over until they were solidified in my mind. I then opened the camera on the iPad and began to film in selfie mode.

"Hey, everybody. This is kind of a video letter to you all, and it has been a long time coming." I sighed, running my hand through my hair, my expression filled with self-reproach. "There aren't enough sorrys in the world to express my regret that it has taken me this long to reach out to you. My fans want to know where and why I disappeared and the truth is, I owe you an explanation. You've all been so loyal to me over the years and I haven't been very good at paying that loyalty back.

"I was very unhappy while I was in Tellurian. Don't misunderstand—I loved my guys, Austin, Brandon, and Micah. They're my family, you know. And I loved the music, I loved my fans, I loved being on that stage. I *didn't* love having my personal life splashed all over the internet and magazines for the world to see. As it turns out, I'm a very private person and I guess I didn't really understand that about myself at seventeen when we signed our first record deal. All I cared about then was performing and writing music. The first time I realized I didn't have what it took to be a 'celebrity' was the first time I saw myself splashed across the front page of a tabloid magazine, the first time I got random, unnecessary negative comments on a benign Instagram post. The truth is they tell us to ignore it, let it wash off us and move on, because attention in any form is good.

"But I found that hard. I was a kid and I was going through all the stuff kids go through, but I was going through it live, in front of the world. Don't mistake me, I was grateful for the opportunities I was given, grateful to be able to support my family financially and make them proud . . . but . . . well, I guess there's no way to really explain how I felt without sounding ungrateful. People will make up their own minds about that, and that's okay. We all have our opinions.

"The point of me telling you all this is that I hid my unhappiness from everyone. I didn't reach out to someone to tell them I was depressed. And I . . ." I took a breath, not wanting to cry. I wanted to be calm and clear and say my piece without breaking down. I blinked back tears and turned back to the camera. "I kept my feelings locked away from the one person I loved the most—my mom. You guys probably know from all the interviews the band did that we credit Angie Finch, my beautiful mom, with supporting us like no one else ever did. My mom had the kind of faith in me that was extraordinary. I mean," I laughed softly, "who really believes their fourteen-year-old kid is going to make it as a rock star? I sometimes think—no, I *know*—it was my mom's belief that got Tellurian to where they are. We didn't have much growing up and my mom spent a lot of money she didn't have on my dream. So when I realized that this life didn't make me happy, I hid it from her because I felt like I'd failed her somehow. The last couple of years before my mom's death . . . well, I avoided her. She was my best friend. I knew if I let her in, she would see how unhappy I was and I couldn't let her down like that. Our relationship was the most important thing in the world to me, and because of me we were not in a good place before she was killed.

"Then," I took a deep, shuddering breath, "as you all know, she and her husband, Bryan, were murdered. They were shot in the house *I* bought, for a stupid painting *I* bought as an investment. A painting. A goddamned painting." I glared at the screen, not caring if they could see my anger. I *was* angry. I'd never stop being angry about it. "I got through those first six months by concentrating on finding the people who did it, so when the cops told me that their leads had gone cold . . . I'm not ashamed to say that I went off the deep end.

"The only healthy thing I did was to do what I should have done a long time ago. I told the guys that I was unhappy and that I was quitting the band. They're amazing people. They were so supportive, and I won't ever be able to thank them enough for always having my back, even when I didn't deserve it." I stopped, feeling my heart race harder the more I thought about this going live. I willed myself to be calm, to continue. "I took off backpacking through Europe. The guys knew I needed time away, but they had no idea how long I'd be gone. For just over a year, I traveled around Europe, staying in hostels, staying away from social media, avoiding the news.

"The longer I was gone, the further I drifted from who I used to be, and the pain, my grief, became more manageable. I had just enough money left to travel to Glasgow, Scotland, and that's where I've been for the last eight, nearly nine months. With no money, I had no choice but to sleep in this little one-man tent I'd bought. I used to set it up in a cemetery, believe it or not. And I'd busk in the city to make money to buy food. So yeah . . . Skylar Finch was homeless for a while," I said dryly. "At the time, it was what I needed. Surviving filled my days instead of grief. But a while ago, I made a friend." The thought of Killian filled me with so much sorrow, I could barely breathe. "And things got better. It felt like I was waking up from a really long sleep and when I did, I couldn't believe how much time had passed.

"I was afraid," I admitted. "I was afraid to reach out to Austin,

Brandon, and Micah, to reach out to all of you because I'd left it too long. I'd been selfish. And I'm so sorry. I'm so very sorry. You should know that the photos posted that outed me as 'alive and well' were taken right after Brandon and Micah offered me forgiveness for letting them worry about my safety for too long. I told you they're great guys. And I spoke to Austin on the phone and we're good too. You may not think I deserve their forgiveness, and maybe you're right, but I have it, and for that, I'm eternally grateful.

"As to the photo that seems to show Micah and I kissing, we weren't. It was a kiss on the cheek taken at an angle that made it look like a kiss. I'm sorry to disappoint any Miclar fans out there, but Micah and I are just friends. I love him and he loves me, but it's in friendship. That's all it'll ever be.

"So . . ." I smiled wearily into the camera, "that's where I've been. That's why. I hope you can forgive me and understand that losing my mom threw me off course for a while. I also want to say, however, that this is probably the last personal thing I'll ever post on social media. I love you all for supporting me, but I need to find happiness, and sharing the finer details of my life with the world media makes me the opposite of happy. I hope you understand, and I'm sorry if you don't. But I have to be true to myself now. That's all any of us can really do."

I pressed the stop button and before I could talk myself out of it, I uploaded it onto both Twitter and Youtube. .

Truthfully, I felt shaky about it. Butterflies raged like wild things in my belly as I got into bed. But I couldn't sleep. Not just because I worried about how the world was reacting as I laid there in that hotel room, but also because I knew what I had to do the next day.

And it was going to be a million times harder than uploading a video to social media.

thirty-two

I was awake when my cell rang at six in the morning.

Knowing who it was before I even looked at the screen, I steadied myself as I reached for the phone.

"Hello?"

"What did you do?" Killian didn't sound angry; he sounded confused.

Sitting up, I laid back against the headboard and sighed. "I did it my way."

"I see that."

"I'm not doing that interview."

"I think I got that memo."

We grew quiet for a moment and then he asked hesitantly, "Have you looked at the comments?"

Those butterflies I'd been feeling all night swarmed upward into my chest, creating a claustrophobic tightness. "No. Is it bad?"

"No, Skylar. It's overwhelmingly positive. Gayle called me and said the media still thinks she's your manager. She's been getting a lot of follow-up interview requests. I told her to deny them all.

You said what you had to say. It was brave. I'm proud of you."

I closed my eyes, inadvertently squeezing out tears, and crushed the phone harder to my ear. "And here I thought I'd get a knock on the door from someone telling me I was being committed," I cracked dryly. "I did admit to the world that I, a multimillionaire, was homeless for five months."

"Yeah, well, your fans seem to appreciate the honesty. They also think a movie should be made about you."

"Oh God," I groaned at the thought. "Just what the world needs."

"You don't have to, but we still have the photographer and style team ready to go for this album cover shoot."

"What time am I expected?"

"About ten."

I trembled as I forced myself to say, "Can I meet you before then? Meet you at your office around 9:00 a.m.?"

"Of course. I miss your face."

Fuck, it was like a stab to the heart. "Yeah, me too." Because it was true. I did miss his face.

RICK AND ANGUS PICKED ME up from the hotel, which was a good thing because the crowd of paparazzi had grown larger since I'd posted the video. They shouted and jostled and grabbed at me as my security guards hustled me into their SUV.

I'd spent the morning in my hotel room not only getting ready for the day ahead but gathering the courage to hop back onto social media to check the comments on my video.

There was a lot of:

Skylar we love u!! Do what u gotta do! Keep healin'! <3

The beauty in their forgiveness bolstered me for what I was about to do. It reassured me that this was the right path to be on, no matter if it broke my heart.

That's why I didn't bother checking the newspaper articles now attached to my video. I didn't care what the press thought. I cared what my fans thought, and the strength of their support carried me into Skyscraper Records.

Admittedly, that strength faltered as soon as I found myself standing outside his office.

Eve got up from behind her desk and hurried over to me. "Oh my God, Skylar, I had no idea! You're so brave." She threw her arms around me and although surprised by her over-familiarity, I couldn't help but hug her back. She was such a sweet girl. I really hoped this industry didn't change her.

"Thank you." I pulled back and nodded to Killian's door, feeling the color drain out of my cheeks. "Is he in?"

"Let me tell him you're here." She knocked on his door and at his "come in," she opened it and poked her head in. "Mr. O'Dea, Skylar is here."

"Thanks, Eve." I heard him cross the room and then he pulled the door wide open. Our eyes met for a second and my courage fled. "Why don't you," he pulled out his wallet and removed some cash to hand to Eve, "head over to Starbucks and order a team's worth of coffee and pastries for the shoot. Get someone to help you. Take a car."

"Sure thing." She threw me a smile as she grabbed her purse and strode off down the corridor.

It took effort, but I returned my gaze to Killian.

He stared at me with such love and affection, I wanted to burst into tears. "Come in," he stepped back to let me pass.

I did and he'd barely shut the door behind us before he hauled me backwards into his arms. I wanted to melt into his kiss, let him devour me and fill me with bliss. The thought of never having this again made me shudder with grief.

Somehow, though, I found strength I didn't know I had and pulled away from his kiss, not wanting to mislead him.

He didn't deserve that.

Reluctantly, Killian let me go, a scowl marring his brow as I stumbled away from him. "What is it?"

I couldn't hide why I was here. The anguish blazed in my eyes as I stared at him.

Understanding flared in his and then anger. "Why?" he bit out.

"Because I promised someone that the next time I committed to love that the man I chose would be a man who loved me enough to put my happiness before his own."

Killian stared at me incredulously. "You know I love you. I've told you that. And I have never . . . told a woman that I loved her."

"I know you love me," I replied. "And I love you. That's why I'm not going to fight this contract. A contract we both know I signed when I was in no fit state to do so. I'm not blaming you for that. I'm a grown woman; it was my mistake. I just didn't realize how much unhappiness I was opening myself up to again when I signed it."

"Skylar." He crossed the room, reaching for me, but I held him off. He wasn't happy but he stayed back. "It'll be different this time."

"No, it won't." I shook my head. "Can't you see that? It's too late, Killian. I'm out there and if I put this album out, I stay out there. Your team can take over my social media and relieve me of that pressure, but that won't stop the fact that my decisions and choices will still be watched and judged. The anxiety that causes will always make me miserable. I love performing and I love writing music, but it comes with this shitstorm that I . . ." I took a shuddering breath. "One album. I only have to get through promoting one album. And then I'm done." Our eyes met, his filled with disbelief and anger, mine with heartbreak. "I'm giving up the fame. That's the only thing that will make me happy."

"Not me?" he whispered.

"I love you." The tears spilled down my cheeks before I could stop them. "I will always love you. And I want you to have everything that you've ever wanted." I gestured around the room, signifying the label. "But I need to be with someone who wants me to have all those things too. It would always be between us, and over time I'd grow to resent you for it. I know. I've been there before. And I don't want that with you."

Tears shimmered in his eyes, the show of emotion almost cutting me off at the knees as he stumbled toward me. "Don't you think I would change it if I could? Don't you think I fucking hate myself for putting you in this position?" He grabbed hold of my shoulders, pulling me into him. "Forgive me," he pleaded, "and we can get through this album and then it's over and you can have the life you want. With me."

"Don't," I begged, trying to pull away, but he held me fast. "Killian, please."

"I love you." His voice shook as he pressed his forehead to mine. "I can't lose you. I don't know what will happen to me if I lose you."

I cried harder. "Killian."

"Please," he choked out.

I couldn't stand it. His plea was like a vise wrapping itself around my chest, the pain was so bad. "I have to go." I pushed him away, fleeing his office, unable to bear his heartbreak on top of mine. He would weaken my resolve. I knew he would. And the thing was, we might seem okay at first, but I knew that just as it had with Micah, over time our feelings would turn toxic with resentment. Knowing I loved him more than he loved me would turn me into a ball of insecurity. I didn't deserve that.

Thankfully, I didn't pass anyone in the hall, ducking my head as I shot through reception to the elevator.

But I couldn't hide my tearstained face from Rick and Angus when I hit the main reception of the building. Angus stepped forward and pulled the hood up on my coat. "Duck your head," he murmured kindly. "Don't let them see."

I shivered, realizing the press had found us at the label.

They'd have a field day with that.

And I was right.

As I tried to erase the memory of Killian's distraught expression, I was surrounded by the paparazzi.

"Skylar, are you making music again?"

"How was it to be homeless?"

"Skylar, what was life on the streets like?"

"Do you think you need professional help?"

Rick growled at that, shoving aside the guy who said it, and he hurried me into the car.

As soon as we were safely inside, I pulled down the hood and watched the city pass me by. I bit my lip so hard trying to hold back my tears, I tasted the coppery tang of blood.

It wasn't until I got back to the hotel that I let the emotion flood out of me. I sobbed so hard, my ribs hurt.

I thought at one point I might actually die from the pain.

thirty-three

The room fell dark as clouds moved through the sky. But as I sat on the floor at the end of the bed, staring at nothing, wishing I felt nothing, I had no idea how much time had passed.

My cell rang a couple of times but I ignored it.

I heard the click of the lock on my hotel door and I whipped my head around. Fear made me freeze.

But it was Autumn.

I forgot I'd given her a keycard when we checked me in.

She shut the door behind her and leaned against it. She looked so sad. "Oh, Skylar."

Renewed tears trembled on my lashes.

Fuck, would they ever stop?

My friend crossed the room, dropping her bag and keycard on the bed, before she slid down next to me and put her arm around me. The relief that I hadn't lost her too caused the tears to fall again.

"Sshhh," she hushed, rubbing my shoulder in comfort. "It's okay."

"It's not." It felt like it would never be okay.

"I know," Autumn admitted. "I know it's not. But one day it will be again."

"Can we get to that place now, please? I'd like to skip this heartrending, feeling-like-I'm-going-to-die bullshit."

She laughed without humor and squeezed me closer. "It'll come."

"I ran out on the cover shoot," I muttered. Like it mattered.

"You weren't the only one." Worry rang in her words as she told me, "Eve called me and told me you and Killian disappeared. That you'd left the building separately, both seeming upset according to Justin in reception. I tried my brother and couldn't get him. So I went to his flat." Her voice broke on the last word and I tensed against her. "I've only ever seen him like that once before. He was eighteen. It was the seventh anniversary of our parents' death. But never again . . . until now."

"I'm sorry." My face crumpled.

"Oh, no, no," she soothed. "Don't. I always knew that one day I wouldn't be able to protect him from himself. As soon as I saw how you were together, how he felt about you, I knew this was it. He manipulated the one person he shouldn't have and now he . . ." Her voice hitched. "Now he just has to live with that."

"Is . . . is he in pain?"

"Yes."

I looked at her. Autumn stared straight ahead as tears slipped down her cheeks. His pain was her pain and vice versa. "I'm sorry."

"Don't be. You've been through so much, Skylar. You need to do what's right for you. And you're right. Even if you stayed together, you'd end up resenting him, always questioning why he couldn't put you first."

Realizing Killian had told her I'd said that, I wondered if he'd told her everything. "I do love him."

She turned to look at me. "I know that. *He* knows that. Otherwise you'd find a way to get out of this contract."

"I can't do that to him. Or to me. I made a promise and I intend to keep it."

Autumn sighed heavily, wearily. "There is a ton of press outside. Do you think they ever eat?"

I snorted. "I couldn't care less. I hate them."

"I know. The world doesn't hate *you*, though. Everyone thinks you're very brave for posting that video. I do too."

"I took back control."

"Yes, you did. As long as you do that throughout this whole ordeal, you'll be fine."

"Autumn?"

"Yeah?"

"Do you think maybe Killian might stay away? I mean, at work. Do you think he could let the team take over and stay away? I think it would be easier."

"I'll have a word with him," she promised.

Good. I didn't want to see him. I didn't want anything to weaken my resolve and I was afraid one more look in those dark eyes of his would snap my determination in half.

AT SEVEN THE NEXT MORNING, after another sleepless night, I had the hotel night manager slip me out of the back service entrance. I'd pinned my short hair to my head so I could tuck it under a borrowed baseball cap and I hurried down a narrow alleyway that let me out to the opposite side of the main entrance to an entirely different street.

I thought sunglasses might make me look more conspicuous and instead I'd layered my clothing so my body appeared bulkier. I kept my head down, tucked my hands into my pockets, and tried not to think about how hot I was, despite the low temperatures, with all the clothes on.

Not really sure what I was looking for, I headed toward Buchanan Street. All I knew was that I couldn't stay in that hotel room one more second grieving for Killian and fighting the need to go to him. To change my mind.

There were no shops open yet and traffic was still light. I wandered aimlessly, pausing whenever I saw a homeless person sleeping in a doorway. Killian and I had been in the middle of setting up the charity I had in mind for the homeless. What would happen with that now? Would he turn it over to someone else to help me with it? My idea was for a soup kitchen / shelter. It would be first come, first serve. There would be plenty of reserves of food and as many beds as we could provide. Too many homeless people's lives were in danger during the winter. They needed someplace warm to go.

Thinking of Mandy, I wandered toward Argyle Street.

I faltered when I saw Ham huddled under a shop doorway near the closed Arcade.

Deciding not to run from him, I made my way over and he looked up at me as I approached, opening his mouth probably to ask for spare change. He squinted at me and I lowered myself to my haunches.

"Hey, Ham," I sounded hoarse from all the crying.

I knew my eyes were still swollen too.

He narrowed his gaze, trying to place me, and then recognition hit. "Busker Girl?"

"You can call me Skylar, Ham. How are you?"

"I feel better than ye look." He flashed me a cheeky grin. "Too hot in all those clothes?"

I chuckled and almost immediately felt tired by the action. "Had a bad few days."

"Aye, I ken what that's like."

"You okay?"

He shrugged. "Same old." His face fell. "Mandy left."

Curious to know if she'd taken my advice, I asked, "Do you know where she went?"

"Aye, one of oor pals says she got help. She's living in shared housing. Got a cleaning job, believe it no."

Relief moved through me that she'd taken my advice. "That's good."

"I dunno aboot that. We were doin' awrite here." He grumbled. "We had each other."

I contemplated him; his cheekbones looked even hollower than before. It was awful but I didn't want to give him money. I knew he'd only use it for drugs. "Can I buy you something to eat?"

He stared at me, seeming to read my thoughts. He pushed, "Money would be better."

Sighing heavily, I stood up. "I'm not giving you money, Ham."

Curling his lip in disdain, he retorted, "Ye're no any better than us, ye know. Whoever ye are now, once ye're like us, ye cannae go back."

No, I couldn't go back. Everything that had happened to me here would always be a part of me. Including Killian.

Heroin wasn't my addiction. Killian was.

But unlike Ham, I would beat mine.

"Goodbye, Ham." I walked away.

"I REALLY THINK IF YOU'RE going to launch this album, you should take some of these interview requests," Gayle said as we talked on the phone a few hours later.

I'd snuck back into the hotel through the service entrance and was safely ensconced in my suite.

"I'm not doing it."

"Yeah, Killian said as much."

I flinched at the mere sound of his name. "Well, he was right."

"But there's so much positivity out there about this, Sky. It's opened up a lot of discussion about so many things, including the importance of mental health. You know how amazing it is when celebrities admit they're normal people too with the same fears and problems as everyone else. You could do a lot of good here."

"At the sacrifice of my own mental health?"

She was silent a moment and then huffed, "You're right. I'm sorry. Anyway, I really didn't call to annoy you. I called because I wanted to let you know that if you want me to, I'd be happy to manage you again through your solo career."

Grateful for the offer, I also knew I had to be honest with her. "Gayle, I would like that, but you have to know that once I'm done fulfilling my contract for this album, promoting it, touring, whatever, I'm out."

"You're out?"

"Yes. I don't want to do this. Be a star."

"Then what do you want to do?"

I'd thought about that a lot and the answer was kind of glaringly obvious. "I want to write and produce music. I want to be behind the scenes."

"Okay. Well. That's not my forte. I don't handle songwriters, generally, but I can make an exception. If you want to be a songwriter, I'll help you do that."

For the first time in what felt like days, my lips stretched into a genuine smile and I felt a glimmer of excitement at the prospect of that life waiting for me. "Gayle Leiderman, you just became my new favorite person."

"Fantastic," she chirped. "I'll send over a new contract to the hotel. We'll keep it yearly for now since we'll have to change the language when you change careers."

"Great. I'll let the hotel know you're faxing it over. And Gayle . . ."

"Yeah?"

"Thank you. For understanding."

"It's hard for me but I try."

We hung up and for a moment I didn't think about my pain. Hope smashed through it in that second. I was only twenty-four, after all. I still had time to get my life back on the path I wanted it to be on.

The hotel phone ringing shattered the nice moment.

"Hello?"

"Miss Finch, I have an Eve Smythe of Skyscraper Records on the line. Can I connect her?"

Those butterflies I'd grown so accustomed to made themselves violently known. "Sure."

I waited until I heard Eve's tentative, "Hello?"

"You've got me, Eve."

"Oh, good. Hi, Skylar. I'm calling to let you know that Mr. Byrne would like you to meet with him today at one o'clock here at the label."

Shit. The last thing I wanted to do was be in the same room with that guy. "Regarding?"

"The current media situation and the launch of your album."

Knowing that this was going to happen at some point whether I liked it or not, I decided to get it out of the way. But first, "Will Mr. O'Dea be in attendance?"

"Yes, he'll be here too."

A burning weight pressed down on my chest at the thought of seeing him so soon. "Okay. One o'clock it is."

thirty-four

I didn't realize how bad I looked until Eve winced when she met me at reception that afternoon.

"This whole thing is really taking its toll on you," she said sympathetically as she led me down the hall. "Can I get you a cup of tea?"

I shook my head. "Let's just get this over with."

"You know, you should ask the hotel for some cucumber slices. For your eyes. They'll reduce the puffiness." She lowered her voice to a whisper, "So people won't know you've been crying."

I gave her a pained smile.

"Bloody tabloids. Bottom-feeders."

I'd agree but *they* weren't the reason I looked like I'd been crying nonstop for a week.

Eve drew me to a stop outside James Byrne's office and knocked.

"Come in!" he barked from inside and I pinched my lips together. *Ass.*

Killian's assistant shot me a commiserating look, I guess

because I had to deal with the prick, and opened the door. "Miss Finch is here, sir."

"Send her in and go."

Ugh.

I stepped into his office and immediately halted at the sight of Killian sitting on one of two chairs in front of a glass-and-chrome desk. His uncle sat behind the desk, a floor-to-ceiling window behind him with a fantastic view along the River Clyde. It would've been a mirror image of Killian's office if the walls weren't so bare. Whereas Killian's was covered in his passion for the job, his uncle's had two probably expensive pieces of artwork on his walls and nothing else.

I looked at Killian. He sat sprawled on the chair, his left ankle resting on his right knee. Although he wore a suit, his tie was loose and askew and he had an overall disheveled demeanor. He hadn't shaved either.

I tentatively crossed the room and slipped into the chair beside him and when I chanced another glance at him, our eyes met. His were bloodshot, his expression wounded and furious.

"You'll have to forgive my nephew's appearance, Miss Finch," James said smoothly. "The boy forgot his manners today."

I sneered at him. "You call Mr. O'Dea a *boy* one more time and I'm going to leave your office and never come back."

James's eyes narrowed and I could feel the heat of Killian's gaze burning into me. "I'm sorry, we have a problem?"

"Your condescending attitude is a problem, yes."

"Skylar," Killian warned. Our eyes locked and if possible, he looked even more pissed at me. "I don't need you defending me."

"Why would she defend you?" James pushed his chair back. "Might it be because you're sleeping with each other?"

Shock rooted me to my chair.

"You're surprised I know? Really? You were carrying on an affair in a building in which I own many of the properties. Including properties my employees rent."

"You had someone spying on us?" Killian curled his lip in disgust.

"No. You don't interest me that much. But another employee saw you kissing as you got out of the lift. He asked me if I knew about the conflict of interest this posed. Of course, I didn't know what he was talking about it. But did I know my nephew is reckless and immature? That I did know so it really came as no surprise."

"We're not together anymore," I said.

He snorted and gestured to us. "Clearly. The angst is almost amusing."

"James," Killian warned him, sitting forward in his chair, "don't push me right now."

His uncle's expression darkened. "No. Don't you push me right now. I've shut up the employee who knows about you and no one else is to ever know. I want all the media focus on Skylar and this album, not on some misguided romance with her A&R exec." He rounded the desk and sat on its edge, contemplating me. "There's a storm out there, Miss Finch. A big, bloody storm with your name on it, and we're going to make sure this album gets caught up in it."

Trepidation filled me. "How?"

"Well, for a start, I've rescheduled that interview with *Good Morning Britain*. And then we're heading to the States. There are a lot of big-hitter interviewers over there who want you on their sofas."

What? No! "But—"

"Lois told me about your deal with Killian. I checked the contract and your little clause about the media is in there." He glared at his nephew. "That was ill-conceived."

Killian pushed up out of his chair and paced behind it. James watched him as if sickeningly entertained by his nephew's distress.

"If you saw the clause, then you know I don't have to do that interview."

"Or post on your social media or engage with your fans, or basically do anything that ensures this album's success."

"We can make this album a success without all that."

"Maybe," he acknowledged, "but look at your social media. No one had commented on your Twitter or Instagram in months until that stalker posted the photos of you and your band a few days ago. Until they were reminded, they forgot about you. That's how it works."

"Get to the point, James," Killian demanded.

His uncle didn't look at him. He focused on me. "My point is that unless you agree to do exactly what Lois advises you to do for this album launch, advice that includes radio and television interviews and sharing every boring minutiae of your life with your fans, I'm going to fire my nephew."

Killian's low, hoarse fury filled the room. "You son of a bitch."

"And not only that," he looked at his nephew now, emotionless, cold, "I'll make sure he never works in the music industry again."

Disbelief slackened my jaw. "You would threaten your own family for an *album*?"

He frowned at me like he thought I was simple. "Not just any album, Miss Finch. An album riding the coattails of an international sob story that has gripped millions. Millions who will buy the album. We've never had an opportunity like that at this label. I intend to make sure we take advantage of it."

Realizing he might be a sociopath, I stared unseeing at the ground. I was trapped. Again. "Fine." I stood, my legs shaking a little, but I refused to let James see me beaten. I glared at him, hoping he could taste my vitriol. "But when this is all over and you and I are no longer legally bound to each other, I'm going to make it my life's mission to ruin you."

I walked away, flicking a look at Killian who stared at me like he couldn't quite believe what was happening.

"You're needed here at eight tomorrow morning for the album cover shoot," James called after me.

My answer to that was to slam his office door so hard after me, I could hear the window behind his desk shudder.

Eve's head jerked up from her place across the room but I couldn't talk to her. I couldn't talk to anyone. I needed to get out of there.

I heard James's office door open behind me and then, "Skylar, wait."

Killian caught my arm, jerking me to halt. I glared at him. "Let me go."

His grip on me only tightened as he hissed, "Don't you dare do what he says. Not for me."

"You want to lose your job? Everything you've worked for? Everything you love?"

Condemnation darkened his gaze. "Not everything I love."

I tugged on my arm, stumbling back from him. "I need to go."

"Don't do it. He's not going to fire me. He can't, Skylar. He doesn't have a fucking leg to stand on. He knows I'll sue him for wrongful termination."

"Do you know how long lawsuits take, Killian? How much money? What are you going to do in the meantime? No label will touch you while you're suing another label."

Frustration blazed across his face. "Fuck!" He turned away, head in his hands.

And I used the opportunity to escape.

Eve stared at me with wide eyes, obviously wondering what the hell was going on. I hurried past her desk.

"Skylar!" Killian called after me. "Don't do it!" To anyone else, he likely sounded angry, but I could hear the desperation in his voice. "Not for me! Do you hear me? Skylar!"

As the elevator descended through the building, I could still hear him shouting my name in my head. He was right. I didn't need to do this. I had a contract that said so. But how could I let James ruin Killian's entire career? For me it was merely a year, maybe eighteen months of unhappiness, versus the man I loved facing a lifetime of failure and disappointment.

Because that was it at the end of the day. The thing James took a stab in the dark at.

I loved Killian.

I resented that love now, but that didn't mean it wasn't there with its claws buried deep inside me.

Love.

Was there anything ever more complicated in this life?

DESPITE MY DECISION TO HELP Killian, there was honestly a piece of me that clung to the belief that he'd turn up at the hotel or at least call to reiterate that I shouldn't give into his uncle's demands. He didn't. No show. No call.

As I lay in the bed in my hotel room that night, my anger toward Killian grew.

He was going to let me do this.

And I know I said I would and I hated being that woman who said one thing when she really felt another, but I'd honestly expected Killian to stand up for me more. That was what he was known for! Protecting the people he cared about.

However, this was his career. It was different. It meant so much to him to prove himself to his uncle, to beat him at the success game, and if I didn't do this, his uncle won a pretty goddamned huge fight between them.

I tossed and turned all night, a mass of confusion and hurt.

When I finally got out of bed the next morning, I groaned at the sight of myself in the mirror. I really hoped the makeup artist for the album cover shoot was a genius with dark circles. I looked like hell.

The paparazzi surrounding the hotel had decreased that morning as Rick and Angus got me into their SUV.

"Do you think that means they're giving up?" I asked hopefully.

"For now," Angus replied.

For now.

As soon as I indulged them again, it would flare up.

Great.

"I should do what Daniel Radcliffe did." I grinned thinking about it. "He wore the same clothes for months to frustrate the paparazzi because every photo they took looked like it was from the same day. They were worthless."

Rick chuckled. "Buy a bunch of the same jeans and jumpers. You could make it work."

I might do that. It was a way of still holding onto that defiance and control James was trying to take from me. "Unless the label has other plans for me, I need to shop tomorrow. I have to buy a laptop, get a phone from this century, and buy a couple dozen pairs of the same jeans and sweater."

Rick looked over his shoulder at me, grinning. "We can make that happen."

A couple of paparazzi waited for me outside the building and one nearly clocked me with his camera before Angus moved him out of the way.

"Come on, Skylar! We just want to know what you're doing here!"

I ignored them and strode toward the elevator with purpose.

"We'll be here," Rick said.

I thanked them, smiled at the building security guard, and stepped into the elevator.

Closing my eyes, I took slow, calming breaths.

I could do this.

Eve greeted me at reception. I frowned. "Where's Justin?"

"It's only 7:55 a.m. The office doesn't technically open until 8:30."

"Oh, right." I glanced around, only now noticing that the place was pretty much empty. "Where is this team? Do we know where we're shooting the cover?" I asked as I followed Eve down the hall.

"Actually, they're not here. Mr. O'Dea asked me to bring you to his uncle's office."

"Why?"

She shrugged but wouldn't meet my eyes.

Hmm.

Exhausted at the thought of another confrontation, I had to force myself to walk into that office. Sure enough, James was sitting behind his desk while Killian stood with his hands on the back of one of the chairs in front of it. Today he looked much better. Clean-shaven, and his suit, shirt, and tie were immaculate. The only thing that hadn't changed was his tired eyes.

He straightened when I walked in, his gaze flicking to Eve. "Eve, I'd like you to stay."

James scoffed, "I'm not discussing business with an intern."

"She's my *assistant*," Killian stressed. "And this morning, she's here because she knows what I'm about to say is true. She's here to testify to it if you don't believe me."

"This isn't a courtroom." James bolted upwards in his seat, eyeing his nephew in suspicion. "What the bloody hell is going on? Why did you call me in here today?"

I waited, studying Killian, feeling clueless. He turned to look at me and I felt breathless at the thousand silent apologies in his gaze. "To right a wrong," he answered.

"Get to the point."

"The point, Uncle," Killian dragged his gaze from mine to James, "is that we have a problem with Miss Finch's contract."

James tensed. "What kind of problem?"

"Well, Eve and I," he gestured to his assistant, "wanted to have a look at the contract again after our discussion yesterday. And . . . well . . . it was the strangest thing. We couldn't find it."

No.

No way.

I stared at Killian, incredulous.

"What?" James snapped.

"We couldn't find it. We can't find the physical copies with Miss Finch's signature on them and we can't find any of the digital copies. They've disappeared."

"No," James grunted, hitting the space bar on his keyboard with almost enough force to destroy it. He began typing, his eyes searching the computer screen frantically. "No," he muttered, hitting the enter button hard. "What have you done?"

After another minute of searching, during which I studied Killian, willing him to look at me and disappointed when he wouldn't, James pushed back from his desk only to lean on it. His face was mottled with unrestrained fury. "Tell me you didn't?"

Killian scratched his neck, looking almost remorseful. "Thing is, after that, we discovered all the digital recordings for the album are missing too."

I swear my heart swelled in my chest as hope seized me. "Killian," I whispered.

Finally, he looked at me and all the anguish and love he felt was there in his eyes.

"You're fired," James spat.

Sorrow flickered over Killian's face but it didn't touch the determination.

"I'll find a job," he reassured me. Then he faced his uncle. "Turns out people in this industry respect me a whole lot more than they like you. It shouldn't be hard."

"Like has nothing to do with it. When I tell them you sabotaged the biggest deal this label has ever had, no one will touch you, boy."

"It wasn't Mr. O'Dea," Eve suddenly stepped forward. "Mr. Byrne, it was me. I accidentally deleted the files and I-I-I accidentally shredded the contract."

Killian's head whipped around as he stared at Eve in shock.

I gazed at her in horror.

But she bravely pressed on, even though she had turned a sickly white, appearing ready to upchuck any second now. "You can't prove it was Killian because I have all of his logins. And if I say it was me . . . well," she shrugged, "he could come after you for wrongful termination. If you're going to fire him anyway." She shrugged at Killian. "Mr. O'Dea might as well make your life a misery for it."

Silence descended over the room.

James seemed disgusted that an "intern" would attempt to strong-arm him. Killian was clearly not expecting this turn of events. And me? I was really hoping the man I loved wasn't going to let a young girl take responsibility for his actions.

"Eve, no." Killian shook his head. "I'm not letting you take the blame."

I think I visibly deflated with relief.

"It was me." He assured his uncle. "I deleted the files. But you can't prove it wasn't an accident."

"No." James curled his lip in disgust. "But I can fire you for negligence. And I am. Well done, boy. Ruining your career over a waif with a guitar. What a fucking disappointment you turned out to be after all."

My heart bled for Killian at his uncle's words, knowing that all he'd ever striven for was his uncle's positive acknowledgment and the chance to officially run the label. Now it was all gone so he could free me from a life I didn't want.

I opened my mouth to argue, to put a stop to it, when I noticed the look on Killian's face. He didn't appear destroyed or devastated. He seemed resolute and at peace with his decision.

"I don't care," he said. "You've been a disappointment my whole life. And I was never, ever going to be good enough. Not for you." Killian turned to me. "But I can try to be good enough for someone who actually matters."

Before I could throw my arms around him or howl in relief, his uncle commanded, "Get the hell out of my building before I have security throw you out. And Miss Finch?"

I glared at him.

"Try getting past the paparazzi without security guards. I believe those men are on my payroll."

Vindictive bastard. But I was one step ahead. "Actually, they switched to my payroll two days ago."

The smug smirk fell from his face and I almost crowed. I smiled sweetly. "Perhaps if you were here more often, you'd know that." I glanced around his office and then looked him straight in the eye. "It'll be a pleasure to watch this label fail now that you've fired the best damn thing that ever happened to it."

I spun on my heel, offering Killian a blazing look that told him he and I had unfinished business. I stopped to touch Eve's shoulder to offer her a silent thank-you. "If you ever feel like working in LA, I know a label that would be lucky to have you. You've got my number."

Her eyes widened with gratitude. "Thank you, Skylar."

I strode out of that office and took a huge lungful of air, feeling it flow through me and loosen all that tightness in my chest.

I was free.

"Skylar."

I whirled around to face Killian. He looked uncertain. "Not here," I told him. "Grab your stuff. We'll take my car."

Killian nodded and marched by me and into his office. By the time he emerged, Eve had come out of James Byrne's office trembling.

"I quit," she told us. "The tyrant was promising to make my life hell. I'm not staying for that."

"I told you I'd help."

"Thank you. I think I might need it."

All three of us walked out, both Killian and Eve carrying boxes with their stuff. Killian stopped at reception because Justin had arrived. "I'm sending someone to come and pack up the rest of my office," Killian told him.

"Sir?" Justin's eyes grew round with shock.

Killian's expression was impressively neutral as he said, "I no longer work here." He dug into his pocket and removed the key to his office. "Can I trust you to only let the person I send in? Not even my uncle."

Justin took the keys, saddened by the news. "Of course, sir."

While Eve said her goodbyes to those who had arrived at the office, I stood in the corner of the elevator while Killian kept the elevator door open for her.

I stared at him, caressing his face with my eyes. "You chose me," I whispered.

Killian turned to look at me and shook his head. "Living without you isn't an option."

God, I loved him, the romantic, convoluted, sexy bastard. "You threw away everything you've worked for, for me. Are you sure that you won't eventually come to resent me?"

"Never," he replied, his tone adamant. "You chose me before I chose you, Skylar. I won't ever forget that. And the truth is this," he gestured out in the office, "it wasn't a choice of picking you over the label. This was about righting a wrong. How could I ever say that I love you and mean it, all the while standing by while those fuckers leached the happiness right out of you?"

"Okay, let's leave because if I have to say one more goodbye I'm going to cry." Eve jumped into the elevator, completely oblivious to ruining the moment between us.

I shared a rueful smile with Killian as he let the door go so the elevator could descend.

If Rick and Angus were surprised to see us, they hid it behind their perfectly professional, neutral expressions. We said goodbye to Eve, who promised to call, and she left the building, totally ignored by the paparazzi.

Then Rick and Angus hustled Killian and me passed them into the SUV. They asked Killian questions. Who he was? What he was doing with me? But he wore that aloof expression he'd mastered and helped me into the car.

"Where to, Skylar?" Angus asked as soon as we were all in.

Killian answered. "Tantallon Road in Shawlands." He felt my gaze and offered, "My place."

Joy bubbled inside me. "Awfully presumptuous of you, Mr. O'Dea," I teased.

His grin was roguish. "I have something to give you there."

"Oh?"

"Mmm." His eyes dipped to my mouth. "A reminder, really."

"A reminder?"

His head bent toward me so our lips were almost touching and it took everything within me not grab onto him right there and then. Especially when he whispered against my mouth, "You're mine. And I'm yours."

And for the first time, I really, honestly believed that was true. "You're mine," I murmured, "and I'm yours."

thirty-five

Every now and then, a car would pass out on the street, the light from their headlamps darting around Killian's bedroom in the dark.

I must've made some kind of noise or movement because he pressed his hand deeper into my stomach and pulled my body against his so my back was pressed flush to his front. "You're still awake," he said, his voice just above my head on the pillow.

"You need blackout blinds," I answered, snuggling deeper into him.

"Get them," he mumbled and then yawned. "Do what you want to the flat."

Had I heard right? I stiffened in his arms.

He gave me another squeeze. "What?"

"Are you . . . are you asking me to move in with you?"

"Aye. Did I not say that?"

Confused, I peeled his hand off me and slipped out of the bed.

"Where are you going?"

Staring at him warily I pulled on my underwear. He sat up in bed, sleepy and bemused.

I strode out of the bedroom, searching for the rest of my clothes. After Rick and Angus dropped us off at Killian's flat, we didn't talk. We tore each other apart. The sex had been explosive. Exhausted by the last few days, we'd fallen asleep until late evening. We'd eaten together but we hadn't really talked about anything important yet, and just when I thought we would, Killian made love to me.

Apparently that still wasn't enough because we'd had sex again before Killian snuggled into me and closed his eyes.

But I wasn't tired after sleeping most of the day away. And now this.

"If you don't like the flat," Killian called out, and I heard the bedclothes rustling, "we can get something else."

It wasn't about not liking the flat. I liked the flat. If it wasn't for the fact that it was a period property, it would remind me exactly of the apartment on the Clyde. It had the same layout, except it had two bedrooms instead of one. There were no French doors overlooking the river, but there was a huge bay window and an original fireplace.

"Where the hell is my phone?" I muttered as I pulled on my jeans.

Killian stomped into the living room in his boxers, his lips thinned at finding me half dressed. "Where are you going?"

"I don't know. I just . . . I don't know!"

"What happened? What's going on?"

I stared at him, incredulous, and then blurted out in a ramble, "You asked me to move in with you without really asking and I don't know what I'm supposed to do with that so I think I'm just going to go."

"Okay, Skylar, I haven't slept since the paps found you. I'm shattered. Can we please go back to bed and discuss whatever this nonsense is tomorrow?"

Was it nonsense? It didn't feel like nonsense to me because it wasn't about the way he'd asked me to move in with him—although, you did not ask a woman something that huge like you were offering her ice cream. I studied him, seeing the sleep-deprived bruising under his eyes. He hadn't slept for worrying about me.

And now I couldn't sleep for worrying about him.

"We didn't talk."

He scrubbed a hand down his face, looking resigned to the fact that he wouldn't be going back to bed anytime soon. He wandered by me into the open-plan kitchen. "Do you want something to drink?"

"Water." I found my T-shirt and put it on as I slipped onto a stool at the island. He reached across the countertop and handed me a water.

"We didn't talk," I repeated. "We ripped each other's clothes off and had at it."

Killian gave me a heated look. "Well, considering yesterday I never thought I'd get to touch you like that ever again, I was feeling a wee bit impatient to have you. Problem?"

He knew it wasn't a problem. "Yeah, you gave me too many orgasms."

He smirked and gestured to me. "What's going on?"

"We didn't talk at dinner. We've not talked at all since the car."

"We're talking now, Skylar. What is going on?"

I frowned at him, forgetting that he wasn't the most patient person. "Are you in denial? Is that what this is?"

"Help me out here and get to the point."

I threw my hands up in exasperation. "You're awfully happy for a guy who just lost a job that meant everything to him. That is my point. And I can't sleep because I'm worried about you and I'm worried about what this will eventually do to us. Oh, and you do not ask a woman to move in with you like that. Ever. And you shouldn't be asking me to move in with you at all because we've only just started dating."

Killian blinked slowly as he processed all of that.

"Are you going to speak?"

"One, I'm happy because I have you back and you're free to do with your life whatever you want now. Two, I have plans for my career. Three, even if I didn't, it wouldn't affect us because I need you more than I need a career. Four, give me a break. I'm exhausted and a lot has happened, so I apologize if I fucked up asking you to move in. And five, we've been together for three months and as far as I'm concerned, that's enough time for me to know I don't want to wake up in the morning without knowing I get to wake up lying beside you."

When did he get so goddamned romantic? "You're too good at this," I huffed, and then I frowned as I replayed his words. "We've not been together for three months."

He smiled like he had a secret. "In my head, we have been."

I shook mine, confused.

He leaned across the island. "The first time you sang 'In the Wind' to me, you became mine. I tried to deny it, but it happened right in that moment."

I gaped at him. "I was still a skinny, bruised waif then."

Killian rounded the island and I turned toward him. He nudged my knees apart and pressed in between them as he wrapped his arms around my waist. My hands settled on his chest as I stared into his eyes, still trying to process that he was telling me I'd had his heart for far longer than I'd known.

"Your voice has always gotten me. From the first time I heard you busking. I was walking down Buchanan Street with Autumn and I heard your voice. I swear to God, Skylar, I felt this prickling sensation all the way down my spine at the sound of it. So I followed it and found the crowd standing around you. I couldn't see you at first because of your hat. I just saw this slight wee thing with this voice that was angelic, but so powerful. You reminded me of Eva Cassidy."

Goosebumps prickled over my skin at the comparison. "That is the compliment of the century, my friend."

He squeezed my waist. "I kept coming back whenever I could to hear you sing because it calmed something in me. And when I first heard you sing an original song, it was one of those magic moments when you feel like someone has reached inside you and found a way to express all the things you're feeling but can't say."

Shit.

He was going to make cry.

"One Saturday it was hot. You didn't see me standing in the shop doorway behind where you were busking and you took off your hat. I recognized you. As soon as I saw your face and put your voice to it, I knew it was you. I couldn't believe it."

"Smarter than the average bear," I muttered, caressing his warm, hard chest and thinking how grateful I was that he did recognize me.

"But that morning you sang 'In the Wind' to me, no guitar, no music, just your voice, you sung it like your fucking heart was breaking . . ." He ducked his head, eyes locked with mine and brimming with intensity and love. "My heart broke too. I was stunned because I realized I wanted to piece you back together again, hoping that maybe you would be able to piece me back together too."

Yep. Definitely crying.

Tears streamed down my cheeks, his beloved face a blur in front of me and I laughed. "You have to stop saying wonderful things to me. I have these uncontrollable and embarrassing reactions."

Killian smiled and kissed my nose. "My point is that even if we've only been together for five weeks, it feels like a lot longer to me."

I nodded, swiping at my cheeks. "Okay. But that doesn't mean we have to rush things."

His grip on my waist momentarily tensed. "We don't have to if you don't want to."

The ridiculous thing was that I did. "You don't think we'll regret it?"

"Skylar, I've been practically living with you. Before the paps thing, I hadn't slept or eaten in this flat for four weeks."

That was true. I bit my lip, contemplating. "I hated those nights in the hotel without you."

"I hated them too."

I laughed a little hysterically. "We're moving in?"

He grinned. "We're moving in."

"Okay." I cocked my head to study him. "Now what's this about a plan for your career?"

Killian's grin widened. "I'm setting up my own label."

Shocked—but good shocked—I slapped my hands on his chest with excitement, making him chuckle. "Really?"

"Yes, really."

"Killian, this is amazing. And I'll do whatever I can to help!" I threw my hands around his neck so he had to catch me, swinging me away from the stool. I peppered his face with thrilled kisses and all the while he smiled boyishly, shyly, like he was taken aback by my enthusiasm.

His expression filled me with so much tenderness, I was overwhelmed by love.

"Bedroom," I muttered against his lips before I kissed him long and deep.

Walking blindly in that direction, he said when I finally let him up for air, "Four times in one night? That'll be a new record."

"Don't even think about making it your new label name," I muttered, kissing him and feeling his laughter rumble in my mouth.

I gave a little "oof" of excitement when my back hit the bed and then squirmed with anticipation as Killian removed my jeans and underwear. Pulling my T-shirt back off, I threw it somewhere on the floor and was unclipping my bra when Killian braced himself over me.

Something in his expression stilled my movements.

"What?"

"You can't let that album die, Skylar."

Horrified at what he might be suggesting, wondering if he was actually nuts to be bringing it up after everything, I froze.

He raised his hands in a placating gesture. "I don't mean putting it out there in the usual sense with all the plans we had at Skyscraper. I mean self-publishing it. Just putting it out there. You don't have to do anything with it. Upload it, and if people want to buy it, great. It deserves to be heard."

I'd never really thought about it, but the idea didn't suck.

"It would be a great advertisement for your songwriting skills if songwriting and producing is the path you want to go down."

It would. He was right. "So I'd self-publish it and maybe send out a tweet with a link, and that's all I'd have to do?"

He smiled slowly. "Aye, that's all you'd have to do."

Excitement bubbled up out of me at the notion. "I could do that."

"Yeah?"

I grinned, nodding. "Yeah."

His answer was to tug on my bra, sliding the straps down my arms. He threw it over his shoulder and grasped my wrists in his hands. He slowly guided my arms above my head and brought his lips to a whisper above mine. I opened my legs wider and wrapped them around his back.

We both gasped at the feel of him throbbing against me.

"Tell me you love me," he demanded.

I tingled everywhere at his fierce expression. "I love you. I love you more than I love anyone."

His chocolate eyes smoldered. "Overachiever."

I chuckled, the sound curtailed by another gasp as he rocked against me.

"I'll never love anyone the way I love you," he promised with a whisper in my ear.

Heat, need, and a rush of wet moved through me at his words.

"Come inside me," I panted, tightening my legs around him.

His answering kiss was long and slow, as if he was savoring me. When we finally came up for air, I was pushing against his hold on my wrists with impatience. Wanting him now.

"Foreplay, my love," he admonished as he held me down. "Need to make sure you're ready."

My eyes widened at the endearment. "I think you'll find I am ready."

Killian raised an eyebrow in disbelief. "I know I'm good, but I'm not that good."

Lips twitching with the need to laugh, I replied, "I had an interesting reaction to you telling me you loved me like you did. Plus—" I pushed against his hold on my wrists and my inability to break it caused another tug of arousal between my legs—"apparently, I like you holding me down."

Lust darkened in his eyes. "Is that so?" he murmured, shifting his hips against mine as he pushed into me. His nostrils flared at finding me wet, and tingles of pleasure scattered down the base of my spine as he glided deeper into me.

The pullback caused those tingles to flare like sparklers.

It was his expression that made the tension inside me stretch deliciously.

And it was something else entirely that made me come hard around his thrusts on a cry of his name.

It was knowing we had the kind of trust between us that allowed me to delight in him holding me down to take and give pleasure. The kind of trust I found when a man who kept himself so closed off to the rest of the world divulged the depths of his feelings for me without fear.

"Skylar," he groaned, letting go of my wrists to hold my hips as he shifted onto his knees to power deeper, harder into me.

Delighted surprise flushed through me as I felt that tension start to rebuild. "Oh my God." I curled my fists around the bedclothes above my head as Killian hit a magical spot inside me with each drive.

As my uninhibited cries filled the apartment, the need in his eyes burned brighter, shooting me closer to oblivion. I was vaguely aware of the headboard smacking against the wall as he thrusted into me with so much lust.

"Come," he demanded through gritted teeth. "Come for me again."

It was surely too much for his ego that I shattered with a garbled scream around his pounding drives on his command.

"Fuck!" he cried as my inner muscles squeezed around him, demanding his climax. His grip on my thighs turned almost bruising as he throbbed with hot release inside me.

His hips jerked in a prolonged shudder against mine. It was

the hardest we'd both ever come and I felt slightly dazed by it as Killian groaned and collapsed over me. Little aftershocks caused me to pulse around him while he was still inside me. He kissed and rocked against me like he wanted to prolong the orgasm even further.

A pounding on the wall behind us stilled his movements and he lifted his head to look at me.

Laughter bubbled on my lips. "Maybe try not to shake the headboard so hard next time."

We burst into laughter and he wrapped his arms around me to roll us so I lay on top of him. When our laughter eventually died, he said, "We need to move."

"But your place is nice."

"Nah." He shook his head. "We need to live somewhere we can slam that headboard as hard as we want."

"Surely your neighbor is used to it," I teased. "Mr. Serial Monogamist."

Killian cut me a look, like he knew my game and wasn't walking into that trap. "Sex has never been like this for me. I'm addicted to making you come harder every time."

I narrowed my eyes. "You're too good at this."

His body shook against mine in amusement. "I'm only telling the truth."

I squirmed with happiness and admitted, "That was pretty spectacular."

"Aye." He agreed, kissing my forehead. "And I intend to repeat it, so we'll look for somewhere more private."

"It doesn't even surprise me that we're going to look for an apartment based on where we can knock the headboard against the wall without pissing off the neighbors."

"Why should it?" He yawned, caressing my arm as his whole

body relaxed beneath me, ready for sleep. "It's the best reason I can think of."

Smiling, I snuggled deeper into him, feeling more content than I had in a very long time. The truth was if he wanted to look for a new apartment so he could do *that* to me anytime he wanted, I was all for it. "I love you."

"I love you too. Now sleep. We've got a lot to do when we wake up."

We did. And the prospect filled me with anticipation.

How amazing was that, I realized. Not just to sleep to wake up to the day hoping to simply survive it.

I was going to sleep to wake up to the day to actually *live* it.

epilogue

The thrum of music vibrated through the walls and right into my chest. Nerves like I'd never felt before caused demented fluttering in my belly.

This was what I'd done for years. Why the hell was I so anxious?

I must've said it out loud because Autumn grabbed my hands in hers and replied, "Because this is different."

This *was* different.

And it was a dream I thought had ended when I gave up a conventional career as an artist.

The small room I was in smelled of old cigarette smoke and beer, and the wall was covered in the autographs of the artists who'd played at the legendary King Tut's Wah Wah Hut in Glasgow.

And now I was going to be one of them.

The door to the intimate VIP room opened and Killian strolled in. "You ready?"

Three months ago, when we'd sat across from each other at the breakfast table in our new small but perfectly formed apartment near Kelvingrove, I never expected what was about to come out of his mouth.

Killian and I found a new apartment pretty fast so he could concentrate on starting his own label. There was a lot of financial stuff involved and it would take a while, so he wanted to get the ball rolling. He wouldn't accept my offer of financial support, and I understood that. He needed to do this on his own.

As for me, I hired a recording booth and a band, Killian guided me through producing, and we re-recorded my album. We still had the digital files from the recording at Skyscraper but to avoid any legal problems, we decided re-recording it on my own money was the safer bet.

After sharing a fantastic Christmas with him and Autumn, we flew first to LA to see my guys and Gayle. And then they supported me when I took my first trip back to Billings to lay flowers at my mother's grave. It was not an easy time, and I wouldn't have gotten through it without my two best friends there with me.

When we returned to Glasgow, I didn't dwell and got back into the studio to wrap up the album in time for an end-of-January release. I self-published it. Posted that I'd self-published it on my social media and something magical happened.

My fans bought it.

They *really* bought it.

Autumn had stayed in Montana to visit with her friend at a ski resort on Whitetail Mountain so she wasn't around for what happened.

But that's another story entirely.

While Autumn was off changing her life for the better, my album hit number two on the US Billboard and charted in the top ten in the UK.

I honestly hadn't expected it and was anxious about the chaos it created. We were still dealing with the paparazzi and Rick and

Angus were still around, thankfully, but the crazy got crazier for a while because of the album's success.

It became clear to everyone, however, that I had no intention of promoting it or going on tour.

By April the chaos died down, people got bored, and for the most part, they moved on. Killian finally got the label off the ground. He'd successfully talked a couple of artists into taking a shot on him and rejecting Skyscraper's offers. Only time would tell but he was already showing his uncle what a mistake he'd made firing him. I had the utmost faith Killian's label would one day overshadow James Byrne's. My guy had a true passion for music and that, along with how smart he was, would prove his uncle's undoing.

Killian had been traveling on and off to hear artists he was interested in, and the traveling had kind of intensified in the past few months. Sometimes it was hard, but his homecoming was always worth it.

When the bands he was interested in were local, I went with him. What I learned and loved about my adopted city was that the people here couldn't give a shit if you were famous. I got the occasional shout-out if I was out shopping with Autumn or Killian, but otherwise, they left me alone.

Killian and I had ended up on the front of a couple of tabloids at first, but we agreed to ignore it entirely and get on with our lives. In fact, there was a positive to Killian's sudden exposure as my boyfriend. It opened doors for the label and although the unfairness of that frustrated me, in the end it was a good thing for him. And I had to accept that it was the way the world worked.

That morning in April I'd returned home from LA to listen in on Tellurian's recording sessions for the new album. When Brandon invited me to come over, I wanted to turn him down because

I didn't think it was fair to Macy to have me there. However, Macy called me. It was awkward, and weird, but in the end, it was okay. I could honestly tell them that I loved the new direction they'd taken with this album and I was happy to see Macy had gotten rid of the rainbow hair in favor of the fire-engine red of her own choosing.

I flew home thinking things with the guys were in a great place. Except maybe for Micah. I didn't know if we'd ever be truly okay. He threw around a couple of caustic remarks about Killian that I had to ignore. It was either that or punch him in the gut. I decided to let it go. I was happy. One day, I hoped, Micah would find a way to be happy too.

"So, I have something to tell you," Killian had said that April morning, pushing his empty breakfast plate away. "And I'm not sure how you're going to react."

"Okay."

Although still Mr. Aloof-and-Intimidating with almost everyone else, Killian was rarely expressionless or grim with me. Autumn called me his happy pill, which he hated and I found hilariously adorable.

"I . . . Now you don't have to do this, but I wanted you to have the option."

"Spit it out, Killian."

"I booked you to play an intimate gig at King Tut's this summer."

Completely not expecting that, I could only gape at him.

"Skylar?"

King Tut's? King Freaking Tut's?

"I know you don't want to perform anymore, but I know this is a bucket-list thing. If the opportunity is—"

"Yes!" I'd shouted in excitement. "Hell yes! Oh my God!"

He'd grinned. "Yeah?"

I'd laughed. "It's King Tut's. I'm not saying no to that. But keeping it small, right?"

"It only has a three hundred-person capacity."

"One hundred," I'd stated. "Let's cap it at one hundred."

"We can do that."

So that's how I found myself getting ready to perform for an intimate crowd of a hundred when I never thought I'd be doing this again.

Autumn hugged me tight. "We'll be out there cheering you on. Remember that."

I smiled gratefully at her and watched her leave before locking gazes with Killian.

"I'm proud of you," he said.

"I'm proud of you."

"Mutual appreciation society," he murmured, strolling toward me.

My love for him was a deep ache in my chest. Would the sharp sweetness of it ever fade? Right now, it didn't feel like it ever would.

Killian blocked my path and I raised an eyebrow. "In order to go out there, I kind of need your sexy ass to move out of my way."

"Marry me," he blurted out.

And just like that, all the air went out of the room.

"Your work visa will come to an end," he continued, studying my face for reaction. "And there's no way in hell I'm putting you on a plane."

The amazed shock I'd been feeling was not so slowly turning to indignation. "What?"

"You're not leaving me for the States, so we need to get married," he said in staccato, as if I was a moron who didn't understand him the first time.

I smacked his chest. "That's not how you ask someone to

marry them!"

Killian looked confused enough to enrage me.

"You don't marry someone to get them a visa!"

Understanding dawned and he had the audacity to glare at me. At me! "Did you not hear the part where I can't live without you?"

"Not really."

"Fuck," he muttered, reaching into his pocket. "I'm doing this all wrong."

"Oh, you think?"

He cut me a dark look and then yanked whatever it was he was searching for out of his pocket.

I stared at the black velvet ring box in his hand.

"I meant for this to be romantic. That you'd walk out there with my ring on your finger. Whole big thing . . ." he trailed off, shrugging.

Despite the awfulness of his proposal, my anger died under the weight of my affection for him. "How can you be so good at the romantic thing but always wreck the big moments?"

He rubbed a hand over his face in distress.

I reached for him, feeling bad now about reacting so negatively. "Hey, hey, it's okay."

"It's not okay." Killian opened the box and my heart stopped at the sight of the engagement ring. It was a rectangular cushion-cut diamond on a simple platinum band.

Simple and elegant, but a little different.

It was perfect.

"Killian," I whispered, my fingers itching to touch it.

"Even if we didn't have the impending visa hanging over us, I would ask you to marry me, Skylar. I'm not a man who sits around and waits for what he wants. I tried and failed spectacularly with you when I was attempting to keep it just business between us."

I grinned, remembering that night after we left King Tut's. "Yeah, you did."

"When I decide on something, I am absolute and steadfast in that decision. And I decided last year that you were the only woman I needed and would ever need. Marry me, Skylar. Marry me because I love you and I will do anything to make you happy."

I hit him again. "You bastard!"

"What now?" He threw his hands up in agitation.

"You're going to ruin my makeup!" I blinked back the tears burning in my eyes. "I'm all ready to perform, nervous as hell, and then you turn me into a pile of mush before I go out there. Good going!"

Killian scratched his eyebrow while he gestured with the ring. "Was that a yes?"

I knocked him back on his feet, I threw my body at him so hard. But he had fast reflexes. His chest shook against mine with laughter as I kissed him hungrily. I pulled back, hanging onto him to him breathlessly, "That was a yes. Guess I'm not so good at these things either."

"That's okay." He flashed me a wicked smile. "Your talents lie elsewhere."

"That's right, make it dirty."

"I don't know what you're talking about. I was talking about your music."

Not fooled, I made a face and then kissed him again, pouring my second "yes" into it.

Killian pulled away only to rest his forehead against mine. "They're waiting for you." He said it like he didn't want to let me go and I knew he didn't when he continued, "I should have proposed after. Near a bed."

I pulled back, my eyes lit with anticipation. "After my set, let's do *it* in here."

In answer, he gently extricated himself from me. "This is a sacred space, Skylar."

Snorting, thinking he was being funny, it didn't take me long to realize he wasn't.

Which only made me laugh harder.

In fact, I was laughing as he slid the engagement ring on my finger, which made him laugh. Maybe it wasn't the most romantic response, but I thought it a good sign. If we entered marriage laughing, maybe it meant our lives together would be filled with it.

Killian kissed the ring on my finger, gave me one last hard kiss, and then handed my Taylor to me. "Now, go get them."

He followed me out, disappearing through the door that would take him into the crowd offstage. Hearing the loud murmurs of talk as they waited for me, I took a deep breath.

I couldn't hear the floorboards creak under my feet since the conversation of a hundred people was so loud, but I felt them solid beneath me, holding my shaking legs upright.

Feeling a hundred stares beyond the stage lights, I didn't look at them as a hush fell over the room. I plugged my Taylor into the amp, slid onto the stool, and adjusted my mic.

Finally, I looked up.

Everyone was a dark shadow against the lights and it was a familiar and yet unfamiliar sight. It had been a long time since I was so physically close to my audience, and I'd never been on stage alone before.

The silence seemed to boom around the room as I stared out at them, wondering what they were thinking. I knew they wanted to be here because the tickets sold out in the first ten minutes, but I was still nervous. I didn't want to let them down.

"Woohoo, Skylar!" I heard Autumn catcall from the crowd.

It made me smile and reminded me she was out there. That Killian, my fiancé and best friend in the world, was out there. "Hey, guys," I greeted.

That was all it took. The room erupted into applause and whistles and a wave of nostalgia hit me with so much force, tears pricked my eyes.

"Wow, thank you," I said as they quieted down, my voice echoing through the mic. "I really appreciate the welcome. I don't know if you know this, but my old band and I never got to play King Tut's. The offer to play here was too great to turn down and I'm really grateful you guys came out tonight to let me tick this one off my bucket list."

"King Tut's!" someone shouted, and the applause started up again.

I laughed into the mic, feeling myself relax more and more.

"Well, let's do this. I'm going to kick off tonight with a song called 'Ghost.'" I strummed the guitar to the applause, noise that died down as soon as I opened my mouth to sing.

They were with me. Right there with me as I retold my story through music. I sang it all, feeling my pain and my anger, owning it, because it no longer owned me. And they sang it with me, singing those lyrics back to me like they felt it too.

I sang "In the Wind," my biggest hit off the album, and felt a rush of love and support from that audience like I'd never felt in my life.

As the set drew to a close, I cut through the wolf whistles. "I'm sad to say this is my final song tonight, guys. This was the last song on the album but it's definitely not a song about an ending. It's a song about the best beginning I could've ever asked for. Killian, this one's yours, babe, just like me."

"I was concrete standing still,
Cemented heart, bricked-over soul.
But there were cracks I couldn't see,
Through them my song called out.

"The river heard me and it came for me.

"I was cold there, forged in stone,
And you were colder on your throne
Of freezing waves that flooded me out,
To free my song upon you.

"The river heard me and it came for me.
It rushed me on toward a waterfall.

"I feel the wind on my skin breathing,
My heart is beating to the feeling.
I catch my soul as I free-fall,
Then your arms close tight around me
Right before we land.

"I'm alive and it's all your fault,
Blood is pumping, burning hot.
Worse, I'm growing addicted to
Being awake, being with you.

"The river heard me and it came for me.
It rushed me on toward a waterfall.

"I feel the wind on my skin breathing,
My heart is beating to the feeling.

I catch my soul as I free-fall,
Then your arms close tight around me
Right before we land.

"You're in my heart, you're like a beat.
You're the air I drink in breaths.
You're the flood that set me free.
The waterfall I'd gladly drown in.

"I feel the wind on my skin breathing,
My heart is beating to the feeling.
I catch my soul as I free-fall,
Then your arms close tight around me
Right before we land.

"The river heard me and it came for me.
Now my song belongs to it."

From *New York Times* and *USA Today* bestselling author Samantha Young . . .

Autumn O'Dea has always tried to see the best in people while her big brother, Killian, has always tried to protect her from the worst. While their lonely upbringing made Killian a cynic, it isn't in Autumn's nature to be anything but warm and open. However, after a series of relationship disasters and the unsettling realization that she's drifting aimlessly through life, Autumn wonders if she's left herself too vulnerable to the world. Deciding some distance from the security blanket of her brother and an unmotivated life in Glasgow is exactly what she needs to find herself, Autumn takes up her friend's offer to stay at a ski resort in the snowy hills of Montana. Some guy-free alone time on Whitetail Mountain sounds just the thing to get to know herself better.

However, she wasn't counting on colliding into sexy Grayson King on the slopes. Autumn has never met anyone like Gray.

Confident, smart, with a wicked sense of humor, he makes the men she dated seem like boys. Her attraction to him immediately puts her on the defense because being open-hearted in the past has only gotten it broken. Yet it becomes increasingly difficult to resist a man who is not only determined to seduce her, but adamant about helping her find her purpose in life and embrace the person she is. Autumn knows she shouldn't fall for Gray. It can only end badly. After all their lives are divided by an ocean and their inevitable separation is just another heart break away . . .

The Kristen Proby Crossover Collection features a new novel by Kristen Proby and six by some of her favorite writers:

Kristen Proby—*Soaring with Fallon*
Sawyer Bennett—*Wicked Force*
KL Grayson—*Crazy Imperfect Love*
Laura Kaye—*Worth Fighting For*
Monica Murphy—*Nothing Without You*
Rachel Van Dyken—*All Stars Fall*

Samantha Young—*Hold On*
Out March 2019

A series of chance encounters leads to a sizzling new romance from the *New York Times* bestselling author of the *On Dublin Street* series.

The universe is conspiring against Ava Breevort. As if flying back to Phoenix to bury a childhood friend wasn't hell enough, a cloud of volcanic ash traveling from overseas delayed her flight back home to Boston. Her last ditch attempt to salvage the trip was thwarted by an arrogant Scotsman, Caleb Scott, who steals a first class seat out from under her. Then over the course of their journey home, their antagonism somehow lands them in bed for the steamiest layover Ava's ever had. And that's all it was–until Caleb shows up on her doorstep.

When pure chance pulls Ava back into Caleb's orbit, he proposes they enjoy their physical connection while he's stranded in Boston. Ava agrees, knowing her heart's in no danger since a) she barely likes Caleb and b) his existence in her life is temporary. Not long thereafter Ava realizes she's made a terrible error because as it turns out Caleb Scott isn't quite so unlikeable after all. When his stay in Boston becomes permanent, Ava must decide whether to fight her feelings for him or give into them. But even if she does decide to risk her heart on Caleb, there is no guarantee her stubborn Scot will want to risk his heart on her. . . .

Read the first chapter over at Hypable.com
Out October 9th 2018

CPSIA information can be obtained
at www.ICGtesting.com
Printed in the USA
LVHW09s1036081018
592794LV00001B/52/P